Dear Natal

Without [illegible] are no books! Thank you for reading! ♡

Tainted Lovers

Sarah Michelle Lynch

I'm so touched that
Ade & David's story
has made such an
impact on you and
I'm so happy that it has!
Enjoy! ♡ Sarah Michelle
xxxx

ISBN: 1530018153
ISBN-13: 978-1530018154

DEDICATION

For those that did NaNoWriMo too –

Here is proof.

Also by the Author

A Fine Profession
A Fine Pursuit
The Chambermaid's Tales Pocket Sized
Unbind
Unfurl
Unleash
Fabien: A Vampire Serial
Angel Avenue
Beyond Angel Avenue

As S. M. Lynch:

The Radical
The Informant
The Sentient

ACKNOWLEDGEMENTS

Thank you to D.B. for the poetry
– for everything really.

Thank you to the readers who keep reading
– superstars that you are.

Thank you to my younger self
– you didn't give up.

Thank you to the organisers of book events
– you make me keep writing!

Thank you.

Tainted Lovers

"I am no bird; and no net ensnares me: I am a free human being with an independent will."

Charlotte Brontë, *Jane Eyre*

ONE

Easter, 2003

I worked as a cataloguist of special documents at Leeds University's Brotherton Library, which had some seriously interesting old scrolls and manuscripts among its collections. I landed the job because I had tenacity. I wanted the job because it meant not dealing with the public. I was waiting until my son Billy was a little older so that I could give more time to my studies and finally do my accounting degree.

Occasionally I left my office but only to make the distance from my workspace to the café nearby. While Billy spent time at the crèche every afternoon, I worked. I didn't need the money, just some sort of sanity.

One day I was leaving my office to pick Billy up on my way home when I spotted a man stood nearby at the self-service units, looking perplexed.

"Excuse me, excuse me," he called in a panicked voice. He held one foot on the floor while reaching high in the air to signal me over the tops of the high booths. Looking around, I saw no other members of staff available to help him. It was getting toward the end of the day for most people and also, it was nearly the Easter holidays and the past few weeks had been the busiest of the year. Most of my colleagues were surviving on cigarettes and bitching sessions to keep them going.

Walking toward him, I asked, "What's the problem?"

It wasn't my job to help him, but I was familiar with the self-service machines.

"It won't let me take out this book."

Part of me had already clocked the fact he was beautiful but I tried to ignore that.

Attempting to take his book out for him, I muttered under my breath, "Where is everyone?"

"I've been stuck standing here for god knows how long waiting for help."

I nodded along, hearing angry beeps from the machine, which refused to let him take out this book. Looking closer at the screen, I realised the computer bore a message:

This title is reserved.

Pointing at the screen, I drew his attention to the message and he answered, "Yeah, I reserved it. About four months ago. So did everyone else. Some shit keeps hiding this and none of us can ever get hold of the bloody thing."

I picked up the book under scrutiny and held it in my hands. It was an old book on medieval chivalry with a brown, warped cover and thin pages nearly falling apart. The book had illustrations in colour but it was at least a hundred years old and should have been a reference title – if that.

"This shouldn't even be on a shelf," I mumbled, "it should be under my care. Look at it."

I felt him staring at me for a while as I examined his long-overdue/reserved book. "A soft spot for battered old books, eh?"

"I'm actually in charge of battered old books," I told him. "Just wait here a second."

"Okay. I'll wait," he said.

I caught a softness to his voice, perhaps affection, and the tone caught me off guard. Looking directly up into his eyes for the first time, I was throttled by what was staring back.

Our eyes locked. I think I burned from every pore. My

belly filled with heat and my heart rinsed off its icy cage in an instant. Staring at him, my feet rooted, I realised he wasn't affected at all, not whatsoever. Cool as ice. I hated him a little for it.

"In… a… wait," I mumbled, not making sense.

I rushed off back to my office and sank against the door, panting, trying to slow my heart. Never had I been so affected. Light-headed, I tried to catch my breath.

Clutching the book in my hand, I remembered I had a job to do. My PC on standby, I started it up again and searched the catalogue number.

It was a borrow, he wasn't lying. Not a reference title. Flicking through it again, I realised it was one of the core subjects our medieval scholars studied – on chivalric courtship. So I knew he was either an MA student or higher. Going by his eyes, he was a few years older than me.

Anyway, I needed to get rid of him.

Quickly.

I overrode the system and did something naughty, cancelling all the reserve statuses so the book could start a new cycle of temporary ownership. No doubt some div hated his fellow classmates and wanted nobody else to have access to the book, a rare title which could make or break a dissertation.

Gathering myself, I took some deep breaths, my bag clutched under my arm and the book clutched at my chest.

Leaving the office again, I walked fast because I really needed to pick up Billy.

"Hi," he said as I rejoined him.

Stepping in front of the self-serve machine with authority, I asked, "Library card, please."

He handed me it and I took the book out for him, avoiding eye contact altogether.

Job done.

"There you go."

"Thanks… how did you…? Thanks!" He stuffed the book

into his rammed-full bag as I began walking away.

I chased down the stairs, not wanting to give him chance to follow me. I had two flights to get down, though. My exit was through the Parkinson building, and the stairs outside were steep and dangerous. I had to slow down to take them.

"Wait, wait!" He caught up with me, a hand on my forearm slowing me down as we got out into the open air. "I know you."

"I have somewhere to be," I huffed, impatient.

"Adrienne, right?"

I dared look into those chocolate-brown eyes again and another electric current shot through me, even stronger though this time. In the light of day, I saw how deeply brown his eyes really were – and smouldering – with umber striations.

I folded my arms. "So what? I saw your library card, David." I sounded pithy. "You saw my name tag. Big deal."

"No," he shook his head, "Adrienne Kyd. I know you. Well," he chuckled, "I know of you."

I examined him carefully and the familiarity became clear.

"You're a Harrogate boy," I said through gritted teeth.

So, my past was inescapable. A boy from my hometown had found me.

But just how much did he know?

"Everybody knows you... or knew you," he said, but while his tone was affectionate, his eyes remained devoid of any feeling. He looked at me like he was looking right past me. It was something about his steady gaze. I couldn't read him. He seemed, guarded.

Anyway, he wasn't lying. Everyone knew me. I was Miss Harrogate 2000, the same year I got together with Marcus, my ex – the donator of sperm that created my child (he was never a father).

"I'm not trying to be rude... I really do have somewhere to be," I insisted, avoiding his eyes at all costs. I couldn't help notice he was mentally undressing me, sizing me up for the kill.

"Can I give you my number?" he asked.

"No."

"No?"

"No. Goodbye."

I charged off. Petrified wasn't a word I thought I understood, but right then, I did. I purposely wore dowdy clothes, no make-up – and worked in the backroom of a library. I hardly ever let my hair down (literally) and I didn't try to make myself look attractive to the opposite sex whatsoever. In fact I was glad to be invisible but that day, my magic cloak seemed to have worn off.

I'd never been so scared before in my life: I'd fallen in love at first sight.

***

Even though I worked at the library, people may not have even known that. I passed through quickly on my way to and from places; always with my eyes focused on leaving, always with an air of inapproachability so that people never stopped me in my tracks. I lived in my office, end of. I wore a name badge I always tried to hide by folding over my cardigan. I wasn't on the help desk. I didn't deal with returns. I didn't want to talk to people. I didn't want people to ask me questions and know things about me. I was quiet. I talked to one girl I worked with, Bebe, and the rest of the staff thought I was some sort of mentally ill person with antisocial tendencies. It worked for me.

However. After that first encounter with David, I was no longer a ghost fluttering in and out of that place. I was a target. David hung around in the afternoons, waiting, watching. He asked if he could carry my bag on my way out. He tried to slip his number into the palm of my hand. He even stalked me at my favourite coffee shop in Parkinson, finding out from the owner what my usual tipple was. The coffee shop owner said David had paid for me to have free coffee for the rest of the academic year. I was molten with fury and longing – torn between giving into my urges and tearing strips off him for refusing to let it go.

Not many days later, I had to run an errand over to the geography department which was expecting a new delivery of old maps. Because of my infrequent escape from the office, I don't think David expected me to catch him with another girl that day. I watched from a distance, hiding myself behind one of the many trees lining the pathways of our campus. I spotted him and a redhead on a bench having a heated discussion, and then a second girl walked up to them. A brunette. The two girls faced off, seemingly fighting for him. David was able to slope off because they were too busy arguing. He chased away once he'd put a safe distance between himself and the two ladies, heading off campus it seemed. Once I knew he was gone, I left my hiding place and walked along to my destination, passing the two girls as I did. All I heard from the redhead was, "He was mine first, keep your hands off."

The brunette replied, "Don't you see? He's playing us both…"

I didn't hear anything more, but I was sure as hell certain David wasn't a man to be trusted. I certainly couldn't afford another man like that in my life.

TWO

Racing out of the library, I was running late to pick up Billy. I didn't have anyone I could call on for help. I had no fallback if I was late and the crèche kept strict hours. I was the only person Billy had and he was my number one priority. We didn't need anyone else.

"Wait, wait!" a voice shouted after me, and I turned to look at David.

God...sake, I muttered in my own head.

"What? Oh god, what?" I demanded as he chased after me just outside the library.

"You dropped your purse. See? Your friend Bebe said for me to give it to you."

There was a matchmaker if ever I met one. I might have mentioned to her in passing I had a stalker called David. I might have pointed him out and she might have admitted her vibrator would be getting some action after watching him reading Kerouac in a corner of the silent reading area.

He handed me my navy, snakeskin purse and I saw my swipe card in the clear window of the ID slot.

"Thanks. I have no idea how I dropped it."

"You seem in a rush?" he said.

I was – trying to avoid him, David, who was still everywhere I looked. Two weeks had passed since the first time I looked into his eyes and my every waking moment was spent thinking about him – and his arms around me.

But he was bad. Bad. And I knew it.

I looked up at him and an avalanche of delight hit me between my legs. His brown eyes had me transfixed yet again. There was something stony and cool in his gaze but a part of me wanted the challenge – of unpicking him. I was attracted to the puzzle, to the reason he couldn't let this go. I wanted to find out if I could warm him through like he warmed me.

He moved closer and I backed away.

"I'm running late again, David. I have to go."

"One moment," he said, moving closer, inch by inch. He was trying hard not to scare me off.

When he was within inches of me, I said, "Why won't you leave me alone?"

"I don't know."

"What do you mean, you don't know."

"I don't know. I should. I know that. I just can't."

"You've used that line before. I've heard it from a dozen other wankers, too."

He snickered and turned his head to the side a little to avoid me examining his reaction. I was enamoured, but I wasn't stupid.

Holding his hands up, he began walking away. "If that's how you feel."

He turned and began walking and I watched him go. He was so tall and so slim, and with eyes that made me feel breathless. He sent shivers through me with his presence alone. How did this happen? How do you go from one day going about your ordinary life to suddenly getting accosted by a boy in a library and then feeling like every breath you take after that hurts without him? Falling happened when my eyes were shut and now he wouldn't leave me alone. I didn't even know if he was my type! What was my type? He was definitely nothing like my ex, Marcus, who was thick-set and with squished features nothing like David's beautiful, elegant face. David was six-four or five and I was tall, but it was like looking up into the heavens looking into his eyes. His hair was brown, wavy, the longest tips caressing his ears. His face, hmm. His face. He had a lovely set of cheekbones and a smile that made me grin, too.

Except I didn't want this. No. I didn't. *Remember that, Adrienne,* I told myself. *You don't want him! Your life is complex enough as it is!*

"David," I shouted and he turned, striding back to me, looking finally triumphant.

If he wanted me, I'd make him work for it.

"What do you want?" I growled. "Really?"

He shrugged. "We could start with a kiss?"

I looked at his lips, small on the top, large on the bottom. He had a tiny bit of stubble on his chin and upper lip. *You don't want a kiss, Ade!* Oh yes I bloody did.

I cocked my head and folded my arms, pretending I had the upper hand. Part of me did – because I already knew his sort – but another part of me (say about 99 per cent) just wanted his body.

Wanting his body was one thing, but what came after bedroom activity was another kettle of fish entirely. I knew myself and I wasn't able to do the whole fuck-it-and-just-bang-him thing.

Glaring confidently, I warned, "Have you not got enough pussy at your beck and call? Miss Red and Miss Brunette the other day not enough for you?"

His eyes grew wide and he said, "God, I think I love you."

I slapped him hard, right across the face. Sneering, I retaliated, "They might not have the balls, but I have. Blokes like you make me fucking sick."

His mouth said I love you, but his eyes still told me I was a piece of meat. A conquest.

I turned on my heels and pelted away.

"Wait, wait…!"

As if slapping his face wasn't enough evidence I WASN'T INTERESTED!

"Bye David."

"No! PLEASE!"

His loud demand stopped me in my tracks. The next thing I knew, I could feel him standing right behind me.

"What do you like to read, Adrienne?"

I turned and looked up at him. In barely a whisper, I begged, "Please, leave me the hell alone."

David searched my eyes and it shocked me when his expression didn't change. He looked interested in me. Actually, interested. Not cold and calculated anymore.

He tried to touch my shoulder and I swung for him. His was just a friendly tap but mine had the potential to be a knockout punch. He managed to duck out of the way of my right-hook quickly, holding his hands up. Searching my eyes still, he spoke slowly, "So... it's true?"

Horrified, I didn't stay to have any more conversation with him. I secured my bag tight on my back and sprinted the rest of the way to crèche.

I once got off murder, and now he knew, I was more than able to defend myself.

The rumours he'd heard were true: I killed my boyfriend.

Billy's dad.

***

The following day when I arrived for work, he wasn't there hanging around the reading section like normal. He seemed to have disappeared. Part of me hated that I couldn't see him. I felt his absence so starkly, I even found it hard to bury myself in my spreadsheets, the one thing I could usually lose myself in come hell or high water.

In spite of myself, when I left the library and found him waiting, I rejoiced privately. Just to see his face made me secretly exultant.

"Can I walk you home? To make sure you're safe?"

"I have to pick up my son from crèche."

He chewed his lip. "That's okay."

He walked alongside me, pensive, speechless. I sensed David was not the sort of person to lose his way around words, not when he was clearly a master of them. The silence was awkward and raking, like a child looking for the right word but not yet possessing the vocabulary for adult conversation.

As we got closer to the crèche, I decided to make myself clear: "You've heard the rumours and now since yesterday, you've probably looked it all up, read all about it on the world wide web. You think you know what happened, but you won't. Ever. Know. You hear me?"

He nodded slowly.

"The details of what happened to me will remain forever stored inside because nobody needs to hear of it and I sure as shit don't need to go over it all, not again."

Another nod from him.

"Now *David*," I said his name like I was raping it through my teeth, "you orchestrated a little plot with the library book to get my attention and get me. All you saw was Adrienne, the girl every guy made a play for. You want the unobtainable, well, go for it. Because it's true. I am unobtainable and you'll be waiting a long time before I put blinkers on to pricks like you." I glanced at him a moment, seeing him shocked. "Keep making that play, because I know your sort. If you think I'm stupid you had better scarper now, because you have got another thing coming."

Anger possessed me, held me in its grip. I shook a little bit as we reached the crèche but as I walked inside, he whispered behind me, "I'll wait."

I exited with Billy in my arms, the pushchair hanging over my forearm. David rushed to help me and unfolded the buggy for me.

He walked me home, the whole way.

Silence.

Comfortable silence, this time.

He surveyed the house I lived in on Hanover Square when we arrived.

"Can we do something, sometime?" he asked with a frown, unwilling to give up.

I looked down at Billy who was asleep in his buggy, meaning I could afford a minute more for David.

"No."

"No?"

"No."

He couldn't wipe that frown away. "Will you ever say yes?"

I looked up at the bright sky. "No."

"Why not?"

I walked close to him, looking directly into his eyes. "Answer me a question... I'll know if you're lying."

"Okay?"

"How many girls are you currently sleeping with?"

He maintained my gaze, still cold and emotionless. His soul hid behind a façade of ice and I didn't know if that was frustrating or arousing. Probably both.

"Three or four," he told me, without a hint of shame.

I smirked. The thought of it made me furious. "Stringing them along?"

"I don't belong to anyone," he said, "everyone knows that."

"Then you don't belong to me, either."

It was his turn to get angry, his teeth gnashing even.

He laughed, "You are impossible!"

"I'll level with you, okay?"

He folded his arms and nodded, his beautiful face and body curling inwards because I wouldn't give him anything but honesty.

"You think having me would be a bed of roses? Honey, I'm the thorn. Parts of me prickle harder than even I realise.

I'm indestructible. I've fought wars... brokered my own life in exchange for my soul... to protect my son. I don't need anyone. I can survive absolutely anything. I don't need you. As you can see," I pointed behind me at my home, "I need nobody. You've heard the rumours but now take it from the horse's mouth, I will never again allow myself to become swallowed by a pathetic, weak man unable to control his dick, his fist or his money hungry, butt licking tongue."

He looked at the pavement, but out of shame or painful emotion – I wasn't sure.

I left him there. Even when I was finally safe inside my house, he still stood on the street looking down at his feet. Through the Venetian blinds, he looked defeated and almost as moody and as much of the enigma as Kerouac was. I tried to ignore the fact he wasn't leaving and busied myself getting dinner ready instead.

When I looked half an hour later, curious to see if he'd finally given up, I saw he'd left the street and hopefully my life – for more empty liaisons that wouldn't get either of us hurt.

THREE

Exactly four weeks to the day since I first got winded by his brown eyes, he was back – waiting outside the library at the end of my shift. When he saw me leaving the building, he straightened up and looked directly at me, challenging me to ignore him.

When I did ignore him, he still fell into step beside me.

"How are you?" he asked.

"Fine. You?"

"You really are hard, aren't you? Like a walking monolith."

I laughed gently. "Harder than that."

I glanced at David and when I looked closer, I realised he looked haggard and grey.

"What's wrong with you?"

"Nothing," he insisted quickly, "nothing. Listen, I mean... Yeah, look..." He struggled for words.

"Are you determined to look a dunce?" I asked.

"Can we have dinner sometime?"

I shook my head. "I don't like dining out, it's never to my taste. I only like authentic Italian cooking."

"Okay." He seemed to wrack his brain. "I can cook. My mum says I'm not bad at it, actually. I could cook for you. You know," he scratched a hand through his hair, "bring shit round, throw it in a pan."

I turned to look at him, stopping in my tracks. "You want an invite into my home?"

"Yes, if it's the only way in, through your stomach I mean. Well, fuck, I mean..."

I snickered at his awkwardness.

"I might be able to get some sleep once you give me the time of day again. I haven't had sex in fourteen days," he looked at his watch, "nine hours and twenty-two minutes. I'm a little fucked up right now."

I held my hands up. "Hey, I've just been doing my thing. Working. Living. I never said you shouldn't do your thing. Whatever your idea of living is."

"Ha!" He threw his head back. "Living? Our ideas of living are definitely a little different sweetheart."

I zeroed in on his eyes. "I warned you I'm cold. I can do silent treatment better than you."

He smirked, reaching out to run his finger down my red cheek. "I'm the one that's cold baby, while you're red all over just looking at me. Maybe I just wanna get warm with you."

"Maybe you should find a hot water bottle, hmm?"

God, you are lame, Adrienne.

"Tried that," he said, "but most of them talk back."

I couldn't help but snicker.

We walked on and I went into the crèche to pick up Billy. David helped me get my toddler in his seat before revealing, "I would walk you home but last time I did that, I lost my way and got a parking ticket and it's not like I haven't already got enough misdemeanours against my name."

"I'm safer without you, anyway," I grinned.

"Maybe," he agreed, "but wouldn't you like to find out how hard this electricity could crackle?"

I smirked. "There will be no crackling because pig's hair gets between my teeth. Seeing as though I've eaten food on six continents, there will be marks out of ten."

"You agree? Is that a yes?"

I nodded.

Tension left him immediately, my agreement brightening his face. He seemed softer and relaxed instantly. "Great. That's good. I mean, yeah, great."

"Saturday night? Seven?"

"Yes, I'll be there. Remind me what number flat again?"

"1A," I told him, pushing off with Billy.

"See you, Adrienne."

"Call me Ade, moron," I shouted over my shoulder.

I left him laughing behind me, and all the way home, I fought the urge to look over my shoulder to see if he was there. I just knew he was.

***

When the doorbell dinged, I walked to the intercom and answered. "Yep?"

"The only thing I could find in the shop was crackling. Sorry."

I smiled and buzzed him in. Waiting behind the door for him to knock on my flat, I heard his soft rap and peeped through the spy hole to see him looking nervous and beautiful, his hair slightly tidier and his dress a pair of smart trousers and shirt with the sleeves rolled up. He was going to think me a nerdy little bint in my denim skirt and plain blouse, with its Peter Pan collar – and I was glad of it.

I opened up and tried to seem nonchalant.

"What if I were Jewish?" I asked, holding the door open while he waited in the hallway to be invited in.

He beamed shyly (yes, shyly) and responded, "But you're not. I happen to know you're a good protestant girl. It was in your Miss Harrogate speech."

I sniggered and pointed at him. "One more mention of that, and your ear will be crackling."

I pulled the door wide open and gestured with my arm he could make his way inside, carrying bags of food.

I shut the door and we looked at one another. He handed me a bottle of red wine and kissed my cheek at the same time. I wasn't expecting that move but it was over so quick, I didn't have chance to hide my flushed face.

Something happened in the moments after that kiss. I noticed things I hadn't before.

His hips.

So slim.

He was rake slim.

But his hips.

I got lost staring into his eyes and before long, I realised my blush hadn't disappeared and we remained stood in the hallway, no idea what we were doing.

I panted, my chest heaving in a way I couldn't hide.

"I've never belonged to anyone," he said in a raspy voice, "until now. Until you."

I frowned. It was a bad habit of mine, and it happened a lot. "Do you mean that?"

He looked deep into my eyes as I did his. "Yes. I won't fuck around anymore if you'll just give me a chance to be with you, be your friend, be here for you. I want to know you."

I gulped. Fractured. But… "I don't know."

"Nobody else has ever seen through me like you do. Nobody. It scares me but I can't stop thinking about how happy I feel when you're nearby."

A tiny voice told me he could still be making a play and nothing more, so I brushed past him and gestured, "I'll show you the kitchen. I still have to mark you out of ten. No half points either."

"Okay," he chuckled.

While I left him to do the cooking on his own, I checked on my son who was sleeping soundly. Then I grabbed a glass of wine from the kitchen.

David peered at me, looking worried.

"I forgot something."

"What'd ya forget?"

"Parmesan. Fresh. I mean, you said authentic…"

"Oh, I have that. Fridge door," I told him. "Maybe I could do half a point, after all. For honesty."

He gave me a sexy grin and pulled an apron over his smart clothes.

"No pressure," he chuckled.

"I'll watch some TV, let you get on with it."

"Thank you, otherwise it could get a little Masterchef in here and I wouldn't want to infect your food with sweat beads."

I had to prise myself out of his presence because now the air was clearing between us, it felt good to be around him.

"Shout if you need something, although not too loudly as Billy is sleeping."

"No worries," he said, lighting the gas stove at the same time as throwing a garlic clove into a pan of butter.

An hour later, dinner was polished off as we sat around the dining table in my large front room.

I smirked. "You asked Bebe what food I like?"

"She said calzone, yes."

We ate the most gorgeous calzone with layers of onions, mozzarella, chorizo, rocket and fresh parmesan. Topped off with a dark red merlot he bought, too.

"Marks then?"

"Eight," I quipped with a tiny smile, "plus a bonus point for this new free flowing honesty of yours."

He rolled his eyes. "Ade?"

"Yes."

"I'm David," he held out his hand to me, "yes, I *was* selfish, for all of my life actually, until you. This is me now. Pleased to meet you."

I looked at his hand but didn't shake it. He had wonderful, big hands.

"How long's all of your life?"

"Twenty-six," he said, lips pursing.

No wonder I didn't know him from school or anything, he was a whole six years older than me. In comparison to him, I felt the elder, the wiser. Maybe I was.

"But you're an English student?"

His eyes danced. "PhD in medieval literature."

"Wow," I gasped, "that's intimidating."

"It's my second PhD. The first was in feminist studies. My undergraduate was half English, half sociology. I'm not at all sure what I'm doing with my life. I may have stayed in education to avoid life. I think I liked the girls here. Maybe... I don't know." He chuckled, half mocking himself, half admitting he was flighty.

He sat opposite me and I watched his fingertips dance on the table, constantly nearing mine to touch my hand, but always pulling back. His eyes continually and intrusively searched mine.

"Are you talking in riddles?"

He smiled ruefully. "Around you, it seems I forget everything that went before."

I snickered under my hand. "I knew you were a player. But seriously, if you're as clever as that, why are you dumb enough to hang around the likes of those hoes?"

I looked away, now hating the prospect he was as heartless as all the rest. With that brain of his too, bloody hell, he was becoming even more attractive.

He finally slipped his fingers between mine and held my hand. Bringing my fingers to his lips, he pressed a kiss to my knuckles. "I told you, Adrienne. With you, I forget everything that went before."

"I need the loo, be back in a sec." I rushed off and with the bathroom door closed, I allowed myself a deep breath and used a tissue to catch the tear resting on my upper eyelid. Had he seen it? Did he know I wanted him?

When I returned to the room, he stood by the bookcase. "First edition Brontë?"

"Fourteenth birthday present from Mother," I told him, pouring more wine. Walking over I handed him a refilled glass and took my prized copy of *Jane Eyre* from his grasp.

"I can't have another," he said, "unless I'm staying. Otherwise I'm driving."

"I have a couch. Even better, a spare room."

He smiled and started on his second glass of wine.

"I've read most of the Brontë canon but Branwell's hard to get hold of," he said, changing the direction of our conversation smoothly.

I sipped my wine, trying to hide how my nerves had my hands and chin trembling. "I was never the bookworm, not a real one anyway. A friend at school got me into reading."

"Yeah?"

"Yes," I paused. "I was in Moscow or somewhere with my mother. I remember I was twelve and I'd read all the *Sweet Valley High* books and those vampire collections that were dog-eared in the school library…"

He guffawed.

"You laugh but they were just my early education," I giggled. He stopped laughing but his eyes still betrayed amusement.

"So, we were there for some business or something my father was on and Mother took me to the ballet one night, just the two of us. It was *Wuthering Heights*. I had to go out and get the book as soon as we got home. Then I got the rest."

"And your favourite?" he asked.

I twiddled my fingers. "This one holds a special place in my heart. It caught me unexpectedly, you know?"

He nodded. "I know about that."

Unlike me, he drank from his glass without his hands or chin shaking.

"I think I read *Jane Eyre* from cover to cover one summer holiday night. And I read it from cover to cover again. I read all their others, even *The Professor* and *Agnes*

Grey, just trying to seek something that could tell me how such humble women did all that, you know? I might have studied English... I don't know. Maybe in another life."

"Being rich," he gestured at my house, "you don't need education. Besides, fat lot of good all the numbers and letters have done for me."

His words made me feel uncomfortable and he noticed.

"Are you judging me for my money?"

"No," he paused, knowing he couldn't back out, "I mean, you always have a backup plan... your father."

I walked away from him to the window and peeked behind the blinds at the sinking sun. "He paid me to leave... to stay away. He doesn't want to know me, or his grandson. My mother knows nothing. He made me sign something saying I wouldn't come back. If I do try to contact them, I'll have to give up my trust fund. Something to the tune of seven figures. I come into it when I'm twenty-one but he gave me this place and set me up with a comfortable allowance until my trust fund arrives... until I'm ex-communicated for eternity–"

"Ade–"

"...and if you think I chose money over my mother, you're wrong. I chose sanity. I chose not having to look at the reason why I got pushed into a bad man's arms. Not to look at the father I was never good enough for."

"I'm sorry, Adrienne. So sorry. I shouldn't have said that. It's just... I'm not rich. It's really me that feels uncomfortable. Not you. I could never match you. Please, forgive me?"

My Georgian, ground-floor flat was comfortable, well furnished. Polished. I think he now saw that far from perfect, I was the opposite, just treading water. I didn't need someone in my life who saw me as a conquest.

"I looked up the meaning of your name," he said, taking my glass from my hand. He put both of our glasses on the coffee table and I slipped *Jane Eyre* onto it too. "Adrienne...

the dark soul, with her bright, light eyes barricading the way to her heart. Now, I'm going to kiss you."

I watched him move closer and froze. "Before, you said we could be friends. Friends don't kiss."

He moved his hands over my cheeks, caressing my skin. "Friends don't have the chemistry we do. It's palpable. Neither one of us can ignore this, no matter how ruined this may make us."

He tipped my head back and stared down into my eyes, his brown globes twinkling in the encroaching darkness, the room needing light suddenly. I wrapped my arms around his waist and he dropped a kiss on my lips. Soothing me, he pulled me tight against him, one hand anchored on my cheek while another held my body. He changed the pressure of his kiss from light to hard and opened his mouth, my tongue meeting his in a heartbeat. I raised my arms around his neck and he stooped a little so I could reach him.

Kissing, I enjoyed the luxurious way he never left my lips. I held his shoulder and we pulled back breathless. Looking at him close-up, I saw tiny fine lines on his face I hadn't seen before then. He was older than me, and worn, but by life? What had him so tired out?

He stroked his thumb over my eyebrow and smiled, showing me a set of big teeth. I smiled back.

"Regarding your residual anger issues," he said, referencing me almost knocking him out the other day, "will I need self-defence?"

He said it with the silliest look on his face, I couldn't help but burst out laughing. Shaking my head, I told him, "You just need to know that when something bugs me, I'll voice it… or demonstrate it."

"Good to know," he sniggered.

"Besides, I can teach you some moves… if you want."

He must have seen something in my eyes because his demeanour changed and he pulled back. Passing me my wine glass again, he said, "We could fuck all night and it'd be as fragrant and as wild as we both imagine. I've had loads of those nights, believe me. But I don't want anymore nights like that. They mean nothing and only make me feel bad about myself. I only want to feel good, and talking like this, being like this makes me feel good. So, what do you say?"

I gawped before realising he was awaiting a response. "What am I saying yes to?"

"Not having sex tonight, but instead hanging out, talking, listening. Maybe pulling an all-nighter, watching TV or... reading a book?"

My smile hurt my face. "It's a light night. I reckon the sun will sleep maybe six hours, what do you think?"

He picked up my first edition *Jane Eyre* and I shook my head. "Wait."

Venturing to the shelves, I reached to the back and pulled out two, very scruffy, dog-eared Penguin copies. Books I'd thumbed almost to dust.

"Let's go. My bedroom gets great light, we'll see the sunrise together."

As we settled on top of my queen bed, he burst out laughing, noticing I'd underlined words and annotated sections too. I checked the copy I had in my hands which had no marks and chucked it at him. "Read that one instead."

"Oh my god, I'm not giving up this window into your mind, not for love nor money."

"What about violence?" I lurched for him, trying to wrestle the book from his grasp. He fought me off and we tussled around the bed.

"Does a kiss get me this book?" he asked, chuckling.

"Maybe."

He kissed me and I surrendered, utterly lost to bliss. He tasted of wine and decadence, and beauty; such warped, sensual beauty.

Peeling himself off me after a long, immeasurable length of time spent kissing, I relented. "You can read it. But no laughing!"

I smiled quietly to myself as we spent the night simu-reading. While he'd been pressed up against me during our kiss, I'd felt the size and shape of his enormous cock.

No wonder women used him.

"Adrienne, you're missing it. Come on, look."

"What?" I mumbled, groggy. "Missing what?"

Light pierced my eyes and I tried to hide myself in his belly, fending off the sunrise.

"Dawn."

"I'm tired. You enjoy it for the both of us."

"Okay," he whispered, stroking my hair.

I peered through one eye and saw him laid beneath me, the book still in his hand. He looked about three quarters through which meant while I'd fallen asleep around halfway, he'd no doubt make it to the end. He was a real slave to words, I could tell.

"Sleep, Adrienne. You should sleep. Sun's up now, but I'll tell you about it later… it was a sexy sunrise combined with this, let me tell you."

"Nothing sexy about *Jane Eyre,* David."

"I beg to differ. Your notes are most evocative."

I giggled and with him stroking my hair, rolling strands of it around his fingers, I fell asleep buried in his chest.

FOUR

It continued like that for four weeks more. We'd spend Saturday nights eating his cooking and then reading. It was always calzone, albeit with different flavours and ingredients every time. We never ever got to dessert and I would end up eating that for breakfast after awkward morning kisses goodbye.

I truly hated saying goodbye to him.

Somehow we'd got ourselves into a state, thinking sex would ruin us somehow. So it was off the table.

Even during the week, we'd exchange glances across the library but like religious fasters, we'd avoid talking or touching, or even acknowledging that we were sort of seeing one another. David briefly mentioned he didn't want anyone to know about us because he didn't want anything spoiling it. In the back of my mind, I wondered whether he feared a past girlfriend trying to warn me off if she saw me and David together.

During our all-night reading sessions, we got through *Middlemarch, Atonement* and *Wuthering Heights*. The latter sort of made me wonder about David's background. Was he a poor boy; would he never feel good enough for me?

"Do you think love really is like the eternal rocks beneath?" I asked him as we lay on my bed at four a.m. after reading about the Earnshaws and the Lintons all night. He laid propped up against the pillows, feet almost hanging off the end of my queen bed. I rested perpendicular to him, my head against his stomach.

In the weeks since we'd started reading together, he'd put on weight, he looked less haggard and his lines less defined. He seemed, I don't know – content.

"If we write it down, love becomes eternal. Like this book. Can you imagine a day when it won't be in print?"

"No, I can't," I mused.

"I don't like Cathy," he said, mumbling, "she gave up love, and for what?"

I sniffed. "For pretty dresses, I guess."

"No, I don't think so," he decided.

I moved off him and rolled onto my stomach, looking up into his eyes, my upper body raised on elbows.

"Then, what?"

"Fear," he muttered, "she was afraid love would take her under, take away the wild girl she enjoyed being when she was with her roguish lover Heathcliff. She loved the wild creature she was when she was with him, but feared real life… a family. Growing old with him… and that eternal love being diminished. The fantasy will never be broken, because she never married him."

"Do all books need an unhappy ending to be remembered? To be romantic? And then, re-imagined over and over… in film, TV… plays. Ballet…" I questioned.

"Hmm," he sniffed, "not always."

"But in your heart, do you think… love can be eternal?" I asked, but he didn't respond, looking away. "David?"

He looked at me and smiled. "I don't believe in eternal. I don't believe in afterlife."

"What?" I sat up and pulled my legs beneath me.

"I don't believe in religion or anything."

"You don't?"

He shook his head, crossing his legs. Placing our books on the side, he shrugged. "I don't."

"Then, what's the point of us being here? What will happen after we're gone? Who will remember us, David? There has to be more to this world. Something on the other side. A place where we'll all be together, in peace and serenity."

"Maybe, or... maybe," he whispered, reaching out to stroke my chin, "there's just love, in the moment, and that's all there is. The rest of life is about taking what you can, when you can. That's all we have."

I gulped, my face frozen in sadness.

I shifted off the bed and walked to my chair in the corner, where I kept clothes and stuff. Shifting everything off it onto the floor, I curled up and hid my face in my hands and knees.

He'd made me cry and I wept, tears absorbed by my jeans. What had happened to him?

"Why do you study all this shit if you don't even believe the romance of it all? Why?"

He remained on the bed, keeping his distance.

"Perhaps I'm searching for something, but I don't know if I'll ever find it."

"I don't understand you," I protested, "it's like you've been avoiding life. Like you don't care about anyone, not even yourself."

"I didn't, not until you," he laughed, "you were right, so right. You had me figured out so early on. I don't know why you even give me the time of day."

My lip trembled. I was full of emotion and had no idea where it had all come from.

Was I tired?

Had the book ruined me?

Had he ruined me?

I lifted my head from my knees and wiped my eyes. "Do you want me?"

"Yes, I want you Adrienne."

"Is there anyone else? Has there–"

"No!"

"Then, why can't you be a bit more optimistic?"

"I don't know," he shook his head, most probably at himself, "because I know myself. I'll fuck this up. I'll hurt you. You don't deserve me, you deserve happiness. You need protecting, someone better than me. Someone worthy. I don't believe in much, and if we were together, you would have to believe for the both of us."

"So, why won't you go?" I challenged him, my face full of anger. "Walk away, now, if all you think is that we'll muck this up and it's bound to end badly before it's even begun."

"Because–"

I waited. And waited.

"What?" I begged.

"…because nobody will ever love you as much as I do."

"What? You don't love me!" I protested, trying not to appear shocked.

I gazed through a mountain of tears at what was undoubtedly a broken soul to match mine. Both imperfect, he was right – we would surely fuck this up.

Everything seemed stark and sharp, now – with him in my life. Food tasted better and I hungered more. I got out of bed quicker everyday since I'd known him, leaping from the sheets some days at the prospect of seeing his face. My heart hurt more, everyday, and I couldn't imagine ever saying goodbye.

"If you want me to immortalise this… pass me a pen," he demanded.

I grabbed one from my bag on the floor and passed it to him. He opened up the front cover of his beaten-up copy of *Wuthering Heights* and tapped the pen against his front teeth, muttering to himself for at least ten minutes before he wrote something down.

When he was done, he passed the book to me and I read the inside page:

To That He Cherished

I met you in the gallery of stars
And drank the ether of your eyes.
Sense. Sight.
My wares obliterate.

Beyond the orchard walls
You became my soul, at the water's edge.
Let us go then you and I
Out across the waves and pastures
Of the sinking world.

Come and rest your head awhile.
My memory is hazed adrift.
As the cloud parts from the blissful shore,
My joy departs to thee.

Sleep in the solitude of my love's cascade,
And wake in the shroud
Of all things beyond the blessed.
Endless joy assured,
My one. My truth. My love.

"No," I whispered.

"Yes," he insisted, "yes, I love you. That's how I see you."

I couldn't explain what happened next but overcome with emotion, my heart felt like a bloody battlefield of two warring sides and each was almost depleted. Neither side of me wanted to admit how very lonely and withdrawn from society I had been. Locking myself away, hiding in my house. Taking Billy to crèche, barely socialising with the other mothers.

I ripped the cover off the book and tore it to shreds, ripping and ripping, until all I held of his words in my hands were tiny little pieces.

This man loved me and I couldn't bear it. His words tore me open, tore me to pieces. I'd dreamed about a man like this my whole life.

"You'll be like the rest," I stomped away from the bed, "you'll hurt me like you said. You'll bruise me and leave me ruined. I don't want this! I want you to go!"

"I want you," he said, "in spite of everything."

He remained calm on the bed, keeping his distance. Maybe he knew I needed space. I turned to look at him, so peaceful and calm, waiting for me. Had he been waiting for me, these past four weeks? For me to admit I felt the same way, too?

"You need to be fucked, Ade. Let me show you how much I want you."

"No."

My chin wobbled up and down and the pieces of the book caught my eye and I ran to them, picked them up and let them slip through my fingers.

"I didn't mean to! I didn't," I wailed, "please, let me... let me tape them together!" I yelled and he took my hand and held it tight.

"Up here, Ade. All up here." He pointed to his head. "Remember?"

He took the other copy, the one I'd been reading, and wrote the poem down again. Passing me it, I madly checked it over and it was just the same.

"I'm in love with you. I want nobody else. There's more... the two weeks I spent thinking, after you dressed me down that time... I wrote a lot. There's loads. It's all for you. I love you. I want you, Adrienne. You're stunning and I love you."

I was wet already, blood pumping wildly around my body. I took the book with me to the window and tried to read his words again, but every single one robbed me of any understanding of my own. My thoughts waded treacle, my mind desperately trying to absorb the significance of his meaning. I moved across the room and stood by his side of the bed as he sat propped up still, calm and collected. He was so composed, I didn't understand it. I was crazed and in love.

I wound my fingers around his. "Will you one day write this, so it remains eternal? Our story I mean. The full thing."

He shook his head. "No, because you will."

I climbed into his lap, smiling, and he tugged my blouse over my head. I'd started wearing my hair down and he pushed it all back over my shoulders, stroking the skin around my neck and shoulders, his gaze heated and intense – the cold all gone away.

I unbuttoned his shirt and found my man beneath, taut and slim, defined and delicate. Pulling me closer once his shirt was off, I felt his pumping heart against my chest. Roaring. His lips began to explore my skin and I closed my eyes, swaying in his arms, his body hot against mine.

"I never realised how horny *Wuthering Heights* might one day make me," he said in a husky voice, "all those withdrawn feelings, buried deep, hmm?"

"I know," I whispered as his finger stroked the skin around my bra strap, teasing me, tickling.

My nipples prickled with heat, the lace of my bra uncomfortable. I reached behind and flicked the fastening open, the bra falling away in his hands.

He pulled me close and my boobs pressed against his naked heart, beating wildly. I dragged my hands through his thick hair and kept my eyes locked on his.

"Let's never look back?"

"Never," he said in barely a whisper.

He wrapped both hands underneath my breasts and brought one nipple, then another to his mouth. He suckled them hard, filling his mouth with my flesh. I arched and ground against his groin, boiling hot between my legs.

I looked down and watched him drink of me, my nipples

a deeper red, the smell of my arousal and his filling the air. He pulled away from my ample breasts and threw me onto my back, his lips on mine, pressing his tongue into my mouth. I wrapped my legs around the back of him, desperate to have my jeans off.

Grasping a tit in his hand, he kissed my throat and I begged, "Please."

"You don't need to beg."

He pulled away and stood by the side of the bed, undoing his trousers. He pulled his boxers down and it was as I thought – he was enormous.

I swallowed, afraid, yet enthralled.

While he undid my jeans and pulled them off, he said, "I got checked recently. I'm clean, always have been. But–"

He lifted his eyes to mine, his breath increasing in pace as he slid my knickers down.

"I'm on the pill, David. Please, be with me. I want you."

I raised my arms above my head and spread my legs.

"You're beautiful, Adrienne," he groaned.

Panting, I wanted to cradle his sexy hips between my thighs. He was still very slim but there was a breadth and strength in his body I delighted in. He just needed a little rebuilding.

He lay between my thighs carefully and held me close, kissing me, never messy – always careful. Little tugs on my lips, little pecks, little licks and caresses and breathtaking, oxygen-depriving French kisses in between.

"David, please, please," I begged, and he reached between us and felt for me. I was slick and sticky and we heard the sounds of his finger sliding around, his lip bitten as he realised how he made me feel. Massaging and stretching me, I had to hold my breath a couple of times to stop myself coming.

"You've got this sweet, wet cunt, just for me?"

"Just for you, David."

He pushed inside me, all the way in, with just one, swift

move. I'd never not know he was in, never would I have to ask. I knew he was *there* because he was just so big and delicious. His eyes shut, he waited. I wrapped around him and waited with him.

"I'm–" he said, barely audibly. Slowly, he dropped a tiny kiss on my nose.

"Me too," I urged, and pulled his buttock. "Just fuck me."

He held my cheeks and kissed me before he reared back and struck hard. My head hit the headboard and I screamed.

I screamed.

Every move he made sent every single nerve ending in my body on fire. Dragging his cock along my fizzing, sensitive muscles, I felt so full and hot. Raging with desire, I wanted and needed it to end – and to last forever.

It was exquisite, no other word.

Hoarse in my ear, he told me in ragged whispers, "I love you."

"I love you," I moaned, holding on tight to his neck. I bit his bicep and licked his skin, tasting salt, taking life from him.

He lifted slightly and fucked me hard, and fast, just a few times. My lower back burned with heat, tension evaporating from there, all the way up my spine and back down again. I screamed for him with the release. I'd never screamed before in my whole life.

I wanted the sensations to end, they were so good but so perishing, and the convulsions gripped me so I was no longer in control. He thrust through my contractions and shouted, "Fucking hell!"

He fell on top of me and our bodies, wet and tender, embraced. I held him against my breast, my legs still wide open with him between them. As he softened, he slowly slipped out and I watched his cock lying on my open thigh, purple and raw from our love.

When he'd caught his breath, he raised himself slightly on his arms and searched my eyes.

"You love me, Adrienne?"

Stroking his face with my fingertips, I smiled. "I knew it the moment we met."

"I knew it the moment you saw right through me and loved me anyway."

We rolled over so I was on top and we kissed each other everywhere for the rest of the night.

There was no looking back now, but like in *Wuthering Heights*, everything salient you try to ignore always comes back to haunt you.

If not today–

Eventually.

FIVE

In the morning I was woken by Billy, squawking in his crib next door. He didn't really cry if it was warm when he woke – he usually enjoyed talking to the toys on his mobile before I yanked him out of bed. David's arms were around me, his nose buried in my shoulder blade. I wriggled and he started to rouse, his body rubbing up against mine, his soft lips brushing my skin. When he fully woke, he stopped dry humping me, remembering there was a kid in the next room.

"What time is it?"

I lifted my head and read, "Half eight. Billy must've needed a lie-in, never sleeps this late."

"Whoa."

"I know. I feel strange. Three, whole hours of sleep this time!"

"I'll go get him." David slid his legs out of bed and put his boxers on. He walked out of the room and down the hall.

I overheard him say, "Wanna come up?"

"Yeh, yeh, yeh," said Billy.

When David walked back into the room holding Billy, I exclaimed, "You don't have to."

He threw me a grin across the room. "I want to."

I stared, gob smacked. On the edge of the bed, he bounced Billy. "Sleepy boy. You hungry?"

I'd never asked David to ingratiate himself with William.

Before then, he'd never offered either. On a Sunday morning after us reading all night, he would normally kiss me awkwardly goodbye when Billy woke at six and that was it. So the night before seemed to have changed everything – literally overnight.

I picked a t-shirt up off the floor, pulling it on to cover myself up. Watching David hold William brought back terrible memories of the last man to hold my child and I reached out for my son.

"Come here, Billy-Boo."

David handed over my son and folded his arms as he watched me plaster kisses all over my baby boy's head. I stared over Billy's shoulder at the lean, dangerous ropes of muscle on David's arms. He was compact but strong. He could overpower me if he wanted to and had done last night during the act of love – in the most wonderful ways.

We exchanged glances and my lungs felt tight. My heart tingled. It was undeniable that I was in love with him – and he with me.

"I love you," he whispered and his words made me smile.

I love you I mouthed, adding, "...both of you."

David rested his palm on my cheek, leaning down to kiss my hair. "Some tea or coffee? What's your poison?"

We'd never done this before – but I rose to the occasion, painting on a smile. "Tea, lots of milk, no sugar. Thank you."

"And Billy?"

"Water and just a tiny, tiny bit of squash."

David searched for some clothes and settled for my oversized towelling robe which fitted him alright except for the sleeves, which almost reached his elbows.

He pottered in the kitchen and brought out drinks. While Billy drank his juice, sat up in the middle of the bed, David and I quietly sipped our tea.

"I have some questions. I... well, you have this house, and I don't..."

I covered my mouth with the back of my hand, wondering what he meant. Was he still intimidated by my money? Billy looked between us, chomping on his sippy cup. I read more in my little boy's eyes than he could communicate at that age. He sensed a new addition to the unit and I think he was weighing up whether it was a good or bad thing, too.

"...I guess what I'm asking is, well... I live with Mum, so I'd–"

I laughed to disperse some of his unease. "Please explain what you're asking!"

He chuckled nervously. "I don't want to spend another day without you."

"Oh... oh, I see!"

David burst out laughing and covered his mouth. Billy joined in, laughing too. I couldn't help but see the funny side of it as well.

After the laughter died down, I explained, "I feel the same, David but I'm understandably cautious. Perhaps we could work on a compromise?"

"Okay, tell me."

I took a moment to think. "I can give you a drawer or two and a key but you're not officially moving in, not yet. Let's take it slow and see how it goes."

"That's brilliant." When he smiled, I realised taking it slow was not something we were capable of together. I wanted him all the time and he felt the same.

"I'm gonna finish this academic year and then get a proper job that pays. It's time."

"But," I frowned, "didn't you say you had two years left on this PhD?"

"Yeah but it's just... it doesn't matter to me as much anymore. I will never earn loads of money doing this... it has just been something to do. I want to do... more."

My eyes widened and I held my heart. "I love that you're an academic, doing it for the love. I don't want you to be like me… I want you to have your own thing. I don't need you to earn loads of money; it doesn't matter to me at all, I promise you."

He chuckled and hid his shyness. His nose whistled when he breathed in sharply. "I want you to do your degree, Ade. I think it'd be really good for you."

"You do?"

"Yeah. What do you want to do with it afterwards? Your degree, I mean?"

"Investments," I told David even though my plan to use my father's money, multiply it, and shove my higher worth in his fat face didn't seem as attractive anymore. All I wanted was this man.

David reached for my hand and stroked my fingers, dusting his fingertips gently over the back of my skin so that hairs were raised and my heart rate soared.

In barely a whisper, he asked me, "You know I would never intentionally hurt you?"

"I know, David." A grimace contorted my face and I rubbed at my forehead. Turning my attention to Billy, I asked, "Son, do you want some breakfast now?"

"Yeh, yeh, yeh! M'ungry!"

"Okay." I looked at David. "And what would you like?"

"Toast will be fine. Is it okay if I take a shower?"

"Sure."

I carried William to the kitchen, plopping him in his highchair. Handing him a spoon to play with while I warmed his breakfast to tepid, he was soon making his own music, banging his utensil against the plastic tray.

When David came into the kitchen showered, he smelled delicious as he put his arms around me from behind.

"You smell of coconut!"

He chuckled. "I kind of like it. I also liked your saucy bath mitt. I reckon I know where that's been."

"Shut up." I handed him a plate of toast and we sat with William around the breakfast table.

David looked different as he stared at me. "I have to tell you something–"

"Oh yeah?" I said feeling buoyant, trying to ignore the warning tone in his voice.

"There's something you should know."

"Okay?"

He rubbed his index finger under his nose, over and over, looking awkward as hell. "Okay," he took a deep breath, "I have no money at all. None. I don't have anything. However, I'm going to get money, I promise."

"David, don't be daft. I told you–"

He squinted. "I want you, Adrienne. I want to support and look after you while you do your degree. I meant what I said, I love you. When the time is right, I want you to marry me."

"David!" I reached over and kissed his lips, pulling him into me, trying to alleviate his worries. "I love you! I don't care if you're not rich! The rich people I know are all arseholes."

He dragged me onto his lap and all that protected my modesty were my panties and an old, knackered t-shirt that had seen out its use as a frequent bed shirt. He stroked the edge of my lace underwear but there was no smile for me for some reason.

"What is it?"

I stared into his eyes and he eventually told me, "I've done stuff in the past for money, stuff I'm not proud of."

"Like what? Robbery? Fraud, something like that?" I scratched my head and wanted to cry. It was the look of worry in David's eyes. "Just tell me."

"I… it started out as modelling, but it didn't pay enough. I ended up being in porn films. There, I said it. I did porn to fund my education."

I stared blindly, wondering if I was having a psychotic episode.

Tell me he's lying.

"When? When?" He didn't answer. "When? When was your last... film? If that's what they're really called?" I always thought porn was fucking disgusting people doing even more disgusting things.

"It was before you. Long before you. The PhDs... they're funded through research grants and teaching, blah, blah, blah. I don't even know why I signed up for another doctorate... I don't... I've felt for so long that I've had no direction, but now... that's all changed."

I stood from his lap and cleared away Billy's bowl, pretending to busy myself around the posh kitchen that he no doubt hated me for. He was trying to plan a future with a woman he felt he couldn't match up to and that made me feel brilliant. (NOT!)

"I don't know why I need to know about your days as a porn star."

He leapt from his chair and threw his arms around me from behind, his rapid breath biting the back of my hot, angry ear. He squeezed my breasts over the t-shirt and I was glad Billy didn't understand yet.

"Don't say that, Adrienne. Don't say that. They were adult films... and I know, I shouldn't have told you, I know. I should try to protect you. I'm sorry. I just don't want any secrets."

I clucked my tongue. "So you got what you wanted last night and now it's okay to dump all your shit on me."

"I hate myself, Adrienne. Please don't be upset."

"No, David, no."

I ripped myself from his embrace and grabbed Billy from his highchair, taking him into the bedroom. I plopped him down in the playpen while I took clothes and things out of drawers. David did the unthinkable and handed Billy a talking bear to play with for a minute. Before I had chance to protest, he carried me back to the kitchen and ripped my few clothes off. I couldn't see for how fast he kissed, held and touched me.

He unbuckled his jeans and lifted me up against the wall, slamming straight into me. My walls tugged on his cock with every thrust. It was wonderful. I came over and over, just because he had me up against the wall, savage and depraved, his mouth bestowing nothing but passionate declarations on my skin, love bites appearing, my body blissfully punctured by his love.

He finished and we stared at one another, a mist of sweat and lust clouding our rational thoughts. Pinning me still, his hands stroked my cheeks as he kissed my lips over and over.

"I'm going nowhere. I'm going to marry you one day, Adrienne Kyd, I'm going to carry you there if I have to. I will love you forever. I know I love you, like I know which way my cock swings. I'm scared of fucking this up... but I love you."

We burst into laughter and I kissed his elegant, long neck. Every bit of him had me on fire. The way his small, tight butt hugged his jeans. The heat of him through his shirt. The spiced scent of him. His tall body, arms, strength. His voice. The way his lips moved. He was so magical, I'd almost forgotten that magic preceded a wicked spell – it was the way of life – it was what I'd been taught. Balance meant nothing beautiful lasted forever, and that was life. I'd learned that the hard way.

He helped me on with my panties and t-shirt, then French kissed me for what felt like hours. I ducked in on Billy and after seeing he was fine in the bedroom, happily playing, I rejoined David in the kitchen as he tried to tuck his deflating bulge back into his jeans.

"I'll leave some things here then?" He held me close and I could only nod in response, my shaking body clinging to him. "It'll save me some trouble. Otherwise I'll be driving a lot between here and home, just to see you."

"Your mum's is in Harrogate?" Harrogate, a place I hated. People talked and swapped gossip there. He might find out more about me – things to change his mind.

"Live here, with me. Live with me," I begged, tears falling from my eyes. "Bring everything. I love you. Live with us. Don't leave me. Stay."

He pressed his nose to mine, holding the sides of my head. "Are you sure?"

"Yes, I'm sure. I know this is insanity, but I'm sure!" I kissed every inch of his face, holding him to me. "Tell me you are, too."

"Adrienne! I'm sure."

It was that simple, or so it seemed. We knew nothing but that we loved one another and it felt so right. He gripped my butt in his hands, moulding my flesh in his palms. I jumped up and encircled him and he spun us both around. Ravenously, we kissed – before he drove straight home to pack. He'd tell his mum eventually what was going on, he said – but for then nobody needed to know how close we were becoming.

Maybe I was blind. Maybe I couldn't see straight because of him and knew I never would be able to. It's why I tried to run from him at the start – and also why I miserably failed at it.

But does love negate reason?

Or does love bury the bad, to preserve the good, and protect itself?

SIX

Even within the first week of us living together, a lot happened. For a start he easily found room for his things because he had nothing much more than clothes. I asked why no books or DVDs or anything, but he said he always borrowed things like that. He told me material possessions meant nothing much to him, but he'd always look after us. He noticed Billy's room was plain and bare and spent two days putting up posters of trains and planes. He bought images from charity shops of vintage cars and put them in new frames. Rugs and all kinds of cute toys soon filled Billy's room and my son came alive with male company. I'd always done the best I could but to see my baby boy with a positive male presence set my heart on fire.

He began buying me presents, too. The first thing he bought me was a ceramic black slide for my hair, so simple, with little diamante details. I put some curls in my long, blonde hair so I had use for the slide and within days, I noticed myself getting more attention from the opposite sex. David bought me a couple of tea dresses from a charity shop which were lovely. Flowery, with little pencil-thin belts. He couldn't afford new ones but he wanted to surprise me and I wore them with pride. A couple of guys on campus asked me out for a coffee and I declined, realising my happiness had put a splash of colour on my cheeks and in my wardrobe.

I didn't know myself and quickly realised things were moving so fast, I was beyond caught up in his love for me – I was invested as deeply as David was becoming.

One day I found him riffling through my underwear drawer and when I questioned him, he shrugged. "I was going to buy you something special… you have everything in different sizes though!"

I pursed my lips. "Yeah, I'm a different size in different shops!"

He burst out laughing.

"It's not funny," I protested, "we've barely been together a week! This is well beyond my comfort zone."

"An F in this shop," he held up one label, "and a D here? What the hell?"

I snatched my undies from his grasp and slammed the drawer shut. "Some stuff I had while pregnant, and I just haven't thrown it out yet. I was an F while pregnant. Thank you very much."

"Let's get you off the pill asap," he grinned.

"Shut up, you knicker-drawer invader."

He folded his arms. "All you wear is white or grey. We need to do something about that."

"And you're an authority after a few nights in my bed, hmm?" I looked away, feeling embarrassed because he was right. "Anyway, I like white or grey. What else are you going to dictate, eh? What I eat."

"You could do with putting a few pounds on actually."

Now it was my turn to fold my arms. "I can eat loads… and never put a pound on!"

He smirked. "Me too. If we have kids, they'll all be stick insects. With large sex parts."

He motioned at my tits and his cock. I laughed and fell on the bed, delirious with happiness.

Once I caught my breath, I turned to look at him and whispered, "I'll buy myself something. You're right. There are plenty more colours of the rainbow."

I didn't say it, but I wondered if I'd be getting second-hand undies off him. That was just the sort of thing you didn't want second-hand.

"Okay," he agreed. "I can hardly wait."

"I'll go on Saturday afternoon. Can you watch Billy while I'm shopping?"

"Sure can," he whispered.

"Okay, fine. I'll go and buy lots of nasty stuff for you to peel off me."

He crawled across the bed towards me and kissed my cheek before laying his head in my lap. "That's my girl."

I shook my head at him, my heart pounding wildly. He seemed so adamant to better my life, to make an impact so quickly, I felt dizzy.

"We've still got so much left to learn about one another, haven't we?" I asked.

"Yes," he agreed, nodding, "and I've got so much left to teach you."

I bit my lip. "Sexually?"

"Oh, that... and so much more, Adrienne."

I dropped my lips down onto his and whispered against his mouth. "Like filming us?"

His expression darkened and he slid off the bed and away, turning his back on me. I feared I'd upset him and began to apologise when he turned and held up his hand.

"You're more to me than that. Don't ever underestimate your worth to me. I'll never treat you like that."

"I didn't mean–"

He held his hand up to me still. "Adrienne, by god, the only thing that will ever make me angry is you, talking nonsense like this. Don't ever discount yourself, you're wonderful. You're nothing like those other women I had in my life."

I stood and threw myself into his arms, weepy, and he bundled me against him and kissed my hair repeatedly. I knew I'd upset him and at the same time, I was glad to fracture his cool exterior and grab some reaction from him.

"I love you," he said.

"I know."

***

I arrived home from the shops late on Saturday, carrying bags and bags of things. It had started with a little trip into La Senza and had then escalated into shoes and dress shopping. I hadn't bought myself any nice things in months.

When I crossed the threshold of the house, I didn't smell his usual Saturday evening cooking. I also heard a female voice. Walking into the living room, I found the teenage girl from the flat next door playing with Billy on the carpet.

"Jenna's going to look after Billy this evening, Ade. What do you think?" He searched my eyes, hoping I would say yes. "We'll put him down to sleep and then Jenna will sit and watch TV. If he wakes, he'll know her face now, won't he?"

"Hey Jenna," I nodded, having bumped into her a few times in the hall.

"Hey Adrienne. You had a good shopping spree?"

I looked down at my bags. "I went a bit crazy, actually. David… a word…" I gestured he follow me to the bedroom, and he took my bags from me, carrying them there.

I pulled the door slightly closed. "We haven't known one another long enough, David. You don't get to make these decisions."

He shook his head. "You know Jenna. She's trustworthy. Plus," he turned his lip upside down, "we've been seeing each other all this time and haven't had a proper date, yet."

I huffed and puffed, annoyed and aggravated. After I sat on the edge of the bed, he asked, "Can I tell her to come back later, or not?"

"I guess I have little choice, now. She's no doubt looking forward to the pocket money."

He smiled and beamed. "Great, I'll go and sort it out. Why don't you have a bath, do your hair, pick out something nice for tonight?"

"May I ask what we're doing? So I know how to dress."

His smile grew wicked. "You'll need practical clothes and shoes, with filthy underwear beneath."

I sat, stunned. He left the room, totally cool, calm and collected as always.

"If I didn't love you..." I whispered to myself, and began getting ready.

We put Billy to bed and Jenna plonked herself in front of the TV with numerous bags of crisps and sweets. I made sure to put the child settings on the satellite box and she pouted. I also locked our bedroom door so she couldn't go snooping in there. Anywhere else was fine, just not in there where all my new lingerie still sat mostly in bags or partially on display.

"Remember my mobile number is on the kitchen notepad, Jenna."

"I'll be fine," she said, "if I have a problem, I can always call next door and ask my mum, can't I?"

"See, she'll be fine."

We got into David's old VW Golf outside the building and I stared at him, annoyed.

"I don't feel completely comfortable about this."

"He'll be fine, she said so. Come on, let's go and have some fun."

He drove us out to a cinema on the outskirts of town and we watched the second *Lord of the Rings* film. All throughout, we were kissing, barely watching it. Sat in a sparse theatre because the film had almost seen out its extended run, David made me come a couple of times with his fingers, roaming beneath my jeans.

Afterwards, we went somewhere close by for a burger and chips at a common or garden pub.

Sat together in a little corner, huddled away, he fawned on me. I loved the way he touched my hands constantly, kissed my fingers and my cheek. I'd never known such affection from anyone else but my mother.

"What are you thinking about?" he asked me, when I found myself staring into space.

Putting my burger down on my plate, I wiped my hands on a napkin and grimaced. "My mother."

"Yeah?" He looked downcast at the mention.

"It's not easy to think about her."

"Why?"

I put my hand on his thigh and my head on his shoulder, letting him stroke his fingers up and down my arm. Warm outside, and light still at almost ten at night, it felt strange to have just been in a dark cinema for so long to come out into this. At his earlier request I wore sensible clothes including leather boots, jeans and a black top with little detail except a scooped cowl neck. I think anything sexier and we would have laid down and made love, right on the cinema floor.

"Because... I miss her, I guess."

He sniffed. "You don't want to cross your father and call her, or something?"

"Yes... and no." I nodded, agreeing with him in some respects. "I guess, oh I don't know... I'm stronger than her. Maybe I know she needs him, but I don't."

"I know so. You have been doing fine."

I looked across at him, reading the tone of his voice. "What do you know about him?"

He looked nervous, uncharacteristic of him. David patted his mouth with the napkin, hiding behind it. "My mum's a bit of a gossip. She heard he sort of... did the dirty on your mum... a few times."

I nodded. "Yep. Anyway, I don't want to talk about this."

"But you looked sad... and you said it was because of your mother."

"It was actually because," I paused, checking my words,

"you remind me of the last person to treat me well... it was her. Before I grew up and developed an opinion of my own, we used to be close. We used to be as familiar as you and me are being tonight."

David sipped back some of his beer and after deliberating, he pulled me closer in our bench seat. He whispered huskily, "We're not familiar, we're in love."

He brushed his lips over mine and the room evaporated as I was held captive by his strength and his zeal. Since he'd moved in, I'd watched him perform 200 sit-ups and 100 press-ups every morning. No wonder his arms were so strong. He rose from bed, dropped and did his exercise on the carpet, then snaked his sweaty body on top of mine to eke out the last of his energy.

Pulling my hands through his hair, I murmured, "I love you."

He nudged his nose through my loose hair, whispering against my ear, "I can see a navy strap beneath your top. We have the first colour of our rainbow, then?"

Running my hands over his shoulders, I smiled shyly. It was good we were tucked away in a corner of the pub because we were almost performing, unable to keep our hands off each other.

"The first of many," I whispered back.

While David paid Jenna and tidied up all her empty confectionary cartons and packets, I undressed swiftly in the bedroom so that I could be ready and waiting for him.

I'd waited all night, what was a few more minutes...

I dimmed the lights and lay on the bed, in the centre, sprawled out.

Eventually I heard him set the hallway alarm and he crept into the bedroom, touching the door shut.

When he saw me, he drew breath.

The bra was navy, as he'd guessed, with little light-blue stars in the trims. The panties I'd matched with it were waist-high and pure lace.

"You said you wanted something to unwrap."

"I did, didn't I?" he chuckled as he began to undress himself.

He wore black, tight boxer shorts which hung below the dramatic indents either side of his hips where muscle intersected with more muscle.

"It's been a week, Adrienne. And you're not bored with me?"

I shook my head repeatedly. "More than anything, I want to know more."

"I do my communicating only one way, Adrienne," he said, repeating my name again, so I knew he was serious.

"What way?"

He circled the bed, wearing only his socks and underpants. I'd noticed he liked to keep his socks on for some reason, but still I had no idea why.

"Fucking, and teasing," he said, "and Saturday nights were made for all-night teasing, don't you think?"

"I don't know," I murmured, "maybe you will have to teach me."

"Maybe. Maybe I like to screw you loose on weeknights, and screw you tight at the weekend. So tight you'll be wound up for a long time to come."

"Just fuck me."

"No, Adrienne," he said, continuing to circle the bed, "you have no idea how insanely beautiful you are, do you?"

"I don't know what–"

"Men would kill for you, darling. I need to know you're mine. If I give myself to you, I need to know. I want to know before I teach you how to be my perfect lover, my perfect mate. If I invest in you, you have to invest in me."

I knelt in the centre of the bed and beckoned him over but he kept his restraint, waiting for words to spring from my lips.

"David, I don't see anyone but you."

"All those men this week, since you became mine and I put the smell of lust on you, you weren't tempted by any of their offers?" His eye twitched and I feared his questions. What if I tripped up and said the wrong thing? Didn't he know I'd had all these mind games put on me before?

I'd admitted to him I'd been suddenly pursued by other men this week and now – he was questioning me, when I'd already told him I wasn't interested in any of them.

"They never saw me before, they only see me now I have you, who brings out the best in me. Please come into my arms and love me," I begged, desperate for him.

"Answer me, Adrienne. Are you mine?"

"Every piece of me. Every inch. Every mark and blemish and scar, it's all yours. If you asked me, I'd wait here all day with my legs spread for you, waiting. I'd wait all day, aching, and in pain, in the hope you'd come running into my arms and come straight inside me. When you're with me, I don't fear anything. I only feel loved and adored and pleasured. Being without you, even when I'm at the library for only four hours a day… it feels like purgatory, without you inside me. Without you, I burn with yearning."

The straps of my bra dug into my shoulders harder, my breasts so heavy. I wanted him to slice himself between my wet folds and mark me again, fill me as full as he'd been filling me all week long.

"Come and touch me," he said, "crawl on your knees to me."

I did so willingly, happy to please him, serve him.

I touched his erection over his boxers and he held his hands behind his back, restraining himself from reaching out and throwing me beneath him.

Sitting on the edge of the bed, I pulled him between my open thighs and my mouth met his stomach, kissing him. His skin smelt of cookies and milk, of cinnamon and subtle spices. I kissed his body as I rubbed my hand over his bulge.

"Slowly peel down my underwear," he instructed, "keep

eye contact. I want to see the look in your eyes when you see me spring out and into your mouth."

Slowly, I eased his pants down, kissing his slender hips – licking over each delicate plane of skin as it was revealed. Looking up constantly into his eyes for reassurance, I noticed him watching intently, still steely but curious. He wanted me to know he was in control. Something about David made me trust him, something reassuring. I'd never known another man like him, so clever and sensitive.

When his long, thick cock finally sprang free, I licked him into my mouth and maintained eye contact, showing him how greedy I was for his length. He helped me take his pants off his legs, over his ankles, and then he put my hand on the base of his cock and gestured I squeeze. When I flicked over the underside of his swollen head, he sucked in breath suddenly.

This was the first time I'd gone down on him and I knew he hadn't expected me to know what I was doing. Before Marcus, there were others. Nice boys who reciprocated my need to release. That was all they were.

"I've had men," I told David, "but I've never had a lover as beautiful as you."

"I somehow thought you'd–"

"Thought what?" I growled low and quiet, as I nibbled the spine of his mighty fine cock.

"I needed to bed you in. I thought–"

"You mean..." I licked his balls in between speaking, "...you saw the cardigans," I licked them again, "imagined some frumpy bint beneath the oversized clothes. When in fact I was just hiding away on purpose, concealing myself for a reason. I don't need or want love. I want passion. I want fire. I want a real man who claims me, and wants me to claim him. I want you. You're all I want."

I kissed his cock, everywhere, marking him. My hands squeezing his buttocks, I controlled him, spinning his world on its axis. Sweat began to bead between his pecs and I knew he was so close.

"Ade," he called, a warning he was going to come.

Unperturbed, I continued, relishing the control. The power he was giving me. Using my hold on his bum, I spun his hips, asking him to circle.

Inside my mouth, I sucked and licked around his head, pumping my fist hard, up and down, saliva running in rivers over the milky flesh of his sex.

I felt the spasm in his pelvis before he realised there was no stopping it. I pumped his semen out of his cock and into my mouth, letting it coat my lips and tongue. Massaging his balls gently, I eased out the last of his ejaculation and swallowed his cum.

Looking up into his eyes, I asked, "Do you love me?"

"I fucking love you."

I grinned, sniggering. "Oh yes you do, baby. I'm going to enjoy performing many more ceremonies like that, let me tell you."

"Fuck. I haven't even got you out of your lingerie yet."

I bit my lip and crawled back up into the pillows, leering suggestively over my shoulder. David followed me and laid by my side, stroking his hands through my hair.

"What do you like?" he asked.

"I love oral pleasure," I murmured, because we'd not tried that yet either. "I expect you think one taste might make you addicted. Well, it will. I've been told I taste fucking amazing... and I should know, I've tasted myself."

He leaned over me and kissed my mouth so hard I thought I'd die of breathlessness. He unclasped my bra and lying on top of me, I cradled his head while he pushed my breasts together and lapped at one nipple then another, over and over.

Moving down, he buried his face between my thighs and chewed my clit over my panties. I realised I never knew what dying felt like until right then. As he pulled my knickers to the side, thousands of nerve endings connected with a tongue I was in love with. I felt a fire ignite, rippling along my every surface. I rocked to his rhythm, my hips in the palms of his hands. I arched and danced with him, my fingers through his. He licked inside me and made me come with his tongue darting against my upper wall.

I barked so loudly, I felt like I'd just run a marathon.

He wasn't willing to wait, however.

He pulled me onto my knees and moved up behind me. He seized me on his erection, making us whole. Arms wrapped around my breasts together, I craned my neck back and we kissed each other's tastes off each other's mouths, silencing each other's cries.

David sweated all over me, from every pore. His hair wet, it clung to his forehead and around the nape of his neck.

Sitting on his cock felt like the cruellest kind of pleasure, because I'd remember what it was like to have had him there later in the night – when he was spent and I was still needy, my lust endless. How could I live with this gaping hole inside of me? I needed him as often as I could have him.

He bit gently against the side of my throat where he knew my hair would cover any marks. I panted, sucking in breath frantically as he began rolling my clit beneath his middle finger. He pulled my hips back onto him, holding us tight together while my body tried to expel his – a fierce orgasm consuming me. He filled me full of heat, his strong arms tight all around me, cocooning me.

We fell down together and he spooned up behind me, his leg covering both of mine. We breathed deeply and eventually sweat cooled our skin. David brought the summer sheets over us and we rested blissfully together.

"I love you."

"Buy more underwear," he groaned, before starting to snore lightly.

SEVEN

August, 2003

From across the restaurant table, David poured wine into my glass. I saw him mentally counting how much this meal was going to cost him and a part of me wanted to hand over my credit card. Another part of me knew it would upset him for me to do that. He wiggled the bottle to eke the last drop out into my glass and I noticed while mine was full, his was only a quarter full. He went without to let me have everything – I knew it. His love for me was extraordinary and beautiful. I could never imagine being out of love with him because he was my world and along with Billy, he was the only reason why I woke up happy everyday. Three months living together had only made me love him more.

Summer had arrived and with it nothing but thunderstorms and sticky nights. I'd rather have had winter, which I preferred, having been born in February.

Celebrating David's twenty-seventh birthday, we were at an Italian near the city centre. It was nice but I could've cooked better at home with a few ingredients from Waitrose. David knew I'd been brought up to know the finer things in life but he didn't yet understand that it meant I knew good food from mediocre and I wished he'd just cooked for me that night – because his food was made with love.

I painted on a smile anyway. "Are you trying to get me drunk? You've barely had anything."

He chuckled. "I'd rather I was performance ready, that's all."

I grinned. "Oh?"

"Yes, *oh*. There will be lots of those… later." He held his hand under his chin and stared at me. "But first I want to talk."

"About?"

"Us. Life. Me. You. Everything."

"Okay."

Since David moved in, there had been nights we laid in one another's arms completely naked, nights we both wore t-shirts around Billy. Nights we only made love the once, nights we didn't make love at all. There were the nights I lost count of the times we made love. There were the couple of nights Billy was sick or had a bad dream and slept with us. There were times David read to Billy until he fell asleep, times David read to me until I fell asleep.

In short, our life was perfect. Well, aside from his insecurities about money.

"I told them I'm not coming back in September, so they dropped me. With immediate effect. I'll not get severance or anything. I knew that would be the case, but… it's left me a little short. Only for the time being, mind… I *will* get proper work, I always said that."

"Oh." That explained why he'd recently started counting his pennies.

"Yeah," said David, dejected. "Only thing is, there's nothing else for me out there. Either I'm not looking properly… or I'm over qualified."

"Oh but you don't have to–"

He held his hand up. "This is something I will handle."

I frowned and he looked at me strangely. It was so ironic. "You're willing to give up academia… for me? The job you want to do?"

"I'd give up my left arm for you, Ade. Never mind a stupid fucking job. I told you, it's only been something to do. I want to see what else there is out there for me. I know it's not going to be easy. I'll figure it out. Do I have your support?"

I took his hands in mine. "Always... although... we could just go travelling for the rest of the summer, and then come back fresh–"

Shaking his head, I knew that wasn't an idea he found attractive. "I'll lose valuable time and besides, I'm not taking your money, Adrienne. I'll take everything else, but not your money."

"Well, you may have to."

"For the meantime, but... I *will* pay my way. I will support you. This is something I want to do for me, okay?"

"I won't need support, not when my trust fund matures. David, it'll more than cover my tuition fees and everything else. I wish you'd stay and finish this second doctorate, I don't understand–"

"I need a fresh start. That's all."

I pursed my lips. "Fine, but I... I don't see what the rush is. You didn't have to tell them anything, not until you found a new position."

He swallowed his quarter glass of wine in one gulp. "I hate this... this, I don't know. I never thought... I never..."

"It's fine."

The waitress came over to collect our plates. "Anything else guys?"

"The bill," I said with a smile.

David stared at me, but I couldn't read him. "You can have pudding if you want Adrienne?"

"I'll have pudding when we get home," I grinned, playing footsie with him under the table.

I didn't know where this complex of his stemmed from. He seemed insecure about his status as my protector and shield against the world. It wasn't my fault I was moneyed.

Even my attempt at flirtation didn't rub well with him and his mouth twitched side to side while he stewed. Could we live a whole lifetime, like this? Words going unsaid? I was terrified if I asked him questions about his past – his situation – that what he had to say might break us.

"Here you go," the waitress said, placing the bill on the table.

I snatched it out of his grasp. "David, it's no biggie."

He held his hand against his cheek and flamed red, hating himself and the situation.

The waitress saw my card laid on the plastic tray on top of the bill and gestured she would put it through the card machine. Maybe she read the situation that was brewing – a man's ego at risk – an occupational hazard for her perhaps.

While we waited for the card machine, I told him, "I read in the *Guardian* it takes the average graduate six months to find work so it may be much longer for you. You're so qualified… and the only thing you're really qualified for, you've quit. We could even sublet the flat and go travelling for a few months… a year, forever. I have savings, plus what's coming to me. We don't have to worry about a thing. People come and go at the library and I could easily return as a casual, whenever I want."

"I don't buy into statistics," he said, vehement, "if we go by those, it's going to take me years to find a job. Fuck that. I'll lie, cheat, do whatever I have to. I'm not going to be a bum anymore."

"Strong words."

He chewed his lip and I stared – wondering what to say.

When he smiled, it was an anxious smile and he blurted, "Ade, I've spent all these years with no direction. You don't know what you've done to me. I don't want to be nothing anymore. I want to be a support to you. You have to understand this is a man thing. I can earn big money, too… I just never cared before. There are things I can do, I know it."

"I'm independent," I said gently, "just get used to it."

"I'm okay with that," he gesticulated as if giving up on that one, "the problem is, I want to be your equal."

The girl came over with a slip for me to sign. From my purse, I slid a tenner in her apron pocket and winked. "If a penny of that goes to your bosses, I'll be disappointed to hear of it."

She giggled and winked back. "Thanks."

"Find something better," I told her straight. She'd given us good service and hadn't tried to hit on David once while she served us. Under my breath, I mentioned, "I overheard them in the kitchen. They don't deserve you."

She snickered. "You know Italian?"

"Yes, I know Italian," I admitted, "and they've got bets on who will get in your pants first."

She smiled broadly. "Well I should really give this back. Now I can have some fun with them thanks to your tip. Pity I don't bat for their side."

"You two could really fuck with their minds," David said grinning, pointing between the two of us – me and the girl.

I stood up and he stood with me. "Keep dreaming lover boy."

She giggled. "To be honest, I wouldn't mind."

David and I left the restaurant laughing as the waitress began clearing the table with a big, broad smile on her face.

We stood outside for a minute, mingling with all the people on the city streets, moving like ants from one bar to another.

"You hated that meal, didn't you?" he asked.

I stared into his eyes. With heels on, we were almost eye level. "I have a business mind and I see inefficiencies where there are inefficiencies. Like crap staff getting the same rewards as better staff. Like fake Italian food instead of real Italian food. What you cook at home is better, even though you always forget the cheese!"

He laughed, tossing his head back. "We just went to the biggest Italian chain in the world."

I turned my lip down. "I've eaten real Italian food, my darling in real Italia and that was from a jar and a British bakery, not authentic from the fields and the kiln."

David stared at me, toying with my fingers in his. "Can we go home now?"

"Not until you tell me what the problem is," I demanded.

"I don't know how I will ever be able to match you!" His words came quick, so at least I knew they were honest.

"Maybe..." I looked around us and assessed our bustling surroundings. "...the world constructs concepts which are unachievable. The notion opposites attract might actually have merit however. Maybe I'm rich and you're academic. Maybe you're kind and I'm hard. Maybe you're soft and I'm businesslike. Maybe we could teach each other a lot? We're not unequal at all. We were sad and alone apart, but now we're together, we're both better. What does that tell you? There's only quality here, and it's equal. Therefore we have equality."

He shook his head. "You're getting fucked tonight, baby."

"Oh, I won't be the only one!"

"Oh, no," he said, tugging my hand to start pulling me home, "go easy on me honey, my mind's already had the flogging of its life tonight."

We began walking, the heat of the night enveloping us, the urge to be together naked spurring us on to walk faster.

"I want you to meet my mother," he said.

"Yeah? What's brought this on now?"

"She rang the other day and seemed to finally accept I was serious about you. She asked to meet you. I've thought about it and I think we're good for it, what about you?"

My steps slowed. "We'd have to visit Harrogate?"

"Would that be a problem?"

"Yes, but... I mean, I could go... for you."

"Good. Then, we'll go. Sunday lunch? She'll enjoy cooking for us."

"What about your dad? Do you have brothers or sisters?"

He heaved a sigh. "Rob's in America and my father died

when I was twelve. She lives alone."

I stopped him in his tracks. "Well, why didn't you say? It's not fair to leave her all alone."

"I love you, Adrienne. I wanted these first few months for just us, you know? No interference. But now I think it's time."

In the street, I looped my arms around his neck and kissed him, really kissed him.

"I heard they left for Spain," I told David in a whisper against his lips.

His every facial feature twitched with shock. "How could they leave you?"

"You don't want to know my father. And my mother does whatever he says. Anyway, it doesn't matter now."

"It does matter. You're a perfect angel and they tossed you aside."

I chuckled slightly. "I'm no angel."

"You are."

"No, David, I love you for trying to put me on a pedestal, but I'm not perfect."

We walked onwards, holding hands, and he professed, "Say you're not perfect again and I'll not make love to you tonight."

"I'm not perfect," I said giggling.

He laughed. "I haven't been able to resist you, not since I found out why you go round with so much hurt in your eyes. I just want to take it all away."

"Don't."

"Adrienne–"

I bypassed him. "David, I'm stronger than you know."

"I know, but still."

"I love you, but you need to shut up," I told him, my chin almost to my chest with emotion.

He wrapped his arm tight around my shoulder and kissed my temple. "I know."

"Is your mother nice?" I asked.

"She's nice," he assured me, "she might be a little hard to convince, but I'll work on her."

"Convince of what?"

He choked on the disease that was guilt. "That I've changed. When she sees Billy is a part of this equation, too... she might go mad knowing what's at stake. I know she's already decided I'll fuck this up, but I'm not going to. It's because of what's at stake that I won't fuck this up."

"Hey." I turned into his body, fisting his shirt. "So you did things in the past. So what? It doesn't matter what anyone else thinks. It only matters what we think and we know what we have."

"But I can't help wanting to have her support... her approval. I can't help it."

I nodded heavily, feeling the weight of his relationship with his mother – it was obviously important to him.

"Hey man! Hey... Dave! Dave!" we heard someone shout from just outside a trendy bar. We were almost out of the city centre and onto the more residential streets when we saw a man around David's age waving and shouting.

"Oh it's Si," he said, "we'll say hello and then I'll take you home and fuck you."

"I just love it when you get all commanding." I giggled and he pulled me by the hand in the direction of Si.

"Hey man," Si said when we reached him, and the guys shook hands. "We haven't seen you in so long."

His eyes swept up and down my body and David growled, "You touch one hair on her man and you will be spitting cactus needles for the next ten years... from your dick."

Si held his hands up in defeat. "Can I get you both a drink? We're just having a few before heading to Mission."

David looked to me and I looked at my watch. We had about fifteen minutes before the babysitter expected us back.

"A really quick one."

"Okay," Si said with glee and we headed inside the

refurbished pub, once a bank or something.

"Eh lads, look what the cat dragged in?"

A big group of eight blokes all looked at us, especially me, and I didn't know where to put myself as David got dragged into several man hugs at once.

I heard the words, "Where have you been?" and "Is this the reason you've been gone?" and "Introduce us, will you?"

Eventually David took my hand and we had two drinks thrust at us as he told everyone, "This is Adrienne, the love of my life."

Wolf whistles started up and I turned a shocking shade of red. I could see myself in the mirrors above the bar, flaming almost purple.

One of the lads (I noticed) gave me daggers and I gave him a stare back. I held out my hand to him while David stepped to the side slightly to quickly chat with his other pals.

"Adrienne, and you are?" I asked the man with daggers for eyes.

"Callum," he said, "once Dave's best mate. Seems I've been relegated."

"Are you all celebrating?" I asked.

He gave me a funny look. "What?"

"Well, you're all dressed up and there's so many of you."

He chewed his bottom lip. "Just an ordinary Thursday night sweetheart, just an ordinary night. Dave should know. He used to be out with us all the time. Now I see what's got him hooked... a bit of alright, aren't you?"

I decided this was a group of David's university friends because Callum had a cockney accent and many of the others were speaking London, too, among other tongues.

"You gonna look after our Dave then, girl?"

I shot him eyes. "What do you mean?" It was clear this guy didn't know who he was dealing with.

"You know, don't hurt him," Callum said, and my eyes locked onto his.

"Do you think you have the right to tell me how to live my life?" I grinned, untouched by his insinuation.

He smirked. "Knew you were a fucking crazy bitch. It's why most of us stay single."

I looked down on Callum, who was about half a foot shorter than me. He was clearly gay (in denial) and had feelings for my boyfriend.

"Real friends welcome another's happiness, they don't try to strip it down the first moment they get."

Callum kept my stare and I saw his eye quirk at the corner. He knew I meant business.

"There comes a time when people move on," I counselled him, "maybe this is your time, huh?"

I could see him seeking words, but none fell out.

"Hey, Adrienne, hey... come meet Hugh... come here!" my lover called and I grinned smarmily at Callum, moving on. *Bring on the rest of these jealous bastards.*

Hugh, in contrast to the others (with their designer togs) was dressed in drainpipe jeans with a Breton striped t-shirt. Hugh smiled warmly and bent down for my hand, kissing the back. The other guys turned their backs and got back to their banter.

"You done nice for yourself, son," Hugh said in a thick Essex accent.

"She's my world," David said, and I thanked the stars for one nice friend.

"Nice to meet you," I said.

I wanted to mention the cool reception I got from Callum but I realised that queen was not worth giving airtime to.

"We should 'av coffee sometime, all three of us, and Adrienne can get me hooked up with a nice bird. I daren't touch the ones round here in case any of this lot's already had their way wiv 'em."

I laughed at Hugh and replied instantly, "I'm not from round here and the only girls I know are librarians."

Hugh snarled. "Fucking hell, I love me a librarian."

"Me too," David said and squeezed my side, pulling me close.

Hugh grinned knowingly and while David finished his bottle of beer, I put my half-empty one in Hugh's hand.

"We've got to go and get back to my babysitter."

"Oh yeah we have," David added, "catch you later then Hugh!"

I noticed as the guys hugged, Hugh looked at me, shocked. *Yes, I have a kid.* He kissed me goodbye and whispered in my ear, "Good luck, you'll need it with our Dave."

David and I waved as we left the pub. He didn't bother to hug any of his other mates and as we walked out, I felt all eyes on us. Once we were outside the place, we began walking away quickly but I looked through the windows and saw all the guys doing shots. Just Hugh stood there, watching us leave, standing quietly with his pint held at his chest.

"What's with that Callum fella? He was sort of trying to warn me off!"

David chuckled. "Yeah... he's got a little soft spot for me."

"Hugh seemed nice though?"

"Hmm, he's unlucky in love that one. Good guy though."

"So, why would he just tell me to be careful with you?"

"I'll tell you at home. You got money for a taxi otherwise we'll be late now," he warned.

"Sure."

We grabbed a taxi and we were silent on the short drive home.

David paid Jenna in cash and walked her home. She was fourteen and only lived in the apartment next door, but that's what he was like – he had manners. He was a gentleman.

I checked on Billy in his crib and he was sound asleep, in the same position we left him in. The babysitter had left a ton of empty snack bags everywhere but it was a small price to pay for a night out, just us.

I cleared the coffee table of her litter and headed for the kitchen to put the kettle on.

David returned to the flat just as I was draining the teabags and adding milk to our cups.

"So what did Hugh mean?" I asked him.

"I was a player, that's all, and you already knew that."

I turned and looked at him. "Does he mean the porn stuff, or what?"

My heart was beating so fast. Had I got myself involved with another bastard?

While I thought about that, one answer screamed at me incessantly: NO.

He was not a bastard and how did I know?

Well…

He put the toilet seat down.

He cleaned.

Washed up.

Made me come, every time we had sex, whether with his fingers, tongue or cock, it didn't matter.

He cuddled me and kissed me and told me at least once a day he loved me.

He woke with Billy some mornings when I was tired and needed a lie-in.

He still wore socks during, but I sort of loved it.

And the main reason I knew he wasn't a bastard was that he wanted me to meet his mother – so I knew he was deadly serious about me.

"None of them know about the porn," he said clearly, "the only people that do know are the people I did porn with and the people watching porn. Thankfully it wasn't really my face people wanted to see, just David Dare screwing women senseless with a big cock."

I gulped. "Is there some sort of personality defect I should be aware of? I'm struggling to understand why a friend of yours would try to warn me off?"

He sighed, wiping his brow of sweat. It was a hot night, but still…

"Everything before you was just sex. I love you. I've loved nobody else nor will I ever love a single other woman. I love you."

"That's not what I'm asking." I stared over my mug at him. "But now you mention it, how many women have you had?"

He gazed into space and mentally started counting, then lost count, if his confused expression was anything to go by.

His chin wrinkled. "I honestly don't know."

"More than a hundred?"

"Look, Adrienne…"

"More than that?" His guilty looked confirmed it.

He moved toward me and took my waist in his hands, "…the guys were probably shocked but that's just because they don't know what love is yet. We're lucky that we've found it, right? And when you find it, it changes you. I changed because I love you. I only want you. The rest were just sex. You're the only honey I want now. Nobody else."

I pouted. "You think it's because they don't appreciate what love is yet?"

"Precisely," he ducked down and kissed my neck gently, "when you find love, it blows everything else out of the water. Sure I was happy to see them all tonight but I haven't missed them. I've been too busy loving you."

His lips moved from my throat to gently caress the tops of my cleavage instead. His fingers eased the straps of my maxi dress over my shoulders and he stroked his fingers over my bare skin. Pushing his hips against my thigh, I felt him already hard.

"David," I groaned.

He kissed my throat loudly, so I heard the smack of his lips drinking my skin. When he reached my mouth he French kissed me wildly, overpowering me. I clung to his arms and arched into him, my longing growing heavy.

He eased my dress down over my breast and rubbed his thumb up and over my erect nipple, flicking and pushing. I reached for the other side of my dress so he could have both breasts. He grinned and pulled out a chair from the kitchen table, sitting on it.

He held my hips and pulled me so I was standing between his open legs.

"Adrienne, you've got fucking perfect tits." He buried his face in my breasts and sucked them, making me fling my head back with joy.

Gradually my dress fell and pooled at my feet. His mouth moved from my nipples to my stomach and he directed me to lie back on the kitchen table.

Holding my body in his hands, he said, "Adrienne. You don't need to worry."

"Please take me," I begged, dying of need and want in the face of this heat between us. The cold wooden breakfast table stuck to my skin beneath me.

David kissed over the blood-red lace of my panties and pushed his tongue and my lace gusset inside me.

"Oh, fuck," I moaned, covering my face with my hands.

The tip of his tongue licked the sensitive skin between my thighs and core, teasing me.

"Please, please."

When he peeled the panties from my body, I moaned and shivered, so wet I could feel my arousal trickling down my crack. After three months of sleeping together, there was not much we hadn't tried.

He rubbed a single digit through my slit and made sure his finger was soaked, then popped it inside my ass. I lifted my hips from the table, groaning in ecstasy. David buried his mouth in my pussy and sucked rhythmically, not taking his mouth away. He pressed his thumb inside me while a smaller finger fucked my ass still and I came hard, crying his name.

He stood and pulled his cock out from behind his zipper, leaving everything else on. He held me down and buried himself into me as deep as he could. I looked up into his dark eyes and he whispered, "Tell me you love me."

"I love you."

"Then that's all that matters," he commanded.

I lay back, my arms flung behind me, dangling over the edge of the table. He fucked me, long and deep, just how I liked. He took his time, making me feel every inch. I coated him and the sounds of his big dick slipping in and out aroused me even more.

"So big, David," I murmured, rubbing my breasts.

"Adrienne, my lady."

With that sentiment, the atmosphere changed. He knew I liked it down and dirty like this, but sometimes I knew he needed it to be more loving and intimate.

I lifted up and wrapped my arms around him. "Make love to me in bed, David."

He didn't pull out as he picked me up and carried me to bed. Slowly, I unbuttoned his shirt and helped him shift his jeans down.

When he was naked aside from his socks, I ran my hands up and down his body and let him kiss me slowly. The skin of his back was velvet-soft, softer than you'd imagine a man being.

"Ade, what would I be without you?"

"I don't know," I whispered in his ear.

"You don't want to know."

"Never stop loving me."

He looked down into my eyes. "Never."

"Oh, oh," I hummed and tested his desire by squeezing my pelvic floor muscles around him. He yelped a little. "Please don't stop, David."

He madly kissed me so that I struggled to kiss him back. He rolled onto his back so I could ride him and it got so out of control, I didn't care how loud we were or how fucked the bed would be. Laid cuddled in each other's arms afterwards, I continually pecked his mouth and rubbed my nose against his, my hands diving in and out of his thick hair.

"Will you marry me, Adrienne?"

I wept the moment I heard the words, tears sparked by our fraught sex, combined with his desperate plea to have all of me – to have the final proof of how much I loved him.

Marcus never asked me the same question, but expected so much more of me. All David asked of me was my love.

I leaned up and looked down into his eyes, searching his. He breathed hard, waiting for my answer. I didn't have one. Not immediately.

"I said I wanted no presents for my birthday and I meant it... but this, me and you, I want. I want you." Caressing my face, he pleaded, "I have nothing but love for you. It's all I have. Somehow I figure, with the richness of your love, I can make it too. If you'll be my wife and stick with me? Say yes?"

"Yes, David, oh god, I love you!"

He pulled me into his arms, kissing me, holding me tight to his body. Our hip bones locked and our legs wound around each other's and I honestly did not think we could have been any closer than what we were then. I loved how his belly panted against mine as he struggled to control his erratic breathing.

"Oh god, Adrienne. You're a dream."

We made love again and I reminded him I didn't need trinkets, just him. Just a plain wedding band and his promise never to leave me, either. I bawled into his arms and told him I had been so lonely without him – that he meant so very much to me. It seemed like we'd already made our pledges and the rest was just law and a piece of paper.

EIGHT

On the road heading out of the city in David's battered, old VW Golf, I looked over my shoulder and Billy was already asleep in his car seat, the vehicle hot and stuffy, just the right conditions for a snooze.

"What will I make of your mother?"

"You'll like her. She might be surprised by you."

"Don't you get on with her?"

He coughed and scratched a hand through his hair. "It's not that; it's just that she knows me far too well, if you know what I mean."

I nodded. *The porn.* No doubt she also knew he was a bed hopper before me.

"A payslip got sent home and she realised. We fought and she said some terrible things, which I probably deserved." He held the wheel with one hand and repeatedly rubbed the sweat off his other hand onto his jeans. "She'd never kick me out and she didn't. I've spent most of the past eight years chancing it, on friends' floors or whatever... in Leeds most nights. I always went back home and she washed my shit and fed me. Sometimes she could barely look at me or talk to me, but she has just been here for me. I didn't want to take her money, Ade. I wanted to put myself through school. I couldn't afford to live in halls and party every night, though."

Tentatively, I asked, "So you're not from a poor family?"

He glanced over at me and without emotion, talked about his Dad. "He was a dentist. Left Mum comfortable enough."

"What?"

"Yeah," he nodded, "my older brother Rob's got a couple of kids and last time I heard, he was super successful. I'm the black sheep if you like. I have debts up to my armpits. I don't wanna bore you with it all. I'll sort it all out, don't worry."

"I don't get it? Debts? What debts?"

"Living too hard and fast, Adrienne. All my old uni mates now have the jobs to fund fucking about, but I never left school did I? It's a mug's game. But it's all a mug can do when he's bored senseless and disenchanted with life."

I asked myself whether he was living in the shadow of a super successful brother, or whether there were other factors in play.

"How did he die?"

"Rare heart condition that'd gone undiagnosed. I was twelve and Rob fifteen when he died. He wasn't a nice man but it was cruel that his life was taken, just like that. He was only mid-forties."

I nodded along, letting him talk.

"So, your mother never remarried?"

"No. As far as I know, she's not interested. If you'd been married to my father, you'd be put off for life too."

"Was he violent?"

"No. Worse. He was a manipulative arsehole."

"Oh." It explained why David didn't want to take any of his mother's money while at university, putting himself through higher education, at the expense of missing out on student digs. In a roundabout way, his mother's money was his father's.

David had higher morals than me, it seemed, although I had a son to think of and the only big thing my father's money had so far bought me was a roof over our heads.

I reached over and kissed his cheek. "I understand and I love you."

He smiled and made a proposition out of the blue: "After we marry, I want to adopt Billy."

"You do?"

"Of course. Why not? He's sort of mine already, don't you think?"

"Okay, but..." I tried to think quickly about this. "What about when Billy grows up? Will we tell him who his dad–"

"It's up to you, Ade."

I bit my nails. "I think we could tell him, maybe when he's older. But it would be a lot to deal with, hearing about his biological father."

"I just want you to know, I'm going to love him as my own and maybe it's better all round if everyone thinks he is my own."

"Okay, David. Okay."

We drove a few miles more with the radio turned up, singing along together. For some reason I sensed David was desperate to close the deal with me and Billy as quickly as he could.

We managed to find a space on Beech Grove, a leafy street overlooking a large green playing field. David pointed at a gigantic, limestone mansion with three floors and when he saw my face, he said, "It's flats, Adrienne. Hers is quite a big flat, mind you."

I was nervous for some reason. Maybe I feared his mother would tell me something I didn't want to know. David, my fiancé, was perfect as far as I was concerned and I wanted nothing to ruin that.

I grabbed a grumpy Billy from the back while David walked ahead and opened a cast-iron gate leading onto his mother's property.

He signalled for me to follow him and I did, walking through the landscaped front garden with trepidation. He went to the main entrance and pressed a buzzer with *3A – Mrs Lewis* beside it. We waited patiently for a response and one eventually came.

"Hello David, come straight up," said a crackly voice, "did you forget you have a key?"

"No, I'm just trying to demonstrate that I'm a guest now." He smiled nervously in my direction.

"Stop dawdling and come up!"

The door buzzed open and we walked quietly inside the entrance hall. In my arms, Billy looked around, wondering what was going on. He was very taken with the different architecture of the place, a deceptive building where the ceilings were enormously high, with chunky, original wood skirting boards and ornate Victorian cornicing.

"Whoa," I said, "nice."

Collectively, the building of six flats was worth at least £10million I thought.

"We used to have a big house but moved here after Rob went to New York."

David carried our toddler as we climbed some steep stairs and once we'd navigated that leviathan of a building, we found an open door and a fifty-something woman waiting in the doorway. She dressed in something similar to what my own mother would have worn: a tailored navy Jaeger dress with short sleeves and a belt.

"Mother, I'd like to introduce Adrienne and William."

Speechless, she tried to move her mouth but no words came out. I saw immediately where David got his brown eyes from and I walked over, pulling her into a hug.

"I'm Rachel," she managed to say.

I pulled back from her. "It's so nice to meet you!"

She searched my eyes fast, trying to remember where she knew me from. "You seem familiar, Adrienne."

"Yes, I'm Adrienne Kyd."

Her face instantly paled. "That Kyd?"

"That Kyd." I nodded.

David shut the front door behind us and plonked William straight into her arms, overwhelming his mother so she didn't have any more time to digest who I was.

She looked aghast even though Billy started fondling her earring. Cocking one eyebrow, she exclaimed, "You need a place to stay, don't you? Or money, right? Finally, you want money. I knew the time would come. I knew it. I put some aside for just this."

I didn't know where to look but I felt embarrassed and decided to keep my mouth shut. All she saw was a single mother shunned by her parents. Little did she know my father had everyone in his life on the payroll – to ensure they did exactly what he wanted them to do.

"It would be lovely if we could catch up, and you know... tell you our good news" he said, vaguely explaining himself.

She tutted, loudly. "I knew it. She's pregnant! You got her in trouble."

We moved through the hallway to the kitchen at the end where several pans bubbled on a gas-fired stove. David peeked in on the vegetables as he said, "I apologise for my mother, Adrienne. I don't think she's taken her medication yet. That or else she's taken leave of her manners."

Rachel pouted. "What news, then?"

"Well, we're getting married. If you deem Adrienne worthy, I'd like to ask for Grandma's ruby engagement ring... to keep it in the family. That's all I've come for today. Oh... and to give you chance to meet my future wife."

I watched her struggle to find words as she held a wriggling Billy in her arms.

"Need any help with the food?" I asked.

She nodded, lost for words, her tongue twisted. David directed her to the kitchen island and poured her a glass of water. I nursed the pans on the stove but when she caught her breath back, Rachel said, "Take the ring. Blimey!"

***

After Sunday lunch, David and Rachel went into her bedroom where she handed him the engagement ring I knew nothing about until that day. When they emerged, David told me the piece needed a polish so he would have that done before asking me to marry him – properly this time.

Late afternoon by that time, we decided to put Billy down for a nap in David's old bedroom and while David settled the toddler, it left me and Rachel alone, sharing wine together.

"Do you know about the… you know… what he used to do."

I nodded. "Yes."

"Phew." She held her chest. "Adrienne, I think you should know about something like that if you're going to be married to the man."

"Please call me Ade."

"Okay, dear."

Her flat was huge, and beautiful. Neutral and clean, expansive and airy. The rooms were sprawling and super-sized, everything set out like it was a home for giants, not just one, little lady. It seemed Rachel had been abandoned by her older son and now, by the younger one too – when she would no doubt have preferred her home filled with grandchildren and extended family, than be large and empty as it was.

"You read the newspapers?" I asked her straight.

"I do," she hummed, "but more than that, I know *people*. I heard about the case… and I was glad you got free. Every woman I know was glad. Especially the mothers."

"Nobody was gladder than me!"

We giggled awkwardly, both sipping more wine.

"David knows?" she asked, gently. "Have you discussed it with him?"

"He knows." *Not everything, but enough.*

It was reported in the press that I killed Marcus to escape

captivity, just a young mother trapped inside her own home by an obsessed partner. It was self-defence, so clear-cut, it was said not a jury in the land would have convicted me. Nowhere in the papers, nor outside of the courtroom, was there any mention of the catalogue of physical abuse I endured. The plastic surgery was on my father but I still felt the marks, nowhere more so than inside my head. Scars can be erased, memories cannot.

"Well," she began, "this is all very sudden, but he does seem different... he seems happy. He seems together. Is that right?"

"We're both very happy," I gushed, "we have lots of plans for the future, lots to look ahead for."

"I love David more than anyone else on Earth, I do," she said, so certain of that – such clarity in her eyes. "But from one woman to another, it's best to be made aware. He's flighty. Easily bored. He will make plans... then forget them a few days later. He might write essays about his plans... and never follow them through. Like I say, I adore him, but I never figured him for a family man. Never. He's enormously intelligent, possibly the cleverest man you'll ever meet... but that doesn't mean he's for this world, Ade. He's hidden out in academia for a reason."

I allowed her words to go over my head and responded, "He's changed, a lot. I guess our love has changed him."

She poured more wine into my glass.

"We all say that, Ade. We all believe it too, at first anyway. In my experience, however, men don't ever change."

David peeked his head in around the living-room door and announced, "He's almost asleep. I'm just going to hang a few more minutes to make sure. Everything okay in here?"

"Fine." I smiled, acting my ass off. I wanted him to leave me with his mother a little longer, so she could make me aware of what else I might be up against.

He smiled back and left us alone again.

I cleared my throat. "In the car today, it was the first time he ever really spoke to me of his father."

Recognition set into her eyes, her head bobbing gently as her mind filled with memories. "Nobody was more affected than David when he died. As though a curse had been lifted, but the price for freedom... extreme sadness. Sometimes I look back and wish I'd been stronger, but I wasn't. My husband wasn't a good man."

I was sure she knew I'd been there and got the t-shirt.

However, it didn't seem appropriate for me to tell her that I got out before it was too late and I was strong enough to escape an abusive partner. Billy would never know disappointment like David had – like I had.

Everybody's reasons for staying or going are different and the truth was, I didn't love Marcus enough to stay. I was able to get free because I knew getting together with him was the biggest mistake of my life. If David's father was as charming, handsome and as intelligent as his son, I reckon Rachel's love for her husband made it difficult for her to leave him.

"Rachel, I just want to say that we're not here to sponge off you. I have money but David's proud and wants to start our married life by finding himself what he calls a proper job. I work at a library and I've just been accepted to start a degree next year. He wants to support me in every way he can. He looks after me in all sorts of ways. Cooks and cleans. He–" *fucks me very well...* "hates it when he can't pay for things. He wants to work, wants to support me finan-cially... he adores Billy and vice versa. We're so happy."

She smiled, pleasantly surprised. "Brains and beauty? No wonder he's changed, eh? Swept off his feet, I'd say."

"I think it actually makes him feel more insecure."

"Oh yes, well, yes," she agreed, sipping more wine. "But it sounds like he really has changed. I didn't think it possible, but you're right, he's changed."

"I love him so much!" I cried, with joyful tears, and Rachel seemed to finally soften.

"Who wouldn't love him? He's utter perfection. I made him, after all." She paused, working something out in her mind. "So... what sort of wedding will you be having?"

I tensed and she saw me grow rigid.

"Your parents moved to Spain, did you know that?"

"I heard."

"Your father sold everything... everything! Every last scrap of the farm and the factory... everything! Apparently your mother was devastated when you left."

"How do you know this?" I felt that horrid, deep frown of mine bury itself into my forehead and I rubbed at it, trying to smooth it out.

"Everyone who's anyone heads to the Turkish Baths, darling, and women talk."

I breathed deeply.

"I'm not judging you, Ade," she said, using my name repeatedly as a term of endearment it seemed, "I'm just saying... if you want a little help toward the wedding, I'd be more than happy. I do have a little set aside and I don't have a girl of my own. It'd be my pleasure."

I burst into tears. "That's so kind of you."

When David returned to the room, he found us with a notepad and pen, and some plans already forming for the big day.

NINE

For two months, David did all sorts to try and get himself a job. He walked round job agencies in a suit and tie with a professionally made CV under his arm, offered himself up as a volunteer at several sales firms. When nothing came up trumps for him, I worried about how it was affecting him emotionally. The only work that seemed to be available was in telemarketing or recruitment consultancy, the one profession unwilling to help him. His degrees were niche and unless he was willing to wait, we knew he wouldn't find the kind of job he wanted – not just like that. Patience and David did not belong in the same sentence.

We'd had Rachel over to our house for Sunday lunch a few times, and we visited her place again and again too. I'd learnt she was a legal secretary and worked part-time. Sometimes she even worked from home. Either she had been good with money since her husband died or he left her a massive insurance policy. I knew she had money because she liked to take me and Billy shopping and spoil us rotten.

It was a Tuesday night when David came flying into the house, eyes wide. Standing in the kitchen, looking at his family sat around the kitchen island, he said quietly, "I got a job."

I was sceptical. Could it be that easy? I didn't even know he had an interview that day. Him actually finding a job seemed a miracle. The Saturday before, David had virtually consigned himself a sous chef at the local Indian restaurant.

"Didn't you hear me? I got a job!"

Mirroring his happiness, I stood and rushed to him, flinging my arms around his neck. "I'm so pleased for you!"

He picked Billy up out of his chair and cuddled us all together.

"Aww, I'm so happy," he said into my hair and kissed me lovingly before pecking Billy's head, too.

"What's the job?"

David left my side, carrying Billy under his arm like the toddler was nothing but a small package. Heading to the wine chiller, he pulled out a bottle of something with a foil wrapper at the top. Something fizzy.

"Marketing."

"What are you marketing?" I asked, excited. A real job!

"Listen, I'll tell you everything later. I called Mum earlier and she's on her way so we can go out and celebrate while she puts Billy to bed."

"Okay…" I thought celebrating was a little premature but then he'd been searching for a job for so long, maybe this was the real deal after all. Maybe I should've jumped right onboard with this news, but something told me this was too easy.

He popped the bottle open and Billy screamed, "BANG!"

"Yay! Bang!" David shouted and Billy giggled his head off, never one easily scared.

"You got a job!" I joined in with the frivolity.

"I did!"

He could tell me we were living in 2D and I would still have believed him.

**

On Rachel's advice he took me to Carriages, a lovely, intimate wine bar cum restaurant in rural Knaresborough. I had to laugh when we stepped out of his beat-up VW, me in a Jaeger dress his mother bought me and David in a suit, no tie.

It was lovely, not too posh, but the food was good. We enjoyed calves livers for starters and we were waiting on our mains when conversation started to flow.

"You look wonderfully handsome tonight, David."

He grinned, a glass of water in his hand because he was driving. "I do?"

"Oh yes, probably because you're relaxed for the first time in ages?"

His smile fell and he nodded, prepared to own up. "It's a job."

"Doing what, then?"

He hunkered down at the table, elbows on the tabletop (error, error!) but anyway, etiquette aside, I was desperate to know what he had to say…

Whispering as we both leaned in to one another, he told me, "I'll be selling sex products."

"Oh my god." My hands rushed to cover my mouth before I said something awful like, *No fiancé of mine is going to sell sex products!!*

"It was funny really," he explained, pouring some more merlot for me, which I drink immediately. "I was wandering Leeds city centre and bumped into one of the girls I used to do… that thing with, you know?"

Fire, not the nice kind, erupted between my ears.

"*Those films,*" I deduced.

He covered my hand with his. "Yes. Anyway… that's not the point. She asked me what I was doing with my life and I told her I was going out of my fucking head, using my paltry dole payments to pay for parking while I tried to scrub up some proper work! She told me about a company she's now working at called *For Mutual Pleasure* and said they were looking for new people. They never advertise and only seek people within the family, you know? Friends of friends?"

"What's this girl's name?"

"Her name's Violet," he said.

"In the past, you did stuff with her?"

He shook his head. "That's irrelevant."

I steamed with anger. "I don't want you working with someone you previously had down and dirty with, David. No way." I threw back my wine and poured myself more from the bottle.

"Adrienne, I'm marrying *you*. We're adults. I never had any feelings for her. I love you. I absolutely love you."

"I need the loo."

I rose from the table and when I spotted the waiter bringing our dinners over, he watched me heading for the toilet and contorted his face, his steps taking him back to the kitchen to hang onto our food a little while longer. Good service.

I hid in the toilet cubicle for a little while, sitting on the toilet seat even though I didn't need to pee. I didn't know why I felt like this but I didn't want him selling sex products and working with someone he previously had sex with. Lust or no lust – love or no love – it made me ache inside to think of him… with anyone else. He was mine.

Part of me knew I should have supported him, pleased he'd found something at least, while another part of me didn't understand why he couldn't wait for his dream job to come along. It wasn't as if we didn't have money. We were young, there was no rush to marry, but he seemed determined to lock me down as soon as possible. My gut feeling was that this new job might ruin everything.

I walked back into the restaurant and hot on my heels was the waiter who didn't even give me chance to seat myself before he plonked our almost-curled dinners before us.

I had lamb cutlets while he had rainbow trout.

Silence reigned as David tucked in and I observed him, wondering how to communicate how I felt about all this.

Speaking after chewing, he told me between bites, "It's

£30,000 per annum plus bonuses and the interview Luca Van Duren gave me... the boss... it was like an interrogation. I didn't even think I'd got the job. I thought I'd failed but then as I was crying into my Starbucks at the end of the day, he called and offered me the position. I thought you'd be proud. I thought you'd be happy."

"I am proud, I am happy," I returned, prodding my lamb with a fork, trying to conjure some appetite. "I love you more than anything. I want nothing more than for you to be happy, David. But you're so insanely clever, you could do any job. It's just a matter of time."

He reached for my hand. "Please, trust me. It's not forever, just a starting post. I never thought I would get into marketing either but this is an industry I have some experience working within and I know what's what. It'll be easy money and one day, I'll escape to do my own thing. It's just a stop gap."

I managed a few bites of potato fondant. "So, we'll tell your mother you're working in... what?"

"Jewellery or something. Who cares? As long as we're honest with one another, who cares what anyone else thinks."

"I guess."

He finished his plate while I barely even got through one cutlet. While I ate slowly, he continued to reassure me with what I was sure was sales speak: "I've wasted so much time already, why not waste a bit more time, while getting paid for it though? Yes it's not ideal but I don't want to have people pay for my mistakes. It's time I earned money to pay off my debts and settle things before we get married. Plus I'd like to lavish you with a luxury honeymoon. I want to do everything right."

I'd been down this path before, however with a similar man thinking money made everything right – namely my father.

He gestured to the waiter we needed more wine and soon

enough, another bottle was delivered for my delectation. Maybe he was trying to get me drunk so I would accept all this without quibble.

"What will you be selling exactly?" I drank as much water as wine, trying to save myself embarrassment and a headache in the morning.

"Products. Of the erotic variety. Toys. Outfits. Films. Everything."

I coughed. "Everything?"

He laughed, avoiding my eyes. He must have known deep down I wasn't ever going to be convinced, but I'd put up with it because I loved him. "My job title will actually be Market Research Lead. As in, I'll ask men and women to test the products, set up questionnaires and video reviews for the company website. I'll present a group of products to the companies Luca sells to and they choose which ones they think can go to mass market. I might get to visit India and other countries where the factories are."

"The films," I stumbled over my words, "what about those?"

"I won't be involved in the making or selling of those. They have an arm for that side of the business. Besides you can pretty much get porn online anywhere these days. What Luca will really want to focus on in future are the sexy hotels he plans to architect and develop."

"What, like with dungeons and stuff inside them?" I managed to finish my plate, putting it to one side.

"See, you're not entirely naïve are you, dear Adrienne?"

I snickered. "No I'm bloody not... I went to boarding school after all. Now, about these hotels?"

He chuckled, folding his arms on the table after our plates were collected by the waiter almost silently.

"By sexy hotels I mean cool, kitsch places. Adults only. Not for families, but couples oriented. With options like private Jacuzzi hire, suites with one or two or three beds."

A shiver ran through me, hearing David talking so calmly

and coolly about all this. Maybe the wine had gone to my head or maybe he was the perfect person to sell sex because he was so incredibly beautiful.

"Dessert menus guys?" our waiter asked, appearing at our table.

"No, no thanks," I said, "I'm full."

David waved his hand, too. "Just the bill."

The waiter put the cork in our bottle so we could take away what was left of it with us.

On the drive home, we were passing a place I knew was hidden from the road. "Pull in there, will you?"

He looked across at me. "Why? Are you sick?"

"Pull in, before you miss it!"

He pulled into a lay-by and I suggested, "Reverse into that bit of farm track there and kill the lights."

When he did as requested, I climbed onto the backseat and he followed.

"What a great idea, milady."

I climbed into his lap and began licking his throat. He groaned and started breathing hard. The material of my dress felt awfully constricting and tight, my hard nipples housed when they should be exposed and sucked instead.

He gasped when I revealed my naked breasts and cupping them in his hands, he licked and nibbled my nipples, his warm breath staving off the cool autumn air creeping into the vehicle now the heaters were off.

"David, have you ever had anal sex?"

"No," he breathed, "I'm way too big."

I laughed, tittering. "No, silly! I mean, the other way round. A man giving it to you. Or a strap-on, or something. Sometimes I think about doing you... up there."

He ground his teeth and grunted, nibbling my mouth.

"I could think of nothing sexier than you with a fucking hard-on for me, Ade."

I laughed dirtily and chimed, "My husband getting butt-fucked. It'd be glorious."

Now I knew the drink was definitely talking; I would never admit my fantasies while sober.

"What else do you think about?" he asked, and slipped a hand beneath me so one of his fingers could toy with the seam of my pussy.

I had gone commando. Just like he often did.

"I think about the times we used to do it in the library toilet. I miss those times. Some days when I'm working now, I imagine you storming through the doors, chucking me up into your arms and slamming me in front of all the horny, sex-starved students desperate to wank themselves off while watching us."

He grunted. "What a show they'd get."

"Ah!" He dug two fingers straight into me. "I know."

I pumped up and down on his fingers and he used his free hand to unzip his trousers. His cock sprang up and stood there between us, aching to be touched and fondled. I just stared at it instead.

Grinding on his fingers, I fucked them and moaned, my breasts pointing out into his mouth as I threw my arms behind me and rode them. Continually catching his nails against my clit as he slipped in and out made me eventually come. As I orgasmed, he pumped into me hard. I screamed his name.

"Oh baby, I love it when you scream," he groaned.

"Hence this spot. I don't want my son or our neighbours hearing how hard you really need to fuck me, how deep, how savagely and tenderly, lovingly and fuckingly."

"Fuckingly," he chuckled.

"Hmm," I moaned as he gave me his fingers to suck, letting me taste my desire for him on them. "Now then. What would you like me to do to you?"

He grinned. "First, take your dress all the way off."

I did as he commanded, sitting on the backseat next to him, letting my dress fall into the foot well so I was naked.

As I sat there, moonlight bathed my naked body in a silver glow that made me feel even more uninhibited and beautiful. I lifted my feet to the seat edges and spread them, lazily rolling a fingernail around my clit.

While he watched, I made myself come again, and he smiled with glee as I spurted onto the red dress at my feet. "I'm not sure dry cleaning will sort that, baby."

"You're so fucking horny with red wine in you, Ade. Now, I want you to finger fuck my butt while you suck me off. Talk of you fucking it has got me all inquisitive."

I laughed loudly and he laughed too.

"Oh David, and you think I'm the bad influence. Just you having this fuck-off cock makes me fill my panties."

"Baby, you don't have panties. You must be filling chair covers instead."

We shared more laughter before I crawled across the seat and started sucking him, my arse in the air, exposed should anyone poke their nose against the steamed-up car window behind me. With my fist around the base, I sucked the head and flicked my tongue over him.

"Ah, that's it, yeah, just chew, ah... a little... yeah, like that, like that..."

I bobbed my mouth over his enormous cock head and used one hand to spread his legs. Putting my fingers inside his mouth, he wet them with his saliva and I moved my hand down, carefully prising his legs as wide apart as possible.

Sucking his balls, he squealed, "Ah, god, Ade! Slower. I'll come otherwise."

I knew how he loved them to be touched, and how sensitive they were too. God, he tasted musky, salty... him.

I eased a finger over and around his anus, feeling for where the pucker sank and felt softer. Using my finger with the shortest nail, I pushed into his butt and felt my digit gathered at all sides by his tight hole.

"Fuck!" he yelled, "fuck!"

I spat on his cock and sucked harder, washing my tongue

around and around his erection. I wriggled my finger inside him and lifted my mouth off his cock to spit in the direction of his butt, too.

Wetted, I began slipping my finger in and out of him, seeking the hard nub of his prostate. He was so tight and gripping me hard. "David, just relax. Relax otherwise it'll hurt."

Did he know I'd done anal before? Not just given, but received, too? I used to be the girl who experimented with everything. Then I learned the price of passion, or rather, the wrong kind of passion. In the past I might have been even more experimental than David, for all we knew.

He listened anyway and seemed to unwind.

"Just let yourself relax a little more, as if you're on the toilet, but without pushing," I suggested, "just bear down gently. Let it happen."

He chuckled. "I'll try."

As soon as I felt him relax, I pushed another finger in and he howled. "Oh fuck, so tight, Ade! Jeez. That feels so good." As soon as I found his prostate, his breathing got out of control and he started losing more pre-cum from his cock, which I eagerly licked up and swallowed.

I started sucking him off again and his head grew enormous inside my mouth, a sign he was ready to come. I fucked his butt, fighting with the tightness, but winning. I enjoyed the scent of his saltiness, the scent of his ass, too. There is less bacteria in the ass than the mouth, but it just tastes a little more flavoursome that's all.

"Come now," I muttered with my mouth full.

"Fuck!"

He pumped his hips and his cock hit the back of my mouth. His body tensing, he barked out his pleasure noisily, ravenously tensing around my fingers. His cum slid down my throat and when I pulled away, he was covered in sweat and gleaming, red-faced. He was a picture, writhing with pleasure – all because of me.

I wiped my fingers clean on my filthy dress and he started pulling all his clothes off.

"There's a fantasy I have," he explained, "and it's gonna be exacted tonight. Now, get out of the car and lay in the mud outside."

"Shit, shit."

I got out of the car as soon as he was fully naked too. This was dangerous and exhibitionist. We could have got caught. Which is probably why it felt even naughtier. The cool night air made my tits prick up even harder and the smeared wetness around my pussy felt more *there*.

I was just his fuck, right now; and I was ready to be fucked hard by my future husband.

He joined me on the cold, hard ground and slid right inside me, his cock as rigid as rock.

Staring into my eyes, he asked, "Don't you know how much I love you?"

"I don't know," I admitted, as he drew whimpers from my throat with slow, deep thrusts. "Maybe it's just too good to be true."

"My love for you makes me crazed, Adrienne. It makes me wild. You're the only woman. No other woman exists."

He kissed me with his heart, pouring his love into me, his caresses and licks gentle and tender, tasting and seeking. He moaned as he fucked me, my legs around his back as I was pushed harder and harder into the cold ground.

When I was close, he warned, "Don't scream. A farmer might hear."

I covered my mouth and he hit me deep and fast, drawing muffled squeals of pleasure from me. I came so hard, I ached all over. I could hardly stand.

Afterwards, he dressed us on the backseat, holding my dishevelled, shaking body in his arms as I held him too.

"I'll bring toys home for you."

"Maybe it won't be so bad."

"Just know, it won't be forever, Adrienne. You and me,

we won't be here forever. Before we're forty we'll be living it up in Gran Canaria or someplace, sunning our lives away."

For a moment, I wondered if I was marrying my father!

Then he said something that totally smashed everything else out of the water. "Let's drive to Gretna this weekend and do it. Say yes? Let's just promise our love and the rest will take care of itself. Say yes, Ade?"

His eyes were glassy and I saw nothing but sober love. Agreement was on the tip of my tongue until I had a thought. "Your mother has plans... she wants us to have a summer ceremony in the outdoors. She wants a cake made out of books... she wants me to wear a princess dress."

He stroked my cheek. "What do you want?"

"You. Just you."

He pulled me close and kissed me. "*It is as if I had a string somewhere under my left ribs, tightly and inextricably knotted to a similar string situated in the corresponding quarter of your little frame.*"

"*Jane Eyre.*"

"Be my wife. Be mine. It's all I'm asking. Bind with me, and never let go. I'm nothing without you."

"I love you. Let's do it."

He shouted in celebration and when we got back home, we celebrated again in the shower. Thankfully his mother slept soundly in the spare room – ignorant and under the influence of the sleeping tablets she regularly ingested. It wasn't in our plan to tell her what we were going to do.

TEN

Christmas 2004

I was through the first semester of my degree but my education had suddenly been put at risk. *Happy fucking Christmas*, I said to myself as I sat on the loo. I was at the library, where I still helped out on Fridays for a bit of the social thing (because nobody on my course liked me). In the staff toilet I peed on a stick, hoping and praying I wasn't with child. How could I do my degree with a baby in tow? How would I make this work?

When the result appeared in the window, I cursed myself. It was those antibiotics I had when I caught the flu a couple of months before. It had to be those. I thought we were safe but I should've maybe made David wear condoms to make sure my system was clear.

"Fucking hell," I said to myself. Calculating, I decided I was due in the summer sometime, which was good. It meant I could still complete my first year, as long as they didn't mind a woman with a bump falling asleep occasionally in class.

I left the toilet, having wrapped the test in tissue and hidden it inside my bag. Leaving for the day, I told my colleague Linda, "See you next week. Happy Christmas!"

"Oh, happy Christmas, Ade!"

I walked from the university library toward home. It was Christmas Eve – and I'd been looking forward to time with my husband, son and mother-in-law. Rachel had only just forgiven us for absconding to Gretna – so I knew she would never forgive me for getting rid of what could be her first British-born grandchild.

Watching my breath heat the air in front of me as I walked through the frozen city streets, I knew they'd all be waiting for me when I got back. Full of festive cheer, they'd ask why I had a sour look. I had to get my game face on.

Abortion was an option but I just couldn't. Even though this was inconvenient, it was a miracle really. I had a second and third opinion after I was examined during the court case. All of them said the same – I might not carry more kids to term because of the tears to my abdomen. The beatings after Billy was born were extensive and brutal – and all while my body was meant to be healing from having just given birth. I wasn't sure this pregnancy would sustain. I could miscarry at any moment. Anything could go wrong. The question remained, should I tell David? He was already under enough stress as it was, having been made a manager at work, still getting to grips with another new role all over again. He had enough to contend with.

I walked up to our flat and stood outside the front door, trying to figure out what I was going to say once I got inside. I stood there for a long time until other residents in the same building forced me to make a decision because they wanted to get inside, too.

I let myself indoors and in the hallway, Billy chased over to me and showed me an early Christmas present from Grandma, a choo-choo, as he called it. He almost skidded on his way back to the living room where I saw a railway set had been laid out – my son under its magical spell. In the kitchen, David was busy plating up festive snacks before the main event the next day.

Kissing my cheek, he asked, "What's wrong? You look pale."

I couldn't hold it in. I'd been trying to since I missed my

period a month ago. I'd known the truth then and decided, *what's the point of holding it in any longer?*

"I'm pregnant," I told him, "about two months."

He turned to face me and took my hands in his, staring down into my eyes. When he smiled, I smiled, and he threw his arms around me, cushioning me from the angst I felt deep down inside.

"Oh baby, that's wonderful. I don't know how... but that's wonderful news."

I pulled back from his tight embrace and blinked tears away, kissing his lips. "I think we should've used condoms when I took those antibiotics that time but I thought a week or so after, I'd be fine, you know?"

He pulled me into his arms again, kissing my head. "I don't care. I'm just so happy. A little sibling for Billy."

I burst into tears in his arms and he cuddled me close. The scent of him – spiced cologne and David – enveloped me. I buried myself in his neck, where his scent was richest, where I felt safest. Rachel entered the kitchen wondering what was happening.

"A grandma again, Mum."

"Oh my god," she said, and put her arms around us both. "How wonderful. Oh Ade, how wonderful."

Didn't she know how punched up I was? Didn't she know this was a miracle?

She seemed far happier about this than I ever expected her to be. I knew she loved Billy but things between her and David still weren't quite right and I always wondered why. However, she was going to be a grandma to David's child this time and I felt sure it could bring mother and son closer – if it all sustained and she saw him holding his own child. Her legacy. Maybe they'd heal then, finally.

My hormonal mind running away from me, I excused myself to go to the bathroom and there, I wiped my cheeks and checked my knickers. I knew I'd be checking them all the time from now on, to make sure I wasn't miscarrying.

ELEVEN

July 2005

"Push, Push! Push, Adrienne!"

"I literally can't!" I screamed. "I've given birth before and I literally can't! She's too big! I know my own body!"

The midwives conferred and asked me to puff on the gas and air while they cut me. David rocked in a corner, disturbed by all of it. I think he needed a drink by the look of him.

I breathed the stuff quickly while they cut me and stuck a sucker thing on the kid's head.

Within moments, the baby was out and the midwives exclaimed, "Golly, she's big. You'd have been lucky to push her out without an aid."

I breathed a sigh of relief. I'd gotten my body back again. My heart could relax once more. It was all okay. It was over. I'd made it through almost 280 days of constant agony, wondering if this baby would survive. I felt utter relief, there was no other way to describe it. My body and my mind were free again.

I could sleep on my side without it hurting. I could rest without having to take a dozen antacids every night. The list went on...

The mental agony had been the worst thing. Doppler checks every night. Counting her movements. Extra scans. The whole lot. No matter how many times they told me she was healthy and so was I, it never sank in. They said I had massive scar tissue to my womb but that I was fine. I was holding her inside me okay.

The scarring to my mind was the worst element to deal with.

All while I was pregnant, the devil on my shoulder told me this baby was something I didn't deserve. I wasn't destined for happiness, not really.

David crept over and when I was handed the baby, I said to her, "Hello Lucinda, I love you but you bloody hurt Mummy."

David burst into tears of joy and cuddled me, tears rolling down his cheeks and into my hair.

"That was horrible, Ade!"

"I've been through worse."

He attempted a smile while I went into a second labour.

"Here, take your daughter," I asked quickly, reaching for the gas and air again.

"Here's the placenta," the midwife explained as I delivered that, too, in absolute agony.

David cradled our child in the sitting area of the room while I was stitched up and repaired.

I cried against the midwife's shoulder as she led me to the bathroom, my body entirely naked. She helped shower the blood off me, avoiding my horrid stitches.

I could barely walk and said, "I need painkillers now she's out. The strongest."

She nodded and headed out of the room. I was determined to labour painkiller free like I did with Billy but this labour was horrendous in comparison. The midwife returned with an injection and warned me, "You may get drowsy."

"That's fine."

I was asleep before I knew it.

TWELVE

January 2006

Six months old already and she was utterly beautiful and the spitting image of her father. While Billy had my blonde hair and blue eyes, his sister had her father's brown hair and brown eyes.

Even though I was exhausted, I knew in the back of my mind things were strained between David and me. We hadn't had sex since before I found out I was pregnant. It wasn't just that, either. When I tried to cuddle him – just connect with him – he was distant.

I had Luce in the summer and went back to university in September. The university arranged my timetable so that I could have two clear days a week. Rachel had been an enormous help, right from the day Lucinda was born. She was there whenever I called. She stayed in the spare room so often I almost asked her to move in with us. I only got a 2.2 average at the end of my first year, but I was back to 2.1s, now I wasn't wrestling with pregnancy tiredness, just sleepless tiredness.

I was afraid of having sex and hurting the baby while pregnant. And since I'd had her, I'd been healing. Thirteen months without sex had to have been difficult for David, I knew that. Whenever I tried to talk to him, he said it was absolutely fine and I believed him.

This night, however, I wanted to give it a shot.

We were kissing in bed but every time he touched my side, I wondered if I felt too thick, having not lost my weight yet. I couldn't relax. Billy had been an easy pregnancy, an easy labour, but Lucinda had changed me irrevocably. It was alien for me to feel self conscious; I'd always loved my body, but now there was nothing I could do to get back to the size ten I used to be.

"Ade, I love you," he told me, "I've missed you so much."

His kisses were welcome and beautiful but I still couldn't relax. Maybe we should have gone out for a meal and got plastered?

He tried to touch me down there and I almost lurched away from him.

"Let me," I said, and I touched myself because I could handle the difference down there, but I wasn't sure he could.

"Yeah, Adrienne," he said, watching me touch myself.

He bit at a nipple through my nightshirt and groaned.

When I was wet, I held his body and gestured he climb on top.

Spreading my legs around him, it hurt when he pushed inside. It hurt more than I wanted to say. I didn't want to spoil the moment.

"You okay, Ade?"

"Umm," I nodded fast, "just been a while."

He continued even though we both knew it wasn't good for either of us. I was a million miles away from reaching an orgasm.

He finished quickly and laid by my side. "It'll get better. Your body was put through the ringer."

I nodded, on the verge of tears. "I know."

He cuddled me close, his body snug around mine. "I love you, Ade."

"I know. I love you, David. I'm sorry I'm not the same, but I'm just…"

"It's fine. I love you," he repeated, but even after all this time, it was just so difficult to believe.

"You're still so handsome and still the same," I said, lip trembling, "and now I'm just this whale who lost her libido. I'm just so sorry!"

Overflowing with emotion, I poured my heart out onto the pillow. He brought me onto his chest and let me cry. "I want you to take a break from university. You're too tired and coping with too much!"

"No, no! I can't. I've waited so long already. I just want to keep going."

"Why can't you just give yourself a break?"

I rolled over and away from him, muttering, "You just don't understand."

"No I don't, and that's just the problem. I don't know half of what happened to you to make you so bloody stubborn, working yourself like a dog, like this. You have a little baby and you won't stop working yourself into the ground. You'll make yourself ill."

"Then I'll make myself ill!" I shouted.

"I'm not arguing with you, Ade. I'm not your keeper. I'm just saying what I see. Now I've said it, we'll leave it at that."

"You don't understand," I mumbled.

"You're right, I don't," he growled under his breath, "because I work hard so I can spoil you and give you the life you're accustomed to. I want to care for you, see you right. You went back too soon, there, I said it. You're nursing a cold every five minutes. You're barely yourself. I want my wife back."

It was the first time we ever went to bed with an argument still hanging over us and it left me feeling sick. I wanted to call him out on things, too – like his mood swings, him working too many hours as well – but I didn't have the energy.

Things got much worse after that night.

THIRTEEN

January 2007

A morning like any other, William laughed at the television fixed to the wall above the breakfast bar while Lucinda spread her breakfast everywhere she possibly could. We'd moved to a large, Victorian house in Harrogate so we could be close to Rachel, our priceless help and support. It was wonderful, actually, having a proper house, altogether. However, recently I had admitted to myself that marital strife had hit our perfect quartet. William was six and Lucinda, eighteen months old, but problems that surfaced during my pregnancy still hadn't been resolved. My sanity hung by a thread.

I glanced over my shoulder as my husband breezed into the room in smart jeans and shirt, smelling gorgeous as always. With my back to him as I prepared Billy's packed lunch on the countertop, his voice as he called to our children sent a delicious, snaking thrill down my spine.

"Luce, not again! Your mother has enough to clean up without you adding to the pile!"

Billy made a derisive noise in his sister's direction. The age gap had been a bit of an issue in that Billy felt pushed out – and all he knew was that all the other boys at school thought all girls were gross.

"Morning baby," David said, his hand brushing my upper arm, his lips whispering a sweet kiss across my cheek.

"You got a busy day ahead?"

"Ball-busting day."

David people pleased all day long, leaving him exhausted at the end of every day. We still told people he marketed jewellery for a living which explained all the trips away and all the high-end jewellery I wore. People never asked for specifics and anyway, they'd only turn their noses up if they knew how much money was in selling sex products. I never told them that half the sex products David brought home for me to try out – I ended up keeping.

"I have seminars this afternoon so she'll be at the childminder's a few hours. I'm hoping this will more than tire her out because I can't take any more dried-on foods for me to scrub off various clothes and surfaces."

I heard my voice back and knew I sounded tired and sad. I couldn't help feeling this way.

David touched my elbow and I instinctively turned to look at him. His hypnotic, brown-eyed gaze always stumped me, every time. He smiled knowingly. "Ade, I've been neglecting you..."

I pouted a little. Maybe he had. I tried to avert his gaze, moreover, hide my encroaching tears.

We were still deeply in love, more than ever, but there was something wrong and I didn't know what.

"I'm sorry, I'll make it up to you. I'll ask Mum if she can have the kids overnight on Saturday and we'll do something special. I'll arrange it."

My heart soared and excitement rushed into my chest, a small smile teasing its way out over my reluctant lips. I didn't want to have a problematic marriage. I knew we did, but I didn't want to admit that to anyone. It had been hard enough admitting it to myself. Him suggesting time for romance made me happy, of course, but it was what came next that always scared me. There had been a few nights out recently, followed by rubbish sex, only ever making me feel worse. Still, I couldn't help feeling hopeful that this time he might organise something wonderful for our rare alone time together – something that would magically reignite our passion, simmering beneath the surface.

"I love you, David."

He leaned down to kiss me, but it was just a consolatory peck, as though he knew it was difficult being married to him but he loved me too much to let me go. Or maybe he loved me too little, I didn't know. The highly sexual man I first met had left the building and I didn't know if he was coming back.

"I love you so much, Ade," he said, stealing a slice of toast from my plate. "I'll grab something from the breakfast buffet at work. They've had those mini pancakes recently with fresh fruit."

"Sounds yum."

"Missing you already."

The thing was, I believed him, but I wondered if marriage really was a passion killer. Should I have just got down with this and accepted it?

He bit a corner of toast and while chewing, kissed the kids goodbye. "Why don't you get a new dress for the occasion?"

"I might do." I half-smiled, because I was only half-sure we'd make love on Saturday night.

"See you."

"Dinner at six. Will you be home in time?"

"As always," he assured me, but he often wasn't.

I listened out for the clang of the front door shutting and my happy façade dropped instantly. I noticed Billy watching my expression change. He never said anything but he wasn't stupid. No wonder he was determined not to understand girls.

***

Harrogate had more than its fair share of good restaurants

but David decided to take me out of town that Saturday night. In fact, he drove me all the way up into the wilds of the North Yorkshire countryside, to the Black Horse Inn just outside Northallerton. The drive was scenic, the destination gorgeous, with its black timber beams, exposed brick and roaring fires. It being a dark and dismal January outside, it was nice to be somewhere homely and colourful, somewhere away from our usual four walls. Even better, the food had a home-cooked feel but was more than normal pub grub.

"I want to talk about us," he said, sounding almost defiant, after the first course was done with. I had a beef pie and chocolate dessert to get through yet and part of me wondered if I would enjoy the rest of my meal after hearing what he had to say.

"Yeah?" I stared down at the table, my elbows on the surface. I thought about removing them but it was stupid to worry about manners when our whole marriage was at stake.

"I forgot to say how utterly beautiful you look tonight by the way. You take my breath away."

The catch in his voice made me stare into his eyes. I saw only sincerity. My heart melted, the words of my love the only ones that counted – his compliments the only ones I wanted to hear.

"I bought it for you. I'm wearing it for you." I gestured at my new dress.

"I know, Ade."

"David," I managed to get out, my voice croaky.

He stared at me, his eyes so kind and loving. I wore a simple navy dress, silk with a lace overlay. The sleeves stopped at my elbows and the length was just to the knee. David loved me in Peter Pan collars because when we met, I was wearing a simple white blouse with a navy collar. My navy dress that night had a collar made from the most delicate lace crochet.

He took my hands in his from across the table. "You love me, and I love you?"

"Yes, yes!"

His expression softened in an instant. "But it's not been the same, has it? Not recently."

"No." I shook my head.

I should have been glad to hear he felt the same way, but I was terrified. Was he going to tell me we should break up?

"Ade, I just want you to know, I'm never going to leave you. You stole my heart so long ago."

I nodded fast, twisting my lip, waiting for the 'but'...

"However," he paused, "it's hard having kids, having a job as stressful as mine, and you with your course at uni and... I just want to allay your fears. I feel the same way. I feel like we've lost something, but maybe it'll just take time. Maybe when life quietens down, we'll find us again, you know?"

My beautiful husband. Perfect in so many ways. Yet fatally flawed.

I sat twisting the sleeves of my dress and biting my lip. I had an answer, but not one I thought he would like.

"Say we're on the same page?" he asked.

I looked up and into his eyes. "About loving one another, but knowing something's gone from our relationship?"

"Yeah?" His nose wrinkled, looking worried.

"Honestly?"

He nodded, expecting me to agree with him. He seemed so full of hope, judging my patience endless, when it wasn't.

"David," I sighed. "No, we're not on the same page. I think we should try to do something about this... you know?"

He waited for me to elaborate and instead, it turned into a staring session.

Eventually he found some words. "I don't know, Ade."

My lip wobbled as I spoke and I hated myself for it. "I feel unwanted. I feel unloved, David. Sex used to be every-thing to us."

His mouth twitched at one corner and he seemed

disappointed. "We're older, we're different. I couldn't love you more. So, we just don't have sex as much anymore. So what?"

I sniffed, tapping the table with my finger. The old David would never have tried to fob me off. He respected me. Who was this man?

"I'm twenty-four and you're thirty. That's old? Are you kidding me? Seriously, David. We don't have sex as much? Try not at all!"

He rubbed his index finger under his nose and brushed me off with a shrug. "There's nothing wrong with us."

"There is." I was insistent, both with my tone of voice and folded arms. This man underestimated me. Most did. "I'm a woman with needs."

He looked shocked and I added quickly, "I said it. So now there is something wrong because we disagree. We both know we've lost something. It's just that neither of us has wanted to admit it, that's all. However, I'm telling you, I want to make this right. I want my hot husband back again. I love you and I want you. I want back what we had."

He stamped his foot under the table and groaned. "I don't know. I don't know."

"It seems like," I paused, "like you don't want to admit there's a problem."

"I love you, therefore there is no problem."

"David, please–" *don't be ridiculous.*

Our main courses were delivered in an untimely fashion and after the waitress left, he said, "I was going to suggest we see if they had any rooms here tonight, but what's the point now? Hmm? It's ruined. I don't even want my dinner now."

I closed my eyes and searched the insides of my eyelids for some sense. Wisdom had left the building, of that I had no doubt. There was no progression to be had here. None whatsoever. So either I put up and shut up, or did something about this myself...

FOURTEEN

With my marriage failing, I started to wonder if karma was catching up with me. Or fate? Maybe I'd earned this trial. Perhaps I would rest easier at night if I didn't have all this weight of the past weighing down on me. I couldn't escape what I was. Deep down, I was still my father's daughter – unable to turn a blind eye to what was going on around me.

The train from Harrogate to Leeds used to be comforting, a sort of slice of time for myself, but now it was just punishment for me opening up the debate. All I could do was spend time thinking about David shutting me down – David ignoring my needs – my vile, disgusting needs. That was how he made me feel.

I made my way to the campus of the University of Leeds on foot. It was a fair walk from the train station to there but I enjoyed it, passing through crowds of city people, as well as street artists and musicians. Leeds, like Harrogate, had hills but still, all my walking hadn't helped me shift that extra weight I now carried after having a big baby.

David didn't understand why I needed to do my accounting degree. In some respects, he knew what I was – a Kyd – but he didn't know exactly what that entailed. Not really. It wasn't that I wanted to achieve a BSc so I could make money, I wanted to do it for myself. I had a brain and I needed to use it. I also had something to prove to myself.

Two men I'd loved in the past both said I would never amount to anything.

If there was one thing I had to give David, though – he never asked me for the trust fund money which I had invested. He never asked for a penny. We'd bought the Harrogate house after selling the flat, but aside from that, he was still determined to become an equal to me.

Having been together for four years almost, I'd still never told David the intimate parts of what happened with Marcus – and I didn't intend on doing. That man – Billy's father – was evil. I didn't want to give him any airtime whatsoever. I didn't need to go over all that again. My status as an ex-Kyd and an ex-abused girlfriend weren't impacting on my current life whatsoever, I told myself.

If only that were true…

"Ade, are you listening?" my tutor asked as I sat in a seminar later that day. I was lost, staring at the towers of the Leeds skyline outside the window. For a second, I wondered why I wasn't skiving like the MIA members of this class, no doubt hanging out at the union bar. Fat chance of me learning anything, what with my mind elsewhere. Maybe it'd be more productive to get wrecked with strangers. Pour myself out of a nightclub at midnight. The police would escort me home but I'd suddenly remember I was a mother of two, and a wife, and while other people my age were busy fornicating and getting smashed, I shouldn't.

I knew if I unleashed the part of me screaming for release, I'd end up in the gutter. I was tightly contained and simmering, but only for the time being.

I turned my head and stared at Christian, my forensic accounting course tutor. I didn't know why I took this module. It was about the psychology, the ethics and the criminal aspects of fraud.

"Sorry, I'm so sorry," I apologised falsely.

"Did you read the case file at home?" Christian asked.

I nodded. "Cover to cover."

"What did you think? How would you handle the case if it was passed to you? If you were a fraud investigator?"

I cleared my throat. He'd put me on the spot a tad and I looked around the room at all the twenty year old students, most of whom were oriental or American, or from London. The Yorkshire ones were all getting pissed.

I sighed. "Can I tell you what I think personally as opposed to professionally?"

He opened his hands, his grey woollen jumper ugly and vile, like the sort I used to see on our Bishop every Sunday. The knit large, the wool larger, it buried his lithe frame. I wanted to rip it from his back and put a nice, crisp shirt and blazer on him instead. Christian's hands and face were handsome, such a pity he hid himself. Maybe he belonged in a warmer climate.

"Tell us," he said.

The case accused a family business of making false claims they were victims of fraud. Independent accountants discovered they'd 'stolen' their own money because their floundering family business – a delivery company – was in dire straits.

"I think the family accused of fraud deserve leniency and care. They're people. We might be studying pages of black and white, evidence and numbers, you know? But at the end of the day, these are people. They're not perfect, nobody is."

"Ade, but you know—"

"Christian," I persisted, "it's an open and shut case on paper, yes. They're guilty. The money stolen from their accounts was going to a dummy account set up by their own accountant! Those same accounts set up and shut down were always closed with cash withdrawals at the same bank on Teesside. Aside from a few more pieces of information, the evidence was all there. In their accounts." I gestured at the paper wallets spread around the desks in front of us.

I knew that in real life, 'evidence' told a court very little of the bigger picture – the story very few got an insight into.

"Were any pieces of information missing?" he asked the room, but nobody had an answer for Christian. This was an open and shut case. Why would anybody delve deeper? Well, I would and my teacher knew it. Because I covered all angles in life and on paper. I was a Kyd, after all.

"Adrienne?" Christian asked, seeing I had an answer mingled with my smile.

"The family accountant failed to provide itemised expenses for the years 2002-2003."

All the other students quickly snatched their folders up and flicked through. Most of them missed that tiny trinket. It's the little things in life that trip us up. Perhaps, the little things shine light on a lot of the bigger things, too.

"Ah, so what does that lead us to believe?" Christian eyed his students, even knowing I was the only one with the balls to answer.

"That's how it started," I explained, "first fiddling the expenses, then fraud. Start small, think big. That's how this thing works. You have to have accumulative evidence. It underpins the case. The plaintiffs would back down straight away and save everyone the hassle."

"Very good, Ade, I'm glad you were listening after all."

"But I still think the family deserve leniency, that's my personal opinion. They took on the company in 1999 when there was a lot of hidden debt in the business. Maybe they knew that, maybe they didn't... if this wasn't so open and shut, the investigators could have taken that into consideration and extended leniency. A few grand in fines instead of prison."

"Regardless of personal opinion," Christian exerted his voice over the room, "what Adrienne has done is examine all corners, all leads... good work. That's what forensic accountancy is all about. Taking evidence... picking out the circumstantial from the evidential. While I understand you see people Ade, accountancy only sees figures and malpractice if there was any. That's the life we've chosen."

I smiled, hating myself. *I can do this standing on my fucking head,* I thought, but I wouldn't tell him that. I'd always been clever and ever since I could remember, people told me I was clever. I got three grade As in my A levels: one in maths, one in Spanish and another in English language. I did all that while being involved with an abusive boyfriend. I still felt unworthy, though. I always would. I didn't know why I needed to do this to prove something to myself. Maybe I was still the wounded girl, the one made to feel puny.

The thorn was weaker, and more fragile, than she seemed.

The class continued and I lost myself staring out of the window again. Christian sort of peered at me as if to say, *I know you'll still pass this, but it would be nice if you were here for classes, not with your head in the clouds!* I sometimes wondered why the hell I chose accountancy. It was a soulless profession, completely ruled by rules. David hated rules. Always had. He was leagues and fathoms more intelligent than me, though. I'd always loved his intellectual freedom, something I wasn't in possession of.

It always came back to the past. Dad wanted me to become his accountant. All these years on, it still seemed like my only avenue. Still, proud was not a word Dad would ever utter about me, accounting degree or no accounting degree. Ashamed, more like. So much so, he gave me money and said if I took it, that was it, no more contact. I'd brought too much disgrace on the family. The money was really his way of easing his guilt and making sure I was gone. I even had to sign a contract to say I would never contact them again. The worst thing was, he made sure Mum never knew a thing about it.

After my seminars, I picked up some books from the library to take back with me on the train and bumped into Christian on the stairs as I descended the rotunda. I'd never seen him in the library before. *What is it about libraries? Ha!* David and I got together in this very library four years previous.

Maybe Christian was stalking me or maybe it was innocent. Perhaps he had been holding another seminar in a study room upstairs or something, I didn't know. Just seemed coincidental to bump into each other at such a large and sprawling campus where people came and went, irrespective of day or night. We walked down the staircase in silence until we got outside the oak doors of the library.

"Ade, do you mind me asking you something?"

We stood in the cold outdoors and I looked at my watch. "I have five minutes before I have to dash for my train."

"Are you happy?"

I stared, agog, and my jaw dropped. "Of course I am!"

He shook his head. "You don't look happy."

I fake smiled, despising the wisdom he possessed because it meant he saw me in a way my own husband didn't.

"That's your opinion, Christian. Anyway, I'm a third year so in five months' time, I'm going to be gone from here and then you'll never have to worry about me again, will you?"

The smile dropped from his thirty-something, handsome face and we stared at one another, challenging each other to say what was really going on here. Maybe he had begun to realise this was his last chance before I was gone from his life forever?

"A woman like you, she's rare. If he doesn't appreciate what he's got, he's a fuckin' idiot."

I bit my tongue and pointed at him, shaking my head. It was true Christian and me were ordinarily friends and got along, both of us sharing wry humour, but this was well out of order.

I decided not to dignify him with a response and instead, I swivelled on my heel and started jogging away, making sure not to be late for my train.

Finally on a train pulling out of Leeds Station, I said to

myself, "Who does he think he is?"

A woman sat next to me nodded and I covered my mouth, realising I said that out loud.

"I say that to myself most days, hun."

I quickly put my headphones in, avoiding a discussion I wasn't cut out for with anyone, let alone a stranger on a train.

For the duration of the journey home, I only got angrier thinking about his words.

FIFTEEN

Much later that night in the home study, I was working on my dissertation on ethical practice. For some reason, I'd had to rewrite it a few times already because my main course tutor, Alice said I kept writing it like it was a paper on how to earn the sympathy vote. I just had to write what was right according to law – not according to my own principles.

"You okay in here?" David and his shadow filled the doorway, hands in his pockets.

"Fine."

I kept my eyes glued to the laptop screen, deleting paragraph after paragraph of my romantic notions of forgiveness and leniency. Self-doubts spun round my head like, *I'm going to be such a failure as an accountant, aren't I?* I could've taken the optional year in industry or a year abroad to lessen the academic load if I didn't have a family and a husband.

"Well, I'm going to bed." He sounded dejected and I felt bad about that, but I worked late most nights, it wasn't anything new. I had to work late every night if I was going to get everything done and pass my degree.

He might have picked up on the fact that all evening, I'd been grumpy and obtuse because of Christian's words earlier and I couldn't bear to face the fact that people outside of my marriage could tell I was unhappy.

"Night, baby," I whispered, giving him a small smile which I hoped would get rid of him. I didn't want David to ask me what was wrong.

Please don't ask me, please don't ask me…

"Ade, are you–"

"Bit stressed with this dissertation," I answered quickly, "it being my last year and everything. There's loads to get through. I'll be okay once it's all out of the way."

"Sure, don't stay up too late now."

"I won't. Be there soon."

He headed to bed and I breathed a sigh of relief. I was a crap wife but I was trying, in a roundabout way. It's why I asked David at the weekend about our sex life – something that took balls to do. If Christian could see it, David must have known how unhappy I was, too. He was simply unwilling to do anything about it.

I stared at the walls with my pen tapping my bottom lip, wondering if Christian was right. Was David a prick? If he was, did that make me blind? Maybe I was too fucked up inside to see beyond the thicket and out into the clearing. I just had to finish my degree, that was all I knew, and deal with the rest after that.

When I finished working at midnight, I was about to close my laptop when I decided to check my university emails. Sometimes I forgot to check that account and would miss an important update from a course buddy or something.

In my inbox, I found only one unopened mail – and it was from Christian. *Shit.* I wondered what it could be. Chastisement or reparation? One or the other? Perhaps both!

I opened the email and read:

Dear Ade,

I'm sorry about the way I spoke to you earlier but you're distant in class, you look tired and unhappy all the time. You look sad. You cannot deny you are!

I've watched you over the past two years or so and I know you've gone from sad to sadder, it's clear to see in your beautiful, expressive blue eyes.

I see so many people come through the doors and never have I met a woman as passionate about life as you! I don't see women like you on these sorts of courses.

We have always got on, you and I. Maybe because we're nearer in age than myself and my other students, we have an understanding. While I would love to get to know you more and be a friend to you, I fear if I was a friend, I'd ultimately end up wanting something so much more than you can give and that's not fair and not right, I know that.

So I'm just going to say this . . . Adrienne, you are absolutely breathtakingly beautiful, clever and wonderful. You deserve better. Please remember that and make sure you make yourself happy, first. I can't get involved, I know that, but I'm asking you to seek help or seek something – I don't know – that will help you come out of the other side of your sadness.

I'm asking you to make yourself happy. I care enough to say it so you see – someone sees you, for you. I see enough to know you are unhappy. Please don't ever imagine this is what you deserve. You deserve all the safety, security and happiness in the world.

Love, Christian x x x

I swallowed hard and reread his words over and over. Something about them wasn't sinking in. *Someone sees you, for you* got to me and I wondered if he really did see me. Did Christian see me? Did David, even? I didn't think either of them did. His words, rather than helping, tore me up inside and ultimately made me feel alone. All alone.

I walked across the study and pushed the door shut, walked back to my desk chair, curled up in it and stewed. I needed to decide what to do.

What was the truth? From now on when I walked down

the street, was everyone going to be looking at me thinking, *Poor, sad woman, probably suffering marital issues. Yeah, don't ever get married!*

But I was a Kyd and we didn't back down.

When I gathered myself together, I replied:

Dear Christian,
Your comments are completely inappropriate and uncalled for. In some parts, you sound like a madman. And three kisses? Take them back and choke on them. I don't appreciate them and you're getting far too involved by even sending me an email like this, which I'm sure is contrary to university policy. If you're feeling pleased with yourself for finally striking up the courage to tell me how you feel, then do not feel pleased. I feel disgusted.

Stay out of my private life. You know nothing. I truly love my husband.

Stay out. I mean it.
Adrienne

Feeling better for having told him what for, I started to clear up my books and pens into piles when a ping on screen let me know a new email had arrived:

You're right. I apologise profusely. I'll stay out of this.
–Christian

Feeling victorious, I began to shut down my laptop, when I halted. My mind wandered. I was left thinking, *Why is it only ever the wrong men who want me? Why doesn't my husband want me?* I held my head in my hands, elbows on the desk. Is this what life was? Pain… and confusion. Misunderstanding? Was it better to be as the monkeys and be polygamous? My marriage over the past year had caused me some serious heartache and pain. It started when I fell pregnant and just got worse. Ever since we had Lucinda, it'd been harder for me to orgasm and David found it traumatising when I didn't come. He started making excuses and avoiding sex. We never said it but the problem was there and he wouldn't talk about. I'd been brave and tried to talk about it all with him, but like always he shut me down.

I'd tried, I'd really tried. Perhaps sex toys were the only way forward? I chuckled to myself, so weary, but too upset to go to bed yet.

I opened Google in a new browser and searched: *David Dare, porn.*

My husband used to do porn, a thing I never liked to admit. The thought of anyone else touching him made me boil with fury. Even just the idea of it.

However his former life as an actor in adult films was half responsible for how he got his current job in marketing. I couldn't remember when exactly, but he once let slip that David Dare was his porn name. David Lewis playing *David Dare* – it made me sick thinking about it all.

I was at the end of my tether and needed to know. I needed answers – who was this man I married? Really? Who was he? Since we met, he'd said all sorts of wonderful things to me, but did he mean them? Was I his trophy wife?

The Google search returned thousands of hits, all archive stuff from around 2000-2002. So, he never lied – it was all before we met. I was shaking just thinking about clicking on one of the search results. I could barely contain my shock that he really did do porn. I'd sort of always tried to block it out and tell myself I'd never find the real David on screen. However, I was so desperate by this point, willing to do anything if it might help me understand him better.

I clicked on one labelled, *David pounds Candy hard...*

I gulped and pressed play.

The video seemed grainy and bad quality. People actually got paid for this? I knew this was a few years ago, but still...! I watched as (onscreen) a naked woman with en-hanced breasts circled around a beautifully dressed king-size bed. She bent over, showing her crack, as she picked some saucy underwear out of a drawer. David, *my David!*, caught her hand and said, "You don't need these."

He picked her up and tossed her down on the bed and she squealed with glee. I swallowed and tried to catch my breath. Could I deal with this? Should I shut it down? My heart was pounding and I couldn't think, morbidly engrossed by what was onscreen, wondering what'd happen next. I saw the film was twenty minutes long and was contemplating if I could handle a second more when he started to lick her pussy – and the screen froze!

"What the–" I began protesting to nobody. Like car crash TV, I needed more. Wanted the drama, the story, the end.

A website pop-up told me:

If you'd like to watch the whole film, buy a subscription today... new accounts discounted.

Paying for it? Golly. All I could see on the screen was my husband's tongue on pause, about to engage in licking another woman's pussy – and all I could think was, *I need to see the rest.*

I signed up for an account using a fake name and paid using a debit card belonging to an old account I didn't share with David. A few minutes later, I was watching the rest...

Insta-porn.

He licked her slowly, differently to how he licked me. When David used to go down on me, he was a man possessed, licking everywhere, fast, burying himself and with no pattern. On the screen, I saw him working in sync with the camera, building the suspense of the scene, angling his head so you got a good view of his tongue going into and around her labia and vagina.

The fake-breasted woman rubbed her tits and moaned she was going to come. David slid two fingers inside her and sucked her clit and she came, although it didn't look like a real orgasm to me. There was no fluid spurting from her, her thighs weren't jerking, and in the past when I came good and hard, I clawed the sheets and probably pulled some extra-ordinary facial expressions as I writhed beneath my husband. If only we could get those days back…

I watched as he put on a condom and flipped her onto her belly. The camera panned and captured the sight of his large cock buried in her tight pussy and still, I couldn't see as much pussy juice as there usually is when a woman is really aroused. I once read that prostitutes pump themselves full of lube so maybe this is what the woman on screen did too, but who could be sure? Anyway, I wasn't at all convinced of what was going on here…

He pounded her hard doggy style, then lifted her into his arms, her legs thrown over his shoulders. My David's strong but lithe body held all her weight, pulling her bum back and forth, fucking her hard as she hung onto the back of his neck, grunting and faking screams of pleasure. All the while you got a good view of his big cock and how the position only worked because of it. Still, I didn't believe she was enjoying it as much as I enjoyed sex with him, but then Candy Kitten (the woman on screen) didn't appear to be in love with David.

I thought it was sad that this was what really got people off – watching people not in love, having mediocre sex.

Is a condom a get-out clause? A barrier to intimacy? Really, she could have just fucked herself with a sheathed dildo and it would have been the same. They hardly kissed and when they did, it was not heartfelt. There was no meaningfulness on screen. No intimacy. It was just porn and I never realised until now how fucking bland porn was.

When she screamed the house down, faking Orgasm Number Six, he dropped her on the bed and ripped off the condom. He fisted his hard cock really fast and spurted cum all over her body. Covering her. It was in that onscreen moment I saw the real David. My David. He wasn't able to come in her because he didn't care for her or find her attractive. He had to masturbate because he wasn't really all that aroused. Sure his cock was hard and solid but I'd known David go to work still hard and solid because that was just how sexual a man he was. I knew that getting him to orgasm was often difficult because he could go for hours and never come unless fully aroused. He had the stamina of a race-horse.

It was as he spurted on her body that I knew the promise of seeing himself on her skin was what made him finally reach orgasm. My stallion, my lover... with his filthy mind. Always the filthy mind needed more stimulation than anything else. If only I could get inside his mind again...

"Clean yourself up," he said to Candy in an angry tone and left the bedroom.

The camera focused on Candy's face as she giggled to herself and rubbed her fingers in his ejaculation. She licked some off her fingers and then some seedy music began playing as the video faded out.

The website suggested I watch more videos of him and his harem going at it but it was late and I was as horny as hell.

I wiped my browsing history and shut the laptop down, turning the light off in the study as I left.

Walking down the hallway to our bedroom, I felt my knickers wet between my thighs. I needed to do something about it.

Closing the bedroom door behind me, I stripped my clothes off and swiped a finger through my slit, finding myself drenched through. In the dark I fumbled around the bedroom and walked to the bed naked.

Climbing in, I reached for David and felt him semi-hard in sleep. I slipped my hand under his boxers and he grew harder as I played with him.

Before he was really awake, I already had him fully erect.

"Adrienne?"

"Hush, let me touch you."

"Hmmm, baby."

120

Pulsating down below, I was humming. I hadn't been so aroused in years. Seeing David – marking his territory on that woman's body – had made me all hot and bothered. It reminded me of times he used to do that to me.

I threw off the bedcovers and he was about to ask what I was doing when I yanked his boxers down and threw my leg over his body. Pulling him on his side, I slid his cock through my wet lips.

"So fucking wet, Adrienne," he groaned.

"Wait," I growled, warning him. I was sloshing. We both heard it as his cock slipped and grew stickier, our bodies almost joining.

I was drenched and deep in my hips, throbbing. I was starved of him. This man. My husband. The only man aside from my father who really meant anything to me.

I tapped the tip of his cock against my clit and came instantly, crying out, pulling his face into my breasts as I rocked my body against his slippery, swollen cock.

"Jesus Christ, Adrienne."

"Fuck me, David, fuck me hard. Like an animal."

"God, fuck, fuck," he whimpered.

He rolled me onto my back and I pulled his bed shirt off over his head. With my toes, I pushed his boxers the rest of the way down his legs and he toed them right off. He was still wearing socks but I didn't mind if he kept them on. In fact, him keeping his socks on reminded me of how it used to be.

He pushed straight into me and I gulped, terror washing over me for a second before pleasure took hold. He was so big, always a shock. Even in the dark, I saw his eyes alight.

I thrashed his arse and he pinned my arms above my head. "You asked for it," he warned, and began fucking me hard.

"Yes, yes, yes!"

After half a dozen thrusts, I came a second time, my head twisting side to side, my fingers squeezing his. I was so aroused, my lower back crunched under the weight of another fierce orgasm.

I couldn't forget how he controlled Candy onscreen and I wanted that, too.

"You like that, hmm? Hmm?"

"More," I begged.

He pulled out and flipped me over onto my stomach so the cool sheets rustled against my searing belly, my sensitive nipples. Pulling my hips up off the bed, he buried his face in my crack from behind and tasted me, his nose and mouth everywhere. His tongue pushed into my ass and I reached beneath myself to finger my clit.

I came again, moisture trickling down my thighs. He pushed his monstrous cock deep inside me and the slap and squelch of his body against mine drove me to the edge of insanity. I pushed back against him as he rammed into me and pounded me much harder than he ever pounded Candy.

"Fuck, you're so fucking wet for me Adrienne, so fucking wet, honey."

"David, oh god."

"Fuck. You're so wet. I love you like this."

He pounded me until I had to bite the pillow beneath my face, my fist punching the mattress, signalling I was coming hard around him. I tried not to make too much noise and wake the kids. The sound of his balls whacking me was loud enough. He pulled out and came all over my ass and lower back, spreading it all over me, his warm velvet seed staking his claim. He fell on top of me, panting hard, his arms shifting around me, scooping me into his embrace. I welcomed the weight of him, the feel and the smell of him in all his sweaty, manly glory. He squeezed my breasts in his hands and held tight, licking and kissing my throat.

I turned my head and he kissed me with his tongue, gently loving me. I opened my eyes and he opened his, both of us staring at one another in the dark.

"I've been a fucking prick, I just–"

"Please no," I started to protest.

"I was scared we'd lost the magic, I was just so scared Adrienne."

"Oh god, it was never lost, just temporarily on hold."

"I built up a barrier, I'm sorry." He laughed, sounding elated and relieved. "I love you! Jesus, I love you. Whatever got you so horny tonight, thank fuck, Ade. Thank fuck!"

He cradled me so tight, I was surrounded by him at every point of my body. I reached for the blankets and we fell asleep bundled together, his socks the only item of clothing between us, just like old times.

SIXTEEN

The morning after, I woke to find myself bundled in our messy sheets. Lifting my head to look around the room, I noticed he wasn't with me.

I checked the clock and it was past ten in the morning!

Rubbing the sleep out of my eyes, I noticed a note, left lying on his pillow. It looked like a poem. He hadn't written me any poetry in a long, long time.

It read:

All Saints Day

A young poet went walking on a summer's morning,
and found something he did not expect.

A lady of paradise who was built of the forests and the meadows,
appeared and granted him peace.

For all his words the poet could not find the thing to say,
but this did not matter.

In that moment, nothing needed to be written or said,
or recalled as a tale to be told.

For if he blinked or moved she would be gone,
so he resolved to do nothing.

And there he remained for all ages, in bliss
And still he moves not, as all else is nothing...

I love you.

God, he was beautiful. I raced out of bed and down the stairs in my robe to be welcomed by the sight of my husband in casual clothes, playing with our daughter on the floor of the living room, building blocks together.

"Where's Billy?"

David smiled. "I took him to school. I switched the radio alarm off so you wouldn't be woken."

"What about work?"

"In all these years, have I ever called in sick? I thought it was about time."

I stared, flummoxed. "Okay."

"Coffee in the pot," he said. "Did you like the poem?"

I nodded, showing him I had it in my pocket. "I love you, too."

I didn't have seminars or lectures that day, just lots of reading to do. I normally did that while Luce had her morning and afternoon snoozes.

I stood in the doorway with my mug of coffee. "I'll do some course reading in bed then?"

He smiled, unfazed. "Knock yourself out. You deserve a pyjama day sweetheart."

He stood up and kissed my lips, murmuring against them, "Absofuckinloved last night."

I grinned and tore myself away. "I won't get anything done if you're bad."

"Me? Bad?" He cocked one brow.

I climbed the stairs, wondering how he knew I was exhausted enough to sleep so late. I normally rose at seven every morning and jumped straight out of bed because I was one of those people who didn't do snoozing.

Maybe a hard fucking made me sleep?

As I settled with my course books and got comfy propped up in bed, the memory of Christian's emails hit me and I felt dirty almost, thinking about him and his inferences about the state of my marriage. Ah well, I supposed he saved the day really because looking at porn after that got me the hard shagging I needed.

***

Later that night, I sat in the study finishing off one of the core chapters of my dissertation when David popped his head around the doorframe again.

"Maybe I'll see you later?" he asked with a big grin.

"We'll see, won't we?" I tried to be sultry, sucking on my pen.

He winked and headed off to bed. "Night."

Did he know I used porn last night to get me wet? I didn't know. Maybe he didn't care. After all, it was still him I was getting wet to, wasn't it?

I thought back to how all this awkwardness started. After I had Luce, I became a bigger lady, going from a size ten to a fourteen. David said he didn't mind but then they all say that, don't they? I sat wondering what really went on in his head because I had no bloody clue.

I'd gotten down to a respectably curvaceous size twelve but I didn't know if it was my lack of confidence over my new curves or his insecurity over pleasing me that was the problem.

When we started having sex again after Luce, I found orgasm really difficult to achieve and sometimes I didn't want the light on. Sometimes I didn't want him to go down on me. I wondered if he judged it all as rejection but I didn't know how to tell him I just felt different and it was a lot of getting used to. I snapped back fairly quickly after Billy but he was a small baby and Luce was a whopping nine pounds. Not surprising considering the height of her father and also, second babies generally are bigger.

Anyway, putting all that out of my mind, I piled my books up and shut down my dissertation to find that porn site again. Logging in with my secure username and password, I searched for more films featuring David Dare.

This time, the film was a little different. David was tied to the bed blindfolded and spread-eagled. Two women worked on him, one kissing his mouth, the other licking his knob.

"Jesus," I said to myself.

I was instantly wet and instantly, also, outraged. How could he?

I told myself over and over again, day after day, his porn life was a past life but it had always been niggling the back of my mind, ever since he told me. He'd done risqué stuff (clearly) like this (no, not even risqué – that wasn't the right word). He'd had experiences I wouldn't feel comfortable re-enacting with him. He must have thought me so boring, with my size-twelve fat ass and my insecurities and my inability to just sit on his face like this girl was going.

Whoa.

You could see everything.

You could see her folds and his chin, slotted nicely between them, his stubble making her skin shine with red chafing. You could see how bald she was! *Should I go bald?* I thought. I did once but the re-growth was fucking hell!

I got a close-up of her arsehole and – golly gosh – now the other woman was sucking him off.

I was unbearably aroused and I didn't know whether I could handle any more of this. I couldn't look away even though I hated it. I rubbed my thighs together, the itch so heightened, I knew I might run the batteries down on my vibrator while trying to scratch this ache between my legs.

"Oh my god," I whispered to myself.

While one of them rode his face, the other one started riding his cock. I realised as I was watching, just how big my husband was. You could see how stretched she was because of his large member and I wondered if that's what I looked like to him when he watched his cock go in and out of me. He must have felt like the King of Pussy whenever he fucked a woman.

I was shocked to realise that this time, there was no condom. She was fucking him without protection. It made me wonder, did he get regular checks?

When Miss Facefucker had finished her deeds, she joined Miss Cockfucker in licking David's cock free of pussy juice.

Still no male cum in sight.

I was outraged.

Fucking livid.

That was my cock.

Get off!

Together they worked on his cock until he erupted all down their cheeks and all over their breasts and stomachs, in their hair and everything. It got smeared everywhere and that's when I realised David used to sometimes come twice with me and he was still more than capable of it, I felt sure.

So, they just made him come twice.

Well, I could better that!

I wiped my browsing history yet again, livid that the end of the film had them untying David, both girls snuggling into his sides for naked, after-sex cuddles.

Two women.

Two.

How could I compete with that?

I couldn't!

I wasn't enough!

Still, I'd go down fighting.

I crept into our bedroom and into the walk-in closet where I picked a pair of heels off a shelf and put them on.

Red heels.

Come Fuck Me heels.

In the dark I removed all my clothes and left them there, walking back into the bedroom, naked aside from the heels.

"David?" I whispered.

"I've been waiting, what were you doing in the closet?"

I laughed dirtily, gutturally, wandering around the bed.

"Seriously, what have you got on?"

I laughed. "Wouldn't you like to know?"

He switched the bedside lamp on and saw me naked, in only heels. He immediately rubbed his cock and winced. "I'm so fucking painfully hard, look how wet you are. Sit on me, now!"

I climbed onto the bed and crawled slowly to him, maintaining eye contact.

Creeping, I asked, "How bad, David? How bad do you want my gash to swallow your filthy, fucking, fat, cock?"

(I may have learnt some new language from porn films.)

"BAD!" he exclaimed, grabbed me, and sat me on his rigid, blazing hot cock.

"Uhhhh," I groaned, tipping my head back, "you're such a fucking bad husband. Arms above your head. Where I can see them. I'm going to fuck you."

Arms above his head, he bit his lip, his nose wrinkling as I began to screw him.

On the bed, I squatted in my heels, the spikes digging into the mattress as I hovered over him. Hands on his chest, I bounced up and down.

"You want this, every minute of the day David?"

"I'd fuck you for a living. Six, seven, eight times a day. I'd be dead, like…" He grunted, eyes squeezing shut as I slammed down hard on him, "…dead within a few days of screwing you like this. Nobody ever got me this painfully hard."

"Tell me David, tell me how fucking hard, you filthy fuck," I growled.

He smiled, gazing lustfully up into my eyes. "It feels like if I don't wank off or fuck, I'll die. I feel like I'll die. I need your sweet, wet cunt to soothe me, calm me. It throbs. It hurts. I need to come like I need a fat slash after a long night drinking. I need to put my cum in you. You're my drug, my lifeline, I need you. Your body is the paradise I'll gladly die inside of, worshipping forever. You drive me wild."

With that, he took me in his hands and turned me onto my back, fucking me with my red heels on, his ass moving fast. So fast. He was wild. I watched him maul my body with his hands and teeth. My heels bucked to and fro with his moves. It was so sexy.

Slosh.

Spurt.

Thwack.

Fuck.

Cum.

I smiled.

Just noises.

He came twice.

I barely knew what'd happened when I came round.

I knew he went wild using me and I blacked out as I came so hard, I wasn't me anymore.

He removed the heels and lay his head on my belly.

"Are you happy, Ade?"

"I think so."

"Do you want more children? What will you do after you finish university?"

What was it with all the questions?

I tugged my fingers through his hair and enjoyed his warm breath against my belly. "I'm happy and I don't know what I'll do when I finish. I don't know if accountancy is me. If you want more children, maybe we could think about it, although I'm happy with the two we've got."

Honestly, I didn't want my body pulled apart again.

"How about being my accountant?"

"Huh?"

He lifted his head. "I'm getting out. I've built up enough contacts. I'm going solo."

"Really?"

He nodded. "Sure, yeah. I can do it from home, don't you think?"

"Of course you can and I'd love to be your accountant!"

He went back to snuggling on my stomach and a few moments later, I asked, "I thought you loved working with Luca?"

"I do but there's more to life than the nine to five. I've always wanted to be my own boss, Ade. You know that."

"I'll support you, of course I will. If I do this with you, I might freelance as well, just to keep my hand in you know?"

He sneered. "Why?"

"Well, just because, it's good for an accountant to have a portfolio, you know? Otherwise I might be seen to be practicing favouritism?"

"Well, you'll still be favouritist, if that's a word?"

"Ooh, I've always been partial when it comes to you David Lewis."

He laughed and moved up into the pillows with me, switching off the bedside lamp.

"Is that why you pulled a sickie today?"

"Sort of," he replied, "just needed a bit of time to think, you know?"

"I understand."

"I love you, baby. I'll wake you in the morning. You have lectures, right?"

"Right. Night, night."

"Night." He smooched me and I had no reason to doubt his love, except when I dreamt, all I saw was him and other women loving him.

SEVENTEEN

For a couple of weeks after that, I used porn to get me wet and willing for David every night. However, one night he caught me out by suggesting we take a bath together and slip into bed right after.

Finally in bed after the bath, I wasn't as horny as I usually was. I was warm and aroused but not as abnormally aroused as I got after watching porn. Wrapped in each other's arms on top of the duvet, we lay naked. I still found his body wonderful and comforting and sexy but I just wasn't gushing. I think he noticed because he was kissing me slower and touching me slower, too.

"I want to reconnect with you, Ade. It's not been the same but I think…" He kissed my throat with little pecks and I sighed. "…we could be hotter than we've ever been."

I started thinking I could raid my drawer of toys to speed up the process to super wetness, but I knew he might get annoyed by me bringing a third act into the equation. I was never sure what was going to upset him or not. Why couldn't he just be David Dare, as he was onscreen, so cocksure and in charge, so sexual and deviant. The David in my bed that night was struggling with his ego and needed me to be coming at every turn for him to feel confident in what we had. I had no idea where this went wrong!

All I knew was, for him to make me come with

penetration, I had to be extremely aroused otherwise it did not happen and when it did not happen, he got upset with himself.

"David, will you lick me baby?"

He slowly kissed his way down between the valley of my breasts and gently over my stomach, toward my sex.

"How do you want it, Adrienne?"

"Messy," I told him, because that would certainly get me all wet.

"Okay," he replied with glee.

He pinned my legs to the bed so I was spread wide.

"Fucking beautiful, Ade."

He turned his head sideways and used his lips to seal mine in an envelope of his mouth. Sucking greedily on my whole labia, his cheeks hollowed as he kindled the flames in my belly.

"Shit, what is that?" I asked him.

"Something I read about in GQ," he offered.

I laughed and grabbed his hair, "Don't stop."

Now I was getting wet, he slipped two fingers inside me and began fucking me hard with them. It was a little painful but when he said, "Feel that, do you?" I sort of felt more turned on hearing his dirty tone.

Moisture started to make it easier for him to slide in and out of me and he grunted, "So wet."

He started noisily licking me, all over, doing that dog thing of slobbering around and around, up and down, like an animal. I pressed the heels of my palms into my eyes and wondered why the hell I decided I didn't like this anymore. I loved this! I loved oral pleasure. So what if I wasn't the same down there anymore, he didn't seem to care, and I was horny as fuck.

I spread my legs even wider, my feet on his shoulders.

"Oh David, yes, don't stop. Don't stop–"

He did that thing I saw him do on camera. He sealed his whole mouth over my sex and the suction meant he could dip his tongue in and out of my pussy at will and slip upwards toward my clit at intermittent moments.

I breathed heavily and panted, my voice getting hoarse with all the breathing. I jumped my hips up and down and when he felt me coming, he darted his tongue in and out of my vagina and I swam in ecstasy, a fireball rushing from one side of my abdomen to the other, my walls trembling and fluttering around his delicious tongue.

In the past he would have been straight inside me after that, enjoying the trembling of my body around his. That night, he had different ideas. He rose to his knees and started beating himself off really hard and fast. I watched, laid there exhausted, my legs still spread wide.

"Oh, god, oh, god, Ade," he moaned, and came shooting all over my body. Throwing his head back, his cock bobbed up and down as he stopped masturbating and held his hips, his body overcome.

He lay down beside me as he recovered too.

"Are you okay?"

"I just had to come quick. I was so hard, it hurt. I love licking your pussy."

On the inside, I winced. "Does it seem different, down there? I mean…"

"You taste and feel amazing and along with you coming as hard as that, that's all that counts."

I laughed and he cuddled me in his arms. His cum had dried on, but I didn't mind. I loved his scent all over me. So did he. I loved him marking me, claiming me, making me his.

"The duvet's pretty soaked," I told him, "maybe I should change it?"

"No way," he growled, "I want to smell us all night."

Beneath the covers he curled up tight behind me and I reached for the light, switching it off. I wondered if I'd really pleased him. I thought I had – and all without porn being involved, too. It occurred to me, maybe I should try to lay off the videos and just have more baths with him.

The thing was, David wasn't a man you could love half-heartedly. If you were going to love him, you had to do so properly, otherwise his huge erection just didn't find a home. Being with a guy with such a huge cock was a problem – especially when he said lube reminded him of the past.

If only we could have gone back to the early days of lazy loving while Billy slept in his crib – the sort of loving that didn't require thought and had no responsibilities attached.

"I love you," he told me as he was drifting off, and I wriggled back into him, making him groan.

***

Walking in through the front door a couple of weeks later, David announced, "Well, that's it! Officially unemployed now."

In the kitchen where I was cooking dinner, I laughed before walking through the hallway to meet him at the entrance. We kissed and cuddled and I asked, "How was it?"

"Okay."

"Come tell me in the kitchen once you've said hello to the kids."

He strode into the living room and kissed his children hello before sliding his arms around me in the kitchen.

"I got a £1000 gift voucher," he said, "and a lot of tears from some of them. If I hadn't have been driving, they would have got me smashed at lunchtime."

"Really? So you all went out for lunch in Leeds then? A leaving meal type of thing?"

"Yep," David admitted, "I'm sort of glad I won't be working in the city anymore. The noise can get too much."

"So, what did Luca say?"

His eyes glazed over and he piped up, "No tears from Luca. Just anger. I don't think he appreciates why I want to go it alone. He even offered me five grand more, today."

I turned and with my arms around his neck, told him, "He obviously knows what he's losing. You've been selling his stuff successfully, but you were never going to be his forever. Surely he knew you would move on, I mean…"

"Right." David stole a carrot from a steaming pan off the stove and tossed it about in his fingers to cool it down. The man had asbestos hands, I was sure. "Anyway, that's that."

I turned back to the stove and started draining vegetables. "So what is the voucher for?"

"Oh, it's a one-for-all so we could spend it on a holiday or a new computer, whatever."

"Well, I've been saying for ages we need a holiday and I have a study break coming up, so we could use that to get away?"

For so long, he'd been saying he couldn't get away but now, he didn't have an excuse, did he? Not when he was unemployed, so to speak!

"Sounds good. You book it and we'll go. I'll go set the table with the kids."

"No problem. Dinner's ready now," I told him, serving vegetables and steak pie onto plates, and some mushy versions for Luce in a plastic bowl.

Soon we were eating dinner peaceably in the dining room, Billy telling us all about the types of rocks he'd been learning at school.

Except as I stared across the table at David, I didn't fail to notice a tiny imprint of pink lipstick on the inside of his shirt collar. Not outside. Inside. How bizarre! Maybe it was someone getting too close during the goodbye hugs today, or maybe it was something I should have worried about.

Anyway as we crawled into bed that night, I didn't initiate sex and neither did he. Since I stopped watching porn, it'd virtually gone back to how it was before. I.e. unless I was absolutely gagging for his hard cock, he wasn't interested.

EIGHTEEN

July 2007

"Once more, I think. To Mummy," David toasted again, but I could hardly believe I had done it. I had my degree. I scraped a 2.1 but I did it. I actually did what I wanted to do. It'd taken more than blood, sweat and tears – it'd taken guts to get to the point I was at now.

"To Mummy," Rachel and Billy cheered, while Luce looked bewildered in her highchair. Almost two, she'd been with me on this journey all the way and I felt like we'd come so far together. While she was teething, I was writing essays late into the night. Sometimes the only way to get her to sleep was in our bed so as David cuddled her to sleep, I'd be laid next to them with the laptop, working late.

"Thanks everyone," I gushed, "it feels strange but wonderful."

I wouldn't pick up my certificate until the graduation ceremony in December but I doubted I'd go to that anyway. I decided to have the certificate sent home because then I didn't have to see Christian, who'd been funny with me ever since those late-night emails.

"Isn't Mummy clever, Lucinda?" David asked.

Lucinda grinned, and suddenly shouted, "Pretty Mummy!"

"Oh! Aww." I clutched my chest and smiled at David, who took my hand. Billy rolled his eyes and his grandmother chuckled to herself quietly.

"Well done, Ade. Seriously. A baby and a degree in under three years. I don't know how you've done it darling," Rachel said, draining her champagne glass. We all sat around the dining table, in our best clothes, eating a dinner I bought from M&S to save me cooking.

I looked at David. "Blind stubbornness right, love?"

"Something like that," he groaned.

He'd now been working on his business for six months and had a few clients already. Money had just started to roll in but I always knew that starting up would mean a little break in his income, so we'd been digging into my savings a little. Not that I was worried, but I felt as though a discussion about the future beckoned, given I've just gotten my degree and all. I didn't know why money was such an issue for us both, but it was. For me, I grew up never worrying about where money came from or where it was going. That carefree attitude was stolen from me when suddenly, I had a child to provide for singularly. Sure, my father set me up, but what if I lost everything suddenly? He'd paid me off, sent me packing with no way back. I had no fallback anymore, whereas for the first eighteen years of my life I had all the fallback I could ever need. Abandonment was something that traumatised me – feeling so desolate and alone after I moved to Leeds and left my parents behind. I never stopped thinking about my mother and how much I missed her. How much fun we had together. As I sat round that table with my husband, children and mother-in-law, the grief of not having my own mother there to celebrate with us hit me like a sledgehammer and so out of the blue. And it was meant to be such a happy day.

"I think we should fill the dishwasher tonight and let Mummy put her feet up and relax, don't you Billy?"

"Suppose," he said, "maybe."

David chuckled. "That's settled then."

"I'm going to get off, if you don't mind," Rachel said,

helping David clear the table of our dessert bowls.

"Yeah, got a hot date?" I asked her, sipping more champagne.

"No! I've got a book club meeting with some friends. I started going a few weeks ago. It's been really good so far and the discussions are enhancing, I must say."

I grinned over my glass and picked up on her vibe. Maybe it was a group of women whose tastes were embedded in the more fragrant books of our time. Like sex books.

"Have fun!" I said as she kissed me goodbye, letting herself out of the house.

When I heard her car engine start outside, I breathed a slight sigh of relief. In David's study we had several black rampant rabbits stored away. Three dozen of them. We had to keep the room locked until David could afford office or storage premises of his own. Rachel still didn't know what he did for a living! So that's how it was going to be for the foreseeable future. I.e. him locking sex toys away in our study, or the attic! Even just housing those sorts of items while Rachel was around made me feel icky, not to mention our kids...

"Phew," I told him in the kitchen, standing behind him, my arms slipping round his waist.

"Go sit and chill out. I'll put Luce to bed and Billy's fine. He doesn't need a bath tonight."

"Thank you, David." I kissed his cheek and left them all to it.

What a day.

Waiting for the post.

Seeing the words in black and white.

Hardly believing it.

Now it was real.

I had a degree.

I switched some classical music on and lay back in the cushions of the living-room sofa, my head a little woozy from the bubbles. I wondered if we'd have sex tonight. I didn't know. How ironic he was selling sex products and the most sex we'd been having lately was the kind where you wake in the middle of the night; he would finger me, I'd wank him off, and that was that. It was dreamlike, so it was barely remembered as real in the morning.

I think he hated it that I didn't get fully engorged anymore (well except when I watched porn, but I didn't do that anymore... and he still didn't know I once did that). I stopped watching porn because it made me feel down on myself afterwards – that I needed porn to get me aroused.

Sometimes when he was out of the house and the kids were at nursery or school, I'd take out one of my toys and masturbate to thoughts of what I wanted him to do to me. I wondered if he knew I did that? Sometimes in my fantasies, I imagined him coming home unexpectedly to find me spread-eagled and helping myself. I imagined he'd be shocked but desperately horny having caught me out – therefore wild, angry sex would follow.

Did he know he was the only man I'd ever really loved, or would ever love? My fantasies about my husband ran deep and rugged. I didn't know how to unlock the connection we'd lost even though it was still there, somewhere.

Recently, since I hadn't had lectures or seminars, I'd spent time searching the web for sex tips and also speaking to people anonymously online.

I exchanged messages with people who thought sex was bound to dwindle after marriage, but I decided those people were defeatists. I wouldn't be defeated! I also spoke with people who admitted to bringing in a third person now and again, to spice up their love life, but I knew I wouldn't be able to watch David with another woman. I also knew he wouldn't want to see me with another man. It had been bad enough watching it onscreen, even though it had aroused me...

I also met people online who openly admitted to cheating

on their partners, believing it the only way to hold their families together and also get sexual satisfaction without hurting anyone. One woman, a mother of six, told me she went out with her sister at weekends and had a different man every Saturday night in a pub or club toilet. Did her husband know? I doubted he did. I bet the sister covered for her. I couldn't even contemplate the thought of cheating on David. I'd feel sick.

From what I'd garnered from these sex-chat forums, where everyone was anonymous, more women than men cheated. Most romantic literature I'd read seemed to forgive the cheating man while despising the cheating woman which was strange – because it seemed to me, women cheated more often than men. Were we emasculating our men? What was happening to the world? I didn't know! How were we meant to get what we wanted from the bedroom when there was the risk that if you opened up to your partner, you'd offend, upset or demean them by revealing you were not happy. Sometimes I did wonder if marriage reached the point of loving someone so much, lies only crept in as you tried to protect that other half of yourself. If this was marriage, I was fucking tired of it, that's all I knew.

His large hands suddenly dropped on my shoulders from behind and he massaged me, cutting me off from my meandering thoughts.

"Hmm," I groaned, "feels good."

"Yeah? Why don't you go and relax in the bath and I'll... rustle up something."

"Yeah? What?"

"Hmmm, something good baby."

I stood up to see his eyes glittering.

"See ya in a bit then." I tried to sound seductive but half the time I didn't know if I was just dorkier than dork.

I squashed the thick carpet beneath my feet as I wandered through our house. It was a lovely place, with little original features like tiled fireplaces and window seats. Built-in cupboards. Stuff like that. I felt warm and safe there, never cold and alone, as I did when I was growing up on my parent's estate just outside Harrogate. I went to a boarding school but never boarded, though the discipline made me rebel. Maybe I was spoiled or maybe I saw my mother dealing with a constant sadness I didn't want for myself. Maybe that's why I decided my privileges were a load of crap.

Mother and me used to rise early everyday to ride and groom the horses before she'd drive me to school. Sometimes she was so happy, she would race me beyond the paddock and into the nearby woods, where it was dangerous to ride so fast. I used to fear the look in her eye then, like she wanted her life to be over, like she wanted to prove something. Sometimes she would be the opposite, sombre and tired, and I would be the one bringing her tea and biscuits, or maybe something even stronger.

Growing up, I yearned for a brother or sister, though in some respects I had made my mother somewhat a sister. We used to chat for hours about what would be my first car, where would I go to university, what would my first boyfriend look like. We had a secret club outside of Dad. Mum used to confide in me about how deeply unhappy she was and how she wanted to be free of him, once I left home. With hindsight I looked back and realised she was wrong to confide in me about her unhappiness, but I understood she had nobody else to turn to. I never had close friends at school because my father had such a bad reputation and it was like David said when we first met, I seemed untouchable because I was. Dad told me never to get too close to people because they'd only shaft you if given half a chance. His workers knew him to be pretty uncompromising and as the years went by, he let go of more and more staff as technology improved and he updated the business. He was never the type of boss to redistribute someone, rather, he'd prefer to pluck out the chaff.

Sinking myself in the deep tub, the door creaked open and David walked in with another flute of champagne.

"Trying to get me drunk?"

He shut the door behind him and winked. "Might be."

He sat on the edge of the bath while I sipped my bubbles. "You happy?"

"I think so." I nodded.

"Still a bit strange for you?"

I sighed. "It's still sinking in. Doesn't seem real. Surreal, maybe."

"Well, when you get that certificate in your hand at graduation, it'll seem real alright."

I laughed. "I'm not going. A cap and gown affair? That's not me and you know it."

He squinted. "Seriously? After everything you've been through? You're not going to the ceremony?"

I pouted and threw back all of my champagne. "One of my course leaders, Christian came onto me a little once… and well… he said some slightly inappropriate things. I don't want to bump into him again… and I mean, I never made any real friends on my course, anyway."

I was digging myself a hole, but…

He frowned, his pupils dilated. "What, things?"

I shook my head. "I put him straight, don't worry. It's just awkward with him."

"I think you should go, baby."

"I don't need to, they can send the certificate here. Besides I did that degree for me and it's done now and we can move into the future. I don't want to wait around for months thinking about that ceremony. I'll opt for the certificate to be sent here and that's that."

He stared at me, confused. "He didn't touch you?"

I shook my head. "Not once. I'd have ripped his arm off before I let him touch me."

"So, then, what did he do? Or say?" David peered at me, disconsolation in his eyes.

I stared at my husband, feeling self-conscious as I lay in the bath naked, so I directed some bubbles around to cover myself up.

"He told me I looked unhappy and he said some things that were out of order, made some assumptions about us. I put him straight, told him he was acting unprofessionally and crossing boundaries. He was a dick and just didn't like it that I aced his class without banging on his door everyday for study group."

He chuckled lightly. "Oh, god, I thought it'd be something so much worse than that! Ade, baby, don't let a moron like that put you off collecting what's yours and enjoying the rewards of all your hard work."

I glared at David. "My mind's made up. I'm done with university. I want my life back."

He nodded, relenting. "I would like to find that fuck and thump him, just a little, you know."

He wore a tiny grin and I touched his hand with mine, happy that he still got jealous.

"Academics like him… they don't understand real life. All he saw was a pretty girl sitting in his class when it's usually just geeks and girls way younger than him. Living and breathing books, how can he even contemplate the life we've led, supporting each other, with two kids in tow, and all of our–"

His eyes shot to mine after I cut myself off. "All of our what, Ade?"

"Pasts," I said, because sometimes – it seemed to me – the past was very much our present.

He stood abruptly and turned his back on me, his hand around the doorknob. Pausing before leaving, he said softly, "Enjoy your bath, baby."

He left the room and I was left wondering if it was me, was I the only one fucked up? I mentally kicked myself and remembered how Marcus used to make me think there was something wrong with me, when there wasn't. It was always him. I might have once been rich and spoiled, but I was never a nasty bastard, not like him.

Then my thoughts turned to Christian: the easiest way to spy on him and find out what he'd been up to lately was through Facebook. I rarely used it but I was on there because a Japanese friend had told me it was going to be the new craze. I picked up my new, first-generation iPhone from the shelf behind me and logged into my emails. This gadget was amazing, but I'd had to import it from America at an astronomical price to secure one. David didn't understand my love of technology and still had a brick of a phone, but this thing... it boded of things to come. My father always said technology was the future and I had the money to jump right onboard that train, so I had with this phone.

I didn't get many emails anymore, not since I finished uni. I was hoping for some messages of congratulations from people on my course, but there was nothing. There were a couple of emails from Sandra at the university library asking me if I wanted to work more shifts now, which I could while I was deciding what to do next. Library work had never been bad money.

I mailed Sandra back and told her I could take some overtime if she had it.

While I was scrolling through Facebook, I saw all the usual eventide posts. I only had thirty 'friends', most of them library colleagues and old school friends. I smiled at pictures of people having their dinner, plus pets/babies etc. A couple of people from uni did friend me on Facebook but I suspected only so they could be nosey because they barely talked to me otherwise. Anyway they'd both posted pics of themselves downing shots at their local pubs in celebration of their results. Suppose I should have been doing that too.

I saw nothing from Christian in my feed even though he was my Facebook friend, too. I searched for his page and went to it. He was like me and rarely updated his status, I noticed. Scrolling down, I read boring updates like:

At Manchester Airport flying to Corsica…

Determined to get my students through the year… etc etc.

When I remembered those emails we exchanged were around January time, I scrolled all the way back to then and saw a status he'd likely wrote that night which read:

I tried to help somebody today. All it got me was a kick in the gut. Feeling fed up.

My stomach tumbled. Here was a man who (like me) never wrote much on social media but had obviously felt so upset that night, he had to reach out. A few people had responded to that status with words like: *Chin up. You'll be fine. They don't deserve you… She's not worth it mate.* Or… *Fuck them. Life goes on.* I laid back in the bath with a sinking feeling. Had Christian been trying to help me? Really help me? Not just get in my pants.

As I was scrolling through the rest of my own Facebook feed, I noticed the friend request icon flash red and when I looked at it, I saw the request was six months old. I must have missed it one day and it'd remained on my profile all this time.

When I clicked on the person, I realised who it was.

Violet.

What did she want? I'd never met her, never met any of David's colleagues in fact, except Luca who once came to our house for dinner, to speak with David about a trip to India that never came to fruition (we found out soon after that I was carrying Lucinda). Luca was Dutch but with Italian looks he got from his mother. He seemed a fair boss and a good friend to David.

Before accepting her friend request, I scrolled through her list of friends and found Luca missing – and David wasn't on Facebook so it was no surprise he wasn't there. In fact, among her list of friends, there were no names I recognised, not one person David mentioned working with at *For Mutual Pleasure.* Maybe she had left now, too? It seemed strange she would get in touch with me when she neither knew me or cared about keeping in touch with her own colleagues.

Curiosity had me intrigued so I accepted her request. I may have missed it six months ago because my privacy on Facebook was set to high but maybe their settings had recently changed, bringing this notification up again now.

As soon as I had accepted her friend request, an avalanche of messages fell into my inbox.

What the hell?

Maybe Facebook hadn't let me see them until I accepted her request. Gulping, I reached behind me and stretched my arm out, locking the bathroom door. I wanted no interruption. Scrolling to the very first message she ever sent (six months ago), I read:

Hi Adrianne,

You don't know me. I'm Violet. He may have told you we work together. He may not. Well, today he walked into the office and told us all he was leaving the firm. At the same time, he told me that he and I were quits. I'm sorry to tell you that we've been having an affair...

Fuck.

No.

I couldn't breathe.

What?

This had to be a joke. A lie. In denial, the words became blurry and I refused to read on.

Palpitations gripping me, I suddenly had to know more, to have this woman's lies read in their entirety before I took this to David. Tears pricked my eyes... and I knew... I just knew.

Shaking violently, the warm bath suddenly felt ice cold.

I wiped my eyes and continued reading, though I wanted to retch into the toilet. That, or boil my brains out with acid so I physically couldn't read anymore of this. However, I just couldn't stop myself…

We worked together in the past, David and I. He was a jerk back then, a total fuck-up. You clearly changed him but one day, he came to work really sad and one lunchtime, we had a drink together. One thing led to another and that's when we started spending our lunch breaks fucking. Evenings he was 'having a drink with Luca' were actually spent with me.

I think you were pregnant and he was upset that you seemed different. You seemed changed.

I was a body for him to lose himself in, that was all I was. I know that.

However, now he's leaving, I feel desolate. I feel ruined. I couldn't help falling in love with your husband…

I covered my mouth as I began to sob, as I began to blub like a child. I didn't want him to hear me crying. Somehow, I summoned the courage to read the rest…

Something tells me you and he are back on track and that is why he is leaving the company to start from scratch again (even though he has it so good here).

I think you should know the truth. He is not the man you think he is. He's a compulsive liar. He's broken, inside. Our assignations sometimes involved drugs. It's why he used to do porn, to pay for the drugs. I used to do it for money to get me through university. David's never needed money, except for drugs. His mother was never going to pay for those.

If you don't believe me…

What followed were numerous picture messages of them in bed together, pictures taken while he was unawares. I vomited into my bathwater, the images wrenching everything from me. My dinner, and my champagne, ended up swimming with me, staining my chest and my hair. I puked and puked, coughing and spluttering.

148

Violet and David had taken what little I had left. Now I had nothing.

One of the last messages she sent included: *P.s. does he still wear his socks with you too?*

If I was ever in doubt, well I wasn't now. She wasn't lying to me, I knew that.

Still swimming in my own sick, I frantically directed my thumb around the phone and searched on Google for *'David Dare and Violet'*. Soon, a film popped up on Tumblr. It wasn't even one you had to pay for.

Without the sound on, I played the film. My internet connection was slow, but I caught enough of the things they had done together…

I vomited more acid sick and felt grateful I had a sense of feeling, even though he'd gone around fucking another woman behind my back – guilt-free and cold. He must have been dead inside, doing this to me. At least I still had a heart.

They didn't.

She didn't… sending me all this.

I watched as he fucked her. You could tell he didn't love her. It was evident.

There was no love; nothing but her playing with his cock and then them fucking.

She wasn't pretty. She had slim hips, no breasts, an ugly mouth that had no grace as she sucked his dick. While the David in this film was very young, the David in the pictures she Facebook messaged me were of him looking older – so they were definitely taken recently.

It should have made me feel better that he just used her for sex. He could never love a woman like Violet, I knew it. In fact, if he did love her, he would have carried on like he was doing, working for Luca and fucking her on his lunch breaks. Nothing need ever have changed except I started watching porn and we started getting more amorous in the bedroom again. That must have been why he quit *For Mutual Pleasure*, right after I jumped him that night.

I wondered if he came inside her. Was she taking pre-
cautions? Was he? Did he come in her hair? On her body? In
her mouth. Did he lie and say he loved her? What happened?
I didn't think I'd ever find out.

He'd made me feel like there was something wrong with
me and I couldn't believe this had happened again. To me. I
was cursed, destined to only love bad men.

I calmly placed my phone beside the bath and pulled the
plug. Reaching for the shower curtain, I waited until all the
floating bits of sick had been drained down the plughole and
I pulled the shower curtain inside the bathtub and switched
the overhead shower on.

Standing under the rain, I cleansed myself. Dirt could be
washed off. Hurt would eventually be forgotten. I'd started
fresh before. I'd survived. I would again.

Like a chick flying from its nest for the first time, I took
Billy with me all those years ago, leaving my hometown
behind with an allowance from Daddy between my teeth and
a feeling of serenity at finally getting free of the Kyd family
and their cold-hearted ways.

But why was this happening, again?

I shampooed twice and became a new woman. It wasn't
me that was at fault. I wasn't ugly. I wasn't shit in bed. It
was him. He was just a coward.

All this time he allowed me to start believing that
marriage made sex rubbish, when really, he was just too
exhausted to do me after doing her for most of the day.

I didn't have to remain in a marriage like this.

I had a choice.

I could go if I wanted to!

I wasn't trapped in this marriage.

I knew what I had to do. I had to leave. After I was gone
with the children, I hoped his soul would lie ruined in the
wake of my strength, my anguish. I hoped he knew how
strong I was and how much he underestimated me. I didn't
need him; I never had. I could survive and go on without

him. He was the pollen of a dandelion, flying and scattering into the wind daily, while I remained the stork, and the head, forever replenishing. I could overcome again. I could rebirth, once more, always rejuvenating. At last, I realised that life shouldn't be like this. I shouldn't have been left in constant self-doubt, wondering whether my husband loved me. I should have just known he loved me, but all I knew now was that he had no conscience and he'd been fucking someone else because it was easier than loving me.

Having scrubbed myself raw and cried all the tears I had to give, I emerged from the shower an hour or so later. I dried off with a towel and put my robe on.

Pocketing my phone, I had a thought. He knew my pass code. What if he sensed something was wrong and tried to look at my phone's contents?

I changed it quickly to something he would never guess: my mother's birthday.

Leaving the steamed-up bathroom behind, the fan still running to dehumidify the room, I walked quietly to the bedroom, wondering if he was waiting in bed or still downstairs watching TV.

I entered the bedroom to find it empty (great!), only to be knocked off course. He'd scattered rose petals over the duvet. Chocolate-covered strawberries laid in a decorative bowl on his bedside table and a fresh bottle of champagne chilled in a bucket at my side of the bed. On my dressing table, three candles burned, all smelling of vanilla and strawberries. On my pillow, he'd laid out some new lingerie. White lace, like a bride again, or the bride I never was. Just a woman walked to her fate, her destiny – to always be alone, in the end.

So… he thought this would make up for his mistakes, did he? What did he think…? I locked the door as I tried to decide what to do.

"Ade, are you getting dressed?" He tried the handle from the other side of the locked door.

"I'm… getting ready, making myself pretty for you. Give me ten. Or fifteen?"

"Okay," he said, with warmth in his voice.

I quickly slipped into the lingerie, thinking I could maybe fuck him and then leave in the night. He'd be clueless.

My eye caught sight of something else. Another poem on the pillow. Did he think meaningless words could fix this, did he think I was stupid? Did he not know that all I needed was his arms, his smile, his heart – for me to be happy? Why these fucking, meaningless words? The poem glared at me until I read it:

Eterna

Full many a gem and bloom, in thy youthful garden,
In temperate season.
Where walls will yield to vine and country blessed,
Have time will not wither.
O, that I could go with you at all moments,
Your ageless aura is untamed.

I have walked these searing, dusty roads,
Unkempt and unfinished.
Flesh will age and billow in songs unwritten,
You steadfast yet ceaseless wonder.
No god shall ever govern thee, or break thy visions,
Your ageless aura is untamed.

Phantom rains, and long, warm thunderous nights,
These, the things unkind and furious.
Shall only bring out thy flourishes, and wondrous feature,
All is verity and increase.
But are you still unborn existing, and not wonderful
complete,
Your ageless aura is untamed.

What was he trying to say? That he was sorrowful? Or sorry? That he loved me? What? I swallowed my bile back, angry and shocked that the poetry which used to mean everything to me now meant nothing. Numb on the inside, I would have to mask that and pretend I was still the same – still sparkling and young like he said – when I wasn't. I felt a hundred, I felt dead. I felt withered and aged and as though youth was never mine, nor happiness. Only jewels dulled with jaded hues, hung around my neck.

All those romantic notions we'd shared in the beginning were now folly – and disease. They made me feel – and I couldn't afford to feel anything, not anymore.

I went into the closet, pulled out a suitcase and began filling it with essentials. I could pack the kid's stuff within minutes. I only needed to tip their drawers upside down.

A thought hit me: why was I leaving?

I couldn't take Billy out of school.

Lucinda had baby massage and Swim Tots. How was I meant to take my family away from everything they knew?

I took everything out of the suitcase and put it back.

I had a better idea but it'd keep, for now.

"Baby, are you ready now?" he called out.

"Just a minute," I called back, fixing my underwear right.

NINETEEN

Like a phoenix rising from the ashes, I would overcome. I was going to fuck David one last time, and I was going to make it so good that when he realised he would never get the chance to touch me again, he'd die of sadness knowing exactly what his selfish actions had cost him. Did he even realise how grossly he underestimated me?

"I'm just doing the finishing touches," I said to calm him as he stood behind the door still.

When I eventually opened up, after ensuring the closet still looked the same, he had his hands in his pockets and looked worried.

I smiled and excused myself. "Why don't you warm the bed while I dry off my hair a little?"

"Okay." He nodded, and in walked the Moving Filth, the degenerate that was my husband, hiding his vile, rotten carcass beneath a beautiful, fake mask.

I could have forgiven him anything; robbery, fraud, forgery, anything... just not this.

At the dressing table stool, I sat in my lace shorts and matching balconette bra, watching carefully as he stripped out of his clothes. Looking down at the roses, it was as though he knew I'd become the thorn again – and with the awkwardness of a jilted lover, he swiped the petals from the top of the duvet cover and climbed onto the bed in his boxers. He must have known something was wrong because I hadn't thanked him for any of the treats he'd pre-prepared for our night of 'romance'.

"Why don't you start playing with yourself?" I giggled, smiling into the mirror so he could see my amusement.

If he wanted fake, he was getting it.

"How much champagne have you had?" He chuckled over the warm whirring of my hairdryer, a nervousness carefully folded inside his demeanour – but there.

Calmly, coldly and collectedly, I brushed my hair slowly and alluringly as a gentle stream of warmth dried my blonde locks.

"Not enough," I replied slightly aggressively, reminding myself to check my anger at the door and leave it there... for now.

He didn't know I'd thrown up all my dinner and my champagne. I was also seeing more clearly than I had in years – another advantage I held over him.

He laid on top of the duvet and I smiled smarmily as I watched him lazily roll the palm of his hand up and down his length.

"You like that, David?" I asked, biting my bottom lip.

"I'd like you sliding up and down me more."

"Hmmm..." I giggled, licking my lips. "...what else would you like?"

"That underwear on the floor. Your legs around me. Your hands in my hair and those gorgeous lips on my mouth."

A thought struck me. I didn't clean my teeth after being sick. I finished drying off and smiled. "One moment lover. I need to be lover ready."

I strutted out of our bedroom in my lingerie and down the hallway to the bathroom. I brushed quickly and used mouthwash just to make sure I didn't taste of acid, even though that's all I felt.

Acidic.

Acrid.

Angry.

Strolling back to the bedroom calmly, I shut the door and locked it.

His eyes wide, his cock fully hard, he asked, "What are you locking us in for? What have you got planned?"

"Lots and lots of fucking."

I'd never love another man so I figured I might as well make this count. After tonight, I was dead inside. I'd never trust another man. I'd never love again.

I'd raise my children and that's all I was going to do. I could be strong for them. I'd mother them and that's all I would do. I would never feel again.

I'd die tonight.

A mother was all that would be left of me.

"You wanted me out of these things?" I asked, standing at the foot of the bed, looking down on him. I teased a finger under the waistband of my knickers and he grinned.

"I just want you, Ade. Naked with me."

I smiled, though my smile was stained with betrayal. Could he see it? How betrayed I felt?

As of tomorrow, I would no longer feel. I'd give myself permission tonight, but no other night.

"You remember the meaning of my name?" I muttered, watching as he stroked his long, thick length. No doubt his cock – and his beauty – was what got him work in porn.

"It's a beautiful name," he explained, "however, I know that they made you cold, made you live up to that name. I know that what they made you means I will never have the whole of you… and it's not your fault you're like this."

Breath caught in my throat. "Not my fault?"

"You shut down… hold back. You refuse to talk about Billy's father."

"You're his father," I almost screeched. "I told you it's done, what more do you need to know!?"

"Everything? I want to know everything!" He sat up and swallowed, holding out his arms. "But for now, come and be with me. Just be with me."

Did he know that something was wrong? Did he know that buried beneath layers of skin was a cold, barren heart – dead now that I knew he had betrayed me.

Did he know?

I couldn't push the words out to tell him about what really made me like this. The real Adrienne, the one I used to be, got buried with Marcus. She rested six-feet underground with him, in the grave I put him in when I acted out of self-defence. Didn't David know that? He was intelligent.

Couldn't he deduce for himself what was going on here?

For years, I'd hoped and prayed... I'd yearned for David to know how sad and barren I felt sometimes. I'd hoped he would figure it out and I wouldn't have to say the words, because pushing words out was much harder than it seemed. Words like: *Marcus stamped on my chest, on my ribs. Told me I was too stupid for university. I was a bitch, he said, that needed taming.*

I wondered whether David had ever gone behind my back and asked the family doctor for details. Throughout the pregnancy, I had lied and kept him at a distance. I didn't want him to know everything... to know about why... why... and how. At the scans, he never knew why I was so nervous, why there were so many scans. Sometimes, I didn't tell him I had a scan appointment and I went alone.

Maybe, if he already knew, I would never have to tell him. I wouldn't have to spell out the words. Speak the words. Make them real – and remember.

I could never say the words.

Never.

I killed Billy's father... because he beat me. Blue. Black. All the colours, actually. I escaped... on purpose.

I shook off my demons as I unhooked my bra and slid down my knickers.

Crawling onto the bed, he captured me in his arms and pulled me close, pulled me so my chest touched his.

"I love you, Adrienne. I love you, sweetheart."

For the first time in years, I switched off like I learnt to do with Marcus. I wasn't me. I was playing a character and that's all – a character he wanted me to be.

As he kissed my throat, I evacuated my mind. I imagined I was another creature – a much smaller one – sat on high in the clouds, swinging my legs beneath me. Looking down from my vantage point, I watched a beautiful, naked goddess become entranced by a naked god in a tranquil, tropical hideaway with a waterfall on one side, a wading pool in the middle and lush greenery on all the other sides, just a stream lined with protruding lilies the only other focal point.

The naked god swept his goddess into his arms and lay her down in the lush, mossy earth. Beneath her back, she felt cool, dewy grass give way beneath their weight. When her lover swept his hands down her body, she arched and moaned, his lips finding her breasts. Sunbeams on her face made her wildly happy and she rolled gently from side to side as he ran kiss after kiss all over her.

Standing her up on the ground, he lifted a leg of hers over his shoulder and she swayed on her feet as he kissed the wet flesh beneath her maiden hair, rubbing and caressing, his tongue dancing between her thighs, his large hands spread out across her buttocks.

"I love you," she moaned, "oh I love you."

"Adrienne," he called to the goddess, but she didn't respond to that name.

"Ade," he corrected, and she sighed.

Laying her on the ground, he entered her soft belly, weeping with pleasure. His arms beneath her, he angled her head back so that he could kiss her exposed throat, his stubble and lips marking her every dip and tendon.

"Oh, Ade, I've missed you so much."

They swapped positions so she sat astride him and with her eyes shut, she gazed into the sunlight so it didn't hurt and with her eyes to the heavens, she grabbed his hair and made love to him.

"David, David!"

He groaned, holding fast, his fingers trembling as he stroked her arms. "Oh god, Adrienne. Oh god."

Their bodies ripped and rode over the tumult together and he held her so tight, his face pressed against her heart. He cried, really cried, for the first time in his life, weeping into her arms. She'd never seen him cry before – not really cry, with snot and noise and heaving sobs – and as she looked down into his tears, she saw within them words of love he'd spoken and images of times they'd shared. He shed them all away for her sake – because no longer could she cry.

He loved her, but he was a bastard, and the fantasy was over.

As he rested in her arms, cuddled against her breast on the bed, she hushed him and was thankful for him crying on her behalf.

TWENTY

David

It's pitch-black but I know she's not with me. Feeling around, it's as I thought – the bed's empty.

"Ade?"

No answer.

Reaching for my phone, I press a button and it glows, telling me the time.

3.23a.m.

I lift my head and look around, waiting for my eyes to adjust.

In the corner she's sitting in a comfy chair, on top of clothes we pile onto it at the end of every day. Ade never crumples things. She likes the house neat and tidy and she keeps every single thing in our lives clean and dust-free. I watch her, day after day, caring for everything but herself. In part, it's why I love her – and why I feel pushed out. She won't let me take care of her, she never really has done. Her soul's out of my reach.

"What's wrong, Adrienne?"

In the dark of night, I can only see her shadow but I notice her legs are pulled to her chest, she's wearing her dressing gown and staring out of the gap between the curtains of the window by her side.

"I can't leave you," she says in a weak voice.

My heart starts pumping. I sit up in bed and switch the

bedside lamp on.

She immediately hides her eyes in her knees but I got a quick look at her face then, blotchy and streaked with tears.

So she knows.

I hoped she would never find out, but maybe it's best this way, I don't know.

"Why would you leave?"

"Check my phone," she says.

I look on her bedside table and her normal code doesn't work.

"You changed the password?"

"25-6-62," she says, and I punch in the number.

"Where am I looking?" I ask after finding nothing at all in her call logs or text messages.

"Facebook," she mutters.

"How the–" I gasp, "I don't know... I never used this... what... what am I... looking for?"

"Messages."

"Oh... oh!"

I see what's rattled her and gulp. I always knew Violet was a bitch but I never thought she'd stoop this low.

I slide the phone back onto her bedside table and sit back against the headboard. I hated technology before, but now I'd gladly piss in the face of anyone who makes these things.

I have no idea what to say. She's not hit me. She's not left. We made the most incredible love even when she probably knew...

"Ade, were you going to leave me, even after last night?"

She nods against her knees. "I wanted one, last time... one thing to take with me, one moment of perfection... but I can't leave you. I just can't go. Uprooting the kids... it's not fair. It's also physically impossible for me to leave you. Which means you have to leave me."

"No," I reply, my broken soul hoarse.

"I was going to get the locks changed. Shut you out. Toss your things on the lawn. Set fire to your products. I don't think I deserve the humiliation of people knowing what you've done. I just want you to go… quietly."

She's shut down. She's not looking at me. I dare not touch her. Sometimes you can tell she doesn't want to be touched and now's one of those times.

"I know about Marcus," I blurt out, "about the smaller details… the things he did. Who he was. I know."

She lifts her head, tears pouring from her red, sunken eyeholes. Her chest heaving, she whispers in barely a breath, "How?"

I rustle my hands in my hair and try to tell her without it sounding cruel. "When you were up and down through the pregnancy, I was beside myself with worry. You completely shut down and closed yourself off. I sought advice from Mum. Speaking to her, she told me about him… about what she'd heard from people, what she'd read… she's a legal secretary, remember? Her chambers happened to have the records and she stayed late one night to open them. When she told me everything, I didn't know how you could keep something like that from me. I felt like you didn't trust me."

Her chin wobbles so hard, she has to push it back into place in her jaw to stop it breaking off with the unbearable agony of all this. I always wondered why she didn't like me coming to antenatal appointments with her – why she wouldn't let me touch her when she was pregnant. I got my answers, but I got no solace in the explanation I found.

I shake my head, tears falling from my eyes too. I catch my breath and chew two fingernails at once. Clearing my throat, I try to explain, "I always wondered about the marks I couldn't see… but I didn't ever want to upset you. When I first read up on the case, how you got acquitted and everything, I thought you'd escaped bravely… like in a soap opera. I don't know what I thought… I just thought you were unlucky and you'd done what you had to, for you and Billy. I thought you got away scot-free. Unblemished. The victor, the heroine, an inspiration for women everywhere in the same situation. I didn't know about what had happened in the lead up. I never stopped to think about the events that led to you... doing that... I never–"

She swallows her sobs as I continue, "...then, I couldn't believe that this beaten-up woman Mum told me about... this wronged girl... was my wife! I felt like for you to not tell me about what you went through, you didn't trust me and... I didn't know whether to talk to you. Carrying Lucinda, you were stressed enough as it was. I just let things get on top of me and things with Violet got out of hand. I don't know what she's told you... but she pursued me. For months. She also knew my weakness for blow... and she just, I don't know, offered herself. Like she was nothing, like I was nothing but a dildo, like it was all nothing... and nothing's what I wanted. It became just like before, meaninglessness. Me... feeling nothing. I just wanted to feel nothing, Ade, I wanted to feel nothing!"

She shoots to her feet and points her finger at me. Gathering her strength, she says through wobbling lips, "David. Do. Not. Speak. To. Me. Like. That."

Her eyes threatening, I see a tiny spark of the lioness that had to fight for not only her life, but that of her child, too. She acted out of self-defence the court decided – after an overwhelming case of abuse was brought against Marcus Spavin. It wasn't like she woke up one day and he slapped her out of the blue, it wasn't like she knew he was a bastard from the start. She'd suffered for months before she escaped him and I'd brushed the reality under the carpet – the same as everyone else had.

It all killed me, to think of her in pain. It killed me.

Apparently he was an admirer she met in a nightclub. The wealthy socialite, wronged. The only thing is, I know how gentle and fragile she is, beneath. I doubt she ever realised how cruel people could be, nor how strong she was until she had to fight.

"Do you..." She tries to take deep breaths, to gather

herself, "…do you know… how it makes me feel… knowing this happened because of what he did to me? Do you? Do you? The repercussions… I had to spit out my soul to survive. Now from beyond the grave, he's still trying to ruin my life."

"No. I can't imagine, honey." I shake my head.

"I thought I left all of it behind…" She puts her hands on her hips, looking down on me. "…started new. But it just follows me. Everywhere I go. The spectre… he's right behind me, just here." She signals over her shoulder. "He whispers, still. Whispers of things he used to say, things I've not forgotten… 'Adrienne, if you do this… it'll make me so happy,' he would say. Never mind how degraded or disgusting the things he would do would make me feel, I'd do them. 'Adrienne, let me look after you. Let me protect you,' he would say, when he was the only one I needed protecting from. 'Adrienne, nobody is a better friend to you than me,' he would say, no matter the fact he was my one, true nemesis. 'Adrienne, aren't your dreams inclusive of me and me alone? Why do you need to leave the house?' When I told him I wanted to spend evenings out with friends instead of carrying out his sexual demands, he'd beat me so hard, I'd get winded. He'd cradle me afterwards, softly asking me not to defy him again. One day, I woke up and wondered how the hell I ended up in such an abusive relationship. I had no idea but the more I thought about it… the more I realised."

"Oh god, Ade." I weep, thousands of tears dripping between my fingers. I can't look at her. Her pain's too much for me to bear.

"He just kept sort of turning up, hanging around the same clubs as me. He seemed handsome and kind. He had the kindest eyes. I was seventeen when we started up and we kept it quiet because my father was very strict. Marcus seemed so wonderful and loving. I'd already had a boyfriend. I started having sex when I was fifteen with a stable hand my mother employed. That was no big deal. Sex,

I mean. I was experienced. However, when I was eighteen Marcus wanted me to move in... he wanted me to forgo uni so we could be together all the time. I did everything he said, everything. I was wildly in love with him. All I knew was, he made me feel so happy and I wanted a man in my life who made me feel safe. My father and me had never been close. Didn't hug. Didn't chat. I don't know why. Mum and me were very close and it put distance between Dad and me because I was her confidante. I knew he was a philanderer and I knew he drank too much. She talked of escape so long, maybe I decided to make my own escape. I went and moved in with Marcus. I thought it was the greatest decision I'd ever made and there was no clearer path for me to take. Right then, he was my saviour from an unloving family."

"What, then?" I ask her, needing answers, though hating them too.

"It was about six weeks into us living together. He'd say things about my weight, even though I was slim. He'd say things about my intimate areas... asking whether normal girls looked the same as me. To all of his questions, I didn't have answers. Slowly I began to feel he was right, there was something wrong with me. He would reply he loved me despite my imperfections and I would feel grateful. Eventually..."

She sobs and it kills me. There's nothing I can do to save her. Everyday she relives this and there's nothing I can do. I can never live up to her. Adrienne is so much better than me.

"...the abuse intensified and it got to a level where I decided obeying was easier so I was indoors and I was better that way. Then... I fell pregnant. He changed, he completely changed. It stopped. He was wonderful. I was so happy and thought William was my redeemer, the one thing that would protect me, because Marcus loved his son so much, he loved me for giving him that."

She shudders and takes a deep breath.

"Then one day, I don't know the exact date, but one day

Billy wouldn't stop crying and I... didn't know what to do. I got hysterical. I had no support whatsoever and Marcus kept yelling for me to shut the kid up. When I retaliated, that's when it all happened... that was the day he died."

I want to give her space so I wait patiently for her to tell me more. Eventually, she explains, "I pushed a knife right into his gut. He could hurt me but not my baby."

She cries for a minute and gets the rest out...

"He looked shocked. He stood there smiling, looking down, as if it was nothing. He didn't notice his blood was everywhere, he was bleeding out heavier than he realised. He dropped to the ground and died with minutes. I called the police, as cool as anything. I was calm as they put him in a body bag. He was finally gone. I was questioned and let go on bail. Mum brought up Billy for the first nine months of his life while I was useless. Eventually they let me go, Dad's solicitors got me off. I had plastic surgery to lessen my scars, my damage, and went home to my son. It was almost as if none of it had ever happened. Dad tried to wipe the slate clean for me."

Calmer now, she takes a deep breath, no more tears left.

"However, one night, in the library, Dad was drinking malt heavily as he handed me an allowance schedule and deeds to the flat in Leeds. I remember he said, 'I can forgive but I cannot forget. I thought it would get easier but I cannot stomach the sight of you. I can't bear that you're my daughter so now, I'm willing to pay you to leave and never come back... to save me feeling sick everyday of my life. Your face is like a slap to mine, every, single day."

"'But, Billy, Mum...' I tried to protest. He replied, 'Your mother is attached to that baby but she'll get over it. Just like I've gotten over you. I don't think, in that puny head of yours, you will ever understand the shame and disgrace you brought on us. So I want you gone. You've done nothing but disappoint us.' Of course, I wanted to bawl and yell, tell him if only he'd loved me more, I wouldn't have found such a desperate need for love elsewhere. He didn't deserve my tears. He didn't deserve my anguish, my emotion, my pain. So I took the money, and left. I placed a note on Mummy's bedside table saying sorry and I took my son and was gone. I haven't seen them since."

She needs me to be strong for her but all I feel is hollow. I feel empty, devoid, derelict. I'm bewildered and in shock. How did she survive this? How did I not see it all? I hid from it, that's why. I thought killing her partner was a joke, just a bad night gone wrong, not a never-ending cycle of abuse. I've been hiding from it since the day she told me about Billy's father. I wish she'd gone into details so long ago!

"Ade, please don't leave me. Please don't make me go. I know I cannot make up for this, but please don't leave. Just stay, for the children. We'll work this out over time. If we have to part, so be it, but for now please stay. I'm begging you. I'll do anything you want me to. Please just let me hold you. I promise I just want to hold you."

She nods slightly and crawls up beside me. I turn the lamp off and in her robe, she lies on top of the covers next to me. I ease my arms around her shoulders and pull her in closer. Resting her chin on my chest, she begins crying.

"David," she cries, "David!"

A womanly cry falls out of her, desperate, weary. A full-grown woman crying, beyond repair, lies in my arms and I've no idea how to put it all right.

"I meant what I said. I'll love you forever. Whatever happens, that'll always stand, Adrienne. Always. I just wish you'd let me finally show you... how much I love you. Let me prove it to you."

"Ohhhhh David, I just don't know! I just don't know."

We cry and cry.

I feel like I'm dead already, living in a body that doesn't want me. But I'll stay. We'll both stay.

TWENTY-ONE

The morning after, she has pulled away from me in the bed, the stark light of day reminding her what I did. I'm as ashamed as she is sad. Now we're glued together by this horrible paradox: needing each other, but knowing it will be the hardest thing we ever do – staying together.

"Mum? Me and Luce want breakfast," Billy says, peeking his head around the door.

I wonder if he heard her crying; he's never this calm in the morning, usually boisterous.

"I'm coming, Billy," I say, knowing Ade is in no fit state.

"Aww but Dad…"

He starts to say something but I cut him off, shaking my head. "Mum's not very well. I know she makes better porridge than me, but that's life sometimes Billy. It's not fair."

I throw on a robe and visit Lucinda's bedroom to pull her out of her cot. She has so many kisses and cuddles for me, I may die of shame.

With my infidelity, I nearly risked all this.

I just wanted out of my own head. I wanted the images of Ade, cold and afraid, laid in her own blood at the hands of that monster out of my head. It's not even an issue that she killed him. I would kill him twice over if I had the chance.

I know what I am. I know.

It's that I feared telling her I knew.

I knew she was punched and kicked by a grown man.

A man who was meant to love her.

So, why couldn't she tell me?

Sitting the kids at the breakfast table in the kitchen, I ask them, "Drinks first?"

"Yeah," Billy says, hand against his cheek, moodily changing channels on the TV with the remote.

"Want, want!" Luce squeals as he flicks from CBeebies and onto CBBC.

"Nah, that's for babies," he says, ignoring the bright colours of a cartoon on the little toddler's channel.

She frowns at him, obviously upset.

"Put it on for your sister, Billy. Be nice."

"Fine," he huffs and slams the remote down.

I take a deep breath and hand him some juice and Luce her beaker. My tether might easily snap this morning but I'll try my hardest not to let it.

I make their porridge and Luce cries when it's too hot. Billy grimaces, telling me with his expression that his food is not up to snuff.

"Be nice to me. I've got a lot of work on right now and Mummy's not very well."

"It's okay," he says, "just not like Mum's, that's all."

"I know, but I'm trying."

Tears threaten. This is all my fault. My wife's upstairs, her heart broken, and my kids are eating my shit porridge because of me. It's all my fault.

I concentrate on feeding Lucinda.

"You okay to get dressed, Billy?"

"Yeah." He heads upstairs after finishing his breakfast.

When he's gone, I call Mum.

"Early isn't it, son?"

"Oh Mum," I cry, but when I notice Luce getting upset seeing me cry, I cover my eyes and take a deep breath, spooning more food into her mouth.

"Oh, it's happened then? She's finally talked about it?"

"Hmm."

"Are you okay?"

"No. No. I'm not okay. She's hurt. She's only admitted it because I made a fuck-up Mum, I did something–"

"Fucking men," she curses, "bloody hell, David! For–"

"I know." I shake my head at myself. "I need your help. Will you take the kids to school and nursery this morning? I just can't face leaving the house."

She groans. "Okay. I did have a meeting this morning but I can cancel it."

"Thank you, thank you!!!"

"I'll see you soon."

She puts the phone down and I take a deep breath.

I hear the TV switch on in the living room and I look in on Billy as I head back towards the stairs.

"Combed your hair?"

"Yep."

"Brushed your teeth."

"Yep."

"School bag ready?"

"Yep. Yep. Yep."

"Good boy. Grandma's coming to take you and Luce to school so I can look after Mum."

"Okay," he says, his voice taking a lower tone than usual, "will she be okay?"

"She'll be fine, son. I'll take good care of her."

He nods. "Okay."

"Come on then, Lucinda, let's get you dressed."

In my daughter's bedroom, I lay her on the changing mat while picking out some leggings, a jumper, socks and vest. While my back's turned, she almost rolls herself off.

"Whoa, whoa!" I almost shout and she bursts into tears, wailing. Adrienne's suddenly right behind me, asking what's wrong.

"She nearly rolled off! I forgot she's into gymnastics!"

Adrienne picks up her child and cuddles her close. "It's okay, baby girl. It's okay."

Lucinda is soothed and I stand back, feeling useless as Adrienne expertly changes and dresses our baby. Brushing her hair gently, Ade pops a band in Luce's hair and she looks so cute with a ponytail.

"Mum's taking them for us this morning, she'll be here soon."

Ade vaguely glances at me and nods. "Nice of her."

"I know. She's furious, though... she despises me."

She shakes her head. "She doesn't deserve to know her son can't keep it in his pants."

"I know." I hang my head in shame.

When the doorbell downstairs sounds, she hands me Lucinda and puts the nappy bag over my shoulder, reminding me, "Don't forget this."

While she trudges back to bed, I take my baby downstairs and find Billy's already let his grandmother inside.

"Go get your stuff, William," she says to Billy with a strained smile.

I hand over Lucinda to my mother and she says, "You look like shit so at least you have a conscience."

"It ended six months ago–"

She holds her hands up. "I don't give a monkeys about the details. Just put this right."

Her face changes instantly the moment Billy joins us in the hall wearing his bag and coat.

"See you David. Say bye to your father, William."

"Bye," I say.

"Bye," William replies, and then it's just me and my dimwittedness left in the house alone to deal with Ade and the fallout of my actions. I don't know how I'll make things right with these shit for brains I have.

I climb the stairs and visit our bedroom, spotting her fast asleep in the middle of our bed. She's no doubt exhausted after reliving her past last night.

I leave the bedroom behind and head for the shower.

While I'm under the rain, I allow myself to cry and cry. I wish she'd just told me all about Marcus from the very beginning. About her chances of carrying a baby to full term being reduced. About everything!

I started up with Violet because I needed to forget. That was all. Nothing more.

Ade does her own thing but I need to be needed. I don't think she understands that. I also need her to be honest with me, but she keeps so much buried deep down. I just want to look after her.

I step out of the shower, all cried out, and make the decision to do whatever it takes to put this right and show Ade how much I love her.

TWENTY-TWO

Past

In the few weeks since Ade told me she was pregnant, I'd been on edge, wondering if this was just how pregnant women got – or whether my instincts were right and there genuinely was something wrong with my wife.

Mum was just putting Billy to bed for me. Ade had gone to bed early and Mum had stopped round for tea. I listened from outside the door as my mother read *The Cat in the Hat* to my son. Something about her jolliness made me feel sad.

I never appreciated the mother I had, not until then. I was going to suggest to Ade we move back to Harrogate so we could be closer to Mum. I knew we needed her.

My mother caught me waiting outside Billy's bedroom door and read the look on my face. After closing Billy inside, she asked, "Want to talk about it?"

We headed to the kitchen. I poured a measure from a whisky decanter while she watched me closely.

"There's something not right with Ade."

"Pregnancy is difficult David, you know?" She defended my wife, folding her arms as she leaned back against the sideboard.

"I know that." I nodded, pouring a double measure this time. "But something tells me there's something really wrong."

"Hmm, what like?"

I took a deep breath. "She visits the bathroom every five minutes. She won't let me hold her, at all. She's completely forgotten she has a son to tend to and I'm doing most of it. I don't mind but I know her and I can just tell, there's something wrong."

Mum frowned and bit her lip.

"Why are you doing that? Why are you... biting your lip?"

My nose twitched, knowing from experience what the biting meant. She'd got something bad to say.

"Has she told you about Billy's father?"

"An overview, but not the full score."

She wore a grave expression. "Maybe there's some trauma she associates with being pregnant."

"All I know is that she was a prisoner in her own home."

To add to the biting of her lip, she tapped her foot on the floor, shaking her shoulders up and down and still – with her arms crossed! BODY LANGUAGE MALFUNCTION! My mother was always calm in a situation, so what the hell did she mean?

Pursing her lips, she whistled out a sigh before admitting, "It was in the paper but everyone knew stuff must've been withheld... her father was well known and he had enough money to shut people up, or keep them quiet, not that you'd have noticed... you were always too busy getting into any girl's knickers to watch the news. Our firm handled it. I wasn't on the case but I know colleagues of mine read the files and said what happened to Adrienne was awful."

"I–I–I've no idea what to say or do to make this right."

"Adrienne had her life wrecked, getting involved with that monster! He was apparently some kind of entrepreneur. Able to provide for her, I expect. It was scandalous when it all fell apart. Everybody knew she was destined for great things, the only Kyd child, the heir to the throne."

Anger boiled inside me. "The fucker's dead and I have no place for this misery to go, nobody to take it out on but me."

She shook her head as I poured my third drink, the amber liquid doing nothing to rectify my soul.

"Adrienne was acquitted after they brought a raft of evidence against Marcus. He beat her, cut her, threatened Billy's life. Not only that, he emotionally and psychologically abused her. He had pictures of her on his computer... horrible pictures. Who else did he do things to? But they never came forward. It was all on Ade. This could have happened to any girl but it happened to her. They said Ade only got pregnant because he replaced her contraceptive pills with vitamins."

My eyes squeezed shut and the word *no* spun and whirled around my head. This wasn't happening.

"Why didn't she tell me?" I ground out, hand on my forehead, rage swirling inside me.

Her voice softer, Mum stroked my forearm. "She just wanted to be happy? Maybe she didn't want to relive it and she wanted to start fresh, with you."

I swallowed. "This hurts so much. I wish she'd told me."

"Well, now you know. Only, I wouldn't go upsetting her fragile disposition, not while she's with child. You just have to try to be here for her, okay?"

I opened my eyes and one tear fell. Mum reached up to hold my cheek and I slammed my glass on the counter behind me.

Cupping my mother's cheeks, I begged, "Tell me how to make it all better for her? Tell me!"

She shook her head again, the negative signals becoming unbearable. Is this what people did when they knew there was nothing they could do about a terrible situation? They shook their heads and got on with it all?

How could I open old wounds that might seal mine, when she was pregnant and vulnerable?

"I don't know what you can do. Except be here for her."

"I asked her to defer university. This is only her first year but she won't listen. She's so tired... but she won't listen."

Mum kissed my cheek. "Maybe studying keeps her sane. Maybe it'll help. I don't have all the answers but if she's sleeping a lot, that's not necessarily a bad thing: it means she's caring for the baby. It means she cares and that means everything David, believe me. Some mothers go drinking and smoking all the way through, but don't you see? Ade's just trying to do everything she can to protect her baby."

I wanted to say, what about me? *What about me?* I'd just sound selfish if I said that. My emotions didn't come into this, did they? I just had to be there for her because that was my job. That was all I had to do.

Mum grabbed her bag and headed for the hallway. I followed behind and hugged her goodbye.

"Give it time, David. She's fragile beneath her defence mechanisms, just remember that."

I kept reciting those words of my mother's: *she is fragile, remember that.* Some selfish part of me couldn't help feeling short changed. Left out. I don't know, discounted in favour of *getting on with it.* I felt robbed of information I should have had ages ago. She was my wife, the person I promised myself to, and yet large chunks of her heart weren't mine!

Now I knew why her father really gave her that money: so she'd leave and never come back, having disgraced the family and their so-called good name. More importantly, so he wouldn't have to look at the face of the girl he'd let down. The great Max Kyd knew he was responsible, for pushing her away and steering her into an abusive bastard's arms. No doubt he couldn't live with the guilt of it all.

My poor, beautiful wife. Nothing I'd ever been through compared. My life was worthless compared to hers. I was nothing and she was everything. She was ten times the person I was. I'd fucked my way through life and never had any comeuppance while all she did was seek love with the wrong man.

She'd never done a thing wrong and it was what made me

realise I was unworthy. I'd done bad things in life and I didn't deserve a woman like Ade. I'd always known it, but I'd always been too selfish to consider letting her go.

***

Two weeks after finding out about the details of my wife's past, I was sinking, and I think people at work knew it. Colleagues knew not to approach my desk while I remained stuck in such a foul state.

Luca got me in his office and I mentioned Ade was pregnant and having a really rough time of it. I even dramatised it a bit, saying we thought she miscarried but hadn't – just because I couldn't bear to tell him the real reason I was all over the place:

I just found out my wife used to live with a bullying psychopath.

Not only that, but Billy's dad was a psychopath. Every day, when I looked at Billy, all I saw was pure innocence but in his veins, he carried the DNA of that fucking bastard. Did Marcus still haunt Adrienne? Did she see the bastard's face whenever she looked at her son? Would she ever be able to move on? Ever?

I didn't know how I was getting through the day. The way I felt – it was like having a truck strapped to my back, and every step I took felt like I was pulling several tonnes behind me. Maybe if she cuddled or kissed me, I'd feel better, but she wouldn't touch me. She was afraid of me and I'd done nothing bloody wrong!

"Want to get a drink after work tonight?" Violet asked me one day, out of the blue. "I got some vouchers for a new place. You just look like you need a drink, that's all."

Absentmindedly, I replied, "I have to get home to Ade."

"Oh. We can do a rain check if you like?" Faffing with her hair, she looked away from me, feigning nonchalance even though she'd been asking me out like this every other week since I started working at FMP.

"Maybe," I replied.

She left my desk, heading off back to her own. She wouldn't give up for some reason.

***

It had been a month since Mum dropped the bomb on me, and I was drinking a litre a day. Now I needed something stronger. Ade was five months pregnant and shutting me out completely. We barely talked except about bills and other things.

"Want to get that drink yet?" Violet asked, noticing me sipping from a hip flask I kept in my jacket pocket.

I beckoned her closer with my finger. "I need something stronger. As I seem to remember, you always knew how to get it."

Licking her lips, she nodded. "Tomorrow lunchtime. I'll have it by then."

"I'll book a table somewhere for one o'clock. Get me as much as you can."

"You know I'm good for it."

She sauntered off and I watched her skinny arse leave. I never, not once in my life, wanted to hit her. I still didn't. However, she was going to get me some blow and that's all I wanted.

***

After taking a hit in the toilets, I wandered back out, feeling slightly better than I had done in months. I rejoined Violet at our table for two in the local burger joint and she grinned.

"So?"

"So, what?" I retorted.

"Good stuff?" she asked, fluttering her eyelashes.

"Not bad. Had better. How much do you want for it?"

She sniffed a half-laugh. "On the house."

"Really?"

She smirked. "Yeah, really."

After eating, I took another hit in the toilets. I'd spent the last month feeling rotten, when I should've just been doing this the whole time. I felt great now and wondered what I was ever worried about.

We left the burger joint and walked back to work.

I got back to my desk, feeling ready to take on the world. I had plenty of blow left to use later. I decided life might be slightly more palatable with drugs by my side. I could live on drugs, I reckoned. I didn't need drink or anything else, not now. It'd be like it was before, just me and my numbness. No feeling, no care. Life used to be so easy before she came along, my wicked goddess, Adrienne.

On my computer screen, I saw a number of emails had arrived throughout lunch: from clients waiting on proofs to be checked or products to be signed off as part of the new line we were currently putting together. The most recent email, from Violet, read:

I just get so horny after blow, don't you? I'm doing to the disabled toilet now... to masturbate.

I didn't see her do any blow, but maybe she did it before lunch? Or at the dining table when nobody was looking?

The thought of a woman masturbating nearby, with her knickers round her ankles, did indeed make my cock twitch. I felt horny, too, and I hadn't been laid in months.

"Fuck," I said under my breath.

I told myself off for even entertaining the thought of going to listen in as Violet wanked herself off, but the seed had been planted and now I knew she was willing – she'd become a temptation.

***

Six weeks since Mother dropped the bomb...

Violet and I were lunching everyday. She got me blow and in exchange, I paid for lunch and humoured her flirtation tactics.

We were not sleeping together and nothing whatsoever about her turned me on, even with drugs in my veins.

However, I was gagging for sex.

She was not my type. When we did porn films together back in the day, I had to think of Goldie Hawn or Ursula Andress to get myself hard enough to perform. Violet was not beautiful and half of her body was filled with collagen.

I got back to my desk as usual and she mailed me:

Same time tomorrow?

I replied:

Sure. As usual.

She said:

Just one thing. It will have to be at my flat tomorrow. I'm getting a delivery I need to be in for, you see.

Feeling wary, I still replied:

Okay. Fine.

I wasn't going to sleep with her. No way.

The next day, we were at her flat. It was nice, in the city centre, a high rise. It was expensive to live there, no doubt.

"What's your husband do?" I asked as she faffed around in her bedroom, where she apparently kept the drugs.

"Barrister."

"Ah, I see." Explained how she could afford blow... and living here.

She emerged from the bedroom, where she'd alleged the drugs were, wearing only lingerie.

My jaw dropped but before I could say anything, she said, "Listen. David. I've gotten you quite a lot of blow now. I think I'm due a bit of payback... unless of course... you'd like me to cut off your supply?"

I stared at her, grinding my teeth. There was no way I was going to risk getting drugs from a dealer. I already had previous drug arrests on my record and it's why I couldn't afford another blot – and perhaps a court appearance this time.

"What about the delivery? The one you had to be here for this lunchtime?"

"What delivery?" She smiled. "Just fuck me, and we're all good. I don't need any romance. I just never see my husband these days. I think he's fucking his secretary. Got bored of me, or something. We both know what this is… just snorting and fucking, yeah? It's not an affair. Just an exchange. Nobody need ever know."

She crawled onto the sofa on all fours and placed a condom on the coffee table beside her.

"Nobody will know."

I didn't want this. Yet as I stared at the possibility of blowing my load without all the emotional crap attached, I decided it was an attractive offer.

"Nobody?" I demanded as I walked over, unzipping my trousers.

"Nobody," she repeated.

I slid the condom on, pulled my trousers down and her knickers to the side. Slamming straight into her, I realised drugs and sex were all that made me forget.

Forget the twisting, agonising pain of loving a woman who wouldn't let me love her.

A woman beyond my reach, out of bounds, hiding her pain. Barriers built up. The thorns prickling every time I tried to broach her painful past.

"God, I've never had anyone bigger," she yelled. "Just pound me, Dave!"

I did just that, forgetting my name, forgetting I was married with a baby on the way. I forgot everything. I was nothing, just like he always said. Nothing. To be nothing is to never have any expectations of yourself or anyone else. To be nothing is to renounce responsibility. To renounce pain. I felt so much better, already, just pumping my cock in a hole I didn't even find attractive. I didn't even hold her. She held herself steady.

"Shiiiiiit!!! Shiiiiittt!" she squealed, and I unloaded, not caring if she'd come or not. Her screams told me she had, but I was so numb, I didn't care either way.

Flopping on the sofa, panting away, I guess she was satisfied.

I walked to the bathroom and wet a towel, cleaning around the base of my cock, getting rid of her stink. It was the wrong smell. It wasn't a nice smell, because it wasn't *her* smell. I reached into my pocket and took a hit on the bathroom counter.

She wandered in and joined me. "Don't leave me out."

She took some of my cut and giggled. "That's good shit, yeah?"

"I guess." I shrugged.

"Once more?" she asked, eyes wide.

"Why not. It'll be on my terms, though."

I looked at the slag before me and decided to use her like a slag. Part of me knew the drugs were talking and the drugs were in control, but she'd lured me and she was using me if anything.

I forced her to her knees and for the first time in years, I fucked a woman's mouth like an animal. Afterwards, she vomited for ten minutes, but painted on a happy face as she left the bathroom dressed and ready to go.

As we walked back to the office, liquid lunches in our hands, chemical lunches in our veins, she mentioned, "I'm glad I can please you, you animal."

She looked at me with bloodshot eyes and I fought the urge to vomit, too. She was pleased I had used her like that. She had enjoyed it. Part of me felt justified in my belief that I was nothing and only the nothingness she provided me with was what I was worth.

I laughed her off. "Next time, it'll be your arse, bitch."

She cackled, "Can't wait," because being misused was

clearly what she understood to be love, the ugly fucking bitch. Ugly because she flaunted herself for nothing. I despised her almost as much as I despised myself.

Violet hadn't the faintest idea what love was.

Love was something I'd tasted but now, I didn't want it back. I couldn't go back now. I didn't deserve it, didn't want it, and I couldn't afford to get my heart broken anymore. I was better off believing I deserved nothing, because nothing was easier to cope with than having given up my whole heart to a woman I didn't even know.

TWENTY-THREE

Present

It's lunchtime and I've done all the washing, pegged it out, dusted everywhere, cleaned the inside of the dishwasher and the oven. I don't think there's a spot in the house I haven't cleaned. I even bleached the bathroom.

"Are you insane?" she asks when she enters the kitchen, her nose in the air, smelling all the chemicals. "Open a window!"

I guess my habit of x-number of years has ruined my sense of smell.

She glares at me, wearing her dressing grown, her hair dishevelled, eyes puffy from recent crying as well as last night's crying.

"Sorry," I apologise, and she gives me the 'that's not good enough' look. "Do you want some tea?"

"Suppose," she replies, pulling up a stool at the kitchen island.

She hangs her head, looking into space.

"Are you okay?" I ask as I put the kettle on.

"Honestly?"

I nod.

She pauses for dramatic effect. "I feel suicidal. If we didn't have kids... I don't know what I'd do."

Way to knock the wind from me.

I stare into her eyes and I see she's deadly serious.

"Last night, I sat in the bath, in my own vomit. That's how those photos made me feel."

I turn my back, unable to look at the sadness I've caused.

I dunk her teabag for the length of time I know she likes and add half a teaspoon of sugar and a splash of milk, the way she takes her tea when she's poorly. Otherwise, she never has sugar.

I sit opposite her and she asks, "Tell me everything. If you want me to stay, tell me everything. It can't be any worse than anything that's happened to me before."

So I do.

I tell her everything... about how Violet lured me, using my biggest vice to do it.

After she knows about the drugs and how Violet as much as took payment in the form of sex, she looks at me for a long time, seemingly calm. "What stuff did you do with her?"

I thought I'd be off the hook. For a second there... I'd hoped.

Seems this world has it in for me. "Does it matter?"

"It matters," she insists, "you were fucking her for almost two years!"

I shake my head. "I ended it with her loads of times... she just kept coming back. I knew I had to leave FMP to escape. With her came the promise of cocaine and that's all I really wanted... that was all I was really tempted by."

"You're avoiding the question. What stuff did you do? You must know... it lasted months... years!" she screams.

"Everything," I reply.

Her cheeks blaze red, the colour of passion, the colour of shock, but hers is a shade of hurt and anguish.

"Did you enjoy it?"

"Yes, the physical getting myself off part, yes, I enjoyed that. But I didn't love her. I didn't even find her particularly attractive. She gave me drugs, it makes you horny. I was hurt, I was lost. You were being distant with me and that's not an excuse, that's just an explanation of why I was feeling weak. Violet persisted and persisted, offered herself… freely. On drugs, everything seems a good idea, even when you know it's not."

"I wouldn't know," she yells, stands, and throws her cup across the room so it smashes and splashes her lovingly made tea everywhere. "I've never fucking taken drugs!"

Shocked, I look at the white floor tiles, and stand absolutely still.

Lowering her voice, she asks in a terse tone, "Did you lick her?" I wince, but she paces towards me, slapping my face. "DID YOU!?"

"Once or twice… maybe!!"

She slaps me, everywhere. I wrap my arms around my head and she attacks me, hitting, punching, kicking. The physical pain is nothing, but the rest… hurts so bad.

I fall to my knees and she steps back.

"Look what you've made me do! Look at what I'm becoming! How could you do this to me?"

I shake my head. She slaps me again, no doubt considering me insolent.

"Put yourself in my shoes… I found out I married a woman I didn't even fucking know."

She screams from the bottom of her lungs, making my eyes shoot up to look at her. Hands twined in her hair, she twists at it, screeching and yelling, tears falling, animalistic sounds pouring from her.

"Stop it, Adrienne!" I demand, using the full breadth of my lungs. Standing to look directly at her, she stares at me. Stunted, she quiets down.

"I meant every word I ever said." My lip trembles, my body on fire from her attack, skin bruising and shuddering with shock beneath my clothes. "I loved you from the moment we met. I will always love you. But now every time I look at you, all I see is that he got to you first. He made his mark first and I can't ever undo it. I'll never be able to convince you that you deserve happiness, that the dresses you wear were made for you. When you were carrying Luce, you didn't let me near enough to let me hold you... to let me soothe you. You didn't let me in, to comfort and protect you, to reassure you it's going to be alright. I was left alone, without you, throughout one of the most frightening times of our lives. You went into survival mode, shutting down, switching off. You've done it before, I can understand that. But my survival mode is to get out of my own head." I tap my temple. "To vacate, get high, have meaningless sex. It's how I always did things... until you."

I wipe a finger underneath my eye and she begs, "Please, don't."

"This isn't just about you, Ade."

"Don't, David," she begs again, her voice just a squeak.

"I changed the instant we got together. I didn't take drugs anymore. I started paying off my debts. I stopped with all the girls I was stringing along at the same time. I saw you and it was like bright, white light and pure happiness..." I pause, my heart pounding. I close my eyes as I think back to the day I finally plucked up the courage to speak to her, pretending I needed help with a book. I didn't want that book, not really. I'd been hiding that book in a corner of the library for months. I knew exactly where it was, every day of the week, because I was tall enough to reach the highest shelves and I enjoyed pissing off other people on my course who wanted that book. But all I really wanted was her. I stalked her around that library for weeks before I caught her attention. She was mesmerising. "...I had this feeling I'd never felt before. Better than drugs, better than anything. I looked at you and I felt lighter, unburdened. I felt me. I felt happy, really happy. I stopped all that shit for you, because I love you. I've always loved you. I don't just see beauty, I see a strong spirit, a beautiful soul. I see in your eyes someone wonderful, someone sensitive and intelligent and more observant than any other person I've ever known. I saw you.

I saw you..."

"But now you don't see the same girl!" She screams and sinks to the floor, her back against the wall, legs to her chest. Crying into her knees, she wails, "Love, it's not enough, is it? It'll never be enough. I'm too fucked up, David... I'm too fucked up. You were right... you were right... I'll never get over it. I'll never be me again. I'll always just be her... laid on the kitchen floor... wishing myself someplace better, someplace else. Imagining it all never happened. Living in ignorance, it never lasts. The memory always returns... always. Broken bones and scars, knives on the sideboard, just a temptation for me to end myself. It was him or me, him or me!"

I rush to her and hold her, even though she fights me. I hold her as tight as I can and when she's given up fighting, she howls into my chest, wails, unburdens herself of the weight she carries.

I'm still so in love with her, but nothing's the same, and never will be again. We've lost something. I've become someone else, and so has she. We're not the two people who got married in our casual clothes at Gretna, her kid more well-dressed that day than us. We're just fakes really, with our fancy house and 2.4 kids and two cars and all our degrees, education behind us, plus a grandmother who turns a blind eye. We're just a front now, hiding what's really going on.

I don't know what we're going to do.

When the hysterical crying stops, she whispers little cries into my chest and wipes her nose on my shirt.

I lower my voice and tell her quietly, levelly, "When you started asking why we weren't having as much sex anymore, I tried to brush you off because the guilt was eating me whole. I tried to end it with Violet, but she wouldn't have it. The day I left the job, Luca asked me if she'd had anything to do with it... I admitted everything. I was so relieved to tell someone, and maybe, I thought that was the end of it all. The same day I left, he had security raid her bag, sacking her on the spot. Everybody knew she had her eye on me. She was relentless, wouldn't stop. I was feeble-minded and let her take advantage of the rift in our marriage. I failed to get myself free of her. The only way I could was to leave my job. I had to sell some shares I was saving for a holiday home for us so that I could set up what I'm doing now and keep us all afloat. I had such dreams for us, Ade. Right now, I know everything looks bleak but I'm telling you... the promise that you'll stay so we can work this out, together, and rebuild our love... that could be amazing. That could be beautiful. To me, right now, that seems a dream. Please, give me another chance. Make my dream come true."

Her bottom lip turns up. "Right now, I don't see us doing that. I don't see it."

"Ade," I beg, lifting her chin so she has to look into my eyes, "listen to me. I don't care what the world does to me, I don't care. I still believe nobody will love you more than me, nobody."

A tear falls from her eye. "You did this. Not me. How can you say that? You're the only one hurting me. The man to love me, for real, would never do this to me."

I beg with my eyes and with my declaration: "Adrienne, he's dead. I've got nowhere for this hate to go. Where do I put it? What do I do with this pain, right here," I put her hand on my chest, "like a bullet wound, forever leaking air from my lungs, I haven't been able to breathe properly since I found out. I can't breathe, I can't sleep, or eat. My wife, the woman of my dreams, was treated in the most horrific way and the only way she could escape has left her living with guilt for the rest of her life... how am I meant to process all this? How? Please, tell me how!"

I break down crying, tears coughing out of me. I've never been a crier. Ade knows that.

"I don't know how, Ade," I repeat, and she clings harder to me, our lungs taking a beating as we sob together.

"Oh, David. Oh, David."

"I know, Ade. I know."

I pull her head into my chest as tight as I can and she holds me back, she actually holds me in return and it gives me a sprinkling of hope, dusting my broken dreams with a smattering of silvery possibilities.

TWENTY-FOUR

A week has passed since she found out about me and Violet. Correction. There was no me and Violet. Just a lot of stupid mistakes. We've spent the time trying to be as positive as possible in front of the kids but in bed, she sleeps on her side and I'm on mine, and nothing's said. It feels like we couldn't be any further apart if we tried, even though we're still sharing a bed every night.

She sometimes looks at me and starts to say something, but stops herself.

This morning, she seems unable to keep her words to herself. Now the kids are packed off to school and nursery respectively, she stares over her coffee cup and spits out, "You had anal sex with her?"

I stare. Whatever answer I give will be the wrong one.

"Didn't you?" she persists.

"Yes," I admit, shame making my face hot.

"You said you never wanted that with me. Said you were too big."

"She asked me to do it. I told you... it's difficult with my size. She didn't care about the pain. She was too coked up to care. So was I."

She shakes her head. "I can't deal with this, not when I have to look at you."

"What do you mean?"

"You're working here all day. I can't escape you. I think you need to give me some breathing space."

Breathing space? Breathing space...? The thought makes me break out in a sweat. It means time she'll spend alone realising what a fuck I am. Time she might find someone better. Someone worthier, someone who promises fidelity and maintains it.

"I don't know. I think we should work through this together."

"I want you to go to your mother's. They offered me a job as Finance Officer at the local library here. Full-time. I don't need you, David, and I think you need to feel that so that you know I don't need you."

I frown, squirming. Is she fucking with my head?

"I've got no idea why you're saying all this... I don't know... what is the point? If I leave you, how are things going to be better or worse?"

"I don't need you," she repeats, "I don't need you. Maybe once you think that through, you'll realise that I married you because I wanted you. Not because I needed you."

"I need you," I growl, thumping the air.

She recoils and steps back against the kitchen counter, watching me closely, like a huntress eyeing up her competition.

"Surviving what I have, you need to understand... I'm strong. But you're not. You need to make yourself strong otherwise, you're not good enough for me. I entered this for life and if you want to make it up to me..."

"Ade, are you just saying shit to hurt me? What the fuck are you talking about?"

"Pack a bag, pack your sex toy industry away into your van outside, and go. Today. If you want to save us, you need to go."

Slamming my cup on the counter, I shout, "This doesn't feel like we're trying to save our marriage. This feels like you giving up."

"Whatever."

"No, no, how can you just say, *whatever*? I need you!"

She smirks, scratching at her jaw. "You're just so selfish, David. Putting your needs before everyone else's. I think I've been pretty rational and fair considering the circumstances and now, I want your face out of my face. I want time to think this through because all I see when I look at you... is betrayal. Hurt. Her... sucking you, you licking her, your bodies in the act... you lying. You don't get what this feels like. Imagine if I had done this–"

"I fucked her to get drugs, Ade!"

She nods. "Keep telling yourself that."

"So, tell me why I fucked her then?"

She stands tall, arms folded, and looks me straight in the eye. "Because something difficult entered the equation and you couldn't deal with it. You wanted escape from the tough stuff, to get out of your own head and get high and get sucked off by an ugly, desperate little slut!"

She pants, catching her breath. She's not wrong. Violet was a desperate old slag with a husband who neglected her, no doubt. I wonder if they're still together...

"That's not why I did it," I explain, anger making me want to smash something.

"Then, why?"

I swallow. "I love you so much that–that– I just can't tell you why. I don't know how to deal with it. I love you more than anything, Adrienne. You don't know how much I love you. My love's so strong, it burns me."

"Love. Love. You don't get to spout love and get let off the hook. I'll ask you again... imagine how you'd feel if I'd cheated on you."

My arms flail as I roar, "I'd feel... I'd kill the man! I'd boil his head and start eating the insides while he was still breathing."

She sniffs. "You might think I'm functioning but beneath, I'm a mess. I've been hurt before, so I know how to bury this. How to hide it. I know what this feels like. It's nothing new to me. You don't deserve to understand how much you've hurt me. It'd only serve your ego just that bit more."

"I didn't fuck her to pump up my ego, Ade!"

"Sure, sure, you didn't." She laughs loudly, covering her face.

"I didn't."

"Tell me, then."

"Ah, Ade. Stop this." I wrap my hands around my head, trying to shut out the cringing, stabbing pain of owning up to all of this.

I know it's my fault, deep down, I know that.

I'm just trying to explain it all, but I can't. I did this and that's all there is to it.

"I don't have to stay with you. I don't need you," she repeats, "but you need to realise your culpability here because you're swanning round, fulfilling your orders and doing business everyday like our marriage isn't on the line, when it is."

"I don't expect you to forget what happened," I groan, "I just asked you to stay so we can figure this out."

"David!" she shouts, her arms joining the flailing party, "you can't make me feel how you want me to feel! I'm telling you right now, you've pulverized me. Seeing those pictures, those... words from her... don't you understand?"

I thump my chest. "That bitch was callous and mean. If she had anything about her, she'd have forgotten about the whole thing and left you alone. That would have been kinder."

Slowly, she shakes her head, tapping her skull in exasperation. "I'm not getting through to you at all, am I? Not at all."

I look at her, in her tracksuit, no make-up and her hair brushed back into a ponytail. So she's not wearing her usual dress or jeans and blouse combo, she's not made up or washed her hair, but she's living. So am I. Maybe she's not doing as well as she normally is, but... she's surviving. We can survive together, right?

"First sign of trouble and you fuck someone else. How do I know it won't happen again?"

"It won't, I promise!" Nothing is worse than this feeling.

"I don't know that. Our trust is broken."

"You're the woman who bloody killed a man... maybe it's about time you repeat offended, eh? Because kicking me out will most certainly kill me!"

She sneers, "That's low, David. Well below the belt."

I growl a desperate cry for help and beg, "Please don't make me go. Just... let's stay out of each other's way, I don't know... I'll get an office unit and then you won't have to see my face as often."

She sniffs. "I want you to go to your mother's. I don't see why I should have to look at your face and be reminded of the pain your mistakes have caused us."

"Ade, please. I'm begging you. I know I'm completely in the wrong, but please! Don't give up on me."

She turns her back to me, holding her weight up with her palms pressed firmly against the kitchen counter. "You're so selfish, David."

"Then we were made for one another, yes? Me, the selfish arse, and you, totally selfless. Let me stay and put things right. Please. Tell me what to do... what to say... how to fix this! Please, Ade, tell me...!" I start crying and she turns to face me, a blank, unsympathetic expression in her eyes.

"I need time, David. I need time and space. If you think I'll rush off to find someone else," she curls her lip, "then you never knew me at all."

I shudder and close my eyes. We're not the same, me and her. She's always been better than me. I should've let her be when I had the chance, back in the beginning, when she told me she knew my type. I've been running from what I am, trying to be her loving husband, when all I really am is my father's son. I was right all along, I'm just like him, and the prophecy is complete. But, a part of me still wants to fight... to be better.

I keep my eyes shut as I tell her, "Our emotions are all over the place and nothing makes sense. Not to me, anyway. This is all nonsense. I want to tell you that... when I met you, Adrienne, I was carrying a lot of pain. I used drugs and women to bury that pain beneath a superficial barrier but when I met you, all of that pain left me and nothing that happened before mattered anymore. It all left me and nothing else mattered but me and you. None of the bullying I put up with from Dad and Rob mattered anymore, it was all gone. All I saw was sunshine and you, happiness and you, stars and you, love and you, warmth, comfort and beauty, and you."

She stares into my eyes before saying very slowly, "It was the same for me. The exact same. You came along and everything from the past was forgotten, none of those hurts mattered anymore! So now you know how much you've taken from me by fucking her. Our perfect love is broken, it's broken! I know I've been a shit wife sometimes, I know all that, but I didn't run off. I tried to make things better between us. I asked you if we should get help and you said no. None of this would have got out if she hadn't messaged me because you would have continued hiding your secrets... and I would've lived wondering what I could've done to put things right. I tried, David! I TRIED!"

She sobs into her hands and I know she's right.

I'm just a bastard. This is what I was born as.

I can't undo my DNA.

I got one chance at happiness and I blew it.

I'll never get this again, not with anybody. The way I feel about her comes around once in a lifetime. You get one go and if you fuck it up, that's it. You're done. I should've realised we weren't invincible. I should've known.

"I'll go," I agree, "to Mum's."

Leaving the room to pack, she pulls on my forearm to halt me. Looking into my eyes, she says, "Thank you."

I nod.

Taking the stairs two at a time, I'd rather punch holes in the walls than leave, but I'll go because she asked me and because now I remember...

I've always been a bastard. This is my just desserts.

There's nothing to live for now, except hoping one day she'll take me back.

TWENTY-FIVE

It's been six months since she asked me to move out and Adrienne's found another man. I have even been served divorce papers but I refuse to sign them. I've given up on life. I've given up on everything but my kids, who stay here at Mum's every other weekend and visit twice on school nights so I can to give them their tea.

I'm in hell.

My mother despises me, but not enough to throw me out. She knows I'd be useless on my own and anyway, me living here means she gets to see the kids, too. Ade's even been frosty with Mum. Maybe she blames her for giving birth to me, the bastard. It's not her fault but she did, my mother I mean: she gave birth to a bastard like me.

That's all I am.

Self-pity is my friend. It's the only thing I understand.

I'm driving in my van to pick up the kids and bring them to Mum's for the weekend. Surprise, surprise, as I pull up, I notice the spot I used to have is occupied by Luca's Golf GTi.

Prick.

Knocking on the door, I take a deep breath. I knew it was him she was seeing but I didn't know it'd gotten to the stage where he's visiting our house, making himself at home.

Maybe I should sign the divorce papers because then he'll have to pay me half of what this house is worth.

Ade opens the door to me, wearing a full-length navy dress.

"Come in," she asks.

I'm speechless and try to avoid looking at her. She's gorgeous and she was right, she doesn't need me. She doesn't need me at all, not looking the way she does.

"It's the Christmas party tonight," she says.

Funny, she never liked Christmas parties before.

How many more times can she stick the knife in and grind it?

"Hey, David," Luca says, strolling into the hallway with Lucinda under his arm. The fucking bastard must be ten years older than Ade but looks as fresh as a shitting daisy. I'm not gay in the slightest but even I can see why half the guys at FMP always have a hard-on for him and why all the girls walking past his desk smell of sex. Meanwhile I wake up everyday and find a curly lettuce leaf staring back at me when I look in the mirror, thanks to sleepless nights and too many hours spent crying. He's George fucking Clooney and I'm just me.

Seems the knife can grind harder than I ever thought:

My daughter with another man playing her dad?

I can't have that.

How am I meant to right this?

I feel god-awful.

Apparently (according to Mum), Luca and Ade bumped into one another in Leeds one afternoon while she was shopping and they had coffee. They're dating which might not be inclusive of fucking but either way, the thought of her with someone else makes me feel sick.

Tonight her dress hugs her every curve and she's done something with her hair so that it's wavy and sleek. Her make-up dramatic, I wonder who she's trying to impress. Ever since I've known her, she's always favoured the more natural look.

"I'll have them back by Sunday evening." My head bowed, I know there's no point fighting back.

"Bye, be good for your father," Ade calls after us as Billy trudges at my side, hand in my hand.

In the van I strap Luce into her seat in the middle of the cab up front and Billy puts his belt on in the far passenger seat.

"I don't like him!" Billy shouts after Ade's closed the front door. He throws his arms out dramatically before folding them and scowling.

"He a poo-poo face," adds Lucinda.

Part of me thanks them, while another wonders…

I pull off the kerb and drive away, and as we're heading for Mother's, I ask, "What's so bad about him?"

"He not my daddy!" Lucinda shouts and Billy hides his face, clearly very unhappy about the situation too.

I drive the rest of the way in silence. All this upset is down to me and I've wrecked everything. I don't know how I get through the day sometimes, but somehow I do.

***

New Year. Fucking load of shite.

Last night, while Mum went to a party with her book club friends, I locked myself in my bedroom with six cheap bottles of champagne and drank all of them. Every last drop.

I've spent most of Christmas without my children.

I'm dying. Almost dead. Inside.

I have no idea what to do.

Idly scrolling through my phone as I come back to life, I see I've slept through most of New Year's Day. Probably best. It's almost three in the afternoon.

Surprise, surprise. Not one person has messaged me to say 'Happy New Year'. Not even Ade.

Noticing the email icon highlighted, I check to see if it's

anything interesting.

It actually is.

I've been applying for jobs for a few months, just anything relating to my degree that will get me out of this town... out of selling fucking dildos. It's ironic that working for FMP wrecked my marriage and now I'm going back to the beginning, as an English scholar – the very job I left so I could earn 'more money'. Nowadays, I don't give a shit about money.

(Maybe if I get the job, I'll set up summer writing camps where I invite the students to write shit as maudlin as me.)

Anyway this job at York University recently came up and might be perfect for me. I just have to hope they don't frown on me after doing their background checks. I held favour at Leeds because my professors had known me for years but somewhere, new... I don't know. Maybe enough time has lapsed since my drug arrests that people can now see I'm reformed.

Yeah right...

The email asks whether I can come for interview next week. I hope it might be a liberal university? Or maybe this sort of thing is more common among English scholars than I know?

I need a cup of strong coffee before I even think about forming words to reply to the email.

Meeting Mum in the kitchen, I find she's not much better off than me. In fact, right behind me is a friend she brought home.

"Hey up lad, call me Malcolm," he says, holding out his hand. He appears to be wearing one of my robes from the bathroom but it doesn't fit around the midriff.

From the look on Mum's face, she was very drunk last night and is very regretful. I laugh inwardly. Even in the worst of times, there's always a silver lining. Now Mother and me can cry on each other's shoulders about all the mistakes we've both made, Malcolm being one of hers. He's quite a thick-set chap with a moustache stained by smoking a pipe by the looks of it.

"We've got a thing today, haven't we David? Malcolm, you'd better get dressed because of this… thing. Family. You know?" she says, lying through her teeth.

I don't think she could sound more awkward if she tried.

He makes for his clothes. "O'course, I'll get out of your hair."

After he's left the room, I stare at her, my arms folded.

"Not. One. Word," she warns, nursing her headache.

"I said nothing."

While I'm putting the kettle on, she complains, "Too much noise!"

Stumbling as she stands, she heads for the living room to hide out.

Malcolm passes through on his way out and waves goodbye. "Tell Rachel I'll definitely be in touch. I have her number!"

After the front door shuts, she groans from the living room. "I'm getting a new phone!!!!"

"Least I got drunk without calamity."

"Well, you've learned the hard way, son!"

I carry my coffee and a cup of tea and some paracetemol for her into the lounge area.

"Thanks, David."

I get to work on my phone, writing a professional sounding response from me about that job.

I'm tired of selling dildos. It's not much fun. It's never used my brain and now I work for myself, it doesn't pay great money. Why shell out over £30,000 on my education, just to chuck it down the drain? I can't do that.

"I got an interview for that job in York. Next week."

She grins, as much as she can do with a head full of alcohol and intolerance to light, sound and movement. "I am so pleased, David. Really, I am."

We sip our drinks, a few silent moments passing us by.

"She's not in love with that Luca, you know?"

I look up from my phone, having sent off a message saying I'll be there for the interview.

"How do you know?"

She shrugs. "I know that girl. When I dropped the kids off last week, I could just tell."

I bite my lip. "Do you think she chose him, just to hurt me? You know, because I worked with him?"

Mum shakes her head. "No. I think Luca knows a beauty when he sees one. There aren't many lookers like Ade around, are there? A man like him with money can have anyone he wants."

I struggle to respond or smile at my mother's kind attempt to cheer me up.

"I fucked up big style, Mum. This Christmas has been horrendous."

Christmas morning, Mum and me went to Ade's to exchange presents. Luca sat in the background, quietly observing. I don't know if he's moved in or whatever, but my children don't fawn on him like they do on me, thank fuck.

"He probably says and does all the right things. Acts the gentleman. He's not you though, is he son?"

"A cheating bastard, yeah," I growl, throwing myself back into the cushions of the sofa.

"Doesn't matter," she mutters, "she doesn't love him, I can tell."

"What doesn't matter? I'm a fucking wanker and I fucked up. Even if he's not the one, neither am I. She will never forgive me."

"It doesn't matter, you can't help who you love," she tells me, "and she loves you. I know it. She's just been hurt, that's all."

"I know Luca, Mum. He's had hundreds of women. He knows every trick in the book."

She grins. "So why hasn't she been knocking on our door

everyday, begging for that divorce? If she loves him, she'd want that divorce as soon as possible."

"They've only been seeing each other for three months," I argue, trying to contradict her. I don't want to get my hopes up.

"She'd want a clean slate, a fresh start. Mark my words, if even he can't win her over, she might be sitting there right now wondering how she'll ever get over you. Part of her knows she never will."

I rub my eyes. "Mum, I sincerely hope you're right, but you don't know about the ins and outs of our marriage. I don't know if things can be repaired. I just don't know. I don't want you to get your hopes up. There are children to consider, too... and they are already confused enough. We don't know anything about their relationship yet."

"Son, don't give up–"

"No, come on, Mum," I beg, my hand gestures frantic, "please. I'm trying to move on. I'm trying to cope with this as best as I can and this won't help me do that. I fucked another woman. I can't deny that I did that. This is all my fault."

She shakes her head. "I know you, David Lewis and I know how sensitive you are beneath all the stupid things you've ever done. I know it must have been bloody difficult finding out all those things about Marcus, that bloody evil cocksucker."

"MOTHER!" I explode, shocked by her mouth.

She holds her forehead and groans. "I'm never drinking again!"

I laugh slightly and she winks from across the room.

"You both dove in headfirst when you met. You were young. You had a shock when I told you about Marcus. You were exhausted from second-guessing her emotions throughout her pregnancy and things went south. Tits up. Whatever you want to call it, stuff got bad. Now, listen to me. If she even has a tiny bit of doubt over this Luca guy, you have to beg for her to give you another chance. Beg, plead, on your knees if you have to. Tell her you've sought nobody else, you want nobody else."

I weep into my sleeves a little. "I don't want anybody else."

"Then tell her," she assures me gently, "because she doesn't love him."

"She might grow to love him, though, and I bet he wouldn't cheat on her. He'll be better for her than I ever will be."

"Maybe, maybe not. That's not the point, though. Either she loves you or she doesn't and that's the only thing that matters. You can't force love, David. You can work it out, if she admits she still loves you."

"She won't," I assert, "she's still angry with me. She never looks me in the eye anymore."

"Angry because you hurt her, or angry because she still cares and doesn't want to. But she does. She still cares for you."

I wipe more tears and shake my head. "I don't know whether I should risk it. It's too much to lose. She might tell me to back off for good."

"If you're not willing to take the risk, then maybe you don't deserve her love after all."

I shake my head. "I took the risk once before. This time, there's so much more riding on it."

"You want that man fathering your children, who by the way don't even like him?"

I shoot up from my chair. "No."

Turning, I walk back to my bedroom and head straight for the shower.

TWENTY-SIX

<u>*The East Wind As A Messenger of Love*</u>

"Dum dum da tum"
It will never be broken, though bitter things spoken,
Be here at my side, and filled be with pride,
As winter disperses, and spring offers verses,
Of worship and hope, or bountiful scope.

"De da dum de dum"
Kindly be thee, and laid out to see,
Hush all concern, the past we will learn,
We are all that we seem, the bygone a dream,
From which we'll awake, both nearly not fake.

"La la at dum de dum"
Apple blossom blow, rise up from below,
I cannot turn back, there's nothing we lack,
Fresh and awaiting, beyond love's frustrating,
This point is our time, you shimmer in prime.

"De dum de da dum"
All has been said, look up thy head,
Young and a pair, have crushed our despair,
Grant me your hand, and wander this land,

For all's been addressed, and angels have blessed.

***

I'm standing outside our front door. My knees are knocking, I'm so nervous. I have poetry in my pocket, written on crumpled paper, should I need a last resort to convince her of what I now believe.

I ring the bell and Billy opens the door to me, rushing into my arms. "We weren't expecting you, Dad."

Ade arrives to see who it is, cautiously eyeing me up as Billy madly hugs me. For a seven year old, he's handled all of this pretty well.

"Sorry if this is a bad time, just come to say Happy New Year."

She's wearing sweats and she's not done up at all today. She fiddles with her hair, but it's not like I haven't seen her naked and pure a thousand times before. Maybe she feels naked. Exposed. Vulnerable.

I have to hope Mum is right.

"It's fine. I was just making some sandwiches. We ate out for lunch at a pub."

Billy heads back to the lounge and I follow Ade into the kitchen. With her back to me, she angrily makes cheese sandwiches and I ask, "Luca took you all out, then?"

"No, it was just me and the kids," she replies, taking more slices of bread from a bag.

Her boyfriend's dumped her for someone else on New Year's Day?

Prick.

"Are you okay?" I ask, "you seem a bit frantic."

She swirls around. "What? Are you criticising me?"

"Whoa." I hold my hands up in defeat. "Not at all. I just know this isn't your favourite time of year. I know you miss your mother. I just want to check you're okay... Mum said... she was just worried," I eagerly correct myself.

She turns back to making sandwiches and I leave her there, heading for the lounge to greet the kids. Lucinda climbs up into my lap and cuddles me.

"You okay, buddy? What have you been up to?" I ask Billy.

"We all went to bed early last night. Mum was crying."

"What?" I scratch my head. "What about?"

"Don't know. She forgot to feed us. I snuck down in the night and got me and Luce some fruit and cheese. Didn't want to disturb her."

I look down and find Lucinda has fallen asleep across my lap. Carefully, I unfold her and put her on the seat next to mine. Placing a blanket over her, I ask Billy, "Watch your sister while I go and talk to your mother."

He nods. "Yes, Dad."

I walk quietly through the hallway back to the kitchen and find her still buttering bread like a maniac. She's made enough sandwiches for twenty people, let alone two little kids.

"Ade?"

She stops what she's doing and looks over her shoulder, her eyes red from crying. "Don't come any closer."

Her hands gripping the sideboard, I know she's going through something rough.

"What happened with Luca?"

"I expect Rachel heard and that's why you've come round."

"She didn't tell me anything except she wasn't convinced you love Luca."

She spins and pins her eyes on mine. "Love? Love? Why does everyone have to talk of love? Why can't I just have some fucking fun for a change?"

Oh. So that's why she's like this.

"What happened with Luca?"

She blows out a deep breath. "We were in Betty's last week... Billy was playing up. Luca just lost it and shouted at him. I gave him what for, almost beat the living shit out of him for turning on my son. Lucinda was crying and Luca stormed out."

"What?" I exclaim.

"I know." Ade wipes her palm under her eye, whispering, "He was mostly pissed because he knows my heart's elsewhere. He lost it because of me, because my emotions are all over the place."

"If he's pressing you, Ade... it's not right. It's only been a few months–"

"So then we came back here after Betty's and he was waiting. He was apologetic enough but I told him to go. When he wouldn't listen, I told him I don't love him, because I don't. I never will."

Staring, I wait for more. She catches her breath and tells me, sniffing, "It was all a big mistake."

I just can't stop staring at her. She's magical. From the long curve of her swanlike neck to her immaculate skin, her rosy cheeks and beautiful hands, I can't imagine any other woman ever being so beautiful.

"Say something," she says.

"You said you wouldn't go crawling off to someone else. You said that."

"I know, but he just said the right things. *Did* the right things. Though... when he shouted at Billy in front of the whole restaurant, I saw another side of him... you know. He professed love but I never did. I'm not a liar."

I stare her out.

"But I am," I accept. Looking down at the floor, I ask, "Has he left you alone since then?"

"No. He won't stop calling."

"I'll talk to him, if you like."

"You would?"

"I'd do anything to make you happy again, anything to make life easier for you. I'd give my eyeteeth for you to be happy."

She turns and faces away from me again, her fingers clinging to the counter edge.

I think about what Mum told me earlier and realise, risks are sometimes worth the fall.

Walking towards her, she starts turning when she hears me coming, but my chest hits her back and I wrap myself all around her before she can fight me off. Gathering her in my arms, she sags and sinks, falling back against me. My nose buried in her hair, I whisper her name. I kiss her nape and her earlobe. Turning her, I pull her face into my chest and hold her tight. She clings to my arms and convulses with tears.

"I'm so tired of hurting, David."

"Then please, let me make it all better. I'm begging you. I'll do anything. "

I hold her, stroking her hair, smelling her. I shake uncontrollably, having missed her so much.

"David!" she cries and I pull back and smash my mouth to hers, healing her wounds, suturing her gashes. She reaches her hands into my hair and I kiss every inch of her face.

"I love you, I love you. I'll love you forever."

"David!"

Some part of me recognises the love in her voice as she cries my name and I kiss her throat, her chest and her hands.

Kneeling, I wrap my arms around her body and look up into her eyes. "I'm begging you. Please give me one more chance. I'll do anything you ask of me. Just let me love you, that's all I ask. I don't even have to move back, just let me love you. Please. I'm begging you, Ade. I'm nothing without you. Life makes no sense. I miss my kids and I miss you, and us, being together. Just let me make it up to you, let me love you. I can't function unless you let me just be here for you. I don't–"

She pushes her hand against my mouth and says, "Okay."

"Okay?" I ask as she wipes my tears away. "You mean it?"

She nods. "Okay."

I stand and hold her, staring into her eyes with bewilderment.

"Did you sleep with him?" I ask her, levelling my eyes with hers.

Her mouth twitches before she replies, "No."

"Why not?"

"He's got a small penis," she says. "I brushed a hand down there and he was small, even while erect."

"Really?" That surprises me.

She nods. "I didn't love him... he didn't stand a chance."

I can't help smiling a little.

"I'll never get over you," she says, "you're a man women just don't get over. Clearly, Violet didn't want to part with you, did she?"

Placing my finger over her lip, I warn, "No more, Ade. I'm glad you didn't fuck him because now I don't have to go and pump his guts full of lead, what with him having broken the bros before hoes rule... but none of this is about me anymore. It's all about you."

She strokes my cheek and kisses a tear from my face.

"You never cry, David."

"I didn't know loss before losing you."

She cups my cheeks and kisses my lips. In her eyes, I see seriousness. "I've missed you, but I'm still in pain."

"I know," I reply, "but I can take it away. Just give me another chance."

TWENTY-SEVEN

The morning after, I've never felt so happy to wake up on my own couch. Last night after watching DVDs with the kids, she put them to bed and asked if I minded that she turned in early, letting me know I could take the sofa if I wanted. Of course I wanted. I don't want to pressure her. I'll wait, but I'm happy to be back at all.

The living-room door creaks open and Billy and Lucinda creep in. Lifting my blanket, they get cosy with me and fall back to sleep. I never think to ask either of them where their mother is.

When we all wake up a little while later, I see on the TV clock it's 8.58a.m. I know it's the Christmas holidays still, but where's Ade? Billy cuddles me close and I wonder about his behaviour. Has he been traumatised by me going and now, coming back.

"Where's your mum?" I ask William.

"Sleeping?"

Lucinda snuggles her nose into my cheek and whispers, "Wuv oo Dadda."

"Are you both okay?"

"Missed you," Billy says, and begins crying.

"Please don't son," I ask, but Lucinda joins in, crying too. Ade stands at the door in her dressing gown, having heard us all no doubt. She stares and wipes her eyes, horrified her children are upset. She walks away, too emotional to deal with it all.

When the kids calm down, I explain, "I'm going to try and be nicer to Mummy, okay?"

Lucinda doesn't really understand, she just clings to me, upset because her brother's upset.

"You weren't nice?"

"No, I wasn't, but I'm going to make it all better. I promise."

"Promise?" Billy asks for confirmation.

"I promise. I really do."

He nods his head and climbs out of our sofa cum bed.

Wandering off to the kitchen, I try to peel Luce's arms from me but she refuses to let go.

All these months, me and Ade have only been thinking about our own pain, ignoring the pain of our children. The thing is, the kids haven't really let on it's affected them, not until now.

I carry Luce with me into the kitchen and she's still reluctant to leave my arms, even for the highchair where her breakfast is waiting for her.

"I'm staying here, I'm just getting a drink," I reassure her.

She pouts but when I don't go, she smiles instead, and a few minutes later she and Billy are more interested in their cereal and the TV than the two broken adults stood nearby sipping their tea.

I take a chance and kiss Ade's cheek, briefly catching the look in her eye.

There's so much pain between us; I don't know if she'll ever be able to forgive and forget.

I bite my nails and ask her, "Did you sleep okay?"

"Yes," she nods, "I was exhausted."

I smile a little. "Has he called or anything?"

She shakes her head. "I told him to back off, told him you

were furious about the… scene the other day." She subtly gestures at Billy.

"I see."

Moments of silence pass.

"I have a job interview next week. At York Uni."

"Wow," she replies, "wow. You… god…"

"I know. I was stupid to ever give up on my real calling."

She walks forward and hugs me. "That's amazing, David. I hope you get it."

As we hold each other, I'm sure she feels it too: there's hurt but that's only because there's still so much love here between us. I still don't really know how to explain why I had sex with Violet. It meant absolutely nothing. It was just so I could be out of my own head. I don't think Adrienne understands that yet, but maybe she will give me chance to explain. One day.

When we pull away from one another, I'm stunned by her cerulean blue eyes.

"Ade?" I murmur.

"Yes," she whispers.

"You look so beautiful today."

She loses her breath and shuts her eyes. I don't know how I forgot I have this effect on her. Seeing how she responds to me is all that matters in life. Feeling her love and desire is everything. How could I have forgotten that?

I want her badly. I want her body in my arms. I want all this pain and suffering to disappear so it can go back to how it used to be.

Shaking me off, she moves to the doorway. "Watch them while I get dressed?"

"No problem."

She races upstairs and I'm left feeling desperate to gain a window inside her mind. I wish I knew what she was thinking so I could see things without having to ask questions and search her expressions for the truth. It could take years for me to get her to really open up about Marcus.

"Finished?" I ask the kids.

They both nod and shout, "Yes!"

"Let's go play for a bit, then."

"Yeah!" they both shout, and we head through to the living room to play with some of their Christmas presents, a DVD playing in the background.

***

After my interview, there's only one person I want to talk to. I race down the A59 home, hoping she'll be back from work on time. Cursing the traffic, I slam my foot down and get back into Harrogate at six o'clock in the evening, having sat through several interviews and delivered a presentation for a panel of professors!

When I ring the bell, Billy opens the door and Ade calls through, "You don't have to keep knocking. Just come in."

I stand in the hall and find everyone here, including Mother, who says straight away, "So, so? Tell us everything."

They all stand expectant, waiting for me to tell them all about it.

"It all went better than I imagined. I really want this job. I just have to hope... you know?"

"When do you find out?" Ade asks with a small smile.

"Within the week."

Mum smiles knowingly. "They'd be fools, fools not to employ you."

"Thanks, Mum."

I get crowded by the kids and after being so sad, for so long, happiness feels weird and presumptuous of me. When Mum takes the kids into the dining room, ready for dinner, I walk to Ade and ask, "Can I hold you?"

"Mmm-hmm."

Placing my hands around her back, I stare at her mouth and brush her hair back over her shoulder. She doesn't move, rigid with fear, or trepidation – I'm not sure. Slowly she lets herself lift her hands to my chest.

"I want to be a better man, Adrienne."

She tells me slowly, "I'll be happy for you, if you get it. I know it's the only thing you've ever wanted to do, really and truly."

I nod subtly. I don't know why I ever thought being a big-shot salesman would make me equal to Ade. I know now, I'll never equal her, and I'm okay with that. "What if I don't get it, what if I have to go right back to square one?"

"Nobody can go back," she whispers, "we can only move forward with what we've got."

She holds my cheek and reaches for my lips. Shutting my eyes instinctively, I groan as she softly touches my mouth with hers and whispers against my lips, "You're like a little boy, all giddy with excitement."

I keep my eyes closed. "It means so much to me and I never realised that until it was gone. I never thought I would go back... but... it's true what they say, your true love's always there, it never dies. The only thing that scares me now is, what if it's not enough? What if all I worked for is really lost now? I don't know what I'll do... I mean, I've been away from academia for four years!"

"This is all silly conjecture. Of course they will employ you." Wrapping her arms tight around my neck, she asks, "Now kiss me, David."

I pull her close and tip her head back, licking open her mouth. Her tongue slips out and I touch hers with mine.

I'm rock solid and filling my pants.

I close my mouth over hers and I'm enjoying her sweet taste and warm body in my arms too much to notice we've got company.

Mum clears her throat. "The children are hungry."

"Sorry, sorry!" Ade excuses herself.

She passes over two bowls of pasta for the kids and takes ours through. I can't leave the kitchen yet, not like this.

When Ade comes back into the kitchen for the wine, I pull her to me and ask, "Please don't punish me anymore. Any of us could get run over by a bus tomorrow. Let me love you tonight. It's been a year since I did anything with that woman. There's been no one else. Please let me come home. Please. Let me be in your arms. I love you."

She looks confused so I pull her close again, reminding her of what we have. Kissing her throat, her eyes flutter open and shut and she moans gently.

"Promise me you'll never do it again. Swear on Billy and Lucinda's lives."

I swallow. "I swear. I swear. I'll never do it again. I don't want to lose you. Not you, Ade. Call it a cry for help, a wake-up call... I don't know. All I know is that we have to put it behind us."

"You can stay," she tells me curtly, "but if I say no, if I can't... if I ask you to stay on the sofa instead, you have to deal with it. I'm not sure..." She clutches her stomach. "...just so much pain, David."

"I understand. I understand."

I pull her to me again and clutch her bum in my hands, giving her a ravenous kiss. She groans in my hold and tugs at my hair wildly.

I bite her earlobe, whispering, "I love you, I'm so in love with you."

"I love you," she says in a pained whisper, "but I'll die if you do it to me again."

"Give me another chance. It'll be different this time."

"I hope so," she says, "I really do."

At bedtime, the kids ask if I'm staying for good and Ade tells them, "Yes, he is." I know she's still hurting but I also know with time, I can take the pain away. I tell them I'll pick up my things from Grandma's tomorrow and we're all going to be a big, happy family again.

The kids are fast asleep by nine. Ade and I are watching

TV when she turns to me and says, "You want to head up?"

I nod, gazing into her eyes.

I can hardly speak. I want her back so much.

"Come up in a few, then. Give me a mo to get comfy."

I nod again. It's all I can do.

After she's gone upstairs, I slap my cheeks. "You better make this count, Lewis."

My whole future rests on tonight and on me making the greatest love I've ever made with her. I have to show her how she makes me feel. She has to know.

But what if this is a cruel twist of the knife? Is she going to use and abuse me, then send me out into the bitter cold again, alone and in despair? Is she trying to get my hopes up, just to shatter what little defence I have left?

I stand and decide I can't hang around thinking the worst. I need her, that's all I know.

I check the house is locked and that all the downstairs lights are switched off. Taking the stairs slowly, I edge closer to my judgement day, my reckoning. I just want to love her. It's all I've ever wanted but she pulls away – and she pulls away – every time something bad happens. I have to take the knowledge I have now and use it to my advantage to get beneath her, to sink into her heart and learn more about her scars, her pain, her hurt. I need to be buried so deep inside her, she confesses all her sins and all her hurts to me. I'll negate myself to make her entirely mine. I'll stay the course and I'll wait, for as long as it takes, to get her to open up about the past.

Tapping gently on the door, she calls, "Come in."

I walk inside to find her sat on the edge of the bed. I shut the bedroom door and lock it.

In her black, floor-length, silk nightdress, she looks wonderful. Silk ribbons tied at the shoulders beg me to untie them and free her flesh. Over her shoulder, she looks at me and looks away quickly. I want to dash to her but she asks, "Will you listen a minute?"

"Okay."

"Last year... when... well, when I wasn't sure what was going on... I started watching porn."

"Uh?"

"Yeah, I know it sounds ludicrous, but it just happened. I sort of got addicted to it and that's why I couldn't keep my hands off you. I'd been watching you in porn."

She's too ashamed to look at me, her back hunched as she remains sat on the edge of the bed.

"Me? You were watching me?"

"I was inquisitive."

"I wish you hadn't. That man in those films wasn't me."

She stands slowly, turns and looks at me. "I want you to be like that. I got wet watching you, commanding and mean. I want you to be like that with me, like it was in the beginning."

My chest puffed out, I beg, "You're my wife, not a sex slave."

"In here, I want to be that. I want to be used. By you."

She walks slowly towards me and lifts on tiptoes to kiss my mouth. Whispering into my chest as she unbuttons my shirt, she asks, "I'm not delicate. Inside, I'm diamond cut from granite. If you want me to be yours again, you have to submit to my demands."

"I don't know–"

She shushes me.

Removing my shirt, she runs her hands over my body, kissing my bare chest. The material of my jeans begins to chafe and I let my head fall back as she kisses my neck.

"I'm not a flower, I'm stronger than I look. I want you to pour yourself into me so I can see all of you and you can see all of me. I want everything you are, David. I don't want a perfect man, I just want you."

I don't need any more words; I know what she needs.

Grabbing her buttocks, I throw her up into my arms and stride the distance between us and the bed. Throwing her down, she flushes red and cries with joy. Unzipping my jeans, I throw them to the floor and climb on top of her.

Tearing at her mouth, I rake at her hair, her hands on my face. Sliding her silk nightdress up her legs, I feel her bush against my stomach and growl, "I can't wait."

Spreading her legs, I push straight inside her.

Looking down into her eyes, I see pain and shock, but pleasure, deep, satisfied pleasure. She bites her bottom lip and gasps, "Yes."

I undo her straps and pull her nightie a little way down over her breasts, so her nipples pour out to me. Sucking her, I fuck her too, filling her full, nothing wasted, not one inch.

"Do. not. come," I demand, and she nods, grimacing, the urge there but restrained.

"Fuck me," she asks in a raspy voice.

Pinning her arms above her head, our noses press together as I lever and pound her hard. Her face gets redder, her pussy gets hotter and wetter around me and I can feel the soft vibrations of a climax coming round the bend.

"Don't hold out," she reminds me, and I continue, even when I know I could make her come at any moment. She shuts her eyes to concentrate, to stop herself, and I pound home hard, the sound of her belly being used filthy and dirty, so dirty, my cock solid and the tip furiously full and sensitive.

Biting her nipple, she cries, tears leaving her. I lick her arms and keep thrusting, even when my thighs are caning and my cock is aching like a bastard for release.

"I love you," I tell her in her ear, and she jolts, eviscerating almost – pushing down hard on me. I cover her mouth as she comes so hard, I know her yell would wake the kids.

I have to pull out or risk getting shredded. I wank off over her and come in ropes up and down her body; her pussy hair, nipples, throat, belly button. I rub it over her lips as she lies back.

Cradling her in my arms, I pull the silk nightdress back down her legs to keep her warm. I kiss her back repeatedly, nuzzling her hair, whispering how beautiful she is. She turns her face to offer me her mouth and I kiss her savagely, raking her tongue from her, my facial hair grazing her over and over.

"Uh, yeah," I groan in her ear. "I can't be apart from you. Never again, Ade, never ever again."

"Whenever I ask you to fuck me, you'd just better fuck me, David."

"I'm onboard, I'm right onboard with that."

I run my hands all over her body. I missed her so much. She's got ample breasts for a slim woman, breasts which look fake but aren't. Her nipples are a lovely light-pink matching her pussy lips and arsehole. I want her arse. I want everything.

I want more.

Whether she's satisfied or not, she told me to be David Dare, and that's who I'm going to be. I'm not going to deny my needs anymore.

I flip her onto her front without warning and grabbing the nightdress in my fist, rip it from her. The *scriitch* sound of it ripping thrills me and she groans from her belly.

Rubbing my hands into the flesh of her buttocks, I warm, "Adrienne, I'm going to take your arse."

She nods her head.

Lifting her slightly off the bed, I lick around her arsehole and rub some of her juices into her hole. She wriggles her bum up into my face and I press some fingers into her. It's surprising how soft and malleable she is and she tells me, "I've done it before. But never with a man so big."

"You'll take me," I tell her, sliding two fingers in easily. She groans like an old wardrobe door does when it's opened for the first time in centuries. I spit down onto her arsehole and keep massaging and lubricating her, so much juice from her pussy aiding and abetting me.

Aligning our bodies, I watch as she bears down, her hole opening. I never knew how experienced she was at all this, but now I do, I want to fuck her body until there's nothing but me and my demands in her memories.

Pushing my tip into her, she thumps the mattress with her fist.

"You okay?"

"More!"

I pull her hips and she rides back further onto my cock. The sensation of how tight and how hot she is burns me. Looking down at how she takes me, I still want more.

"You like me fucking your filthy little ass, Ade?"

"Oh my god, David. Yes!"

I start fucking her and she *hees* and *haaws* with all the sensations of us fucking together, so tight.

"It's a fantasy fulfilled?"

"Yes, David, yes. You're my fantasy. I masturbate to you every morning."

I slap her rear and push in deeper. She squeals and I warn her, "Behave, little piggy."

"Oh... god... David!" She pushes back against me, fucking me, and I let her. I watch as she fucks me, like an animal, her body taking mine. The sight of it is fucking out of this world, as she stretches and enjoys it.

Slapping her clit beneath us, she comes and rapes the cum from me, my seed shooting deep into her bowels. Her animalistic noises are muted by her face being pressed into the pillow, but I can hear the meaning behind them.

She falls flat on her belly, her body shaking and shivering. I pull her close and pull the duvet over us. She snuggles into my body, weeping. The shock has set in, the pleasure retreating, the pain edging closer. I hold her and repeatedly caress her cheek with the back of my hand.

"It hurts," she murmurs.

"Do you want something? Some tablets?"

She nods. "Yes."

In the bathroom, I find some painkillers and fill a glass with water. Back in bed, I feed her the pills and she gets comfortable in my arms again.

"It still doesn't hurt as much as when he did it."

"Oh?"

"I didn't want to do it with him. I wasn't relaxed."

"In the morning, it won't hurt baby. You didn't tear, not that I saw. Your muscles will just take a long time to relax again."

She nods into my skin.

"Love you, David."

Holding her close, I respond, "I know. But please tell me we'll make it? Please, Ade?"

She looks up into my eyes. "I don't know if we will, but I want to try."

"Me too."

Caressing her face, I kiss her repeatedly, staring into her eyes. Sedated almost, she stares back not blinking. I worship her like this for a long time, stroking her face, soaking up the feel of her lips with tender, stolen kisses. She eventually falls asleep in my arms and I look down at my poor dick, which she just savaged with her desperate need. I'm sore and aching, like she is, and I feel like she needs to hurt on the outside to feel less pain on the inside. There are so many mysteries to this woman, most of which I do not understand.

She has a past I know little about. One thing I do know – her parents are alive. They're out there somewhere, and someone has to pay for what happened to Adrienne. Why didn't they fight harder to save her from that fuck? Why did her father abandon her? It feels like there's so much I don't want to know, but if I want to know her, I need to find out.

She's not the woman I married but I'm more intrigued than ever, desperate to have all the answers. I always knew she had a dark edge to her. She was never one of those girls who asked me every five minutes if I loved her. When I rammed myself into her, she never once complained, in fact she always begged for more. She never asked questions and never really cried. Sometimes, she'd sit staring into space, such a look of vacancy there, I wondered what she was thinking. I have to ask, how did she survive Marcus? And how might this affect us in the future?

There's only one way to find out.

I just have to stay the distance.

And bide my time...

TWENTY-EIGHT

Ade, July 2008

Everyone else might think we are back on track, although personally, I doubt 'on track' is really a term you can attribute to a marriage; because it seems to me a peaceful partnership of two people in love might be the most challenging achievement on earth.

I stand in front of the bathroom sink, staring at myself in the mirror. What I see staring back pretty much disgusts me. For some reason, though, my sadness, my fatigue, my barely-there look seems to make David want me more. It's been six months now since he got his dream job as a bona fide university lecturer and while it seems on the surface we have everything, beneath we have only a few rocks sparingly placed at odd points around a large pond, and getting from one place in the water to another isn't ever going to be easy.

He walks up behind me, hugging my five-month bump. With his eyes diverted on me, I can watch his reflection in the mirror as he begins to worship me. Wearing nothing more than his boxer shorts, his nose softly caresses me. Whispers of his adoration race over my skin and down my spine. His delicate, strong musculature shifts and ripples as his arms move around me, up and down.

"You're so beautiful," he whispers.

This pregnancy, I've let him touch me. Let him have me. I've tried to be more welcoming, to not shut him out, but every day I keep the truth from him is another day a piece of me falls away and down the drain.

Would he still love me if I told him all my secrets? I doubt it. The thing David still doesn't realise is that a broken woman knows she can overcome just about anything, even losing the love of her life. If we split, I can go on. I've mastered every coping mechanism known to man. He doesn't see how much I can shoulder, how much I can carry without the weight making my knees buckle. He underestimates my strength and just because I'm here with him, carrying another of his babies, doesn't mean I'm all his yet. There are parts of me he hasn't even scratched the surface of and I don't think he could love all of what I am, beneath. He's not as strong as me which is why I spend everyday pretending everything is okay, when it isn't.

He releases the clasp on my bra and softly pushes the straps down my arms. My breasts spill into his hands and he pushes his arousal into my back, groaning into my hair.

I'm on fire, but it burns places scarred so deeply, I barely register the sensation sometimes. The woman he's in love with isn't me; he doesn't even know a tenth of me.

The woman beneath, she's that phoenix, she can always rise, and she doesn't necessarily have any control over who burns as she ascends.

Sweeping me up into his arms, I put my arms around his neck and he kisses me with his eyes open as he carries me to our bed. Gently kicking the door closed behind us, he slips my panties down my legs and lays me on the edge of the bed.

Spreading my thighs, he slips his tongue through my heated pleasure and I push and pull on his head, my toes running up and down his arms.

"Oh, David."

"Ade, I love you."

"Ohhhhhhh…"

He carries me further up into bed, post-climax and pushes

straight into me. Keeping my eyes closed, I cling to every kiss. Any could be the last. He could one day discover the truth and that'd be it. No more David and Adrienne.

Clutching all of his hair in my hands, he reminds me, "You can scream Ade, the kids are at Mum's tonight."

"Screaming is what girls do, David, and I'm not a girl anymore."

He looks down into my eyes, a slight sheen of sweat on his forehead.

He says nothing, questioning me with his gaze.

"No, you're not a girl anymore, Adrienne. You're a complicated puzzle I love more each day."

His gaze refuses to let up as a tear slides from my eye and he wipes it away, pinning my hands above my head so I can't hide behind them. He has one thigh firmly planted beneath my butt so he can thrust deep into my body and I'm so wet, I want to come again already. I'll hold out because the more orgasms I have, the more his love rips me open, and the more I want to tell him everything.

Telling him means risk. I could lose him by telling him.

It all hurts so much. All of it. Him and Violet. Marcus. Mum and Dad abandoning me. Me sleeping with Luca and lying about that, too. I think David would forgive me for that, but I lied to protect him – to save him the same hurt I've had.

Anyway, that lie is the least of my worries.

I guess I got pregnant with this child to try and give us something to focus on, but there's so much pain here, and not even his pure love is ever going to take it away.

"Ade, hold me," he begs, burying his face in my throat as he nears ejaculation.

I wrap my arms around his head and beg, "Please, David! Please!"

I'm ready for him, now. I don't think I can hold out any longer, the urge to bear down so great.

"Let go," he groans, and I relax, my orgasms immediately

flowing from me to him.

"Oh, oh…" I cry out with relief, twisting his hair in between my fingers.

"Oh god… god… oh yeah… oh!" he cries with me, maybe because the kids aren't here and won't be woken.

He doesn't lie with me like he usually would (slumping). He rolls straight to the side because of my bump and he pulls me back against him, his arms trapping me, his legs looping with mine.

I'm so physically tired, I can't fight the urge to sleep. I want to turn and look into his eyes, tell him everything and free myself of the lies, but I don't have any energy to do that. I'm just getting through the day right now.

He signals he wants snuggles, his nose pressing against my back, kisses on my shoulder blades. I reach back and stroke his buttock, crane my neck for more kisses which he bestows immediately.

I love him more than any man on earth. He's everything. One look across a library instantly and irrevocably changed both of our lives forever and now we can't get out – trapped together – because this love is unsurpassable and we both know it.

Will this pain one day leave me? I don't know. Will I one day wake up without the urge to purge myself? Will I wake up with a smile instead of a tight grin? Will it get better?

I reach my arm back and cup the back of his head, running my hands through his wonderful head of hair. He kisses my arm as I massage his scalp and when I turn my head right back, he kisses my lips with gentle, succulent pressure, chaste and lingering.

Panting, he demands, "Tell me."

I tug on his hair, pulling his head closer, our noses crushed against one another's. With certainty, I tell him, "I love you, David."

His face lights up and one hand sweeps down to my belly. "Hmm, my gorgeous girl."

He wraps me tight in his arms and I switch the light off.

I'm just not like him. While he instantly sleeps, I lie awake, my mind wracked by guilt.

I killed a man.

I killed Billy's dad.

More than all that, I told my father I meant to do it. I lied to get myself off.

I lied.

Even Daddy's love didn't extend to forgiving murder, so how will David's?

Daddy – who watched me pour from my mother's womb, who taught me everything I know. A hard man, a challenging man – but always there, always with money, always with solutions to pick up the pieces.

Even he abandoned me.

So, what's to say David won't too?

**

The next morning I wake before David, who is pretty tired at the moment from commuting to work and learning lots of new things in his chosen profession. I lay next to him, watching him sleep.

David's the only man for me. Even when I was with Luca, he used to say to me: "I know it's not me you really love, but that doesn't matter. I'll take you as you come." I used to smile at Luca and tell him he was wrong, even when he was right. Luca was smooth, the smoothest I ever knew, the most exacting lover you could imagine. It's his business after all, but I couldn't help feeling that I was a trophy lover to him. I mean… he could have any woman, but he pursued the beautiful wife of his ex-employee…

When I refused to let Luca come inside me, always insisting on condoms, he'd say to me, "I understand. But one day you will accept me." The reality was, I would never have accepted him, not really. With a condom on, it wasn't even real lovemaking. There was no real exchange and he didn't know me. David may not know everything about me but he still knows me better than Luca ever did.

Pure and simple, Luca was a band aid, covering the pain, and even then he wasn't a very good bandage because look at me now – I'm back in the arms of the man who broke my heart when he was the last person I ever thought I would run back to. The one and true thing I know is this: David is the best father my children are ever going to have. Simple. Billy has a temper but David knows how to disperse his son's anger whereas the only thing Luca knew to do was shut down a problem rather than work through it.

Sex, it seems to me, is just sex. It's become meaningless, in a way. I don't know how it got to be like this for me. Maybe the numbness inside is why I don't feel the things I should do anymore, like guilt, regret, pain, happiness, sadness – you could use me as a pincushion and I'd feel nothing.

David shakes awake violently, his eyes springing open, the bed juddering beneath him. He's gasping for air, so I move closer and notice a cold sweat on his forehead. Catching his hand in mine, I whisper, "Baby, it's okay. I'm here."

His pupils dilated, I watch them gradually shrink and he blinks, staring into my eyes. "Just a bad dream. Just a dream."

He rolls away from me and I feel rejected. He doesn't mean it, I know; he's just trying to protect me from his broken heart. I shift over and press my cheek against his back, my bump pressed against his lower back, my arm around him.

I slowly stroke my hand through his body hair. At thirty-two years old, he's finally growing a little hair. He has some sprinkled between his pecs and also the line running from his navel to his lower abdomen has now started spreading, fanning out across his skin.

I wish sex could seem special again, but it just seems like an exchange now, a cheap consolation. I give so he feels better.

"Oww," he complains.

"Sorry, I guess junior's a little overexcited."

"Something like that."

"Oww," he says again, the baby kicking still. I shift back slightly and he tugs on my bum, reassuring me, "Don't leave me Ade."

We lie still, the baby kicking his father. Silence.

And the pain drifts between us. The invisible. The indescribable pain. The non-physical.

"I know it's not been the same, Adrienne," he begins, the tone of his voice letting me know he plans on initiating a serious conversation. "For that, I'm sorry."

"People say time heals all, don't they? I think it's utter fucking bull."

He takes my hand, presses his lips to my knuckles, and pulls it into the centre of his chest to encourage me to hug him tighter.

"But we still love one another, don't we baby?" he asks, needing to know.

"Somehow, we do," I agree, "which I guess counts for something, right?"

"It accounts for everything, Adrienne."

He turns on his side to face me, the sheets bunched at his waist. I smooth my hand over his chest and a tear falls from my eye.

Tears are like blinks these days. They fall without me being able to stop them. They fall and fall. Maybe I do feel after all, or maybe being in constant pain is something you get used to and tears merely extenuate the bottomless agony I really feel.

"Oh, Ade!" he cries, pulling me tight to his chest. He wraps his arms so tight around me, forcing me into hiding against him. His leg thrown over me, I let out a whelp and cry in his arms.

Maybe it's the hormones.

Maybe it's extenuating extenuations.

"I love you so much, David!"

"Me too, me too, baby!"

Madly dotting kisses across my head, he shudders with tears, too. It seems my tears are the only method of extracting his.

My heart aching and pounding, utter breathlessness caught in my throat, I push my face deeper into his chest, seeking relief. It seems relief was despatched to some far-flung island long ago, however, and all we have left is the search for something else to tide us over while we work through our issues.

"I SLEPT WITH LUCA!" I shout.

I don't know why.

I just have to have it out.

He stills, his fierce hold slackening around me.

"You said you didn't."

"I TRIED!" I cry. "I tried to keep it from you but I can't. I love you more every day and it's painful to lie to you. I can't hold it in. I slept with him. I lied to try and protect you. I didn't love him. I did it because I was in pain. I didn't enjoy it. He was good but he wasn't you, he just wasn't you... you're the one... I don't love him, I never did, I don't... I'm not explaining myself well!" I gasp, seeking air.

"How many times?" he growls.

"I don't know, David, I don't know." I try to push my face into his armpit to hide away from all this, but he pushes on my chest and looks into my eyes, then down at my belly.

"Whose is it?"

My lip trembles. I find breath and murmur, "I don't deserve that."

"Whose kid, Ade."

I shake my head, side to side. "I'm five months gone, David. Five months. Do the maths."

"Whose kid?" he repeats, his bottom lip bitten to shreds.

"Yours. Yours! I made him wear condoms. I dumped him, remember? Since the day we got back together, it's only been you. I got rid of him. I never loved him! I was a trophy to him, David!"

I throw myself over to the opposite side of the bed, away from him.

Burying my head in the pillow and thumping the mattress with my fist, I cry, "I love you, David! Some days I wish I didn't. Some days I wish I didn't know what love is, but I do. I know what love is and it hurts, it hurts so much."

"Make love to me, Ade," he asks, pulling me back toward him, "make love to me. Please. Take charge. I always do but now I want you to. Take me. You can do what you want with me, I've always been yours."

Tears freeze inside my eyes. I have no idea what he's asking of me. Proof I love him? Proof I still lust after him?

"I'm pregnant, David," I whisper, begging him not to force me to be who and what I'm not, "I need you. I just need you. I want this betrayal... this shit we're going through, to fuck off, and everything to just be good again."

"No." He shakes his head. "Make love with me. To me. However you want. Connect with me. I don't want to push myself on you anymore. I'm asking for you to initiate something for a change, anything... that will show me how you need it right now. Show me."

I beckon him closer and summon him to cuddle me, his head on my chest. Laid on his side, tucked against my body, I lie on my side too, my leg over his body. Bringing the blankets up around us, I tell him, "Lie still, David. Lie still and count my heartbeats."

He nods, his hair tickling my nipples as he does so.

"Listen carefully and count them. Keep counting them. Don't stop?"

"Okay?" he whispers.

After a few minutes pass, I explain...

"Every one is for you. Every one. I want to die. I want to die to end this pain, this torture, knowing you felt so alone you sought solace in drugs and meaningless sex instead." He tries to lift his head and silence me, but I keep him locked in my arms and remind him, "Keep counting."

"Okay."

"Carrying Lucinda, I was terrified. After Marcus, never in my wildest dreams could I have imagined I'd fall in love with someone as wonderful as you, my prince."

He groans, and it turns into a wail as he covers his face with a hand. "Please don't, Ade."

"I didn't think I would want another child, and when I fell pregnant with her, it was a shock. I hadn't prepared for it. I've got my mechanisms for every different scenario but there wasn't one for unexpected pregnancy and all the way through carrying her, all I could think about was the doctors that said my chances of carrying a child to term in the future were diminished by the beatings he gave me."

He lifts his head sharply, looking down into my eyes. "No, Ade. I don't want to hear this."

I nod. "I was terrified I was going to lose her. I was petrified. But more than anything, the dull silence came back to me... the numbness... the needing to shut off, to self-preserve. When I found out about Violet, I went to the doc and she put me on anti-depressants. I just recently came off them for this baby's sake."

He caresses my cheek with his hand. "I love you... you should've told me."

I nod, holding his palm to my cheek. "I know. I'm sorry. I'm so sorry. I just... I have it all locked down. In here," I motion, pointing to my head.

He lies back down on my chest and I stroke his hair. "So now you know you can carry a baby okay, you're not as frightened this time?"

"Oh no, I'm still frightened. Every woman is. Maybe I healed better than they thought I would... maybe I got a shoddy medical opinion. I don't know. But I'm still frightened, it's just that... this time I know, there are worse things to fear than losing a baby... like losing you, too. I guess," I sob into my hand, "I just didn't allow myself to really believe... for so long... of course I've always loved you, but I always thought... one day... you'd see through me and go, you'd leave and that would be it."

He presses his lips to my heart and kisses me right there.

"Please, David. I just need you in my arms. I don't need any of the rest. I just need you in my arms. Please! I'm too broken right now for anything else. It's never that I don't love you, but sometimes, I just can't... I can't! I want to be loved, I want to be wanted, I want you to know what I want and I know that is ludicrous," I exclaim, both of us laughing, "but sometimes a hug is enough. I realise that now. I just need you close, nearby, here," I point beside me, "doing your thing, being with me, making sure I'm okay. I'm alright with you taking care of me. I am."

It's simple: sometimes I can't let myself feel, and therefore, us making love becomes just a process for me. I don't want it to be like that, but sometimes, it is. I'm so broken, I don't know where the pain begins and ends. I don't know what's pain or real feeling; passion or insanity; sadness or self-hate. I don't know.

"Please," he begs, his hands stroking up and down my back, "just stay with me. It's all I ask. Don't leave. I'm not going anywhere, I promise you. Just stay. Just stay. Let's stay, both of us."

"I will," I repeat, "but it burns, David. Right now, I don't want to make you feel rejected, but holding you like this, it's enough, it's plenty right now. If I say no to sex, it's not because I don't love you or don't want you, it's because I'm hurting and I... I just need affection. Your love is too much when I'm feeling like this. The way you make me feel is so... it just... breaks me open. I just need your arms and you. I just need you. I don't want to flood out. I want to stay secure. Just while I carry this baby. I just… my heart can't take it. That's it. That's what I find so hard to say, baby… my heart sometimes just can't take it."

"Okay, okay," he says nodding against my chest, "okay, okay. I'm here."

I take his cheeks in my hands and lift his face up to mine. Kissing him hard, the smack of our lips echoes around the room and I keep kissing him, regardless of whether he'll end up aroused. I kiss his face all over.

"I love you so much," I declare, "the day we first met, I knew then."

"I knew too," he says, panting, "I knew too."

His mouth moves around, kissing me back, kissing me everywhere. He's solid against me, his cock pumping and raging with blood, but he won't pressure me. Not David. He's never been like that. He's never forced me to do anything I don't want to. We both tried to live a lie to protect one another but look how that turned out. We learned the cost of lies. Now all we know is the truth is better, but a different cost may be incurred this time.

He kisses my breasts and I warn, "No, David."

He spits from between his teeth, "Fuck, Ade. I want you! Christ, you drive me mad when you're like this… tits and arse and belly… I want to devour you."

I don't want to make love. It'll be painful, like always, having the beautiful man I'm married to make love to me – while the exquisiteness of it all is lost beneath my pain.

"No David," I repeat, "please. Try to understand."

"God you're so beautiful."

"That may be, David," I stare up into his eyes, "but you've yet to see what's beneath."

TWENTY-NINE

May 2009

It's a beautiful, light May night, tropical outside for the time of year. I'm almost finished breastfeeding Marissa, our third child, and I'm sat up in bed naked as I give her what I hope will be the last feed of the day. Six months old, she weighs a tonne now and I'm ready to get my body back. She's wearing just a nappy because it's that warm tonight.

"It's so hot," David complains.

"I know! Try feeding in it."

He flops down on the bed, having just put Lucinda and Billy in bed. The sight of his white cotton boxers against his pink, sweaty skin makes me heat inside. We've not had sex for almost a year and even though we're still struggling to get back what we once had, we do love one another and I do want him back in my arms.

I don't think he's playing away. He's dedicated to me and the kids and he goes to work, always comes home tired, and tells me about the people he works with who are all also parents or middle-aged. It's not like before. I can tell he's not taking drugs because he doesn't have those massive downers he used to have when he got home. I just know in my gut – after having those six months apart and knowing how beastly it was not being together – we're both determined to stay together, whatever it takes.

After finishing feeding Marissa, I wind her and a large

burp signifies she's full and happy. Her eyes droopy, I kiss her forehead and she makes a series of baby noises before dropping off to sleep. David takes her from me and the sight of him holding our baby skin to skin makes me melt. I'm absolutely besotted with my husband, but that little sparkle of magic has disappeared and I'm desperate to get it back. I think he is, too.

He gently plops Marissa in her crib, opposite our bed.

"We can move her in with Lucinda once I've weaned her off, don't you think?"

"Yes, it's safe to, I reckon."

We talk about the kids, about work, but we hardly ever talk about us.

Marissa safely in bed, he stands by the window, looking down on the light world outside. For nine at night, it's still so bright.

I lie back on top of the covers because it's too hot to sleep under them. Arms above my head, I shut my eyes, sleep already on its way. I blow cool air up my own face, but it's just not working. It's sweltering.

"Shower with me, Ade? We'll turn it down to freezing."

I open my eyes slightly and stare at him. Even though I can only see the side of him, I can see he's hard inside his boxer shorts.

"Why don't we get hot first?" I sound lusty so I must be feeling brave, and when he gawps at me, I open my legs to him.

"Adrienne," he tells me lovingly.

"Come." I hold my arms out to him.

He drops his boxer shorts on the way and there are no socks on his feet anymore.

Cold feet... what cold feet?

"Ade," he groans as he lays himself between my legs.

David kisses my lips open with sweeping caresses, coating my tongue thoroughly with his. The exchange of fluids mouth to mouth sends me wild, juices from my pussy wetting my thighs. His taste – there's something aphrodisiac about it – and I feel wildly aroused.

"I'm not on the pill yet," I warn him as he pushes my breasts together and licks them, careful not to hurt me. My nipples hardened from feeding, he need not be so gentle but I love that he is.

"You won't get pregnant. I read about that in your books," he murmurs, enjoying my large breasts, which are not as pert as they once were. However he seems to love them, how ever droopy they are.

"There's a chance."

"It's a chance I can cope with."

He moves back up and kisses me again, at the same time slipping two fingers between my legs. He finds me very wet and gently slips in and out of me, almost bringing me to orgasm.

He stops touching me just as I'm about to come and nudges his cock against my opening.

The discomfort is momentary and once he's breached the sensitive opening, he slips in fully, stretching me wide. I still always know David's there and he's the only man I've ever enjoyed pushing into me without a condom.

"God, Ade," he growls, and kisses my cheek, repeatedly.

"Let's not wake Marissa," I warn.

He rolls over so I'm on top and grins up at me. "Ride me."

I grin back down at him, pushing my hair over my shoulders. I haven't had it cut in ages and my hormones have made it grow wild. It now spills all the way down my back in thick, untamed waves.

David cups my breasts and brushes his thumbs lightly over my nipples.

"You can be rougher. I'm tougher than you imagine, David."

He bites his lip. "I've missed you."

"Me too," I groan, and with my hands holding tight to his

abdomen, I move slowly over him. I know why he wants me on top – because while I have control, he'll last longer. In charge, he might run away with his urges and it'll all be over too soon.

He grabs my meaty rear and digs his fists into my flesh. I gasp, throw my head back, and he tells me, "The tips of your hair are stroking my balls."

I look into his eyes, grinning. "You like that?"

"Fucking love it."

I hum with a dirty little chuckle.

I run my hands up and down his chest and slip around him slowly, trying to be gentle because it's been a while and I don't want to hurt myself or him.

He sits up and pulls on my legs so that they're wrapped around the back of him.

Taking note of my words, he sucks one of my weeping buds and drinks. He sucks my other breast and groans with delight, his hands digging hard into my ass.

"Oh god, David. I'm gonna come, I'm gonna come!"

"Wait, wait!"

He pulls on my buttocks and jumps his body up and down until I'm shuddering around him; aching, bitter tears leaving my eyes as my right thigh jerks wildly for some reason, the other thigh okay. He's so strong, like this, carrying both our weight. I sometimes forget how strong and manly he is, because he's just so gentle and loving. I love him, so much.

He uses so many fingers to punish my clit, my orgasm spins wildly out of control and he throws me beneath him, pounding into me while I bite down on my own hand to stop myself screaming – like a girl once more.

He pours into me, thickening and pumping, throbbing.

Pulling up off me slightly, he looks down into my eyes. Cupping his cheeks, I stare at his face and pull his lips to mine. Kissing gently, he smiles between kisses, twitching inside me.

One hand buried in my hair, he pulls gently on it and slips to the side of me, kissing me with his tongue. Allowing my hands to roam his skin, he comments, "I miss the dates we used to have... when you'd have mascara and lipstick smudged all over your face afterwards. I used to wipe you clean, remember? After I'd fucked you for hours."

I kiss his arms, smiling. I rarely wear make-up anymore. Maybe I will when I return to work.

"I miss those days too, David. I really do."

"Maybe we can make some new, better memories soon?" he asks, holding me close.

"Perhaps... or maybe we'll hit retirement before we get chance."

The perfection of new love – how do you get it back? Does it ever transform, or is that newness something we're always looking to rekindle and it's what makes monogamy so fucking hard?

"I know one thing for sure," he says, blinking fast.

"Yes?"

"Your soul... it's still the same. I see her dancing behind your blue eyes. Maybe one day... I'll get to meet her?"

"Maybe... although my soul's not blue, David. This is an outfit, this body of mine. My soul only wears black, and beneath, she's not pretty."

"I never cared for pretty," he says kissing my fingers, "only interesting... and I always knew it."

"Oh, David," I gasp, holding him to me.

"Oh baby," he says, and we begin madly kissing.

Kissing faces.

Kissing bodies.

Kissing everywhere.

Hands tugging, pulling. Manipulating.

It's hours later I look at the clock to see it's the middle of the night. We skipped the shower, happy to lie sweating and glued to one another, sated and burning with desire.

It hurts but that way, I know it's real.

THIRTY

A month later...

We're at a summer dinner party held at an old Tudor inn up in Thornton Dale, on the North Yorkshire Wolds. The heat is stifling and I hope this summer is going to cool down soon!

David's English department holds a summer bash every year and while I was pregnant last year, I abstained owing to sickness and whatever. David didn't attend either, maybe to be gentlemanly, maybe to avoid temptation. However, I doubt it was the latter. Looking around those gathered with us, the people of his world are mostly men and stiff, middle-aged women who've already sent their three or four kids off to university and are now chasing the career they always wanted.

Anyway, it's quite clear there are no female temptations lying around the office for him to salivate over. Not that I ever thought Violet was a crush for him – just an escape from reality. I'm told David has all his students in the palm of his hand but I know he would never risk his career, not when he fought so long and hard for it – not when he loves me, as well. I know that.

Stood together on the expansive lawn behind the pub, where other patrons are standing with us puffing on cigarettes or watching their kids chase round the park and garden, we hear his boss, Professor Kelvin McCall shout, "Dinner's served, guys."

We walk into the Tudor building, featuring a number of characteristics such as timber beams, low doorways and large, squat fireplaces. I smile at David and he looks at me as if to say, *Don't let this be my life forever!* I think he's terrified he'll end up with a pipe and slippers... sooner rather than later.

As we're seated around a table for twelve (us, David's five colleagues and all their partners), I'm conscious of my short dress riding up in the sweltering conditions, sticking to the wooden chair beneath my butt.

"Adrienne, let me help you," David's colleague Fred says in my ear.

Sitting by the side of me, I try to fend him off, but he's out of his chair and pushing mine in for me before I can resist.

His wife, Trudy, pipes up, "Fred, leave the girl alone."

"It's okay," I reply.

"No, he's only trying to be nice so you'll talk to him."

I stare around the table, because it seems we've got an audience now.

"I'd talk to him, anyway," I mumble under my breath.

"She's just crabby because the last time she looked pretty was in 1975, wasn't it Trudy?"

The little private dining room we're sequestered inside falls silent and I feel my cheeks heat. David saves the day, pronouncing, "Well, my wife could wear a sackcloth for all I fucking care. I find her intensely beautiful whatever form she comes in. I guess I'm lucky."

His words take my breath away. I look down at my lap, trying to hide the furious blushes everyone must surely see.

The rabble around us continue with their own conversations as Fred and Trudy begin squabbling over why they stay married to one another. Meanwhile David takes my hand underneath the table and whispers in my ear, "Let's never be like them."

"Let's," I nod, and turn my face to look at him. Wearing

a navy-blue, sharp shirt, he looks blinding. I dare not kiss him while we're seated so close; with all these people near us in such close confines, I know they will detect our lust if I kiss or touch him. I have to restrain myself otherwise I don't know what I will do. The heightened sex is the only thing that makes us forget about the pain of his infidelity, my mistrust and our mutual yearning to get back what we once had. The sex recently has been filthy, down-and-dirty fucking – I love his body! I'll never tire of it. Luca had a nice body, too, but it wasn't David's. Luca was thicker with muscle whereas I love how lean and slender David is. He's my husband and no other figure could replace him.

I barely remember Luca now. He didn't know about the little places I like to be touched, about the ways in which I like to be touched. David's the only man who's ever been able to make me come with a few touches or caresses because he knows my body so well – and because I'm in love with him.

The starters are served – cod loin wrapped in various things. We're having a set meal because apparently it's cheaper and all these people here tonight with their big houses, their Gold accounts and their holiday homes seem to constantly be watching the pennies. I couldn't live like that. I think if you haven't got it today, you can get it tomorrow. Why waste a day wishing for something, when you can plan to have it in future?

David races through his starter and I look around the room, eating slowly, watching as couples engage in chitchat about the food. Kyle and Naomi opposite me are complaining there are too many spices on the fish. Maybe they should have asked for it raw!

As David talks to a colleague by the side of him, his hand slips beneath the large, white napkin across my lap and beneath my short dress. His finger presses my panties to the side and his digit shoots straight into me. I look down and while his finger swirls inside me as he's otherwise engaged in conversation, I realise nobody will see what we're doing. The serviette is large and the white, starched tablecloth is also partially covering my lap. I bite down on my lip and hold my knife and fork tight in my hands, trying to focus on not exploding. Naomi asks if I'm having trouble with the food too, and I respond, "Too spicy," even though I think it's been done perfectly. They start chattering at me, pretending like they're connoisseurs. Have they eaten at the Lido, at the Ritz, on the QM2? No, well I have, and I know good food because I've been around and this is good food.

When David pulls out and rubs my clit, I quickly reach for my water and down it in one, my eyes shut and my breath gathered by the water as I fight the urge to gasp.

He removes himself, wiping his finger on my leg before taking his hand back to his own lap. I briefly catch him fixing his cock in his jeans and decide I will fucking kill him when we get home.

Melvin's wife Cherry, who's now watching me peculiarly, asks, "How's motherhood, Adrienne?"

"Wonderful, actually," I tell her, and she regards me strangely. I know I'm sweating and flushed, and I have no real excuse for it. I mean, I know it's warm in here, but I probably look like I've just been to the sauna.

I actually just had an orgasm beneath the starched table cloth.

"Sure you're not pregnant again, love?" She peers at me.

I snicker a little, using the napkin to wipe the corners of my mouth as I finish the rest of my starter. I lie and tell her, "I'm still breastfeeding."

I stopped a couple of weeks ago, but she doesn't know that.

She pulls a face at me, as if breastfeeding is the most disgusting recreation in the world. Let's see what she's got to say for herself, then… eh? Then make a mug of her.

"I thought that only lasted a few weeks?" Melvin asks.

I was introduced to everyone earlier at the bar. Most I

hated, except Melvin. There's something naughty about him. Don't get me wrong, he has a slap head and a penchant for trains, plus I tower over him, but he has a cheeky little look in his eye all the time, as though he finds most things privately amusing, so I tell him, "I wish, Melvin. The recommendation is to feed for six months but... Marissa's just turned six months and getting her off the breast hasn't been easy."

Melvin keeps my gaze, not a bit put off by my talk of breasts and weaning. His wife next to him, however, looks horrified. "So, Ade, does it hurt? I always wondered why Cherry didn't feed ours."

She thumps him in the side but I tell him, "Doesn't really hurt. Just means all the responsibility is on the mother. I mean... I froze some milk so David could do the odd night feed but really, feeding is a comfort thing for your baby as well as nutritional."

"How do you... how did you... cover it up?" Cherry asks, her hand touching her face in so many places, I feel dizzy.

While she's awkward as fuck, Melvin is quite to the contrary – he's intrigued and amused.

"Oh I don't hide them, Cherry. Why hide what God gave me?"

Melvin chuckles and she gives him a dirty look. "She's joking," he tells his wife, but everyone around us seems to have left behind their own conversations to hear ours and they're all now looking at me and Melvin, who appears to enjoy belittling his better half.

"Has David tried it?" Melvin asks quickly.

David turns in his chair, breaking off from talking to Geoffrey next to him who's well into medieval shit like David is.

"Of course I've tried it," David tells the table, "why wouldn't I have?"

Melvin raises his glass, "Quite. Why wouldn't you?"

Everyone gets stuck into their main meals of game pie while Melvin stares into space, having a daydream by the looks of his blank gaze. Cherry beside him looks furious and I whisper across the table to her, "Couldn't you breastfeed, Cherry?"

She shakes her head.

"I couldn't with my first," I admit.

"Really?" she asks.

I won't tell her about Marcus and him saying nursing was disgusting. So I just say, "Went dry. It happens."

She nods her head and I spot a woman who perhaps didn't have the confidence or didn't have the support. Melvin seems to be in his own little world most of the time. As I stare at Cherry eating her dinner, I realise the clothes she's wearing look severely out of fashion. Maybe she's trying to be retro, but her raised sleeves and the see-through lace trim at the neck of her dress just appear dated to my eye. Maybe she didn't have a mother to give her confidence. Maybe Melvin sucked it all out of her, or he's just so consumed by himself, never to notice his wife needs a little boost now and again.

"Did your mother help out with your kids?" she asks me.

"She did with Billy. Unfortunately we fell out of touch and I haven't seen her in a while. She hasn't met the other two yet."

She nods knowingly. "I wish I'd had my mother when I was bringing up my kids. Might've helped. Though it doesn't seem to have affected you the same way. Look at you, glowing and so slim already."

"Genes, I guess. Besides, I'm not perfect, but David loves me. It counts for a lot," I tell her, and with my eyes I gesture at Melvin beside her, who's playing with his food, muttering to himself. Oh how I'd love to live like him, constantly in my own, little world.

Cherry's eyes glaze over and become puffy. She excuses herself from the table to go to the bathroom and the funny thing is, Melvin doesn't even notice.

Driving us home later, David asks me, "So what did you think of the crowd?"

"You want me to be honest, or what?"

"You hate them," he states.

I choke on laughter. "Let's just say, when it comes to the Christmas party, I'll allow you a night off on your own if you wish."

He chuckles, clutching the steering wheel tight as he takes us through the country roads.

"What about a hotel, tonight?" he asks, raising his eyebrows as he glances over at me.

"I know somewhere round here, actually," I tell him.

"Oh yeah?"

"Hmm. Keep following this road and we'll see, eh?"

I grin and he does, too. Rachel has the kids tonight. In fact, she and her new hot doctor boyfriend Dr Kers, a beautiful Egyptian man, are looking after the kids. Dr Kers could make even the coldest of hearts break so it's no wonder she's into him. Perhaps that New Year disaster she had showed her what she actually wants out of life – just a decent man. It's not as if she's not got a lot going for, after all.

After a while, David recognises where we are and asks, "Are we going to Castle Howard?"

I nod. "We are."

"Won't it be closed?"

I laugh. "Oh yeah. But I happen to know the foreman. He'll find us someplace to stay. My father brought me up here a lot when I was young. Dad was known by everyone."

David looks across at me. "Really?"

I sniff slightly. "There's a lot you don't know yet, David."

"I know, Ade, oh I know," he says, and reaches over to touch my knee.

Does David realise how badly I tarnished Dad's reputation doing what I did? I don't think he does. Either that or his love is blind.

"Here we go," David says, pulling up on the gravel driveway towards the huge country estate. "I guess we're not going in the usual entrance."

"No, head for the servant's… well, what was the servant's houses!" We both laugh and he shakes his head.

"Sometimes I really forget you were born with a silver spoon in your mouth. You're so fucking normal, unlike my colleagues."

I chuckle and breathe a sigh of relief. "I *am* so glad it wasn't just me!"

"Melvin's a tosser when he wants to be, ignoring his wife. The rest of 'em are bloody snobs."

I laugh hard. "Oh my god! How do you work with them all day, everyday?"

"Well, that's just it," David says, turning the wheel as we slink into a parking space, "we all have our own stuff, our own specialties. None of them have read as much feminist literature as me and I'm quite glad I hold that over them!" We chuckle together. "It's not like when I was in marketing and there'd be meetings around the table every half hour. It's just me teaching and counselling the poor little students through the most angsty time of their lives."

I gauge David's expression and ask, "Do you miss your old job?"

"Certain aspects of it, yeah. Like adult interaction."

His cheek twitches, guilty memories creeping back up on him.

"I know what you mean. So… the dream job, not all that dreamlike, hey?"

He purses his lips. "Maybe our idea of what we should do with our lives is rarely right. Maybe life takes us in the direction we're meant to go, fate and all that. I don't regret quitting that job, but I do miss the varied work I used to do at

FMP, it's true."

We see a man walk out of some outbuildings with a torch in his hand. Thankfully it's Bill, which is short for some long-winded Greek name, but he calls himself Bill and is the nicest man you could ever meet.

"Come on," I say to David.

The moment we step out of the car, Bill exclaims, "Adrienne! Oh my goodness... ADRIENNE!"

So, he does remember me then.

THIRTY-ONE

Bill lives on the estate in what would once have been a gamekeeper's or house manager's cottage I'm guessing. Now it's his home and also his office. He's very Greek in his ways but he's lived over here long enough that he speaks perfect English and loves a pint of mild. His wife and two children are upstairs in bed. He's only up because he's Bill – he never sleeps – preferring to stay up late watching the CCTV monitors on one screen and episodes of *Kojak* on another.

"How come we haven't seen you in so long?" he asks me. "Where's your papa?"

Sitting across from Bill at his kitchen table, I look to my side at David, who's trying not to seem interested in my answer to that question. Maybe this was a bad idea after all…

"Didn't you hear?" I ask Bill.

"No," he says, "hear what?"

I try to sound genial. "Mum and Dad moved to Spain, like they always said they would."

He shakes his shoulders. "But without you?"

"Yes."

The Greek in him looks over David, measuring him up. "Nothing to do with this guy?"

"What? Us falling out?"

"Umm," says Bill.

David looks at me with a little smile.

"I think Dad would be pleased I married anybody. Just someone to take me off his hands!"

Bill frowns deeply. He may run this big house, estate and all its gardens, but aside from *Kojak*, he rarely watches the TV – certainly not the news. He's got no idea what happened between me and my father.

Bill reaches over the table and taps his hand lightly on the back of mine. "What happened?"

I look straight into Bill's eyes and say, "I killed a man."

Bill stares at me, unresponsive. After letting the words sink in, he suggests, "Must have deserved it, then. Known you since this high," he gestures at the height I was at four years old, "never hurt a fly, you. While your father was up here meeting with all his friends, you were out in the woods rescuing clipped birds and flattened hedgehogs."

My heart breaks for Bill, because he has no idea who the real Adrienne is. That girl is long gone.

"People change, Bill," I say, "but one thing's for sure, Dad will never forgive me for what I did so now, we don't talk. It's why I haven't visited this place in a long time. In fact, I avoided a lot of places for years because they were just reminders."

Bill nods in understanding.

"Ade brought me here because she thinks you can give us a place to stay tonight?" David asks, the tone of his voice telling me he wants to get me alone – as quickly as possible. He goes onto explain, "We're a little out of our way here. We live in Harrogate but were over in Thornton Dale tonight for a work's dinner."

Bill examines David for a long time. "What work do you do?"

"I'm a professor of English at York University."

Bill brightens immediately and exclaims, "You're a clever boy, then!"

David laughs lightly. "Sort of."

"He's got more degrees than I can list," I tell Bill, "it was sort of how we met. I was a librarian at the university where he was studying and he asked me for a book. The rest, history."

Bill smiles. "Kids, yes?"

"Yes," David says taking my hand, "three!"

"THREE!" Bill holds his head in his hands. "Mine are teenagers now! Terrible little people! Terrible! Although," he frowns, "not so little all of a sudden. Growing too quickly."

We all sit quietly and David's hand slips into mine under the table. He wants to be close to me and I understand why. It's the first time in so many years I've actually talked about my life before David.

"You must love her very much to give her three," Bill says to David, who looks at me and whispers, "I love her like you wouldn't imagine."

Bill sniggers. "Even tiny little men like me can imagine, mister."

We all laugh and David and I finish the cups of tea Bill made for us earlier.

"So... someplace to stay. Well, one of the tourist guide flats is empty right now. It's one of the nicer ones, too," he says smiling, "nobody will know unless you make too much noise, okay?"

"We'll be like mice," I say, trying to stifle a fit of the giggles.

Bill stands, lifts a key from a hook, and gestures we follow him out of the house he lives in and down to another row of properties at the opposite side of the courtyard.

Gravel crunching beneath our feet, David almost hoists me off my feet when he throws his arm around my waist, the both of us walking behind Bill.

"I love you," he says, his lips pressed against my ear.

We walk into a tall building with lots of flats inside. The walls grey and cool, it's an eerily quiet building inside, compared to the chirrups and tweets of the birds and insects outside. Walking up a sweeping staircase, Bill tells us, "It's a busy time of year. Everyone's resting."

He jiggles a key in the door of a modest flat and lets us inside. It's homely and with little touches like wooden hearts on the walls and houseplants, pictures of farm animals and Castle Howard in its heyday.

"Wilhelmina keeps a good house, hmm?" he asks me.

"Your wife certainly does," I tell him. As he hands me the key, I kiss him on the cheek. "Need us to tidy up after ourselves?"

He shakes his finger. "God, no. Wilhelmina would kill me! Please, enjoy. Remember, quiet. I don't want people to know I've got a favourite, nor that I give out freebies."

He winks and leaves us, shutting the door behind him.

As soon as Bill's footsteps echo no more, David rushes at me, and I throw my arms around him. My chest robbed of air, my lungs burn, because the way he's been looking at me all night has had me in knots I can't untangle without his touch.

His arms tight around the back of me, his bottom lip is secured to mine as he kisses me deeply. His hair is soft and slightly matted with sweat in my hands as I run my fingers from his scalp and over his shoulders, to his skin beneath his cotton shirt, as sweaty as his head.

He takes me to the floral sofa and lays me down. While he undoes the buttons of my dress at the top, I undo his shirt buttons and his belt buckle.

Pulling his cock free, he pulls my knickers down my legs and kisses my exposed breasts as he wriggles into position between my legs. Powering straight into me, I warn him, "I only just went back on the pill."

He thrusts again, deeper, and I gasp, trying not to be loud.

"I don't want–" I try to protest, but he knocks the wind out of me again.

"Hush, let me fuck you."

I take his cheeks in my hands and ask, "Come on my belly. Please."

He nods and continues fucking me. It's not long before my head is hitting the arm of the sofa hard and he's staring into my eyes, waiting for me to come. I'm almost ready to come when he pulls out and tickles my clit with two fingers.

"No, David, no—" I beg, trying not to cry out – loudly.

He makes me come with his fingers, so hard, I'm sweating and spurting all over his hand. He pushes back inside me and the fireball he just created by making me come explodes so that with every thrust, I want to scream. He puts his hand over my mouth and my eyes shut as I focus on the sensations; the heat, the enormity of his cock, the way every thrust hurts and terrorises me yet sends unreal pleasure bolting through me with every movement.

Shaking furiously, my body endures one orgasm after another as he seizes my hips in his hands and on his knees almost, fucks me harder and faster.

When I'm ready to pass out, unable to take anymore, he pulls out and comes all over my breasts, waggling his cock around and smearing himself everywhere.

Trembling, unable to move, he carries me in his arms to the bedroom where we find a quaint little metal-framed bed with more flowery furnishings.

He peels down the bedcovers and slipping my dress from my shoulders, puts me in bed. I lie reclining, my fingers teasing through the sperm on my skin. I notice as he undresses fully, there's a tissue box beside me and I mop myself up as he closes all the curtains and finally, climbs in beside me. I still stink of him but I love it.

Pulling me close, I lie listening to the pulsing rhythm of David's heart as he teases his fingers through my hair.

"Did you see the look on his face?" David asks me.

I lift from his chest to look up into his brown eyes. "What do you mean?"

David caresses my cheek. "He recognised me!"

I stare at him, bewildered.

But then it clicks.

"NO!"

He chuckles, spluttering with suppressed laughter. "Well he does have that room with his TV and stuff… maybe he watches a bit of late-night porn!"

I sit up in bed and cover my face with my hands. "This is horrendous! Why do I want to laugh?"

David sits on his knees too, facing me. "I guess I was more popular than I thought!"

We both fall silent and his gaze falls on my body, whispering desire with his sweet, tender look.

"I want to fall in love with you again," David says.

I swallow hard and for some reason, nerves hit me and I need his arms. He's not in love with me? I don't understand. Trekking over to him through the sheets, I sit in his lap, my arms around his neck while he strokes my sides.

"What do you mean?" I ask, "don't you love me?"

"I love you so much, it hurts… but I want… it to be more. For us to know one another, to love what's beneath, and talk not just about the life we have now, but everything that brought us right here. Get to know one another properly. Like, dating. Finding out about one another. All those things we were too scared to do the first time round."

I pull back, swallowing again. Acid crawls up the back of my throat and I mumble, "We're second timers?"

He nods, his eyes heavy with exhaustion, his body ready for rest.

"I forgot that, David. To me, it's still like the first time."

"I understand," he says softly, whispering kisses at the side of my head, "and I love you but I want the key to your heart and I still feel like you haven't really given it to me."

I pull his cheek so he has to look at me, our noses pressed together, breath mingling. "What do you mean?" I ask again, wishing he would say whatever it is on his mind.

"Every time you speak of the past, like you did tonight, I

love you a little more. I have confirmation that you're the person I always imagined you to be... tending the wounded, hating the snobs, preferring to be in nature rather than being fawned on and flattered. You're the woman I always thought you were, you always will be, but for my sake and yours, I need you to go back into the archives. I really need it."

A tear drops from my eye onto his hand and he licks it into his mouth.

"I'll try," I tell him.

"Okay, that's good enough for me."

We get back into bed under the covers. "Do you think he watches porn for the women or for the men?"

David chuckles. "We're back to this now?"

"Well, you did say he was looking at you funny! He's never tried to flatter me... well, not in that way!"

David wraps his arms around me tight and sniggers in my ear. "I should bloody hope not! The dirty old git."

I smile and weep at the same time. Can I contain this love? After everything we've been through, it just seems to get stronger. Am I fooling myself this is real? Is pain just a requirement of mine, to fulfil my need to self-immolate, or is loving someone so much a genuinely painful thing? Two sides of myself war over that constantly.

I stir up the courage, from deep down inside of me, to say, "I know I'm not meant to admit it... I know having three, healthy children, a stable home and a loving husband is meant to be enough... but will this pain ever go away?"

I burst into tears and he cradles me tight.

After letting me cry for a little while, he looks down into my eyes with tears in his.

"I can't take the pain away, not until you show me it."

I huddle in his arms for warmth, safety and security.

THIRTY-TWO

I stir to find David standing by the window of the flat, watching the world outside. For a moment, he doesn't see I'm watching him so I have time to admire his body. His white cotton boxers hugging his tight ass nicely, desire stirs inside my belly. He's not particularly broad-shouldered. He's slender and in proportion. His skin is flawless and legs muscled, hair perfection. He's my husband and I love him but as I watch him, pangs of anxiety gather inside me at the same time as pangs of lust.

Because he cheated on me.

A slip I would've forgotten about by now. A one-time thing he admitted a day later, guilty as sin and sick with himself. But for months, and years, he fucked Violet behind my back. Some of the times he fucked her, he may have fucked me on the same day too. How can anyone do that? How is his conscience? Is it stuck in a painting, like Dorian Gray?

I watch him watching the world and it occurs to me, he's not as strong as I am, which is painful. That is the matter which provides me with so much pain. Is he worthy of me? I do trust him. I believe he's not cheating on me anymore, but something's gone, and no matter how hard he presses for this second courtship, I know things will never be as good as they once were.

Because he's not as strong as me, I've got no-one to fall back on. I don't have many friends, none that I can really confide in anyway. How would I start to tell a girlfriend about my past? I'd rather not. I have this ache, this constant hunger, for someone who can take the pain away. I wish that person was David but he's the one my pain is wrapped up with and his visage – his presence even – is just a constant reminder that instead of talking to me about our problems, he sought solace in drugs and sex with someone else. Maybe this pain will eventually cease like he claims it will – but – it's been a couple of years now since I realised things weren't right between us. Even though it took forever for me to find out he'd been cheating with Violet – I always knew deep in my gut something was wrong with our relationship and revelations aside, I still hold onto that. Something's wrong. I don't know what, but something's wrong.

In my peripheral vision I spot another poem, left on his pillow, no doubt for me. I don't know if I want any more of his achingly beautiful words, but I lift my head very slightly to read it:

The Time We Walked In The Garden of A Country House

It always starts with a birdsong. And another.
A brash of fireworks, and masks, and cascading waters,
and done things.
In a tender instance, the strings of a bygone event are
resurrected.
These things that are only in our heads.
The dead who linger and laugh in the woodlands.
Lush, whispering ivy chews and courses through the dear-
departed
doors and windows.
A girl perhaps, who watched but could not see.
It is no prison now.
She has left, in the black, and the moss, and the smoke.

And all around is sprang from a grey and babbling history.
Terrible lost. It is good that they are eroded and grant us
chance.
Below, in the crypt, some names have all but rubbed away.
A stranger has found his way home through the godless
centuries.
Because without knowing it, these are the places built by
children
and kept by dreams.
So it goes.
It ends with a birdsong. And another. And I turn to you
again.
O terra, addio,
A terra, addio…

Sometimes I have no idea what he's trying to tell me, but a part of me knows there are depths to David he dare not manifest in any other way but this. I turn my head and watch him again. He's still not noticed I'm awake, lost to his thoughts.

Watching the world, his eyes dart around. His arms are folded, a sign he's resistant to everything around him. He's broken, too, in ways I can't imagine. Will he ever tell me about his own past? Are we two broken people destined to be crap together? Some days I wake up, and I look at all the beauty in our world – our children and our home, successful careers and food in the cupboards – but it's still not enough. The anti-depressants help but my doctor said the infidelity is something we need to work through with counselling and discussion. She said I sounded lucid and logical and I was open about my feelings with her. I don't suppress my feelings like David does. Or maybe I do. I think if one of us started opening up, the other would, but it's difficult to make the first move. I have suggested counselling to David a number of times but he always brushes me off. I told him that in a safe setting, both of us might feel more inclined to confess, but he totally disregarded the idea. Therapy is not something he will consider, he's told me. Which I think is a sign of weakness and is unattractive in a man.

I'm unhappy. There. I said it. Nights like last night just prove it. Nights when I find myself comparing ourselves to other couples, trying to make our marriage seem better than theirs. It's wrong to compare. It's not good. I'm unhappy and the secret ingredient to happiness has evaded me.

I was naïve and ignorant yet happy when David and I first met. Now I'm just kidding myself.

Is it selfish of me to want someone to pick up the pieces for me? I'm broken and I can't fix myself. I've tried. I'm strong but maybe, I need someone much stronger than me to make me feel whole again. Right now I just feel empty and worn. I feel lost.

"You're awake," he says, and sees I have the poem clutched in my hand.

"Mmm-hmm," I reply, gesturing I read it.

He strides to the bed and sits on the edge, taking my hand in his. Sitting up in the pillows slightly, I plump them behind me and keep the sheet tucked under my armpits.

"I was thinking…" he begins.

"Yes…?"

He taps his lip with his forefinger. "Our first date."

I stare at him, not sure if I should break his heart or not. In the fresh light of day, I guess my mind isn't as onboard as it was last night.

I try to smile into his soft gaze but part of me knows David is too sensitive to accept the way my mind works. When I think something's unlikely to work, it's probably because it won't. I guess accountancy has drummed the romantic out of me completely.

"We never had a first date, did we? Not a real one," I comment. In fact, I think I never would've got with him if he hadn't chased me. I never would've got with anyone in fact. I'd still be single right now, Billy my only companion.

His shoulders hunch forward. My words clearly hurt and he repeats, "No, we never had a proper first date. However, I'd like to make up for that."

I stare at a wall and try to sound understanding when I tell him, "I didn't care about dating. I still don't. I just want love, it's all I've ever wanted."

I sigh, the weight of sadness heavy on my heart.

Love should just be love, right?

Daddy didn't love me.

Nor did Marcus.

Now, David.

I must be a wrong sort of person.

They all just keep hurting me.

He frowns and peers at me from beneath his brow. "Why do you sound strange? You were up for this last night?"

I nod. "Last night I had a few wines inside me and before that, I hadn't had a drink in months, remember?"

His whole body tenses and he stands, walking back to the window.

He's emotionally stunted and I have no idea why.

"If I open the archives, you have to, too."

He glances at me. "You've become defensive all of a sudden. Maybe this was a bad idea after all."

Oh, I'm defensive. I'm the one with something wrong with me.

He'll never admit what's really going on here – why he really cheated on me. His problems are part of the reason and he won't admit it. The porn. The drugs. Why did he do porn and drugs? Why did he get caught up with Violet? Surely there was a point at which he could've said no?

He continues, "Well, I was thinking of taking you to a lodge for a night... with a hot tub... a fridge full of wine and food, just me and you. I don't think Mum would mind."

I remain silent. For a minute or so, anyway.

"Don't you think..." I begin, "...that if you were ever going to tell me about the way in which your dad abused you, you would've done so already?'"

He turns fast and points at me, holding his tongue, his breathing hard and heavy.

I keep eye contact with him but it's like I'm looking into the eyes of someone I don't even know. The fury emanating from him scares me and he turns his eyes away again – dark, black eyes of torment.

"You know nothing, Adrienne!" he exclaims.

I can see we'll get nowhere with this. I don't need this hostility from him. I don't want this pain. This hardship.

I've tried. I've tried. I've tried so hard. Until I'm blue in the face.

Truth is, I need to know about David's past. I need him to open up to me – to demonstrate he has the courage and the strength to deal with what I might have to say, too. I don't think he has the stomach to hear about my former life. When I tell him everything about Marcus and me, some tiny piece of me imagines David might run off again and take up with another woman, to avoid the truth and abscond from reality. He can't take the real world but he has children and he needs to see that they come first and right now, they can see I'm unhappy. Billy asks me why I look sad all the time and I have to lie and tell him I'm just tired. Whenever David is in the room, I wear the face of a happy wife to keep the peace.

"I'm sorry," he says eventually, "why don't we... well... let's forget that idea. We'll muddle through somehow, won't we?"

Muddle through?

I take a breath and try not to sound sarcastic, agreeing, "We'll muddle through."

This will never get better, not until he admits the root of why he cheated.

He's been blocking his emotions for so long and I realise it's because he can't deal with them, but he needs to learn to, otherwise my heart is going to die a very slow, painful death – without someone to confide in.

***

Midweek, a few days after the summer dinner, I take Marissa with me into Leeds to buy some new clothes for her and Lucinda. Billy hates clothes and I always get David to buy all his stuff from Primark because everything he wears gathers holes and mud within days of him having it on.

Strolling around, my mind wanders. I don't want to put Marissa into nursery care but soon I will have to make the decision as to whether I will go back to work. As I walk around the Victoria Quarter wearing my Prada shades, I can't find anything I like even though there's plenty of nice stuff here. It must be the mood I'm in, maybe.

While I'm in Whistles, where I always manage to find something to cheer me up, a woman in a tight suit glides over to me.

"You're Ade, aren't you?" she asks.

Popping my sunglasses on top of my head, I look closer.

Violet.

Her sludgy green eyes betray sadness, fatigue and drug-taking. So this is what he broke my heart for.

We get the measure of one another before I ask, "Got another job, then? Must have… to be shopping in here."

She folds her arms and nods. "Big of you to ask."

"I am big. Being big also means I can drag you from this shop by the hair if I wish."

I'm rather cool and calm, to be honest, but I want her to suffer.

"You got the messages then? I wasn't sure," she says.

"Not until about six months after you sent them."

I smile a tight smile and she peers into my pram, wondering if the baby had anything to do with the fact I'm still wearing a wedding ring.

"Sorry," she says.

"You mean nothing to me," I tell her curtly, "and nothing to him, either. Why don't you find someone you do mean something to?"

I lift her left hand for my inspection and notice she's not wearing any wedding rings.

She snatches her hand out of my grasp and snarls, "So high and mighty aren't you?"

Within seconds I lurch for her throat and squeeze hard, so she hasn't got any breath or fight left.

This is what escaping a psycho can turn a woman into.

"Listen to me, little girl. Maybe I should thank you for telling me about his antics. Or maybe I should kill you because you knew he had a wife and family and you made a beeline anyway."

She chokes and thankfully, with her long black hair, none of the staff surrounding us can tell I've got my hand around her throat.

I release her and the instant I do, she falls to her knees.

"He didn't tell you, did he?" she gasps.

"Tell me what?" I demand in a growl that doesn't sound like me. I'm just glad Marissa is sleeping soundly in her pram right now.

"He made me get an abortion. One of the condoms split."

I stare at her. "That's a lie."

She stands, wobbling on her feet. Staring into my eyes, weeping, she admits, "I know what I did was wrong. I was trying my luck. I was lonely and frustrated, I know. I seduced him. I initiated it. However, he could've said no. He could've denied me. At any time. But he did more than fuck me. He ravaged me. Fucked me so hard in the mouth, I was often sick. He did things... he was animalistic. I liked it... I enjoyed it. I wanted it. Looking back, I realise he was doing all that to let out his frustrations, too. It was a mess. He made me get an abortion. I swear. I swear. The baby would be two now," she repeats, wiping her eyes.

She's just the face of the reality I've been burying ever since I found out he cheated on me. David has another side to him he's never shown me.

"Did your husband find out?"

She nods. "We split. I'm better off alone."

Her words hit home.

Better off alone.

Some days I wonder if I wouldn't be happier on my own, I have to admit. Ever since David and me got back together after that time apart, I've been wondering if love is pain, or if pain is knowing the one person you thought you could trust betraying you is something you never get over.

Violet gathers her bag off the shop floor and searches for a tissue, wiping her eyes.

"He's more manipulative than I thought," I tell her.

She nods, ever so slightly, agreeing with me.

"I have to go," she mumbles, "but I am sorry."

I watch as she walks across the mosaic Victorian tiles of the arcade, rubbing her neck as she walks away.

I purchase a red blouse just because it's red and in my size and I have a lipstick at home to match. I don't really want a new blouse, and when I push Marissa (still sleeping) out of the shop, the adrenalin hit that normally follows a purchase is about a million miles away from where I am now.

I find a bench to sit on inside the shopping mall and pull out my phone. Dialling Luca, he answers, "Is that you, Ade?"

"It's me. I'm in Leeds, shopping."

"You don't sound okay. What's wrong?"

"Oh god," I sigh, breathing heavily down the phone, "I just bumped into fucking Violet."

He snickers. "I hope she wasn't actually fucking when you saw her, although I wouldn't put it past her."

"Bloody hell, Luca," I tell him off, because he is absolutely tactless, "I just need someone to talk to. Can you meet me for a coffee?"

"I–I–it's not a good idea. I'm with someone else now and she works with me. She'll ask me where I'm going."

I take a deep breath. "I'm sorry. You're right."

"I'm sorry, too," he says, "but I can't. Now, I've got to go."

"Can I just ask you one thing?"

"Hit me with it."

"Did she get pregnant? Did he admit that to you?"

Luca sniffs hard. "You should ask him."

"That means he did, he got her pregnant. You're not denying it!"

"I have to go–"

"Fine, go then!"

I hang up the phone and throw it into my bag. He calls me back but I haven't got time for his emotional blackmail.

I sit staring into space. Can this be happening – again? How many lies will David try to spin me before he actually tells me the truth?

A message arrives on my phone and I glance at the screen, reading: *Where do I meet you???? God, Ade!!!!*

I reply: *I'm in the Victorian Quarter. Sitting on a bench in front of the coffee place.*

Luca: *Wait there.*

Ten minutes later, I spot him, looking around trying to find me. He's wearing an obligatory pair of chinos, blazer, shirt and a nice tie. He doesn't look stuffy, but he does look like the boss. He eventually spots me, hiding.

He blushes the moment he sees me and sits beside me.

"Come here," he asks, and I dive for his arms. In his embrace, I cry.

Crying is all I can do.

"Why don't you learn? I warned you about him… he will never change. It's not getting any better, is it?"

I sit back and wipe my eyes on a handkerchief he passes over.

"I thought… maybe it was," I confess, imploring him with my eyes to be kind to me today, "…then I asked him last weekend to be as open with me as he wants me to be with him. Then he shut down again."

Luca takes my hand and kisses my knuckles, stroking my skin. "He's not the man for you, Adrienne."

I warn him with my stare. "How do you know that?"

"I know."

Luca's black hair caresses his collar; it's almost shoulder length and glossy, like silk. He's clean-shaven everyday but despite his Mediterranean skin, his beard pushes through with a dark shadow before noon. He's stocky and about the same height as me. The most striking thing about him is that he's incredibly soft-spoken and kind.

I think the truth is, when Luca got frustrated with Billy, it was really because he was frustrated with me. That day in Betty's, Luca begged me to move away with him and start again and I said no. He challenged me to answer whether I still loved David and I didn't reply, which he took to mean yes. So he charged off, sent me a mountain of annoyed, heartbroken texts, and eventually gave up after I admitted that yes, I still loved David and couldn't bear to leave and never see him again. When I reunited with David, Luca backed off, and I haven't heard from him in all this time.

"Where do the lies begin and end, *cara mia*?" he asks, still stroking my hand.

I search his caramel eyes for truth and find it right there, staring straight at me. Luca would've just loved me and I should have met him first.

I smile a tight smile. "You deserve better than me."

"*Cara*, do not say that," he demands gently, in his strange accent. It's sort of Italian but more Dutch-English, having been brought up in Amsterdam. Luca can speak fluent Italian because when Luca's father met his mother, his mother still didn't know a word of English so from a baby, Luca spoke Italian like his mother and Dutch-English like his papa. As an adult he also learnt Spanish and French. Comes in handy in his line of work, I imagine.

"Luca, what should I do?"

He shakes his head. "I cannot tell you that."

"He did get her into trouble, didn't he?"

Luca looks at me, not reacting. He doesn't say yes or no.

"I almost strangled her in Whistles. I'm not joking," I say when he thinks I'm being silly.

"You grabbed her?"

"Yes!" I exclaim. "She was apologetic but so insincere and even after I nearly took the breath from her, she bloody well came out with that bollocks about an abortion."

Luca coughs and covers his mouth, obviously shocked.

"What?" I ask him, sensing there's something on his mind, something he's not telling me. "Please, Luca. Please. Tell me. Put me out of my misery!"

"He told me she just…" He gestures with his hands, like something is floating away. "…lost it. One of those things. His version to me was that getting her knocked up was the reality check he needed."

"Bastard," I mutter.

Staring at Luca, who's rubbing his hands over his face in disgust, I realise Luca has been more of a gentleman than I would've liked him to be.

"You should have told me this back then, Luca," I growl.

"Stop saying my name. Say it once more and I will not be responsible for my actions."

I stand my ground, holding his lusty gaze.

"Take me into the public toilets and have me, will you? Make me as bad as him, will you? Make me as much of a villain as the man who broke my heart, will you?"

He doesn't respond, except his expression darkens, then saddens.

"Ade–"

I shake my head. "Fuck your pity."

Wiping another tear, just another drop to add to the bucket, I stand up ready to storm off. He stands alongside me, holding my elbow in his hand. His grip tight, he won't let me go until he's said what he needs to.

"I wish I had the courage... to promise that I'd wait for you, but if I did, I might be promising forever, because you'll never leave him and I'll never be with the woman I really want."

Strike me down with a lightning bolt. I wouldn't get back up.

I rush at him and kiss him, my arms tight around his neck, his hands holding my back. He smells strongly of cologne and clean cotton. His rough stubble catches my lips as he hungrily and literally eats my face. There's no romantic way of painting it! He never kissed me in public before and this is what I've pushed him to – public displays of denied lust.

Luca yanks himself off my lips, gasping for air, his eyes shut. He's shaking. My nipples are hard and I want to be close to him, to hear him whisper my name as he slides inside me like he used to do.

"I'm sorry," I tell him suddenly, "I've been a fool."

Slowly, he opens his eyes to regard me disdainfully. "A man must protect his heart, Adrienne."

He turns and walks away, leaving me stood here like the ground just fell in and I've no way of crawling out of the crater I've buried myself inside.

I blink and notice he's gone from the arcade and my life.

A text from him arrives on my phone and I read: *I love you.* His words bring me instantly back to life and I shake myself together, checking on Marissa. She's still fast asleep and snoozing in her pram. My little angel. I can't be sorry I have her, but I am sorry I conceived her to try and fix a broken marriage. I get myself together, push the pram and myself forward, and drive back home, ready to confront David.

THIRTY-THREE

When David arrives home at 6.30, he's shocked to find the kids are all tucked up in bed – even Billy – who I fobbed off, telling him Mummy and Daddy just need a bit of time to ourselves to have a nice, romantic meal. I bribed my eldest child with video games while the girls are overfed with milk and so bloated, they're already sleeping.

Despite what I told Billy, when David walks into the kitchen to find out what we're having, he finds the stove cold and my heart frozen.

"Ade, what's going on?" He looks at me, suspicious.

"Sit down, and remain seated," I tell him, gesturing at the small breakfast table.

Hesitating, he seats himself slowly, worry in his dark eyes. Unbuttoning his sleeves, he rolls them up, preparing to get dirty.

"I crossed paths with Violet today."

He stares at me, numb, in shock.

"What happened?" he asks, breath catching in his throat.

"I almost strangled her in Whistles."

He clears his throat. "She's bad news."

"You don't have to pretend," I warn him, and he looks up into my eyes, his worry increasing by the second, "cat's out of the bag now. She told me about the child she aborted. Your child."

He grinds his teeth. "There. was. no. child."

I stare at him, wondering how I could've spent so long with someone I don't even really know. Maybe my self-esteem has always been a bit low, but I must have been really off my head to marry this man.

"With every lie, you etch away at what we had David. You've been breaking us ever since the first moment you lied."

He stands from his chair, legs scraping the floor. "Stop it, Ade."

He stands rigid, fists clenching and unclenching.

"I'm only telling the truth, something you're incapable of."

"She. is. lying," he musters, adamant there was no baby.

"Today, I saw the truth... standing right in front of me... That woman, a shadow of her former self. Broken. From my point of view, she's the result of your point of view. The lies you preach like gospel, the manipulation... your capacity to twist everything to your own advantage."

"You're emotional," he says with large hand gestures, "having seen her. I understand. You're not thinking straight. But I swear, there was no baby. She's lying. Why was she there, today? In a city full of people, she found you! It's too much coincidence. She pounced because she failed to break us up... she's trying to follow through."

"Keep on lying, let's see where it gets you," I snarl.

"I was safe, I was always safe. In the porn industry, we had checks every other bloody week. It's always been drilled into me to be safe. I mean for god's sakes, Adrienne! I wouldn't... what if..."

I know what he's trying to say. He wouldn't dip his nib in her without protecting me from her disease.

I shake my head at him. "Just admit you made her have an abortion, and then we can both move on with our lives."

"Made her?" His forehead furrows. "I couldn't make any woman do anything. This is modern times. How could I make her have an abortion? This is ridiculous."

"You're the only thing that's ridiculous," I scold.

"I'm going for a shower, then I'll order in a takeaway," he says in a strained voice, turning as if to move out of the room and towards the hallway.

Pressing my hands against his chest, I halt him, making him look into my eyes. "Did you insist she have an abortion?"

"No."

Part of me believes him, but another part doesn't trust him.

"I don't know what to think."

"I was careful and I ended it with her, not because she was pregnant, but because I hated her and… I just wanted to be with you. That's the truth," he says.

"Why can't you tell me the truth, David? About your past? About… why you *fucked* her?"

It still cuts deep.

He looks down into my eyes and whispers. "Either way, I know I'm still going to lose you. So why put myself through the agony of reliving my *past* as you term it, when it'll all be for nothing anyway?"

I try to think of a response, but I don't have one. His defence is a bullshit excuse.

There's fear in his eye, which I find difficult to deal with. How do I smother his fear, when all I feel is betrayed and cursed to love a man physically incapable of telling me the truth? I feel sympathy, but I also feel that what we had is lost and we're never going to get it back.

"I'm human. I need love. I need someone to love me," I tell him, "it's so simple."

"I love you," he whispers, husky. "Today was just another blip. Ignore what she said, she's poison."

I shake my head. "You don't know what love is."

"I bloody do," he says, "it's being out of your mind in love with someone and not knowing which way to turn."

"Then I don't want this love," I retaliate, my tone of voice grave, "if this is what you expect me to expect."

"You don't mean that."

He tries to pull me into his arms, but I shrug him off and step away from him.

"The way you treated Violet was disgusting... she told me about you making her vomit... about being an animal."

His expression darkens and I realise I have finally hit a raw nerve. So, he did make her sick. Shaking my head, I whisper levelly, "My love doesn't stretch that far... to forgiving your abuse of another human being to make yourself feel better."

"I love you," he repeats.

I stand back against the sideboard and admit the truth I've been loathe to for so long. "It's not enough. I live in pain every day, knowing you've lied to me, over and over again. I will be happier alone, David."

"No!" he begs, rushing to me, dropping to his knees before me. "Please don't give up on us! I'll do anything."

"Then agree to therapy."

He begins to speak, but no real words come out.

"I thought not," I tell him.

"You don't want to know about me and the stuff I've seen and done, Ade."

"Then we're done."

"We can't be done!" He pulls his hair and stands to pace the room.

"We can't keep going round in circles!"

"Why are you talking like this? Who have you spoken to since you saw Violet? Why are you... who's got in your head? Why are you being like this? I don't understand."

The whopping reality hits me, knocking the wind out of me. David's a control freak and I've let him have the reins for too long. I married my father. I married a less violent version of Marcus. I'm the cliché. The stereotype. Is this my comeuppance for bad deeds done in a former life? How did one glance in a library mean I married a man like my dad? Or am I the lowest common denominator, and it's actually my fault all these men get fucked up because of me?

Part of me knows it's not over. Another part of me knows nothing's going to get better. I choose my ammunition and blurt out, "I lied about Luca."

"What?" He sounds angry.

"He was wonderful. He wanted me to leave and start a new life with him but I wasn't ready for that. Also, he knew I still loved you and he couldn't get over it."

He holds his hand up and begs, "What exactly are you saying?"

"Violet was just somewhere to poke your cock, but Luca was more to me. A friend. He was kind. It wasn't meaningless. He meant something to me, but I still loved you."

Holding his forehead, he asks, "Did you get back with me for the kids? For their sake?"

I shake my head. "No. I still loved you and felt we had unfinished business."

"You've been talking to him... today, haven't you? It's why you're all like this... rabid. Gearing for a fight."

"I spoke to him for five minutes and he said he couldn't tell me what to do! He doesn't try to manipulate me like you do."

"He's got to you! I KNOW IT!" he exclaims.

I turn my back on him, wondering if I'll ever be free of this sadness, this perplexing desire to stay with him and make things work even when every moment we're together hurts. He doesn't understand this from my point of view. If he loved me, he'd let me go.

He broke my heart and it doesn't seem like he'll ever be the one to put it back together. This is one big mess I am unlikely to untangle.

"Do you want me to be in pain forever?"

"Ade, I just wish you would forgive me."

I turn and look in his eyes, a maniacal smile breaking out over my lips. "That's just it, I did. The shame is, I can't forget. I also know something's not right. I don't know what it is... but something's not right between us and never will be again."

"Ade, please–"

I avoid his eyes. "I ate earlier so I'm going to bed. I need space tonight so I'd appreciate it if you slept on the sofa."

"I won't–"

"You will," I growl, turn on my heel and leave the room.

I haven't eaten and I haven't had an appetite for anything in months and months – so that's how I know – this marriage is beyond broken.

***

Dear Christian,

How are you? seems a good enough way to start an email. I guess I should really open with an apology, however. So, here I am – saying sorry. I mailed your work address and it bounced back. Luckily someone I kept in touch with from the course still had your personal email and kindly forwarded it to me, I hope you don't mind.

You were right about David. I shot you down without hearing you out and I was wrong to do so, but I was a woman in love, just trying to make sense of everything. For me, that David could hurt me seemed ludicrous, but here I am now. Yes, he has hurt me.

I wonder if you might tell me if there was a reason you tried to warn me, such as a sighting you had of him with another woman? Looking back now, it seems odd you would suggest to me that I was so unhappy. 1) because you didn't really know me. 2) because I worked so hard at seeming to be happy and managed to convince many other people I was. Am I right? Did you see him with someone else?

Best, Ade

*

Dear Adrienne,

It's great to hear from you. I heard you got chartered status and began working your magic in the world of work. I was really pleased when I found out, actually, because something in me feared you would finish the degree you worked so hard for and then toss it down the drain for love. I guess I just know David's type all too well.

...and you're right. Few years ago, I was having lunch with colleagues one day and saw him with a brunette in a slutty outfit. I knew his face because I'd seen him drop you off for lectures a couple of times.

I watched them barely eat a scrap of dinner. He was in and out of the toilets, and white bags changed hands a lot. There was no romance between them, that much was clear, but from the way she looked at him you could tell she was entranced.

I knew there was something not right about it all. Contrary to what you think, your big blue eyes tell all – and it was clear you were very unhappy beneath the surface. I'm a gentleman and I only confronted you because of what I knew.

So now you know. I saw him. I suspected...

I've given up my lectureship and now I'm in Shanghai, living it up. Earning a nice crust, practicing what I preached for so long.

I married and have a daughter on the way.

Nice guys don't wait forever, Ade – so next time – don't beat around the bush.

I wish you every happiness. Because you do deserve happiness.

Christian

THIRTY-FOUR

While I was happy to hear Christian had moved on – and felt grateful to him emailing me at all – his words still sting, even now as I reread them. Three months have passed since we communicated, but every so often, I reread his email and try to tell myself I do deserve happiness. I wish it were that simple. I also wish I had a time machine to go back and tell myself to shake awake and realise what was right in front of my nose: David is/was a liar.

Christian's email and Violet's confessions were the nails in the coffin I had been loathe to bury. Our marriage is over. Two weeks ago my solicitor resent David the divorce papers I tried to file the first time and this time, he signed them without fighting it.

David lived with his mother for a couple of weeks after I chucked him out, but when she called round and asked to know everything, I told her about Violet's abortion and then she chucked him out too. As far as I know, he's found a flat in York so he no longer has to commute. Despite everything going on, Rachel and her doctor beau have been helping out whenever they can as I try to gather myself together and rebuild.

Now when I wake in the mornings, I feel sad of course, but I also feel a strange sense of freedom. I don't have to worry about how he will react to everything I say or do anymore. After the affair, I used to worry that refusing him sex or affection might give him fuel to go out and do it again. I used to worry if I didn't ratchet up the heat in the bedroom, he might get bored and venture elsewhere. I used to worry if he ever saw I wasn't coping as a mother, he would fly off the handle and go out to find drugs, unable to handle real life. For so long I was not only worried about my kids but about him, too. Now I only have to worry about them. The girls are too young to really know the truth but Billy really hates me – with a passion. Perhaps in time he will understand but right now, I'm the enemy, because I'm the one who's made his father leave. I think some part of me knew this would happen and it's why I put off ending my marriage for so long.

Another part of me feels like a rib is missing. A limb, maybe. The man I pledged my life to wasn't who I thought he was. The loss of him is like a death but the more time we spend apart, the more it seems he was never even really here in my life. He lied so much, my mind often conjures other lies – other lives he led that he's still not told us about. That's what I do – conjure – because he's never given me the answers I've begged and begged him for. All I'm left with is pondering who he really is.

I've been seeing a counsellor my doctor recommended and we've discussed everything extensively. I've been recommended for CBT because it's clear I need to change my way of thinking, having believed for so long that shutting down is better than opening up. I'm willing to try and change, whereas David never was.

Confrontation is something I hate – but only because in the past, it earned either violence or hatred in retaliation for speaking my mind. I have to learn to stand up for myself and what I want. I need to come to terms with Marcus's death and stop blaming myself. I need to move on and start again. Some days, I don't know how I will manage it, but hopefully I will.

I think the funny thing is, over the years I've heard so many girlfriends say, "When we split up... I found out all these things about him... you think you knew someone..."

The proverbial doesn't seem to apply to me, however, because I'm still clueless as to why David lies, cheats, hides from the truth and refuses to fight for us when he says I'm the one he loves. Is the man really so arrogant to submit to therapy, or is there a trauma he suffered that he refuses to admit to anyone, even himself? Guess work might drive me crazy if I let it.

The sad thing is, even now I feel divided about divorcing David. The decree absolute yet to be announced, I sometimes wonder whether there's time to make everything good again. Make reparation. One last-ditch effort maybe? I love David so very much. I've never loved a man more. Living with the pain he caused me for so long was too much however. My soul was dying while I wondered whether I would ever be enough for him.

I sometimes lie in bed at night, wondering if he'll come flying through the door and submit to therapy, to making us work, to doing whatever it takes. To committing himself to making me happy once more.

Then I remember the damage is done. We tried to give it another go and it didn't work.

So the cycle continues. Loving him. Wanting him back. Remembering what he did. Knowing the things he did don't match up to the man I thought he was. The man I married would never have gotten another woman pregnant and then forced her to abort her baby, threatening her he would stop seeing her otherwise.

I'm sat at my office desk right now, wondering about all these things. It's a wonder I get any work done with the amount of stuff on my plate. Somehow I get through everyday and somehow I'm putting tea on the table, too, and my kids are clean, warm and fed, safe and happy enough, I suppose. The sad thing is, David's made no motion to see his kids. Maybe he's trying to distance himself from everything, I don't know, but he's always taken care of his kids and now – nothing.

My phone set to silent so I can concentrate on some reports, I catch it glowing out of the corner of my eye on the desk. Picking it up, I notice several missed calls actually and the number ringing is unknown. Hiding in my office, with the landline switched off also, I have the door locked so nobody can disturb me. Nobody would even know I'm in here without finding a way to unlock the door.

"Hello?" I answer, unsure.

"Mrs Lewis?"

"Yes," I answer.

"I'm Dr Benitez, I'm calling about your husband David."

"Yes?" My heart starts skipping really fast, missing a ton of beats, palpitations in my chest making me light-headed.

"He was rushed to hospital last night. Someone spotted he'd fallen into the River Ouse and he was rescued by a bystander."

"What?"

"You'd better come to the hospital, Mrs Lewis."

"Where, I mean, which hospital, where?"

"York General," he replies.

"I'm on my way."

In a blur, I put my heels on, grab my jacket and bag and leave the office.

Passing the receptionist, I tell him, "If anyone calls, I'm at the hospital. David's had an accident."

George asks me, "Everything okay?"

"That's what I want to know."

On the way to York in the car, I call Rachel from the Bluetooth and she answers, "Hey, Ade. Everything okay?"

"I'm on my way to York General. Haven't they called you?"

"What? NO!"

"A doctor rang… said David fell in the River Ouse!"

"Oh my god!"

I hear a mother desperate for her son to survive, no matter what he's done. "Adrienne, I'll pick up the kids and everything. Let me know what you find out and we'll come if we're needed, okay?"

I nod and she asks loudly, "OKAY?"

"Sorry, I was nodding. I'm just in shock."

"Me too. I'll let you go if you're driving. Take care and be in touch?"

"When I know, you'll know."

In a whirlwind, I leave the car parked on double yellows. I don't have change to pay for parking and I don't have time to search for a space. Besides with the speeding I did on the way here, I'm bound to be banned from driving anyway. I storm into the A&E department, asking where intensive care is. When I tell them my name, there's recognition in the receptionist's eyes and she takes me by the arm, leading me to a quiet room.

"Wait here," I'm told.

After an age of waiting, pacing, rubbing my hands together and pulling chunks of hair out, a tall man enters the room wearing scrubs.

"Adrienne?" I nod. He walks forward and holds out his hand, which I shake. "I'm Dr Benitez."

"Okay. You called me?"

"Let's sit down," he says.

"Okay."

He sits opposite me and I wait, expectant.

"David was brought in with water in his lungs. He almost drowned and would've done had he not been saved."

"Who's this man?" I ask gently.

"We'll get to that, Adrienne."

"Call me Ade."

"Okay," he nods gently. "Did you know David was taking drugs?"

"No," I say, "but I know he had a problem in the past."

"It's a current problem," the doctor says.

"Okay?"

"David's stable, but we have a witness who says he threw himself into the river."

"On purpose?" I ask.

"Yes," the doctor relays, "so for his safety, he'll be sectioned when he comes round. We'll offer rehab and therapy for him. We found a lot of cocaine in his system, not to mention alcohol. Were you aware?"

The doctor's tone and expression aren't judging me, but I'm judging myself. I'm responsible, aren't I?

"We're separated," I tell the doctor. "I tried to help him with his issues over the years but he wouldn't listen to my pleas. I think the drink and drugs have only become a problem since he moved out about three months ago."

The doctor nods. "That bodes well for his recovery if he's managed to stop before."

"Where is he now?"

"He's been moved to a room now. He's sedated. He'll be in a lot of pain when he comes round. We evacuated his lungs so his windpipe and chest will be sore."

"Do you know the name of the man who saved him?"

The doctor nods his head. "A man called Luca Van Duren. He was brought in too and treated for hyperthermia."

"They're friends," I tell the doctor, and his eyes crinkle.

"That makes sense," he says, "that he would jump in to save a friend."

I nod, a tear rolling down my cheek. It's November, not a good time of year to be getting wet in the murky depths of an ancient river. "Luca's been a good friend to him."

The doctor stands. "You're not meant to use your mobile phone in here but you can use the phone in my office to call anyone if you need to?"

I nod. "Let me go and sort my car out and I'll make some calls outside."

"Okay."

I find my car clamped when I get outside. No surprise. They're towing it away as I call Rachel and let her know the score. She tells me she's got the kids and Dr Kers will drive them all straight over.

I'm told by the nice clamp man it'll cost me upwards of a £1,000 to get my vehicle back.

Great!

When I get back inside the hospital, I seek out Dr Benitez and can't find him anywhere. I decide to wait in his office instead, because the door has been left unlocked, like he rushed off somewhere or something.

Half an hour later, he creeps into the room sweaty and exhausted.

"Was there a history of heart problems in your husband's family?"

"Yes," I say, thinking of David's father, who died young.

"David crashed and died thirty minutes ago. We opened his chest and worked on him for as long as we could. We did everything we could, Adrienne. I'm sorry."

I nod.

I nod.

I nod.

"My kids are on the way."

"Okay."

"Can I say goodbye?"

"We'll clean him up."

"Was it the drugs?"

He shakes his head. "The drugs and his fall didn't help, yes."

Is the love of my life really dead? I think I need to see for myself.

Dr Benitez uses the phone and whispers down the line so I can't hear.

"We'll go and see David now," he says.

I walk behind Dr Benitez, a Mexican doctor with big

hazel eyes and a head full of greying black hair.

Before I know it, I'm standing in front of a bed, looking down on a body covered in a blue sheet. This must be a case of mistaken identity! Surely!

"Are you ready?" the doctor asks, and the sheet is lifted down to his neck.

The moment I see his face, I die. Dead. Sealed up. Shut down. The locks are welded, never to be broken open again. I'm obliterated. My heart goes with him.

He looks peaceful, finally. A little blue, bruised and tainted, but peaceful. Asleep.

The love of my life is really and truly dead and I could do nothing to stop it.

I tried, I really tried, but maybe not hard enough.

There's really no cure for a broken heart.

There's no escape from the curse I brought upon myself, to never find true love.

"I love you, David," I whisper, the agony too much to bear, my body turning to walk away – my love left behind.

THIRTY-FIVE

As his coffin's lowered into the ground, I spot some people checking their watches, desperate to get back to their lives and loves. While I have three fatherless kids, they have a golf lesson or a lunch date to make and David's funeral is an inconvenience but a necessary thing to be seen at. Billy and Lucinda stand either side of me, holding my hands, while Rachel wails into Marissa's baby hair beside us.

David's brother Rob is stood opposite us, his wife by his side. He's as rigid as rock, unflinching, grief clutching at him so hard he can't bear to show it. I know that feeling. So far all Rob has done is throw money at the matter and carry Rachel to bed crying every night.

So much more pain than I ever thought possible is now my normal existence. I was born to harbour and wield pain, that is my one, true belief.

I see Luca stood behind the masses in the background, solemn, not seeking eye contact with me. I've tried to call him since he dragged David from the river but he never answers. I just want to ask him to tell me how he came to bump into David in the centre of York – when Luca lives in Leeds and they'd fallen out, too. Perhaps that's why he's not looking me in the eye and is refusing to answer my calls. He might have decided not to tell me how David came to meet his demise in order to protect me.

I don't hear any of the minister's words as he prays for David. When I'm offered the chance to scatter some earth, I refuse. I won't bury him. A part of me knows we never could have put things right, while another part of me wonders if time might have changed all that. Well I've had that possibility taken right out of my hands – the chance to put everything right.

Numb, I watch the crowd disperse and get in their cars to head for the wake. Luca leaves, walking down the hillside of the cemetery and straight for his car. I doubt I'll see him at the wake.

"Are you okay, Mum?" Billy asks me, and I look down to see his clear eyes looking up into mine.

"I will be," I tell him.

"Can we go? I don't want to stay. Daddy's going to be okay with the angels?" he asks me.

"Tucked up warm and tight," I tell him gently, while my heart threatens to shatter into a million pieces.

Someone speaks in my ear, telling me it's time to go, and I look and see Rob's wife Tina beckoning me with her eyes. I take a deep breath and step away. "Let's go then."

My children follow me as we walk to the funeral car and everyone rides in silence on the way to Rachel's where the wake is.

***

"I want a word," Rob says as the guests finally leave, most unsure what to say, what to do. I think most of them think David deserved what he got, the tearaway who might never change. We asked people not to buy flowers and instead to donate money to charity in David's name.

"Let's go to the study, then," I tell him, happy to see my kids and Rob's playing together on the floor, their spirits up even if nobody else's are.

Rob shuts the door and tells me without preamble, "You

shouldn't blame David. It wasn't his fault he was like that."

I stare at the stranger, who looks a lot like David, except he's thicker set and with a less kind face. His accent is slightly American, what with him having lived over there so long now.

"You've got things you can tell me? That might explain it all?"

He nods and points at the couch in the study, gesturing we sit together. His hands folded in front of him, he starts, "It was our dad… he wasn't a good man."

I nod along. "I sort of wondered. He only mentioned briefly, but I guess…"

He smiles a little. Maybe because he knows he doesn't have to convince me of anything. I'm sort of already aware.

"We were kids when Dad used to drive us for days out. He'd tell Mum he was taking us to the armouries or the local adventure park. Instead he'd take us to some car park and leave us on the backseat. He'd go into a woman's house. He'd spend hours in a pub. We'd be stuck on the backseat, sweltering sometimes in summer. He'd warn us not to leave the car but we'd sometimes escape and go stealing from a local shop, taking what we could because we were hungry and thirsty."

I swallow and take his hands in mind. "Go on, Rob."

He nods, relieved. "When you're a kid, you just sorta accept it, don't you?" I nod, agreeing, knowing exactly what he means. "But while to the rest of the world he was the good dentist, to us, we knew what he was. It used to drive David crazy, that everyone else was blind… and couldn't see him for what he really was. Dad even used to sometimes drive us to multi-storey car parks and park high up, opposite tower blocks of flats, take out his binoculars and spy on women undressing in the windows. Sometimes, if need be, Dad would take us into one of his slut's houses and we'd be forced to listen as he fucked her, or her and her friend. We were the excuse he used, so he could keep getting away with it. It'll come as no surprise to you that both of us started early, me when I was twelve, David when he was thirteen. Mum caught him in his room having underage sex... and hit the roof. The angrier she got, the more he played up."

I gasp, shocked. My love never had a childhood. My beloved David... had it stolen from him.

"Dad was dead when David became sexually active, but the influence our father had had on us never died... never. We were barely teenagers when we both watched porn videos... got magazines. Got high. Got fucked." Rob looks insanely sad, wiping his eyes. "When I told my wife, she almost left me. When I told her about Dad sometimes making us watch, she sent me for counselling and they..." He hiccups, coughing out his pain. "...they said it was child neglect and abuse, but nobody ever wants to admit it, do they? Mum neglected us... Dad abused us, making us adult before our time. Making us what we are... and I should've protected him... but I didn't. I could take or leave the drugs but we always knew David had a problem. He'd hide in his room for a week and emerge emaciated and unwashed."

I frown, shaking my head. "David was so sensitive, I think it must have affected him badly."

Rob agrees, nodding furiously. "I was responsible. Dad was my hero, so I did whatever he said. When David threatened to tell Mum, I'd rough him up a bit."

His hands in mine, I feel him shaking. He feels responsible for his brother's death.

"What else happened?" I ask him.

"When David started getting into trouble at school and stuff, Dad found it hilarious, didn't try to discipline his son. He encouraged him to be naughty in fact, telling him that was his only role in life... to be the clown he was destined to be, and me the elder, the one who would achieve and make it in life." Rob breaks down, covering his face. "We were kids!"

"What about Rachel? Didn't she know?"

Rob gathers himself and sniffs back his tears, taking out a handkerchief. "The woman you see today is confident and lively but back then, she was controlled and sad, nervous and… I don't know what the word is… I suppose, needy maybe. The best thing that ever happened to her was that he died. Otherwise, she never would've escaped the misery he brought."

For a few moments, Rob sits and breathes heavily, trying to recover himself.

"That must've been why she got so upset when she found out David was doing porn then… maybe she knew it was his dad's influence and she hadn't been able to prevent him going down that path, too."

Rob looks into my eyes. "Don't get me wrong, Mum and David were closer than I will ever be with her, but she let him get away with things, too. After Dad died, she was bailing him out all the time for things I would never be forgiven for. The stealing. Drugs. All of it. Parents always say they never have a favourite, don't they? But they do."

"I know."

Tormented, he wrings his hands together, shaking his head at himself. I wait to hear what else he has to say.

"You know Ade," he begins, "it sounds like if anyone was going to save him, it was you."

I look at the floor. "I tried."

"You did all you could from what Mum has told me."

I look at him seriously. "We were so happy until I got pregnant with Lucinda and everything went wrong. I have my own past and he couldn't deal with that on top of his."

"I'm sorry," he says, "I really hope you don't blame yourself."

"I do, though."

"I do, too," he admits, "because I got away scot-free, and yet my younger brother is dead in an early grave because of what me and my dad did to him. Bullying him. Silencing him. Forcing him to harbour secrets he hated."

I stand from the couch and look out of the office window, across the green lawns at the back of the property. "When David and I were happy, we were so happy. When we were sad, we were so sad. For so long," I turn and look down on Rob, "I had this pain in my chest, here," I point, "not knowing how to help him, save him from his demons. Now he's gone, the pain's still here, and do you know what I think it is?"

"No." He shakes his head.

"We were once so close, and now I know about your dad and everything, I realise the pain I was carrying was David's pain. I never knew it at the time, but what I was feeling was how he felt. I pride myself on thinking I'm strong, that I've overcome a lot... but even I couldn't live with the pain he harboured. I couldn't cope with it. So if he's lying in a grave now, it's probably better that he is... because the sort of pain he lived with is inescapable. Unbearable. I'm strong but he was sensitive, kind, beautiful... it must have bruised his heart... what you and your father did to my David. He never believed he deserved happiness. He dove off the deep end whenever I mentioned counselling. He lied and cheated because that was all he was brought up knowing."

Rob bursts into tears and even though I pity him, I'm not sorry he's in pain.

"I'll live with this forever," he splutters.

"And so you should. We're all that will keep his memory alive."

I sound calm, though I'm anything but. I'm just trying to get through the day for my children's sake. Being a mother is all that has saved me over the years and it will continue to save me for as long as I live because I live for them.

I open the office door and tell him, "I'm going to rent out the house and leave Yorkshire. I doubt we shall meet again."

He looks up through tears. "I'm grateful he knew love."

"Me too, but I will never forgive you. I ask that when you look at your own children, you try to imagine how they'd feel if they lost you. Then you'll know what you and your father are responsible for."

I leave the room, his shuddering tears echoing behind me as I leave. I collect my children from the living room and Rachel looks worried. "What's happened?"

I smile, faking my intent. "Everything's fine. The air's cleared. I'm taking my children home now."

She sighs. "But I need you all right now."

"I need space," I tell her, looking her straight in the eye.

"You could stay over?"

I shake my head. "We won't be staying."

I hold her responsible as much as I do Rob, because she turned a blind eye. I know about doing that, but I also know there comes a time when you can no longer turn a blind eye – and you either escape or die trying.

My kids are all that matters to me now and I am going to take them as far away from this godforsaken place as possible and never come back. It's a place of pain and misery I don't belong in anymore.

In a way, David saved me, and I'll always love him for that.

The phoenix rises from the ashes once more, taking the love David and I shared with her, my strength multiplied by this loss, my resolve stronger than ever. They try to break me, but don't manage it. The scar tissue thicker than ever, penetrating my walls of defences is something they will now never be able to do.

THIRTY-SIX

May 2011

I step off the train, careful to mind the gap, my eyesight so blurry with exhaustion I feel certain I'll trap a heel and lose half my leg if I'm not careful. I'm exhausted beyond belief. Walking the short distance to our terraced house on Oxford Road in Windsor, I see the lights on in the living room as I approach. My live-in nanny Sarah is busy ironing and the kids seem to be in bed already. Lucinda and Marissa are happy enough, but since we moved here just outside London, Billy's become someone else – and my son is no longer recognisable to me.

He goes to a local school (not Eton) and all the children take the piss out of his Yorkshire accent. He hates me more everyday, I'm certain of it. I moved him someplace alien and I basically killed his father, too, according to his childish rationale.

Shutting the front door behind me, I slip off my heels and throw my coat on a peg. "It's me, Sarah."

"Hey, Ade," she calls, as she's finishing one of Billy's school shirts.

I step into the room with her. "Everything okay?"

"No problems. Just the usual Billy issues, but he ate some chips at least."

My heart sinks. I worry about him. I worry he has a personality like Marcus's. I worry about what David's death has done to him.

It's nine o'clock at night and I tell her, "I ate at the office."

"I'll batch up the leftover lasagne then," she says.

"Perfect. So, if you're alright, I'll go up, kiss the kids and take a shower. I'll see you in the morning."

"No problem."

"Don't work yourself too hard," I remind her.

"It's no problem," she says, gesturing at the TV, "I find ironing and crime dramas a therapeutic combination."

I snicker and roll my eyes. She knows I hate crime dramas. She just doesn't know why.

"Goodnight, Sarah. You save my life everyday, don't forget it."

"Well you never stop saying it!" She winks, flicking me a grin, and I leave behind my young live-in nanny, who has weekends off to go and stay with her boyfriend across in Basildon. If only I got a weekend off now and again…

Upstairs I walk into the girls' room and find them both knocked out. Lucinda gets tired out enough by infant school while Sarah tires out Marissa plenty enough during the day. A live-in nanny sure does save on nursery bills and many other services, too. Not that I'm short of a penny now I work in the city, managing hedge funds. Turns out I have a brain for this after all. Maybe it's losing your soul that does this – makes me more adept at handling the blood-sucking world of finance.

I kiss my girls and they stir but don't wake. I want to hold them tight to me, but I won't. They're tired and don't need me waking them up.

When I walk past Billy's bedroom – which I had to take the door off so he can't shut himself inside – he pulls the blanket up around his head, hiding the fact he's reading comics with the lamp on.

"I love you, Billy," I tell him, but he doesn't flinch at all. I walk in and switch off the lamp, dragging the magazine out of his hands. "You need sleep so your brain works at school. Goodnight, son."

He says nothing and I walk away. He's not happy with me and even started calling Sarah 'Mother' because he hates me that much. With a degree in childcare, she's been a huge help.

Under the shower in the bathroom, water trickles over my face and takes with it my mascara and my fatigue. At work plenty of men have tried it on but I'm so ice cool, I've become known as the 'Frozen Widow'. Perhaps Billy should draw a comic book caricature of me, it'd probably be most apt. I've completely shut down and shut off my emotions. All I do is work, work, work. At weekends I take the kids to play dates, the park, the shops, the swimming baths, but I'm not really present in spirit and I think that's part of the reason Billy hates me – because I refuse to show I'm still hurting. Sometimes I've almost swung for him because of the way he makes me feel but how can I lash out at my boy, when he's been put through as much hell as I have?

Stepping out of the shower, I towel dry my hair and pull on some thick pyjamas, which are all I wear when I'm at home. My bed's frozen every night, like I am, and nothing can penetrate me as long as I bury myself beneath all these layers. Sometimes I don't shave my legs or armpits. Why would I need to? When the kids go swimming, their swimming instructor is the one in the water with them, not me. Nobody sees beneath my clothes anymore. Nobody sees me. All they see everyday now are the shiny grey trouser suits with different blouses and different shades of shoe, just the same peep toe, kitten-heel style. It's all I can manage.

In bed, I drag my laptop from my bag and work for a couple of hours, drafting some important contracts and account settlements I will need to send tomorrow. I'll proof them on the train into work, when my mind is fresher.

When I put my laptop to one side and finally lay down flat, I stare at the photo of David I keep on my bedside and it's staring at him that takes me back to the day we met, a day of blind awakening. I drift off with thoughts of him and this is how I survive.

I wake to Lucinda and Marissa jumping up on my bed to snuggle under the duvet with me. Both of them look so much like David, it's a daily reminder that he's not really left. He lives on in them.

"Hello, angels," I say, "you okay?"

One either side of me, they snuggle into my chest together, facing each other.

"I got lots of gold stars," Lucinda shrieks, waking me up if I wasn't awake before. Both early birds, it's just after six.

"Nanny Sarah take me park and take me ducks and bus and buy sweets," Marissa giggles.

I hold them both to me, twisting my fingers around their brunette locks. "Good girls. You're both very good girls, you know?"

Billy stands at the door, frowning as he watches us. He's never normally up but he stares blankly and mumbles. "I had a bad dream."

"Bill-wy," Marissa calls, opening the duvet for him to get in with us.

He gets in, but with his back to me. Marissa's sandwiched between us anyway and she tightens her hands around his neck and asks him, "Whoa-kay, Bill-wy?"

"Bit better," he says.

"Look after your brother while I get dressed," I tell my girls.

I sneak into the corner and quickly throw some clothes on. I don't want Billy to see me naked but I don't want to chuck him out of my room either. He's ten now and I wonder if he'll one day figure everything out. I don't know.

My suit on, I brush out my long hair and tie it back in a bun. I'll do my make-up in the train bathroom, just a bit of tinted moisturiser, a lick of mascara, bronzer and some pale lip loss. I don't want to be confused with someone trying to attract the opposite sex, but I don't want to be naked either.

"Let's go get breakfast, boys and girls."

Everyone piles down together and when I pat Billy's shoulder, he doesn't try to shrug away from me. Part of me wonders what's made him change his tune.

As everyone tucks into either coco pops or wheat biscuits, I ask Billy, "What was the dream about?"

His eyes are devoid of emotion. "That you died too."

I raise my eyebrows and retort, "Unlikely, since I live for you three."

Billy slams his spoon down and stands from the table. The girls sit in shock, ready to run to my side to try and protect me. They're familiar with his outbursts and none of us like them.

"Why don't you cry? Everybody cries but you!" he screams, runs off and leaves us all shocked, his cereal bowl largely untouched.

From the sound of him chasing upstairs, he almost knocks Sarah over as he races away and she enters the kitchen dining area breathless. "What happened?"

"Bill-wy had bad dream," Marissa says, and I stare at Sarah despairingly.

"Okay, well never mind that, eat up little ladies," she says, and I leave the room to go and find Billy.

When I get outside his bedroom door, or entrance, he's back in bed with the covers pulled up around his head. "I am sad Billy. But being sad doesn't mean people have to cry all the time. Sometimes for adults, being sad means trying to live normally, and hiding how hard that is."

"I hate you!" he cries, conflicted, despising the fact he still cares if I live or die.

"That's fine, but I'm still your mother, and I'm still the only one you've got left."

He throws the covers off and shrieks, "We had Granny! We had Granny!"

His nose is red, as are his eyes. "Get dressed and let's hear no more of this. There are issues between me and Granny you don't know about, Billy."

"YOU KILLED HIM!" he shrieks, and snatches his clothes from the top of his chest of drawers, storming out of the room to change in the bathroom.

I walk to my bedroom and pick up my laptop and all my other devices, plus my make-up case.

Downstairs I put my coat and shoes on and kiss the girls goodbye. I don't know what I would do without them. Maybe Billy feels outnumbered or maybe like me, he just misses David.

I step through the atrium of Berken & Berken, ignoring all eyes on me. I recently won a prestigious contract to manage a healthcare fund and everyone at this firm hates me. I'm saving all my extra earnings for a rainy day – or more specifically – so I can retire within five years and escape twelve-hour days and all these fucking piss-poor excuses for human beings.

In the lift, several sets of eyes stare at me.

"Morning, Stuart," I mumble to a fellow hedge fund manager stood by my side.

"How many accounts are you going to pinch today, Adrienne?"

"As many as the rest of you are incapable of running. Which probably means all of them."

Stuart chuckles. "Never content, Adrienne… bed must be pretty frozen."

"My bedfellows are the robotic and more satisfying sort than your tiny shrimp cock, Stewie."

"Bitch," murmurs whiney Wendy Small beside us. Small by name, small by nature.

I laugh in retort. "All of you are just raw because you never saw the blonde glamazon coming… underestimating me was your biggest mistake." None of them realised I've been dealing with rich arseholes since I was in nappies and I know how to romance the kind of clients we get. I used a lot of my own capital to bring these people in, but the return I get in exchange will be enough to sail into the sunset in just a few years' time. Short-term sacrifice, long-term winnings. Sure I hardly see my kids, but hopefully it'll be better for us all in the long term.

We all filter out of the lift to our various offices and my colleagues, like me, are straight on the phone to check their clients are still happy to sign on the dotted line today. Straight on the laptop to send contracts and latest figures over, and straight on the internet to check the price of oil and how it's likely to affect every other fucking market in the world. It starts and it doesn't stop. Well, not until I am too tired to work anymore. Part of the reason I'm so desperate to make this work is that I've staked a lot of my own cash (from David's estate and the money Dad gave me) and my returns are investments for the future. I have to make sure I take care of my investments and bring the right people in with me to build my portfolio. I made no money at all last year but this year, returns in the millions have started to roll in and soon, I will be ready to roll out. Most of the people I work with haven't got the background I have in meeting and greeting real business people like my father did.

"Your mail, Mrs Lewis," the mail boy says, and I stand up from behind my desk to rush and get it from him as he waits outside the see-through glass door.

"Thanks," I tell him, and rush back to email one of the administrators currently assisting me in transitioning one of Stuart's clients over to me instead.

Tearing my letters open once I've got a moment, I find a number of signed contracts I've been waiting for with instructions to proceed, plus a number of statements declaring various fund activities.

Among the post however is a letter with an embossed envelope. When I open it, I look curiously at a wedding invitation. Along with the invite is a small note, reading:

Dear Adrienne,
I was pleasantly surprised to bump into Rachel recently and
she told me you are doing well for yourself. It's great you're
finally on your feet. I hope you don't mind, but my fiancé
Craig managed to track down your office address so we
could invite you to our forthcoming wedding in a month's
time. (details encl.)
Hope you can make it?
Regards,
Lillian Woodmansey

The invitation's outer card is pure white, with a black and white image of two pinkie fingers crossed, sealing it shut. How lame. I pull open the card and notice the wedding is to take place down at Lake Como. Well, it might be better than looking out of my window at all this rain and the grey rooftops all the time.

My ex-best friend from Harrogate Ladies' College, Lillian has only got back in touch now she knows I'm 'doing well'? Seems fishy to me. She dropped me like a turd in the river when she found out what had happened with Marcus.

The phone rings and I toss the invite on a corner of my desk, forgetting about it for the rest of the day.

At home in the evening, Billy is even more frosty with me than usual. I can't handle it and even though I still tell him I love him, secretly I'm being tested on that. He's making life very hard for me and I don't know what I've done to deserve his virtual dismissal that I'm even his mother!

In bed, I work late as usual and after that, look through the mail I got at the office earlier. The invitation drops onto my lap like a sign and I decide to make a call I should've made a long time ago.

"Ade, oh, is that you?" Rachel asks.

I take a deep breath, sighing so she knows I'm not happy about all this. "You've been tit-tattling haven't you?"

She giggles very slightly. "Maybe."

"I despise Lillian, you know?"

"I do too!" she hastily adds, "but she was banging on about some bloody lavish wedding and she was asking about you... and I thought... I thought maybe if you went to a wedding, you'd need someone to have the kids."

Oh. I just thought her speaking to Lillian was a roundabout way of getting me to ring her?

"I'm not bloody going! The woman's a nightmare. The invite has an image of a pinkie swear on it!"

"Oh, Ade," she murmurs, "I've missed you so much."

I say nothing. Until I feel bad enough to admit, "I've just been doing what I need to, you know? To stay busy and keep going."

"You must need a break, yes?"

"I do," I admit, "but I'm coping. Everything's fine."

"Please, Ade. I haven't seen them in so long... I mean, I'll even come down there. You don't have to bring them to me. I'll look after them the whole weekend. You could even give your nanny a long weekend if you like? I bet she would like that?"

"It does sound like an idea," I agree, though I don't want to give in.

"Please, Ade."

"Rachel, it's not easy for me."

"I know, I know!" she almost shouts. "I'm not asking you to forgive me for turning a blind eye to David's problems. What's done is done... my son is gone, but his children aren't. You have to forgive me."

"I can't."

If there are two people I cannot forgive, the first is my own mother, and the second is Rachel. I judge them as fellow mothers and as mothers, they've failed me and David. I may be failing too, but I've tried hard, at least. I've tried at times when others would've given up.

"Well then, please don't punish your children because of something I did. Please, Adrienne. Think of them. Just one weekend. One. You can go away, clear your head, have a rest. I'm begging you. I'll beg harder if you ask me to–"

She starts crying and I listen to her tears. Choking. Savage hiccups. They trickle along the edges of my icy heart but do nothing to thaw it. But she's right. Billy is being difficult and I am run ragged. Plus it might be funny to see Lillian in a dress. I bet it'll have lemon trims and then there will be doves and all manner of yucky romantic shit.

"You can come," I tell her, "but no spoiling them. You can take Sarah's room and I'll give her Thursday to Monday off inclusive. You can come down on Thursday afternoon and I'll get a flight out of Heathrow that evening. It'll give me chance to settle in and relax at this hotel they're having it at, okay?"

"Yes, whatever you say, whatever you say, I'll be there! I'll do it," she tells me fast.

"I'm tired, Rachel. I better go."

"Thank you," she says, even when I know I should be the one thanking her. She's always supported me and treated me like a daughter, through good times and bad. I should be better to her, but I just can't help thinking about my David as a little boy – younger than Billy is now – being bullied by his elder brother and father. All while she stood by and let it happen. I guess she may have paid the price already, having lost him so young.

"Thank you, Rachel," I manage to say, "I'll be in touch about details."

"Goodnight, Ade."

"Goodnight."

THIRTY-SEVEN

As my British Airways flight lifts off the tarmac in Heathrow, I feel sick thinking about leaving my kids behind. I know they will be safe with Rachel, but the look on Billy's face when he saw her was triumphant, like he's now won the battle and got what he wanted. While he spends most days ignoring or berating me, as soon as she stepped into the house, he had so much love and affection for her. I have to keep telling myself it's just a phase that he'll grow out of.

Takeoff's a little bumpy but once we're in the air, the complementary drinks start to take effect and I relax back into my first-class seat.

When I realised the best flights went to Milan, I contemplated not stopping for the shopping there, but it seemed a shame to waste my trip on Lillian's wedding alone so tonight and tomorrow night, which is a Friday, I'm staying at the Palazzo before a chauffeur drives me up to Lake Como on Saturday morning for the wedding. They're marrying on a hillside at an ancient chapel and then the reception is at Grand Hotel Tremezzo, which they've booked out completely, so I don't have to pay for my room there for Saturday and Sunday night, before I get a flight back to London late Monday afternoon.

It seems like a dream to have this weekend off. In more than a decade, I've never had a whole weekend to myself.

***

Touching down in Milan, it's wonderful to have the Italian sun hit my face as I walk down the steps, onto the dry and brittle brown runway. The aeroplane engines still whirring slightly as they cool down, all passengers jump on a bus and I don't feel particularly strange about travelling alone. I feel great. I can observe the world without having to give my opinion to anyone. It's great to be able to absorb what I see without having to worry whether I'm keeping my partner – or my kids – amused.

"Adrienne?" I hear as I'm grabbing my luggage from the baggage carousel soon enough.

I know that voice but a part of me doesn't believe he's here. I turn and look into his caramel eyes. "Luca?"

He stares at me, really stares, and perhaps I do look nice because I had a spray tan (I'd look pasty compared to everyone else otherwise). I've also had my nails done and for the first time in months, I've shaved parts of my body long unshaved.

People curse us as we stand rooted to the spot, clearly in the way of other passengers still trying to find their luggage.

"I didn't see you on the flight," he says.

"I was in first class. Weren't you?"

He smiles. "Last-minute business trip. All taken."

I smirk. "Oh."

"What are you doing here, I mean, where are you heading?" he asks.

"Milan, then Lake Como for a wedding."

"Milan? For work?"

I shake my head. "To shop. Sudden hedge fund millionaires aren't really reported on, I mean, we're hardly regulated are we, but yes, I can afford a little bit of a splurge nowadays."

He gawps, his eyes blinking repeatedly. "Getting a taxi? You want to talk on the way in?"

I shake my head. "You can share my limo, Luca."

He trails behind me as we walk out and I find my tiny Italian chauffeur, carrying a sign *A. Lewis*. In Italian, I ask him, "Okay if my friend gets a ride, too?"

The Italian chauffeur blinks. "Of course, Mrs Lewis."

On the backseat, I'm suddenly grateful for working air-con because the airport's must have been broken. Beside me, Luca remarks, "You never told me you speak Italian."

"Spanish, too. Mum and Dad retired out there, you know," I say proudly, like the fickle, false woman I am.

I feel him staring at me so I look across at him.

"Who are you?" he asks, a flare of desire in his eyes.

I hold out my hand which he kisses the back off. When his lips touch me, I feel his kiss flutter from there to other places.

"I'm Adrienne. Hedge fund manager. Daughter of a ruthless businessman who disowned me when I killed my abusive ex-partner."

He looks at me, seeing I'm serious, and his eyes darken.

"I'm Luca, a man who's never loved anyone else but you."

His chest heaving, his hands a source of major distraction, I whisper, "I'm at the Palazzo."

"Me too."

"Guess it's fate."

"Guess so."

He leans across and kisses my lips gently, fluttering sweet nothings with his gentle sweeps. My heart flares and I ask him, "You should hate me, shouldn't you?"

He cocks one eyebrow. "I should."

"Haven't you got a woman?"

He shakes his head. "Women, yes but... no woman."

The moment I tug his hair, his lips venture lower to my throat and reality blurs into the background while the driver takes us to the Palazzo.

After explaining to the desk clerk we have two rooms booked but now only want one, I'm charged for my first night's stay at the room I was meant to have but the rest of my rate is scrapped. Luca tries to argue the toss in Italian (violently and effusively) but I tell him it doesn't matter and not much later, we're being shown to our suite in the Palazzo.

Stressed out, he heads straight for the mini bar to knock back a dram.

Amusing myself by the window, looking down over the city from several floors up, I ask him, "Why couldn't you just back down?"

He wipes the sweat from his brow, a mixture of the heat and the stress I think.

"I come here all the time, it's the least they could do for a regular," he explains, "besides, he was mugging off a lady and I really don't appreciate that, especially from some dirty Corsican."

I laugh. "You can tell that?"

"I can tell," he nods.

I lick my lips, dry from the air-con.

"Why are you in Milan?"

He throws back another shot of drink and replies, "Here to see a man about some leather."

When he adds a wink, I snigger, so does he.

"Oh I see!" I giggle. "So, do you come here often?"

He puts his glass down and saunters towards me in the way only Italian men can get away with, a sort of shimmy in his hips.

Putting his hands on my waist, he looks into my eyes. "I come here often, but only to buy leather," he assures me.

"When was the last time you had sex?" I ask him straight, not deterred from confronting him, despite his elegant beauty. For a forty-something year old, he's immaculate.

"Yesterday," he replies without shame, "but I didn't know about today."

"Neither did I."

"So when did you last have sex?" he confronts me.

"About two years ago."

His grip on my waist tightens and I see the cogs turning.

"Aside from me, the abusive dick and David, there's been nobody else?"

I shake my head. "Teenage flings before I met the dick but nothing else serious. Oh, but then there's Cedrick…"

"Cedrick?" he asks, looking disgusted.

"The name of my rampant rabbit."

He throws his head back laughing. "Ooh… we'll get you a new Cedrick."

I snigger. "Will I need a new one?"

He stares deep into my eyes, so intensely, I get lost in his gaze. "You'll need new everything where I'm taking you."

He lowers his lips to mine, gently prising my mouth apart. His tongue flicks underneath mine and whirls and toys with me. I pull him closer with my arms around his neck and he does that thing only he's ever done to me – cups my cheeks and turns my face so he can kiss me fully, tongues wild, lips in line perfectly and suctioned closed so he can devour me.

He pulls back and drops a gentle kiss on my cheek. I stagger on one leg, my other foot off the ground. He holds me up so I don't fall and I ask him, "Again."

He kisses me again and a tiny tear peels from the iceberg that is my heart. He doesn't take me to bed but he takes me to somewhere that isn't just me and my pain – he takes me to a place of peace.

He cuddles me in the sofa after he's finished marking my mouth, his hands running through my hair and his mouth on my cheeks and hands.

We're quiet and it's okay. We don't need too many words.

He gets up when the phone rings and after the call's done, he tells me, "I have a dinner date with the leather supplier

Leonardo but I'll send for some dinner for you up to the room?"

I shake my head. "You must be joking. I'm going to find a hole in the wall. I'm not afraid of being alone, Luca."

"Hmm," he groans, "that's what worries me."

He leaves and when he's gone, I wonder what the hell it is we're doing. I remember to text Rachel and tell her I've landed okay and I'm at the hotel. I think about telling her I'm in a room which won't be under my name – just in case she can't get my mobile – but I don't want to hurt her by revealing I'm already sort of moving on. Or trying to, at least.

She replies to say the kids are fine and that after school tomorrow, she's taking them to a pub and then on Saturday, to Legoland. For a moment, I hover over telling her off for spoiling them, but then think better of it.

After I've eaten real Italian food and wandered the shops a little (I'll do more serious shopping tomorrow), it's time I visited Basilica San Marco. Kneeling inside the ancient chapel, I begin to pray.

"Is it okay for me to be happy, David? I mean... is it chance that put me back in his life, or what?"

I don't hear any response.

"I love you and hope you're happier wherever you are."

Leaving the church, I walk back to my hotel, have a long soak and plan what shops I will visit tomorrow – marking them on a map. When it's midnight and Luca's still not back, I check my phone to find no messages from either him or Rachel.

I climb into bed on my own – wearing a little silk thing I picked up in a local store – and I fall into a deep sleep.

**

Waking gradually, the light of a bright, hot day rouses me. I look around, remembering I'm in Italy, and then I look to the side of me and see no Luca. Standing I walk to the curtain and peel it open further, then hear groans from across the room.

"Why did you sleep there?"

"My neck hurts!"

"I'll ask again," I stalk across the room, "why did you sleep there?"

He sits up and rubs the back of his neck. "Still not a morning person?"

I take a step back because he's right. I have never been a morning person.

"I waited up for you," I whisper.

"I want to do things right this time," he says.

I stare, waiting to hear more. He doesn't say more, because his eyes are fixed on me in the silk slip. I want him to take me because I'm horny and I need him and I want him.

"Right? What do you mean?" I walk back to the bed and under the covers, because I want to know what he means and me standing in front of him seems to have him at a loss for words.

"I was talking with Leonardo, who's actually a good friend, and he warned me to guard my heart."

I sniff. "You said that before. About guarding your heart. Don't you think that I've let my guard down already, just being here with you?"

He stands up in just his boxers, a blanket falling off him to the floor. His skin is covered in male hair, his muscles are solid and hard, and his body is shaking because he wants me so much.

I dash off the bed and run to him and he runs to me.

He peels my slip off over my head and our chests touch. His body hair tickles my fine blonde hairs and my nipples tighten, lifting my breasts to rub against his skin.

His hands under my buttocks, he hoists me into his arms

and lays me down beneath him on the bed.

Kissing me madly, I pull down his boxer shorts and we roll over the mattress, my legs tight around him, aching for him to enter me.

"Do you trust me?" he asks, "enough to come inside you this time?"

"If you say you're safe, I trust you," I tell him.

He groans and leans down to kiss my breast, my central line, my throat and my upper arms and my stomach.

I've lost lots of weight and I feel like Luca might be a man to prefer more curves but then he groans. "Still so soft, Ade. Like silk," he murmurs against my thigh as he kisses me there.

Licking in circles around my ankle, he's baiting me, keeping me on edge.

I can't take it.

If there's one thing I've learnt, it's to go after what you want.

"No denying me, Luca," I threaten and demand, "lie down for me."

He gets down, lying flat in the bedcovers for me. I climb over his face and while he licks my slit, I suck on his cock.

"Oh god, Luca! Luca!" I come spurting all over his face and he laughs loudly.

"Yes, Ade. You want more?"

"Always."

While I enjoy sucking his thick cock, he licks me clean and slaps my bum hard. "Ooh I like you in charge, Adrienne!"

I grab hold of his big sac and tug him gently. He cries out, enjoying it when I tongue the eye of his penis.

"Baby," he growls, and I slip down his body, leaving a trail of wetness all over him, before finally meeting his cock with my pussy.

Sliding down his thick shaft, I grab my hair in my hands and begin riding him backwards cowgirl.

"Oh god, oh god. Oh god. Oh god!"

"Adrienne!"

I can take him right to the root and I do, slamming down hard on him, again and again. He's solid and sturdy, he can take me abusing him. I rub myself against his balls every time I meet the fullness of his rigid length.

From behind me, he squeezes my rear and slides juices up to my crack. He pops a thumb in my butt and slips in and out. In the past, Luca and me tried a lot of things together, but I always felt guilty afterwards and now I don't. Now I just need his body to be mine. Now we can do everything and anything. He's my slave and I want to use him. And for him to use me.

He slips out and tosses me down on the bed on my belly.

"Oh miiiiiii godddddd!" I scream when he lifts my legs up like I'm a wheelbarrow and starts pounding hard into me.

"Pussy has never felt so good as it does right now. Your wet pussy and no condom, Ade. Nothing's ever felt this good."

"Fuck me, fuck me! Luca. Fuck me, always."

"Yes, god yes!" he growls and hammers into me, hammering so hard, it feels like a hard slap every time his pelvis hits my butt.

"I'm gonna fucking come in you," he warns, while I teeter on the brink.

"It'll make me come, having you rush into me," I groan, "your cum in me, Luca. Deep in my belly."

"Raaahhh!"

He spurts into me, hot and fast, and I rub myself the moment he comes to make it all last longer.

His hot cum slips down my thighs even as he's still thrusting and working himself down.

He cradles me back in bed, his body around mine. He kisses my face, all of it. Our legs tangled, I tell him, "I love you. I'm sorry I didn't tell you until now."

He smiles and leans down to nibble my nipple. Playing

with my clit, he draws another orgasm from me, nonchalantly slipping his finger around my nubbin. As he pushes inside me again in the missionary position, I gasp when he's fully buried inside my body.

He looks down on me and kisses my nose, maintaining eye contact.

"I love you, Ade. There will be absolutely no secrets between us."

"Agreed. Agreed," I repeat.

My hands work all over him, my mouth, my eyes taking him all in. His hair in my grasp, I'm shaking violently when he makes me come again, more of his seed spurting into me, his passion so desperate.

He's stroking his hands up and down my body when he later asks, "Are we going shopping?"

"Are you insane?"

He laughs and hikes me out of bed, taking me into the bathroom to wash me and then take me shopping, despite my pleas to stay in bed.

"We said no secrets, Adrienne, and it's no secret your wardrobe needs updating," he tells me, gesturing at the Marks and Spencer jeans and gypsy blouse I arrived into Milan wearing yesterday. "You are beautiful, but do the clothes say millionaire?"

He eyes me and laughs, and I laugh, too. "You're right."

"Always am," he winks.

THIRTY-EIGHT

We spent the day shopping and now we're eating at the hotel restaurant, out on the terrace, because it's nearby, intimate and not too busy like it is out on the streets. I don't normally mind busy but tonight after all the shopping, I just want to chill out. While Luca's wearing one of his new purchases today, an Armani shirt with solid gold cufflinks, I'm wearing one of my own purchases, a Ralph Lauren, lace/cotton dress. It's not the most snazzy of things I bought today but I just want to be casual tonight.

When our empty dinner plates are taken away, he comments, "If you don't mind me saying, you don't seem out of place here... the opulence doesn't intimidate you?"

I laugh smartly. "I'm not intimidated by many things. Besides I first came to this hotel when I was five. My mother used to come shopping here all the time and only started bringing me when I was old enough."

"It's sad," he states, "that all it is now is a grey eyesore with shops, shops, shops. I remember when it used to be more rustic."

I stare over the top of my wine glass, a globe almost as big as my head. "You have your own history with this place?"

"Papa used to visit when he was selling leather in Amsterdam. I suppose it's sort of what got me into the erotic market, although my parents will never know what it is I really do… they think I sell high quality leather dresses, not aprons and pinnys for BDSM play."

I snicker. "Well I think they'd be proud."

He chuckles. "Maybe they'd be proud if they saw me finally settle down. It's sort of a running joke, now."

"Your bachelorhood?" I ask.

"Yes." He smiles across at me, his mouth turning up higher at the left-hand side. He has such a droopy grin at the other side and I really kind of like it.

"You've never been married? Or even close to it."

"No."

"Scared of it?" I ask him.

"No," he shakes his head, "why would I be? My parents are as in love today as they were the day they met."

I nod once. "So you look at them and nothing less than what they have rings true with you? You want the same."

He smiles again. "You're right. Nothing less."

"I thought I had that with David," I tell him, shifting in my seat, "but when I think about it all, and I know it's wrong to speak ill of the dead… but part of me looks back now and realises he never respected me enough to be straight with me."

Luca takes my hand across the table, keeping my gaze. "Some say when it comes to love, respect does not exist. How can passion and respect exist simultaneously?"

I turn my bottom lip down, disappointed he thinks like that. "You really think that?"

He shakes his head, gesticulating. "No, I personally do not think that. I think some moronic turd who went to boarding school and began masturbating to thoughts of his school dinner lady believes that."

We laugh together and I rub my fingers over the back of his hand.

"I've been around the block, if you excuse the term. I've seen enough to know respect counts for a lot. If a man doesn't respect you, then what's stopping him doing all the things his mind is telling him to do?"

I absorb his words. "You don't think men are wired to settle down?"

"I think men are wired to deceive to avoid confrontation with a woman. No respect, no problem. Free as a bird. If respect is involved... then we have a big problem. We have to tell the truth. We can't not, because we respect the lady too much."

"But then the truth kills the passion?"

"Well, yes," he murmurs, lifting my hand to kiss my fingers, "but once a man learns his lesson the first time, he knows never to do it again... that thing he decided he would lie about, but in the end... couldn't..."

I withdraw my fingers from his and sit back. Feeling slightly defensive, I fold my arms. "Do you think he thought about me at all while he was screwing Violet?"

"No," replies Luca, "I think that was the point. He didn't want to think... he wanted to evade. A man is simple, you know? Simple things... simple tastes... in theory. Throw a woman like you into the equation, and the spreadsheet becomes chaos. He wanted to be so much more than he was. The wrong combination of man and woman... and everything has the potential to fuck up."

I scratch my chin, knowing he's right. "David was fine until he knew I had a dark past to contend with... until I refused to bow down and give up my degree. He viewed everything I did without him as competition for my heart."

"Like you said Ade, it's not good to speak ill of the dead, but if speaking truthfully helps you work through what happened, perhaps it's time?"

I blink rapidly, trying to draw back my tears. "He railroaded me into marrying him. Swept me off my feet. Waited until after we were in love to tell me about the porn. He didn't tell me he had a load of drug arrests against his name until way after we met."

"Avoiding," Luca reminds me.

"Most of all, the worst thing he ever did... was the night he took me up into the country and told me I'd ruined the night by bringing up talk of our dwindling sex life... when it was actually him that was the problem. Him, his lies, and the fact he was doing Violet behind my back."

Luca listens, his face solemn, calm.

"She wasn't even pretty," he states, nose wrinkling.

"I watched their porn stuff they did together, did you?"

Luca laughs. "NO!"

I laugh, grimacing, disgusted with myself. "When things got bad, I started watching loads of porn and David thought it was great because I would literally walk into the room and be ready for him, so turned on. Little did he know what I was doing behind his back... but I never imagined the truth... never. He had me fooled. We fooled one another in different ways."

"He had more than you fooled, Ade. I thought better of him, too. What he did to Violet was abhorrent."

I sigh and Luca pours some more wine into my glass. He won't allow the waiters to pour and I think they're all too scared of him to disobey.

Drinking some more Chianti, which complemented our steaks perfectly, I tell him as I set my glass down, "I thought we were back on track. I thought we were good. We had Marissa. I still felt this sucker punch of sadness, but we seemed to be making progress." He watches me thinking and waits for me to say more. "Then that day I saw you, having just bumped into Violet, I realised nothing had been resolved at all. We'd just found ways to muddle through. That's all we were doing. He was happy to have me at home, weeping breasts and all. He took me out with his new colleagues who were so boring it made me want to run from the room screaming!"

Luca bursts out laughing.

"They were diabolical but I sat there comparing my

marriage to his colleagues', trying to convince myself what we had was wonderful and amazing compared to what they had… but it was all bollocks. Why the need to compare, unless you're deeply unhappy?"

He stares down at me, chewing his lip.

"What?" I ask.

"You're just so beautiful when you start ranting."

"Sorry."

"Don't be."

We drink wine and stare at one another across the rims of our glasses. "Do you hate that I have this past?"

I stare at his shirt and how the two open buttons at the top reveal all his chest hair and strong throat.

"Yes," he says, "I do. I hate it all. But I'll listen because I know it helps."

I laugh, exclaiming, "Where have you been? The no contact… what happened?"

He looks down at his lap. Suddenly I remember – he was there the night David died.

"We argued, that night," he begins, reading my thoughts.

"How did you even come to be in York that night?" I sound aghast, because I was, at the time – and still am.

He smiles slightly, but he seems nervous too, tapping a finger on the side of the table.

"He called me, invited me over. He said he wanted to clear the air–"

"And that wasn't the case, was it?"

"No, I should have known, but part of me wanted to clear the air, end things on good terms. You know? We were once friends."

"I get it."

Luca does something I have never seen him do. He touches his hair, which must be a nervous tick. Usually he leaves it alone which makes me want to touch it all the time.

At this point, the waiter asks if I am ready for my dessert and Luca asks for a few more minutes.

"So, what happened?" I prompt him.

"We met at the King's Head near the river. It was late autumn, not warm enough to sit outside, but outside was where he wanted to meet. He was waiting for me by a bench with drinks already poured. I told him I was driving and he gave me daggers." Luca gives me a grave look and I nod for him to get it over with. "It was clear he was high. He wouldn't take no for an answer. I tried to explain again that I was driving and he suggested I get a hotel, that we go out on the lash. It was pointless trying to rationalise with him. He was slurring, under the influence... the David we knew was buried."

I sigh, covering my face with my hands.

"I lost my rag," he tells me quickly, "started telling him he was fucking ridiculous, suggested he beg for your forgiveness, crawl on his hands and knees if he had to. He shook his head at me!"

Luca's slightly fired up now, so I stroke his hand, trying to soothe his anguish.

He catches his breath. "I..." he shakes his head, "...told him if you were mine, I would chase across land barefoot, sell my teeth, break nails, crack jaws to fight my way to you. He laughed at me, laughed at me!"

I look away, unable to stand it any longer. Luca's been here all along, and I've wasted so much time.

"There was no reasoning with him, clearly he was high. I told him I loved you, that I'd always loved you, from the moment we met. I told him I'd tried to forget about you, but I couldn't. I told him that if I ever had you, I'd treasure and love you forever and he wouldn't listen... so I went on and on... I told him about the way you move, how you reacted to the ways I touched you... and something struck a chord with him. Something snapped. He couldn't handle it. He stood by the riverside and moved closer and I shouted for him to move back but he wouldn't. He just said, 'We'll see who she really loves then. We'll see...' and he dropped into the water, like a stone. Like a step forward, but it was a step beneath the surface."

"Oh god," I cry, wiping my eyes.

"I watched, waited for him to surface, and a few people rushed over. He didn't surface. I was going out of my mind. What did he mean? That he would be the memory you'd never get over, or his near-death experience would convince you to take him back? Before I knew it, I was in the water too. I dove deeper than I thought the river could go and pulled him out. He wasn't breathing. I was barely breathing. The rest is a blur–"

I sob and shudder. I don't care if the waiters are watching us. At least there's nobody else out here dining on the terrace with us. I think everyone's too frightened to seat any other diners near us for some reason.

He shakes his head. "When he... died... I couldn't digest it. I felt responsible. I couldn't... something I said took him over the edge, that's all I know. I was so relieved I'd saved him but then... he just slipped away. I saw the look on your face at the funeral, your babies... and I couldn't handle what I'd done. I've spent every moment since then wishing I'd never gone to York that night, wishing I'd never employed him... never met you... never any of this. I wish I'd never left Holland, never had the business. None of it! I can't live with myself."

I stand abruptly from the table and dash off. I can't take this anymore, either. He calls my name but I rush away. Reliving this is the worst kind of agony.

"Adrienne, please!"

I'm in the lift before he can catch up with me and when I get to the room, I put the *Do Not Disturb* sign on and deadbolt the door so he can't get in.

Before I know it, he's yanking at the door handle, shouting from behind the door. "Please, Adrienne! Please, god damn, let me in! Let me in baby. I need you."

I hear his call and my heart lurches. How can I deny him?

I treated him so badly and I don't deserve him.

I walk toward the door so he can hear me speak. "You should escape while you have chance, Luca."

"I love you," he says, "you're my chosen one. Nothing else will do, nothing but what I feel for you."

I sob and erupt with, "But I'm not special!"

"You are," he tells me, trying to keep his voice down, "please Ade, people are walking by, I might get escorted out if we are not careful."

I fly at the lock and unbolt it.

He charges into the room and picks me up in his arms, burying his tears in my breasts. He cries and releases all his pain. I fist his hair and repeat, "I don't deserve you."

"Say that again," he snarls.

"I don't deserve you!"

Before I can protest, he pushes me up against the wall and my skirt is hiked up to my waist. He rips my panties away and unzips.

"No," I murmur, "no."

"What?" he begs, red-eyed and bewildered.

"I love it when you lay me down and love me. I don't like it rough, not at times like this... I want you Luca. I love it when you're with me, connecting. Please."

He nods, slightly relieved I think, and slowly he carries me to the side of the bed where we stand together.

"Show me, Adrienne."

I push his hair behind his ears and stroke his face. "Okay."

Unbuttoning his shirt, I slide it off his arms, running my hands around his body. I kiss his nipple and he shakes violently. Walking behind him, I smooth his back and kiss the skin between his shoulders. He smells like sun and leather. Holding his body from behind, I warn, "If we are going to do this, we have to do it wholly, we have to dedicate ourselves."

He turns in my arms, smiling, and unzips my dress at the

same time as I push his chinos off.

Slipping out of our footwear, I repeat, "I don't deserve you."

"Maybe," he growls, "but you're my special one, anyway."

He smiles and I want to cry, but his smile makes me the happiest I've felt in a long time.

I still love David and always will. Maybe Luca knows that but doesn't care anymore.

Undoing my bra, it falls slowly, and he walks forward and slides my knickers down my legs, kissing my little triangle of hair when he bends for a moment as I step out of them.

Touching my hand to his cock over his briefs, I stroke lightly, feeling the size and impact of him. Running my hands slowly round to his butt, I lick my lips as I feel his buttocks clench and tighten in my grasp. Hands in the waistband of his boxers, I tug his underwear off and mirroring his moves, bend slightly to take them off. I kiss his cock.

Licking him into my mouth, he shakes all over and gasps, "Adrienne."

"Everything led to this, right now. Please say I'm not dreaming this."

"You're not."

He takes my wrist and pulls me to standing. Kissing me, he pulls my leg around him as walks us onto the bed, pulling me beneath him.

Trapping my hands above my head, he kisses me rampantly, then slowly, the tip of his cock teasing my clit. His kisses drench me; his scent and his heat crowd me. My legs wrapped around him, he releases one of my hands so I can feel his hair and he slides his fingers up and down my thigh. His caresses stray and his finger presses in between my crack, tantalising me.

"Luca," I say laughing.

"Hmm," he responds chuckling. "She likes ass play. And why not?"

He gently rocks against my clit with his cock and I'm so wet, I come, clawing at my hair and trying to cover my face with my hands.

He takes my hands away and his chest presses against mine as he prepares to push inside me.

"What do you want, Adrienne? Tell me and I'll give it to you. I love you."

"Sit up, on your butt," I ask him.

He pulls up and I climb into his arms. "Cross your legs, Luca."

He adheres and I sit in between his crossed legs, my legs tucked backwards beneath his, my feet squeezed underneath him, tucked in the folds of his legs.

"Cedrick once helped me get off to a pair of lovers doing this. I might have a few accounts with a few porn sites. I hope you're okay with this side of me."

He laughs and it turns into a low howl as I guide him into me and he feels how tight it is at this angle.

"Oh baby!"

"Yeah, I know!"

"Ah, Ade! I'm so okay with everything!"

I laugh and wrap my hands around the back of his neck, using him to rock myself around, pulling tight into him.

"Fuck that's tight, Ade!" he growls and the tendons in his neck twitch.

"I know, Luca," I murmur and latch into his hair to use that to steady myself. "You have the most perfect fat cock."

"You have the most perfect pussy, perfect for me." I jump wildly and he repeats, "Perfect!"

With me having total control as I use his body as apparatus so mine can act as a pendulum, I get to watch him totally at my mercy and it's the most arousing thing I've ever seen, watching a man succumb to the raw power of a woman's horny needs. Controlling his pleasure so I can take mine, he takes deep breaths and repeats, "Oh yeah, oh yeah."

I take one hand from behind his neck and hold his cheek, press my nose to his.

"What do you want, Luca?"

"To be your slave," he tells me.

"Hmmm, good," I whisper, "now put your finger in my mouth and then touch me."

He slips his thick index finger between my lips and fights the urge to explode as I lick and swirl my tongue around him.

The moment his finger touches my clit, I cry out and begin to shake, eyes squeezing shut. Shock. Awe. He pulls me closer and my legs slip free so he can move and he holds me tight in his hands so he can hit me deep inside.

The orgasm spreads from deep inside my belly to the rest of my body so that I'm liquid warmth and the tremors don't cease even when he stops moving and has ejaculated. He pulls me tight against him and I rest my cheek on his shoulder. Wrapping my arms and legs around him, we cuddle tight and I warn him, "I want everything with you."

I've missed being married, missed everything about it. I've never been a girl to want loads of men, just one, perfect man. He grabs my breast and squeezes so hard, I yelp and gasp, begging him to go easier.

"You can try to tame a beast, Ade," he whispers against my skin, "but when a beast is what you've chosen, he knows you will take it. When and how to fight back are specialties of mine."

I wrap my arms around his head and kiss him, his mouth soft and plump, the fast-growing stubble all around his face not so delicate.

He lies on the bed in the pillows, pulling me with him. I wrap my arms under his. "I don't have to go to the wedding."

"Nonsense. I called ahead to the hotel on Lake Como, asked to speak with the wedding organiser, and they said it was fine for you to bring a plus one because a few dropped out last-minute. So we're going together."

I purr in his ear. It seems I'm a different woman altogether when I'm with him. "I've missed you, Luca. Thank you for doing that."

"My pleasure, my jaded princess. My sweet, dulled sapphire, waiting for me to bring her back into the light."

I trace my fingertip over his bottom lip and ask, "You sure about this?"

"Sure?" He laughs loudly. "Did we not just prove how sure I am?"

I cuddle on top of him and smile. I laugh at myself and hide in his arms. He holds me close, his arms clutching at as much of me as he can. He throws a leg over my bottom and I break down crying in his arms.

"Oh, Luca!"

I cry endlessly, my heart weeping with stored-up, previously frozen tears of pain.

"I love you! Please, tell me this is true."

He rolls me to his side so we can see each other's faces. Stroking my cheek, he tells me, "Give me time? To take it all away."

I nod, sure of his conviction, his desire. He waits patiently and I reply, "I have time."

I kiss his lips lazily until falling asleep, sweetly bundled in his arms.

THIRTY-NINE

Thanks to Luca keeping me busy in the hotel room's mega bathtub this morning, we missed the church ceremony, but I don't think anyone noticed. We've made it to the wedding reception anyway.

"Why has she put all her beautiful friends at the back?" Luca whispers in my ear.

"Two guesses."

He snorts. "Attention whore."

I snort back. "Oh, yes."

I look to the side of me, directly into his eyes, and even though the speeches are taking place we can't take our eyes off each other. I never thought I would love again and now here we are.

The couples sat at the same table as us all hate one another, you can tell. They got married thinking it'd be wonderful, a big rock all that was needed to secure long-term happiness. I reckon most of them had a trek here in their vehicles and getting lost and/or hot and bothered in their cars has really tested their relationships.

"I hate these people," I whisper in his hair, so that nobody will hear me but him.

"Later, there will be dancing," he beams, grinning, "we can dance, and laugh at these morons jigging their bottoms."

I almost laugh out loud and earn myself a few deathly

gazes from the unhappy people sat around the table. No doubt all these guests were obliged to come because they made Lillian attend their own weddings. A part of me feels sorry that Lillian has been one of the last of us to get married, while another part of me knows that marrying Lillian also means marrying her family – and they are a nightmare. While her father is obsessed with vintage post boxes, trains and photography (which he's appalling at), her mother is a doormat with little more in her life than playing the nodding dog and jumping when he says how high.

"Lillian once dated a paedophile. I thought it was curtains for her after that. She'd had no idea at all… until the police took him and his laptops away," I tell Luca.

Lillian didn't come out of her house for almost a year after finding out about her ex. I'm sure she gained a newfound respect for me after that, despite having already dumped me for my own bad choices.

Luca stares, asking with his eyes whether I'm joking. I shake my head, *no.* "The crime rate in Harrogate is off the charts. And it's meant to be such a nice place to live."

Everyone starts clapping and I see Lillian reaching for her mother's handkerchief, which hopefully means it's all over. We've hardly been able to hear a word back here in no man's land.

"What did you buy her?" Luca asks as everyone continues to clap, maybe in the hope the clapping will mean no more speeches.

"A piece of art."

"Very nice," he winks.

"When its worth trebles and she tells all her friends I bought it for them as a wedding present, people will also learn I am in hedge funds and they will see if I have any more sound investments for them."

He grins. "You really do your research?"

I slide my hand around to his buttock and cop a feel. He's got a delicious arse.

"I know my way around these fucking snobs," I tell him laughing. Looking around, at least six women gawp – disgusted because I'm feeling up my boyfriend's arse. They're actually gawping because the closest they'll get to sex this weekend is watching another couple fawn all over one another.

He takes my hand away and pulls it up to his mouth, telling me proudly, "You'll have plenty of chances later... on the dance floor."

We snigger behind our hands and he tosses back the champagne being handed round as toasts get underway.

Toasts and cake cutting and shaking hands dispensed with, it's a starry night outside as the guests begin dancing slowly to a Frank Sinatra tribute band.

Luca has me in a proper hold and he's leading admirably. "You can dance."

It's a statement, not a question. He can dance properly.

"I went to art school baby. I might have dated a dancer or two."

I peer at him. "How old are you?"

He chuckles. "Early to mid forties, and that's all you're getting."

I squint and guess, "Forty-two."

I shock him and he replies, "Not bad, *senorita*, not bad."

I giggle girlishly in his ear. "Are men like wines? They get better with age?"

"Oh they certainly do," he tells me, waltzing me around the floor.

I feel a little woozy on champagne which is perhaps why I'm talking nonsense.

While the band plays *As Time Goes By*, I rest my head on his chest and he sways us gently, slow-dancing me. He's a fit man for his age and he takes care of himself. Part of me hopes he'll care for me as wonderfully as he cares for himself.

Wearing ballet pumps so I don't tower over him, we're almost at the same height but he's just an inch or an inch and a half taller than me, just obviously much broader. So broad in fact that when he lies on top of me in bed, I feel completely covered by him. He totally eclipses me.

"This is a beautiful place, Luca."

"I know."

"Where did you grow up?" I ask, because having a conversation while dancing feels like the most natural thing in the world.

The singer starts crooning *It Had to Be You* and his fingers tease through my hair as we dance.

"I grew up in the thick of it, in the Jordaan part of Centrum," he says, "we had a stunning apartment overlooking the canal and I never knew fear, never knew poverty... until my father fell on hard times."

I pull back, staring up at him. He has a twitch in the corner of his left eye so I kiss his mouth gently and whisper against his lips, "Tell me what happened."

He pulls me close and dances me around, looking at where we're going rather than looking at me.

"Papa had a market stall for years and years, until the time came to open a proper shop on the Negen Straatjes. He was very superstitious and thought a shop was a bad idea but with my mother's health ailing, he knew they couldn't continue to trade outdoors. Besides, he had the money for a retail unit by then."

I stroke my hand through the thickest part of his hair at the nape of his neck.

"Is that why you are an only child?"

He smiles. "How did you know?"

"A guess. Plus you've never mentioned any brothers or sisters."

"And you're an only child, too?"

"Yes," I nod, "my mother couldn't stand to touch my father again, I'm sure of it."

He covers his mouth, trying to stop himself laughing, and we hug rather than hold as we continue dancing. Gradually his arms slacken on me again and he gracefully shifts us around once more.

"My mother has MS," he says, "she's up and down."

"I'm sorry, Luca."

He shrugs. "What can we do?"

"So, the shop?" I ask him.

He looks up at the high ballroom ceiling and tells me, "Three months after opening, he was burgled. No insurance. My father wasn't the practical sort of businessman."

"Oh, no."

"I was ten or eleven. We had to leave Centrum and move to Bijlmer. A high-rise, decaying apartment, hoodlums, I don't know how to equate it... not as bad as your council estates but still bad. I look back and realise I'd lived in paradise up until then, wandering the streets in total safety."

"So then, what?"

"We struggled. No money to replace the lost stock. Father became a cleaner and we struggled for the next few years, until I started up my own business."

His eyes betray fear.

"What business?"

"I sold electrical goods. Stolen from waste sites... repaired. I earned enough to get my father some stock and he went back to the markets. Soon enough, I was selling real good stuff back up at the Negen Straatjes and my parents were able to get a tiny little box of a place back in Amsterdam Centrum."

"And you?"

"When I was nineteen, I left... for London. I had all these plans to become a real artist but the call to become an entrepreneur was stronger. I left college before graduating and started selling other electrical items. Like Cedrick," he says smiling, and I pull him close, kissing him with my arms wrapped around his neck. He pulls back and his tongue traces his lips, tasting me on them.

"And the rest is history?"

"Yes, the rest... history. But I never forgot what it was like to feel hungry, to suffer through sleepless nights as my stomach hurt. To watch my father crushed." His eye twitches again, but a smile lightens the darkness when he says, "Through it all, they still loved one another, and so I know real love when I see it. Despite illness and poverty, they loved me too, gave me what they could and themselves nothing. Now they have a three-storey house overlooking the canal. Papa keeps house and looks after Mama. They would give it up if they knew where the money had come from but I will never tell them. Besides, one day I will sell the business."

"Sell it? Why?"

He strokes my cheek with his fingers and the heat boiling between my legs doubles. I think I really love this man.

"To make money! I started the business and when I sell it, I can pursue other ventures."

"But FMP... it's your baby, your brainchild?"

He smiles, searching my eyes. "In life, people and things have an expiry date. Except real love, which lasts forever."

"Oh, Luca," I moan.

He holds our hands at his heart and not for the first time tonight, I notice we're one of the few couples still left dancing.

"I love you," I tell him, "I'm sorry it's taken this long."

"I'm sorry too," he says, but what does he have to be sorry for?

"I want to go to the room," I tell him, squeezing his shoulders, my voice husky.

"Okay, but you'd better give your best to the bride."

I chuckle as we pull apart and walk off the dance floor, heading for where the bride's standing with her parents, discussing something important it seems.

"Lillian?"

She turns and examines me. "How could you, Ade?"

I look around and look for someone else called Ade. "Pardon?"

"You and this man have completely stolen the show today. Kissing and canoodling at every chance you got. I said yes to you bringing a plus one but wish I hadn't now. Me and Ben just had a right barney because he wouldn't stay on the floor with me! My wedding day is ruined because of you."

I look at Luca, who seems furious. I don't know what to say to the girl.

"Lillian, that's not fair," her father says in a stern manner, eyeing me up and down, "apologise to Adrienne. She's travelled all the way here like all these other guests and you've been ever so ungrateful."

Lillian gawps. As does her mother, Sylvia. For once, the man of the house has backed down. I survey John Woodmansey and he asks me, "Business is good I hear?"

"Sure, business is good," I tell him, slipping my fingers through Luca's, squeezing tight.

"We may have to chat... in the morning? Fresh minds and all that," he asks, a snide smile in his eyes.

"I don't think so. My clients are of the most secular nature," I tell him laughing, "I don't think you have the goods to buy into what I'm invested in."

The Woodmanseys gawp at me but Luca remains amused.

"While we'd love to stay here chit-chatting," I tell them, picking my nails, "I'd prefer to go back on the dance floor and make Lillian cringe for the rest of the night."

"Think you're better than us, now?" Lillian scathes.

"Anything I've achieved is in spite of what's happened to me, not because of. I remember, you know... I was with an abusive prick once and my best friend abandoned me as soon as she decreed it uncool to be seen with me. Now I see, the only thing any of you are bothered about is making your connections and making money. Well, I think I won... because I don't want to dance *or* chat. I'd rather just go and have sex now, though I doubt you'll even get it on the honeymoon, you sourpuss!" I tell Lillian, whose face is blazing red. Everyone around us gawps and I yawn, tired of this affair.

"It was pleasant to meet you all," Luca says, "but while you weren't looking, I tipped all the wait staff because frankly, what you're giving them is pathetic."

We dash away, shocked gasps and coughs echoing behind us. In the lift as we travel upstairs, Luca hooks his hand into my panties and pulls them down from beneath my summer dress. Shoving them in his pocket, the lift pings open. "Run from me panty free... go... I'll chase you."

I laugh and start charging away down a long corridor, shouting over my shoulder, "How cathartic was that?!"

"Run you naughty little bitch!"

I chase away and grab at the key card in my bag, unsuccessfully pushing it into the slot.

Behind me, Luca presses his heat against my back and grabs the card, shoving it in dangerously hard.

"Oh god, Luca," I moan when his hand squeezes my breast over my dress.

We spill into the room so fast once the door's open, I almost fall flat on my face but he catches me and drags me to the bed, throwing me down on it.

Ripping my button-up dress open, he unzips himself and standing by the high bed, rams straight into me with his solid, stocky cock. I'm full and trembling around him, his heat and mine raw and volcanic.

Hands wrapped around my bent legs, underneath my knees, he pulls me tight against him so I can feel his zip scrape against my pussy lips.

Still standing, he starts thrusting inside me, his eyes squeezed tight shut. I undo my front clasp and let my breasts spill out. Lifting my right tit, I lick it.

"Oh Luca, look what I can do," I say and his eyes spring open, watching me lick my nipple.

"Bad girl," he growls.

His next move is to undo the button on his slacks, which fall to the floor. Still watching me and still fucking me, he unbuttons his shirt until his cock is slamming me through just the gap in his boxer briefs. I love that he wears so many different types of underwear. This morning he climbed into the bath with me wearing silk shorts which when wet provided the most succulent view of his package, wet silk glued to hard cock.

"Now you pay for that," he says, grabbing my buttocks.

Lurching me up the bed so he can get on too, he lies on top and attacks my mouth, sucking my tongue, biting and nibbling until working down to my breasts to suck and bite hard. The pain's exquisite but I'm not shocked I enjoy it.

"I want to come," I beg.

"Not until I say, Adrienne."

I yank on his hair to expose his throat, licking and kissing him furiously, producing several marks on his lower neck. In response he pins me down and produces marks all over my breasts. "You're mine, look!"

I look down and see he's written an 'L' on my breast.

"I can't feel your balls, please take them off, Luca!"

He pulls out, removes his underwear, and slams straight back into me.

My eyes are shut and all I can do is feel.

For so long I have been starved of love and a passion like this. How could David have really denied me sex? He must have been mad.

The sounds of our bodies joining permeate my ears and I gasp and cry high-pitch for him to please make me come. He grunts and curses as he tries to hold out, too. The slaps of his body against mine are intoxicating, as is the spurt of liquid from me to him and the occasional air pocket exploding.

"Can you feel my balls now?" he asks.

He pushes deep into me, his balls under my arsehole, almost inside it – he's so deep.

"Fuck me," I beg, my eyes still shut. I can't look at all that muscle and hair on his body. I'll want to come as soon as I look at it.

The sounds multiply and I'm feeling certain of only one thing: when he says come, I'll come. I'm holding onto such burning need, it really hurts, but I'll hold onto it for him.

"Come! Ade!"

"Ah, ah, ah!" I cry out, letting it go, letting the vibrations rush around, pulsing down his length in waves, my body shaking all around him as I go from strong contractions to gentle, short, rhythmic beats.

After we've cuddled and kissed and admired all our marks, he walks to the window naked and throws open the doors to the balcony. The summer wind rushing into the room, I gasp out laughing and he joins me on the bed, watching the stars with me.

"Luca?" I ask as he lays behind me, burying his face in my neck.

"Yes, princess."

"Sex is just sex, you know that right?"

He turns my face to him and frowns. "No."

I smile, attempting to convey I'm not saying this as a bad thing. "I mean… sex is great. I love sex, especially with you."

"But what are you trying to get at?" He seems puzzled.

I roll into him and kiss his lips gently. "That, well… I want everything. I don't just want good sex, which isn't the be all and end all. I want a soul mate. Someone who gives me more… someone I can be at one with. Someone who understands me."

He smiles gently and cuddles me tighter. "Will you listen to me, Adrienne? And by that, I mean listen carefully and try to let yourself believe what it is I am saying?"

"Okay," I whisper into his chest as he holds me.

"You drive me so crazy with desire, I cannot picture a day when I won't want or need you to hold me. There might be factors out of our control sometimes, like work trips or whatever, but I want you everyday for the rest of our lives, do you understand me?"

I pull up and look up into his eyes. "You do?"

"Yes," he groans, "and believe me when I say, I wouldn't ever ask you to settle. I want to give you everything and show you everything. I want to be your everything. I never told another woman that story I did tonight... about Papa and him losing the shop. Loss is something I never talk about, Adrienne. I don't dwell on all that even though it makes me what I am."

"I want to be in your soul," I tell him, feeling desperate, pleading.

Laying myself on top of him, he rubs my breasts with his hands and assures me, "You already are. We just have to give this time... and let me tell you, I'm not going hard on you yet... but I will. Oh I will. And then you'll realise what sex between two people should be like."

I reach beneath me for his cock which is almost hard again. Stroking him gently, I flick my tongue against his and his eyes swirl with desire.

"I love the look in your eye you have for me," I tell him, dropping a soft kiss on his mouth.

"I love feeling like this, Ade. Feeling alive."

Our arms lock around each other's and as I slide him inside me again, we kiss long and lazily. We move slowly and tenderly, making love.

When climax arrives out of the blue, it's with shock I tell him afterwards, "I've never come without a hard fucking or without clit play before."

He sweeps his tongue back into my mouth and kisses me until I'm almost coming again.

"We have much to learn and teach one another," he says.

FORTY

At Heathrow's long-stay car park, we're stood beside my car, making out. I can't bear to be parted from him but he has to go his way, and I have to go mine. For now, anyway.

"Call me," I kiss him, "as soon as you get home."

"Just let me make you come once more," he says, threatening to prise open my jeans. "Just once more. Once more, so I can see your face when you collapse in my arms."

My hands flat on the back of his head, I pull him hard into me, kissing him hard too. Breathing heavy, we're insatiable. We shouldn't be doing this in a public car park, but we are – this long goodbye.

"No Luca. Not here. Soon. Very soon."

He slides his hand over my rear and taps my bum, groaning in my ear. "So mean and nasty."

"I know," I mumble, biting his earlobe.

"You can't do that," he groans, "it's not fair."

I giggle because I know how much it turns him on, having his ear bitten.

"You were the one who threatened to make me come," I remind him, leaning back as he kisses my throat.

"God, Ade, god! Let me take you to a hotel and ravage you for the next few hours. Then you can go home."

I smile a little. "It's not my home. Just a place to be."

"Then leave," he says, "and come and live with me."

I shake my head as he kisses my cheeks. "Can't."

"Why not?"

"All my money is invested. It's going to take me months to consolidate everything before I can leave. If you say you're happy to sell, then sell, because you can… but I can't. Not yet."

He holds me in his arms and shakes me gently, annoyed we're having to separate like this.

"God damn it," he whines.

"I know."

"I hate London," he says.

"It's not so bad. I don't live in London, anyway. I work in London, but live in Windsor, just round the corner!"

"You never said! Now that's a bit more appealing."

I wink. "I'm here baby, waiting for you. Go and do your nasty Luca thing and sell the socks out of that place."

He creases with laughter and smiles with a hint of a warning in his eyes.

"You sure?" he asks.

"Sure."

"Then why don't you look sure?"

I stand back against the car a little and tell him, "I killed a man. Are you okay with that?"

He smirks. "I sort of killed one too, remember?"

I shake my head. "Yeah but… I really actually killed a man. With a knife."

He steps closer and asks, "Just tell me what happened. I'm sure I will forgive you."

I hold his hand and kiss his knuckles. "When I love someone, I love them so completely, it's hard to explain… but it's like I don't see the possibility of a split… so I construct ways to cope when things get tough, rather than getting out. It's what I was brought up on… putting up and shutting up like my mother. Except it got so bad and so insane with Marcus, the only way to break the never-ending cycle of abuse seemed to be for me to take drastic action. So one day when he got violent with me, I showed him that I could cut myself and it didn't hurt because pain had become nothing to me anymore."

Luca looks horrified but holds my hand, so I continue, "I told him he couldn't hurt me anymore so then he turned his eye to Billy and said he knew of a better way to hurt me if I didn't keep my mouth shut and play like a good girl. So then I stuck him with the knife, in a moment of blind rage. The knife marks I later told a jury were his doing. They were mine. My lawyer and Dad had to know the truth so I told them and that's why Dad disowned me because he couldn't bear it that I'd resorted to doing something so low."

"Adrienne," he whispers, shaking his head.

"The plastic surgeon might have removed my physical scars, but what about the rest? The scars inside here?" I gesture at my heart. "I killed a man. In a court of law, they said I was innocent, and I was free to go. Still, nobody knows what it feels like to walk away from that... knowing in your heart you still took a man's life. Being afraid of your own propensity to snap, just like that." I click my fingers. "Nobody knew that I stayed so long because I needed love. I wanted it. I clung onto him whenever he showed me kindness, but then he would show me no mercy–" I say almost choking.

"Go on," he asks me.

"I never meant to hurt him. At the very least, I should've got manslaughter, but a technicality with the knife thing got me off. I don't run from pain, I wield it, I absorb it. I cleanse myself through pain. It's all I've ever known."

I break down crying and he scoops me into his arms. Throwing himself around me, he tells me, "Adrienne, I forgive you. I love that you just told me all that. If he was still alive, I'd gut the fucker, make him watch while I did it too. I'd burn his innards in front of his eyes while they still pumped blood round his body. I don't care about the law or about what's right and wrong, because what he did to you was seriously unforgivable and the world is better off without assholes like him."

I cry harder into his chest, Luca's strength cordoning off the pain temporarily.

"I love you so much, Adrienne that there's nothing to forgive. Let me love you endlessly, let your pain be mine, let us bind ourselves tight and never be broken. I've looked so long for a woman to explore my darkest fantasies with... for me to give my soul to. You're the woman for me, I know it."

He kisses me deeply, a true lover's kiss, his tongue sliding and caressing mine. His hands are in my hair, on my bum, my face, my arm. I cradle his head in my arms and let him kiss me and kiss me, take me in any way he wants to.

"I love you and I'm missing you already," he tells me, "but now you better get back to your babies."

I nod slightly, remembering Billy, and how he hates me these days. I'll just have to face him I suppose.

Luca helps me into my car and waves, blowing kisses as I drive off. I hate us parting, and yet...

A part of me knows that this weekend has brought me closer to another human being, closer than I've ever felt before. What we have can't ever end, not now.

FORTY-ONE

Back in my office on Tuesday morning after such a wonderful, long weekend, I receive a text from Luca:

Think I may already have a buyer. A friend of mine!

Wow, great!

Want to meet again this weekend? Perhaps up this way? And engage your mother-in-law as a babysitter? A hotel, maybe? Or mine.

I shall look into it! Speak later.

Something tells me Luca doesn't want my children as part of the bargain. He barely asked about any of them at the weekend and since I got back from Lake Como, that's one thing that has been bothering me. Is he the best man for both me and them? I guess bumping into him at the weekend shook me up, reminded me I'd been missing out on male company. He felt familiar and safe, so I hopped into bed with him. Now I've had time to think, however… maybe sex had me blinded for a minute. Maybe I need to halt this for a moment and give myself time to think.

My internal phone buzzes and it's my secretary, Trina.

"Yes?"

"Reception say you have a visitor. A Max Kyd. Anyone you know?"

"Really?"

"Umm-hmm."

Everyone here knows me as Adrienne Lewis. They don't know I used to be a Kyd, daughter of the crisps manufacturer Max Kyd.

"Tell him I'm busy."

"He's... oh... he's gone up, with Sharkey T."

"Oh for fuck sake."

Sharkey T is my colleague, his real name Simon Trappor. He's a shark, around my father's age, and no doubt they know one another.

"Catch you later, gator," she says, hanging up.

I walk to the window of my office and fold my arms, looking down on the city.

A few seconds later there's a knock on the door.

He enters without my invitation and shuts the door behind him, the metal blinds clanging against the glass door as it shuts. His familiar, powerful scent carries on the air and invades my nostrils. Still the same fresh cologne.

"Adrienne," he greets me, "how are you?"

I turn and stare at my father, a man who's only ever been good for the money. What else he's given me, I don't know.

"I was good. Until you showed up."

He seats himself without invite too, the leather chair creaking beneath his butt.

"I heard from the Woodmanseys you ruined their wedding. I was quite amused, actually. I feigned shock of course and promised them it was just another of your psychotic episodes."

I smirk and when I do, he glances at me and I catch a look at the same blue eyes I have. Mum is a redhead with green eyes so I was unlikely to inherit her genes, and I got his more Scandinavian heritage, his great-grandfather a Swede or Norwegian, I'm still not sure.

"Where's my mother?"

"She's... in Spain," he says, "you should visit her."

I have the wind knocked out of me. "Changed your tune?"

He shakes his head. "We're not together anymore. We haven't been for quite some time."

"What?" I have to take a seat and look down at my desk, because I can't stand to look at him.

"She's ill. We found out soon after we moved to Spain. She's taken care of, I saw to that. These days I live in Kensington."

"So why didn't you tell her where I was?"

"She doesn't even know where she is. She has early onset Alzheimer's."

"The way you talk," I pause, sucking in a deep breath, "how can you say that with such coldness? She was your wife. So, you've come here to tell me that my mother's been ill all this time... and now, what? What? What are you here for?"

"She's still my wife. I *am* taking care of her, but when she doesn't even really recognise me anymore, what's the point, Adrienne? What's the point of you getting more hurt, and her not even knowing her own daughter?"

I shake my head. "I'd forget about you if I had the option. She would never forget me, NEVER!"

I swipe a tear away. I blame myself, too. I should've fought harder to stay in her life. Fearing looks from people outside the windows, I quickly lurch from my seat and shut all the blinds.

As I'm pacing the room with my arms folded, he clears his throat in a dramatic fashion, letting me know he has something he considers important to say and doesn't want interruption. "You really have no idea about Luca Van Duren, do you?"

My hands become tight fists by my sides and I have the most inordinate need for a punch bag. This man is determined to not only ruin my day, but my entire life, too.

Seated once more, I rest back in my chair, his eyes only able to see me in profile.

"Tell me," I demand.

"He's into all kinds of nefarious activities. Sports fixing being his main thing, drugs being a little sideline. The drugs come in with his dildos, in crates, you know? I also know he owns at least three houses in Amsterdam and I think you know the sort I speak of. *For Mutual Pleasure* is just a cover for what he really gets up to. A tacky cover at that."

Calmly, I steeple my hands against my lips. "How do you know all this?"

"I met him when he was on the Yorkshire Young Enterprise Committee at the same time I was. He doesn't hide his dealings, not among the higher set, like me. When the Woodmansey bloke told me... I had to see you. This can't happen again, Adrienne. Hate me all you want, but you didn't listen to me with Marcus, but perhaps this time—"

"He's a criminal, perhaps," I agree, "but why now? Why are you here now?"

"I know his sort, Adrienne. Marcus was just a stupid punk in comparison. Luca will not put up with your fiery temper. He won't understand your career, your ambition. You know I'm right. Eventually you'll be embroiled, and your kids—"

"What do you care about my fucking kids, your grand-children," I scorn.

When my phone rings, I put it on speaker and tell the secretary, "Hold all my calls."

"Okay," Trina says, her voice crackling as I quickly end the connection.

"So..." I pause, catching a look at my father's frightened eyes, "...my husband dies, and you don't think to visit me. I bear your second and third grandchildren, nothing. But when my money is threatened by a potential husband who's dodgy, you're straight here."

I turn to look at him and glare. He remains staid, as always, tall and stately and unreadable.

"I'm here to warn you. I'm here to ask you to think before you embark on a relationship with this man. He's not like Marcus. Marcus was sloppy, incompetent, and he took out his incompetence on you. No, Luca is smart and he must be, to have never got caught. He doesn't do his own dirty work, he gets other people to do it for him. He's crooked but he uses his mind. He's clever. He even has you fooled."

I think back to the day when Billy was upset and annoyed in Betty's. Luca shouted at him in public and got cross. I thought it was bad, but… we were both stressed that day. He was pressuring me to move away from Leeds, leave the country and be with him. I didn't want to, I wasn't ready.

I fold my hands together on my lap, mirroring Dad's demeanour. "He told me he was in Milan at the weekend for business. Of all the flights he could have gotten, he got the same as me. He's just been waiting to get me on my own, hasn't he? Waiting for the right time."

"To him, you're not a woman, but a commodity. A prize. An addition to his portfolio."

I shake my head. "You'd know all about that, wouldn't you?"

"I know about loving someone, like my own flesh and blood daughter who refused to listen to me when I warned her. My only child. Do you know what it was like? Hmm? Watching you fuck up your life. You almost wrecked everything with a stupid love affair despite all my warnings. It was clear there was no point in arguing with you or trying to steer you right. You needed a reality check so I cut you off. It was the best thing I ever did for you. Coddled no more by your mother, you had to grow up."

I snicker. "Coddled."

"Maybe if we'd had more kids, but–"

"I don't care about your domestic issues."

"Well, I hope the fact I'm here proves just how strongly I disapprove… no, not even that… despise the thought of you with that man. He's not a good man."

"I'd like for you to go."

He rises from his chair and stares down at me. "I tried to

get a file on him, but couldn't. Do you know what that means?"

"He has people bought?" I nod my head because Dad getting files on people is definitely something he would do.

"Yes, he has people bought."

"Do you..." I hate to say it, but I have to. "...think he's capable of killing someone? Like a friend? Would he even kill a friend?"

"He grew up in the ghetto and you ask me that? What do you think?"

I rise from my seat and walk to him. He stares into my eyes and we level. I can see he's genuinely hurt and fearful.

"He was apparently there on the scene, the night David died."

Dad gasps and covers his mouth. "Oh, Adrienne."

My ugly frown rears its head. "Help me?"

He nods slowly. "I'll see what I can do. I can't promise anything. He's armoured."

"You knew, didn't you?" I ask, folding my arms. "You knew what awaited me in this world, so you hardened me?"

"I made you, Adrienne. You're the only one, you're my successor."

I nod slowly and like business associates, we shake hands.

"Be wary. I'll be in touch."

"Thank you, Father."

He leaves as he arrived, quiet and without fuss – utter devastation in his wake.

For the rest of the day, I behave entirely normally. Answer my calls, emails. Chase some leads. Have lunch alone as I check stocks and shares. Answer sporadic messages from Luca and try not to think about him perhaps having killed David. If he did kill David, he's my only link to finding out the truth.

What happened to my husband?

Riding the train home, my mind's a mess of memories and inconclusive evidence. Did Luca push David into the water, did he drug him? What did he do?

When I arrive home, it's late as usual. Billy's been better since Rachel came back on the scene. He even tells me to have a good day when I leave in the morning. Tonight he's already asleep in bed as I pass his door. Lucinda and Marissa are knocked out, too.

I can't be with a man who has questionable morals, not when I have children to think about.

In the shower where I normally have my best ideas, nothing comes to me.

In bed, I tap my hands against my head, trying to think. Lying with my hair still damp, I feel a chill and hug the duvet harder.

A text arrives saying: *Time to talk?*

I don't want to talk to him but then I remember, Luca's my only link.

Sure.

He calls a few seconds later and I look over my shoulder to make sure the bedroom door's shut.

"Hey."

"Hi beautiful, how was your day."

"Strange, actually."

"Yeah? Well, mine was great. I think I can be with you quicker than we thought. How about next month? I move down there. Of course we'll need a bigger place."

"Luca, we can't... just rush it. I have children. They need to be more familiar with you before we move in together."

"I looked into it. Eton will accept Billy, the girls can attend boarding school soon, too."

"I don't want him to go to Eton, don't you think I would have enrolled him if I did?"

"Adrienne, come on! It's the chance few boys get."

"It's my choice and he told me he doesn't want to go."

"He'll do as I say."

"No, he won't. Listen, I'm tired. I can't think right now. I'm sorry."

"I'll call you tomorrow, perhaps as you ride to work?"

"Sure, speak then."

"Okay, I love you."

I hang up, because I know in my heart, I don't love him. I never have done. It's all fucking fake where Luca is concerned. He's just been there, round every corner, surreptitiously planning his assault on me – to take down the SS Adrienne Lewis.

The first time I met Luca was over dinner at our old flat in Leeds, before I had Lucinda, before we moved house. He and David had some business to discuss. I remember thinking he was good-looking, sure, but I also remember watching how David interacted with another man – so confident and vigorous together in their businesslike ways – yet the one thing that set aside David from Luca was the fact I was in love with him and nothing compared. Nor ever would.

After David and I split the first time, I was visiting my solicitors in Leeds city centre when I bumped into Luca outside Café Nero. This was before I had Marissa, and Billy had just started school, while Lucinda was at nursery.

We went inside the coffee shop and Luca just said all the right things, offered me a shoulder to cry on, never questioned why David had cheated. He didn't ask if there were extraneous issues – because Luca didn't really care about my marriage. He just wanted to see what he could get out of the break-up for himself. Perhaps he'd been hoping and waiting for the day he could have me all to himself?

Before I knew it, I'd handed over my number to Luca across the table in Café Nero and he began incessantly calling and texting, announcing his love within days. I was drunk when we first had sex – and I needed to be – because I wouldn't have been able to go through with it otherwise.

Luca seemed to be the fantasy, the perfect lover, but perfect men don't exist and if they do – pigs might fly also. He was always controlled in the way he treated me, in what he said, and how timely it was of him to reveal the story about his father's failed business, right when he knew he finally had me. Now I know why he is the way he is – he watched his father fail and he cannot bear to fail, too. So he has all his backups in place to protect him. Like my father said, *For Mutual Pleasure* is a front and he can run the rest of his businesses from wherever he is in the world. He's not sacrificing anything to be with me. I'm the one who's lost everything. I'm on the losing end of all this.

When I once told David I wouldn't move on just like that, I wasn't kidding – but Luca was just there, in my face, and I got caught up. That thing with Billy was a wake-up call to the real man. David was a troubled man but he never hid his true self from me. Like me, I always knew David was broken and sad, too, but Luca has been hiding the real person he is – he's crooked and a bully. I have to remember he's not a good man – and bad men cannot be fixed. I sure as shit know that.

Grabbing my laptop, I google Violet's full name and sure enough, after a few scrolls, she pops up. According to her open Facebook page, she's set up her own massage business. Oh I bet she has. I message her page, hoping it's not run by an admin:

Hey Violet, remember me? I have something important to discuss. There's money in it for you. Bags of it, if you want. – Adrienne

I'm about to doze off, when half an hour later she replies: *I'm legit these days, what do you want?*

Legit? What does she mean by that? Did she work for Luca, doing his dirty work?

ME: *Info about David.*

HER: *What about him?*

ME: *I don't know, you tell me.*

HER: *Where are you nowadays? I know you moved.*

ME: *London.*

HER: *£5000. I'll be there tomorrow lunchtime. Canary Wharf. Keep in touch via FB?*

ME: *Okay.*

I fear what my father said, i.e. nobody can touch him. I need a plan in case I might be being watched. I have to be careful because Luca could be dangerous, having me watched or anything. I pack my gym clothes, sunglasses and a peaked hat in my bag for the morning, so I can meet her in some manner of disguise.

I don't know what sort of man I am dealing with in Luca, but I doubt my father's visit was for nothing. My father never does anything without agenda.

FORTY-TWO

I sneak out of the building via the toilet in the stairwell, wearing my gym clothes, pretty unrecognisable. The grey suit has gone, replaced by fluorescent clothing I normally wear to spinning on Friday nights when I need to eject all my stress.

I walk quickly to my destination a few streets away, near some trees on Canada Square, by the place where they have the ice rink in winter. Looking around, I find her easily. She told me she'd be wearing a red hat.

We stand on the street, traffic rushing past us. She clearly chose this spot so we'd look like two friends happening to pass one another, not two people meeting for indecent assignations. We're in plain sight.

"The money?" she asks.

"I'll send it as soon as you give me details."

She hands over bank account details on a piece of paper and I nod.

"I worked for Luca as his personal secretary before Dave joined the company. I carried out errands of the unsavoury variety."

"Like what?"

"Delivering photos. For blackmail. Threatening letters. I was his messenger, that was all. It was total coincidence I'd worked with Dave before, in porn."

"So, what happened? I haven't got a lot of time."

"Luca was building a profile of you. I don't know why."

I can only think that perhaps Luca was trying to take revenge against my father... but I don't know!

"More, tell me more."

"When the PI brought photos to Luca, just stuff of you going about your day, I saw them on his desk. I saw Dave with you. I told Luca I knew your guy and he was very interested to know this." She shakes her head, ashamed. "He paid me to follow Dave, see what he was doing. I approached him eventually, aware he was trying to find a job. We recruited him and I was promoted, no longer just his private secretary. I was his way to Dave... and you. I befriended Dave... and when it got bad in your marriage, Luca promised a lump sum if I seduced your man. Your husband didn't take the bait, not for a long time. Then he asked me for drugs. And he was a sucker for those... always was."

I get a look at her empty ring finger. "You're not married?"

She shakes her head. "I never would've interested Dave if I wasn't. Something meaningless, something without a future... I knew that'd appeal to him if he was going through a tough time with you... which clearly he was. He confided in Luca about it all... Luca knew you had marital issues."

I swallow my bile. "Of course he knew."

"Then, the plan failed. It failed again and again because you went back to him. I think the shit luck of it was, Luca had really fallen for you, but he knew Dave was embedded in your heart. It drove him crazy. He didn't want you, knowing you loved another man. But he didn't want you and Dave to be together either... so that was when I found you in that shop in the Victorian Quarter... and told you a pack of lies about an abortion. It was all lies."

My heart's beating so fast, I can feel my pulse shaking my nose.

"He paid you… to seduce my husband, to lie about an abortion. Why?"

"So he could swoop in and save the day, then steal you. Luca's been waiting patiently. He's been enjoying the prolonged anticipation of finally ensnaring you. That's what he's like. Luca can hold a grudge forever, just ask him about what happened to his kid brother."

He never mentioned he had a brother?

I shake my head and try to catch my breath. "What if Luca knew you were here, telling me all this?"

She smiles a tiny smile, her lips twitching. "A few days before Dave died, he caught up with me at my new digs. He looked awful, he was suffering. He pretended he wanted to fuck and I wasn't going to deny him, I mean… you don't deny David! But then… he turned on me, tied me to a chair and demanded I tell him everything. He kept me tied up for two days until I couldn't help but piss myself. I gave up all the details I knew could get me killed. I gave up everything. I never saw Dave again, and you know the rest, apart from this…"

She lifts her top up above her waistline and shows me a deep scar in the side of her abdomen. "He shot me. Luca shot me in the gut… in the countryside… abandoned me… but I survived," she sniffles, "he visited me in the hospital and said the only reason he was going to let me live was because David was dead… and the deed was done. We were finally rid of him."

"Luca never thought I'd trace this back. He under-estimated me. He underestimated my father. Max visited me, after more than ten years' estrangement, he visited me to warn me about Luca."

She nods, blinking up at me through grey, tired eyelids. "So, now you know everything. I'll need that money to get away for a while. Just to be sure, to be safe. I knew what I signed up for… but doing that to our Dave, it wasn't on. It was wrong." She wipes her eyes, still sniffing through tears.

My mind racing, I mutter to myself more than her, "Did he kill David, though? Luca apparently jumped in and saved him."

She shakes her head, pointing at her belly, exasperated with me. "Look at me, Ade! Look at what he did. I can't have kids because he shot me. I had to have a hysterectomy, do you know what that's like? Do you?"

She waggles her head a lot and I shake my head, *no.*

"Okay, yes... it seems like he saved him... but then he died...? So... I don't know what happened exactly. None of us do. But David dead... it seems too convenient for Luca, don't you think? Huh? My guess is that they met that night so Luca could pay Dave off. Maybe Dave didn't wanna play ball."

I gasp, shocked. I can't look at her but I mutter, "You connived with Luca, how am I meant to trust you at all? How did you fake your own marriage? How did you weave these webs, cast these spells?"

"Some doctored photos around my house convinced Dave I was married, alright." She takes my hooded top in her hands and shakes me. "See beyond the illusion... look hard... and see the reality. It's only when you hit strife that people show their true colours... and most people don't care about anyone else but themselves. Not everyone is good, not everyone is like you. Don't you get it?"

Yes, like Luca, shouting at Billy when he had no right to do that. Kids are like dogs, they know a bad penny when they meet one.

I hold my forehead and mumble, "Lightning doesn't strike twice. My ex partner Marcus was a fucker, too. Why again? Is there some connection here... something I don't know about."

"Marcus, who?" she asks, intrigued.

"Marcus Spavin."

Her eyes widen. "You mean Marco Van Duren? He changed his name, I think. To protect himself. He used to

353

supply Luca's drugs around the clubs in Leeds and Harrogate. He used to hang out in them… that's how…"

I'm nodding along when I tell her, "Yes, I met Marcus in a club. One he was probably supplying to, now I think about it… but the brothers, they looked nothing alike! And I never knew either one of them was selling drugs. Marcus told me he was in electrical goods…" Biting my nails as I think back, I remember Marcus telling me all his family were dead. Well, not all of them it seems…

She grinds her teeth. "I knew Marcus back in the day. They were alike, but only when you put them together. It was clear Luca got all the brains and beauty. Their parents died when they were young… something like an armed robbery took their lives. So, Luca brought Marco here when he was a teenager… and Marco didn't have the accent. He was more anglicised, not as dark as Luca. I think there was at least eight years between them. Luca used to spend most of his time in Amsterdam but Marco elected to stay here."

"This can't be happening." I feel all my blood pool in my face and the heat of panic ratchets up my fear. "Why did Marcus never tell me about his big brother–"

"Marco became Marcus to sever his connection to Luca. Luca was becoming so powerful, he feared their enemies would try to use their relationship against them. They left London but like I said, while Luca went home to Amsterdam, Marco went north… to Harrogate, where the drugs culture was just getting started. They tried to live separate lives in case something happened to one or the other of them… and look, that happened, in a sort of roundabout way."

"Oh, god." I hold my throat, fighting for breath.

"Before today, all I knew was that his kid brother was murdered. He used to tell me sometimes when he was drunk and rambling that he knew who the murderer was. He said he could easily kill the one who murdered his brother… or he could spend his life making them suffer. I never knew it was you. It was, wasn't it?"

I nod slowly, gulping down my terror. "I even told Luca at the weekend... I told him how his brother died... I admitted everything! I didn't know what I was saying–"

Taking my shoulders in her hands, she spits words out. "Ade, get your kids, and just go. Get as far away as you can. Take them. And go. I'm sorry... but if it's any consolation," she gestures she needs to leave, "Dave never once fucked me like he meant it."

I show her the crumpled paper in my hand. "I'll put ten in before the end of the day."

"Oh, thank you!"

"Go, before I change my mind."

She scarpers and I start jogging back to the office, pretending I really have been out running to clear my head, which has never felt foggier.

Pacing my office in my hated grey suit, I have no idea who to turn to. Who to trust. All the blinds are shut but I still feel like I'm being watched. All these revelations, what am I to do?

I head for Stuart's office, knocking on the door. He's on the phone but nods for me to walk inside.

When he finishes his call, he asks, "Whassup Blondie?"

"I need out. You want in?"

He frowns. "What the hell, what's happened?"

"Do you want my portfolio, or not? I have to get away. There's been a family tragedy and I have to leave, quietly. We can do this quietly or not at all, up to you. But we both know you want it. You get first offer."

He gestures at the chair opposite his and I sit down. Grabbing his notepad, he writes down a sum:

£5million.

I shake my head at him. "That's pathetic. I have children to feed."

He sniffs. "Stay and make it fifty, or get out now *quietly* and with a decent figure. It's still decent."

"Ten," I demand, "or we'll see who else wants my portfolio."

"Eight."

"Done. I'll sign everything over to you, once you have the money ready to transfer. I'll assure my clients you can handle everything as well as I could."

"Better, even. So, I'll send eight to your usual account?"

"No, here." I take his notepad and write down a new set of banking numbers.

He looks at them, registering I use offshore.

"Okay, then. And here was me thinking you knew nothing."

I stand. "And here was me thinking you had a human bone in your body."

My portfolio's worth at least £10million and he knows it has the potential for so much more.

"Berken won't like this," he warns me.

"I won't be here when he realises I slipped out, will I?"

"That'll cost you. Let's say seven."

"Seven and a half."

"Done," he says, always needing the last word.

On the train home, I phone Rachel. "I need a favour."

"Anything."

"My mother's old friend, Bernie. See if she has their address, will you?"

"Sure, you want to get in touch?"

"Yeah…" I tell her a lie, saying my mother's fiftieth birthday is coming up. I could go through my father, but I'd like to avoid him at all costs.

"No prob."

"Thank you Rachel. I need it quite soon, if you can."

"I'll see what I can do."

She messages me the address before midnight and I book flights.

FORTY-THREE

I booked the first flights I could find so now, I'm driving the kids to my mum's house at the crack of dawn, having flown through the night. They're sleeping; Marissa and Lucinda in the back, Billy in the front with me in our rental Jeep. I don't want to risk my children's lives; I had to get away as quickly as I could and my mother's was the first place I thought of travelling to.

Trekking out to Xàbia, a place we visited often when I was little, I try to remember my mother's face and picture her as she might look now. It's been several years and I threw out old pictures ages ago. I can't remember her much at all, except the clothes she wore and the same Estée Lauder perfume she always wore.

I thought my father would have bought somewhere in Barbados or the Turk Islands but instead he brought her here – somewhere familiar – where we used to come before he made big money. Maybe he's more sentimental than he'd have people believe.

The town's quiet at this time, only a few Spaniards sat out smoking in the dry heat of the summer sunrise. I'm partly glad I tanned a little at Lake Como so I don't look too much like a new arrival.

Passing olive, pine and orange groves, I smell the earth through the gap in my window and the scent takes me right back to being a child. The feelings whirling at the centre of my chest hurt so badly, because that little girl I used to be is gone. I'll never get her back.

Approaching their property by the sea finally, I pull up on the road to admire it. A sixteenth-century manor house, with uninterrupted views of the Med. We could sail to Ibiza if we want, easily visit Valencia or Alicante. Even take a short airplane flight over the sea to Morocco.

I used to love coming here as a child to marvel at the marinas, the pretty, winding bays and deep, blue seas. The markets were excellent and cheap. So many trinkets for such little cash. The truest blues and greens of this land have not changed, not one iota.

"Is that it?" Billy asks, his voice betraying weariness.

"Yes, baby."

"You didn't tell us they were rich?"

"I didn't." I climb back into the car. "We've always been rich though, Bill. Sometimes wealth, and for that matter poverty, aren't measured in pounds or pence."

He frowns at me as I restart the car and begin driving down the long, winding drive uphill to Mum's house, hidden on a hillside beside trees and rushes.

Billy and I leave the vehicle in the courtyard out front. My daughters remain asleep and I don't want to disturb them. As we approach the house, there's something very Moorish about the building, something very simple but regal. The walls gleam white and the windows have those wooden shutters I love.

"*Señora, hola?*" a woman in a navy tunic dress asks, someone I presume a nurse or carer. Leaving the front door open behind her, I realise there is very little security round here. I'm hoping that means my mother has seen no trouble in these parts.

I hold out my hand and announce, "*Señora Kyd? Mi madre?*"

The woman crosses her chest and begins to pant. "Okay,

okay, yes, you daughter, yes?"

I nod.

"I get her. Wait."

Billy and I kick the gravel beneath our feet and he pipes up, "Did you have a row with them?"

I nod slowly. "Over you."

He frowns. "Over me?"

"Over you. You see, when you were a baby, your grandmother looked after you–"

"Adrienne?" my mother almost screams from her bedroom veranda up above us, making sure it is me before she comes down.

"Mum!"

A part of me thought I'd forgotten her, but shaking my head, I weep to realise she looks just the same. Just the same.

"I'm coming," she gasps, running back into her room, no doubt travelling through the house and downstairs to get to us. I'm brimming with tears, I'm dying of longing for her to get outside, and when she does she races to me and we fall to the floor on our knees together.

"Oh my baby, oh my baby," she repeats, and I hide and hide and burrow myself into her, letting all my pain flow out, all my pain and harrowed heart, flowing from me to her. She catches my flying arrows and squashes them to nothing.

"Billy, come to Grandma," she asks, and he's pulled into the embrace with us.

I feel his arms slide around me and he starts crying too. I'm finally crying.

Finally.

When Marissa wakes, she starts crying and Lucinda begins to cry too. Hurrying from our sides, my mum hushes, "I'll get them, I'll get them."

Holding Billy tight while Mum gets my daughters from their seats, it seems to me that Billy's suddenly realised bad things happened to Mummy to make me the way I am.

"Come inside, Grandma's missed you all so much."

Marissa and Lucinda cling to the woman who looks and feels the same as Mummy, watching her with wide, inquisitive eyes.

"Grandma will look after you now, come on."

The care giver woman stares at me and when Mum's out of earshot, she remarks, "She remember now, but later, no remember, you know?" She wiggles her finger in the air, like I'm stupid and don't know what is going on.

"I understand," I tell her.

"No," she repeats, her eyes expressing empathy, "she remember, but later, no remember. No remember... at all. Mean you must go... cannot stay. Understand?"

I gulp. "Not even for one night?"

She twists her fingers together. "I try."

We step through the villa on clay tiles and it feels a little too cool inside after being out in the heat of the day. Mum leads us through dark, cool corridors until we reach a warm kitchen with fresh fruits piled up; grapefruits and cherries, bananas and apples, oranges galore and so much more.

"Are you happy, Adrienne?" she asks, seeming clear-headed to me.

She places the girls on chairs around the kitchen island and passes them a mountain of grapes to pick at. The nurse begins pouring coffee for me and hands all the children glasses of milk.

"I guess I am, although... I don't know," I reveal, avoiding Billy's eyes as I say that.

Mum turns her green eyes onto mine, her expression serious. "If there's any trouble, it's his making. So you're best off with me, away from *him*, away from destruction."

Swallowing, I mention, "I saw him... he told me everything."

"I got tired of waiting around for him to tell me where you were. I *told* him I was leaving," she boasts and I glance at the care woman, who rolls her eyes. "I went away, brought myself here, and valiantly escaped the bastard."

Billy's eyes shoot to mine and he gawps, while she stands around, unaware she's swearing in the company of children. A frown scrunches up her face and for the first time, I realise frowning is something Billy and I get from my mother, Josephine Kyd.

"He told me far-fetched stories of foreign travels, of adventures you were taking Billy on… he was a bloody liar, nothing but," she goes on, ranting about the man she didn't have to stay attached to for all those years.

Part of me now wonders whether fear kept her with him – more than fear of survival – a mental fear she had no understanding of until her diagnosis. We exchange glances and while my mum's help busies around feeding the children, it sinks in that we let a man come between us and all these wasted years have been for what?

"I'm sorry," I tell her, but when I say it, she registers nothing. Stares into space.

"Have you got a name?" I ask the help.

"Viola."

I nod. "Does she have black spots? She's totally vacant."

I waft a hand in front of Mum's face. No response.

"Yes."

We smile awkwardly. It hurts, it all hurts.

Mum suddenly gathers me to her bosom and kisses my hair, holding me close.

"I love you, Adrienne. I always have, always will."

Fighting for air, I whisper, "I know."

Billy yawns from ear to ear and Mum suggests, "Billy, if you want to sleep, Viola will show you where there is a bed." He nods slowly. The poor thing barely slept, either, like me. The two girls are happy and smile at one another, picking their way through their grape mountain.

"Where's their father?" she asks me after Billy's gone upstairs with Viola.

"My husband, David… he was wonderful… but he died."

I don't want to tell her the rest. I don't have the energy to.

"I'm sorry, Ade. Was it an accident... or something?"

I turn my face away. "They told me he had the same heart thing his father had. You might have known his father, he was called Ian Lewis, a dentist? He practiced in Harrogate."

Her face pales. "Not him? He was meant to be riding every woman in that town."

I nod slowly. "Yes, he wasn't a good father to David."

I watch Mum trying to work things out in her head. "Why are you here, girl?"

"Running away from trouble."

"So you've come to see your old mum, well, best place. Don't you think young ladies?" she says to the girls, and they nod, scoffing what's in front of them.

How would I tell her everything? She wouldn't understand, even if she was sane. I've just flown out here, dropped everything, sold my stakes at the hedge fund company I work for, taken my kids out of school, paid my nanny off for a few days. I don't feel safe, I've run here... I don't know what else I'm supposed to do... but hide.

She shakes her head slowly, from side to side. "He's an unwell man, Adrienne."

"What, I mean, who?" I ask, not sure who or what she's talking about now.

"He has no care for anything, not even himself. Except his legacy. He only ever wanted a son."

"Why no more?"

She sniggers. "I didn't want to go through all that pain again, not when I didn't love my husband. It wasn't worth it. Not for him, and not for me. You were enough. You were all I needed."

I hold onto the sideboard. "But what about what I needed?"

She frowns again, trying to reach out and hold me, but I pull away. "Sometimes, Adrienne... it seems like what you get in life is what you deserve, so maybe I told myself over and over that he was all I deserved, but when you left our lives, I didn't begrudge you your freedom, I applauded you for it. I wanted you to go and be free. I hoped I gave you the strength and encouragement to do that, it was all I ever wanted for you. For me, it felt like staying with him was the only way I could give you that freedom."

"I disagree." I sit down on a stool and hold my head in my hands. "Poor, we'd have been better off. I'd have worked, you could have worked–"

"No I couldn't," she interrupts me.

"Why not?"

She taps the side of her head. "This hasn't been functioning for years. He only realised that when we came out here to retire and he finally had to spend time with me."

Her eyes suddenly shoot to mine, blank, and she asks in a different tone of voice, "Who are you?"

That frown.

Except there's nothing worse right now than looking into her eyes and knowing she doesn't see me. "I'm a friend, of Viola's," I tell her, "visiting."

Viola comes downstairs, recognising the bemused look in my mother's eyes immediately. "Josie, let's go knit on the porch? Our guests don't need us."

Mum does as instructed. Maybe knitting is code for something, I don't know. Viola winks and whispers over her shoulder, "I made beds, for you and your girls. Go up... rest."

I rise from my seat and help the girls down from their stools. "Thank you."

FORTY-FOUR

After a nap, we spend time swimming in the private pool. Viola keeps my mother amused in another part of the house, knitting or whatever it is they are doing. I'm not sure if the dementia lasts all of the day or whether this morning was a lucky break – moments of clarity being rare.

Billy asks lots of questions about Grandma – but I don't have the answers to those questions yet and he purses his lips and stews when I refuse to explain.

As I look at my son, Luca's nephew, I wonder if Luca bullied his younger brother – and that's what made Marcus abusive too. If I married Luca, might Billy end up just like his own dad? Thankfully that will now never happen.

At lunchtime, Viola produces a huge tapas feast, laying it all out on the patio tables by the pool. She's an honest woman, treating us as my own mother would have if she were still with us in mind as well as body. It's at this point we all hear a vehicle pull up on the rocky driveway I drove up only hours ago. In the central courtyard where the pool is, Viola looks panicked when she mumbles, "Not more strangers! She won't cope."

I stand and put my dress on over my swimsuit. "I'll go. Just stay with Mum."

Billy wants to follow me but I halt him. "Watch your

sisters… keep them safe for me."

He nods and whispers. "Okay. You will come back?"

I smile wryly. "Don't be daft."

It's clear as I walk through the house, my mother is not expecting a guest. Plus, we only arrived this morning and I told nobody I would be visiting this place, either.

This might not be friendly, so I pull a knife from the block on my way through the kitchen to the front door, just in case.

There's the expected knock on the front door and it reminds me… but it can't be. No. It can't be… *his knock*.

"Who is it?" I bark in an unfriendly voice.

"Me," he says.

This has to be some trick. I swing open the front door, clutching the knife in my hand.

Through the bright glare of the midday sun that's making my eyes throb, I see his familiar outline, although he looks very different.

It can't be–

"D–D–David?"

The ground catches me as I fall.

As I sleep with a breeze drifting in from the Mediterranean, sweet smells pervade my senses. Sea, salt, seafood, citrus, pine and olives. It almost smells – combined – like I'm walking through a market. Yet instead of all the scents overwhelming me, I lay here able to separate them.

I drift through forests in my dreams, I swim the lake I imagine for myself when I'm sad. It's so blue and clear. I scoop some water into my hands as I tread water and I can see right through it, almost as if it's air. Tiny, luminescent fish live at the bottom of the pool and wink at me as I swim naked and free above them, my hair spilling out around me.

While I dry on the moss beneath the hot sun, his body spoons me from behind and he caresses my stomach with gentle, tender fingertips. Kisses at my nape send chills racing down my spine. He pulls up closer to me and I feel his heat at my back, his rough pubic hair against my bottom and his cock between my crack.

"Adrienne," he calls, his voice igniting my senses.

I reach a hand back behind me and he's bearded and has longer hair. His familiar scent brings me to him and I rest on top of his body, kissing his sumptuous lips ravenously.

Hands rub desperately up and down my spine, kneading my skin and flesh, bringing me tight against his arousal. In my hands I hold his bearded face and feast on his mouth, biting, sucking his lips and tongue.

"Oh, David. I've missed you so much."

He throws me over and pulls my legs apart. Instinctively I wrap them around his lower back and he slides into my heat. I squeeze my eyes shut as I bear him; his size and his glory, all mine. I've missed him and I was shut because he'd been gone. He needs to break me in again.

When he's found his rhythm, he lifts slightly and kisses me deeply, his tongue speaking loving words. Slow kisses, then fast, deep kisses, then shallow; kisses all over my face.

When I start to scream, he covers my mouth and finishes quickly, pouring into me with a long and low howl in my ear.

When he's done, he rolls me and holds me on top of him. I'm buried in his chest, listening to the pounding of his heart. He's caressing my face and has me, all of me, at his will.

It's like none of this was a dream, but all real.

FORTY-FIVE

I wake from the most incredible, visceral dreams and find myself warm and sweaty, drunk on the clean air and the dose of vitamin D I got while I was out by the pool. Somehow I sense it's early evening, so I've been sleeping all day? My pillow doesn't feel right, but it feels so incredibly wonderful.

It takes maybe three seconds before I realise I'm not alone. I'm laid in a man's arms.

I shoot up and sit on my knees, edging away from him. This interloper. This ghost.

He can't be real.

It was no dream – but a nightmare.

I fall back and stumble from the bed, scraping my knees on the tiled floor. I back away, until my hands hit the wall of the room behind me.

"This is all I need, now I'm seeing things."

"Adrienne, I'm real. Don't frighten the children."

He steps from the bed as I remain backed up against the wall, my hands brushing against the rough stone to keep myself standing. He's as naked as me and now I'm stood standing, I feel his sperm run down my inside leg.

He's real.

"Why?"

He creeps closer and when he's close, I swing for him. He ducks quickly.

"I knew I'd need self defence," he says.

He smiles behind his beard and breath suddenly leaves me and I'm hyperventilating. I fall on my hands and knees and can't breathe. He panics and begs me to tell him what to do. I push him away from me and crawl on my hands and knees back to bed.

Climbing in, I push my face into a pillow and concentrate on finding my breath again. It takes a few minutes but I manage it.

"I'm in shock," I tell him breathless, "it's okay, I'll be okay in a minute."

This used to happen when Marcus winded me or punched me when I wasn't expecting it. It was the brutality – but more than that – it was the way he did it for no reason, when I was totally unprepared for his attacks.

While I'm trying to catch my breath, he finds his boxers on the floor and pulls them on. I watch him as he paces the floor, wondering whether he's done the right thing showing up.

"You're not fucking dead," I grit out, "and I've been dead alongside you."

"I know. Without you, I'm nothing. When I saw on your emails you'd asked my mother for this address, I had to come and find out what you were doing."

I fling myself up in bed but I can't find any words. I'm still in shock, unsure what the hell is going on.

Frowning, I beg, "You hack my emails? What? Like, everyday?"

"Just your personal ones. The rest I don't care about."

As I observe him, I notice he's a lot more fidgety and nervous than he ever was before.

Plus the hair and the beard…

"Tell me everything, David, please. I love you. I never stopped loving you."

He stops pacing and his head jerks so he can look at me. Stomping across to the bed where I'm sat, he scoops me into his arms and throws me down. His tongue commands my mouth and I groan hungrily, every inch of me on fire.

I push his boxers down over his bottom and he rams straight into me. He bestows wild and untamed kisses all over my breasts and throat as he fucks me savagely, burning into me. I grip his ass in my hands and push him deep inside, scratch my nails down the backs of his thighs and grunt in his ear. We roll so I'm on top and our chests remain pressed together. My lips run riot over his face, licking and kissing him everywhere so fast. He's so warm and so real and smells just the same. I've never felt safer than I do when I'm with him and now he's broader and thicker and heavier, he feels like the only saviour I'll ever need. The only barrier to all the hurt I've endured and still carry inside me.

"My baby, ah my baby," he whispers.

We roll back and I'm beneath him again and his hands are pinning my hands above my head as he aims for my g-spot and fills me so full. He's lapping my mouth when I come and his tongue silences my cries when I feel him swell and vibrate inside me.

"Ah, Ade…"

He remains buried inside me and rests his head in between my breasts, and without sound, he convulses and weeps into my chest. I hold him close and weep silent tears with him, my legs and arms wrapped tight around him.

"I love you, David. I've always loved you," I squeeze myself closer yet, "I'll love you forever, like you said."

"It feels like I've spent decades trying to remind myself of that. I've had to be so strong, for you. I have so much to tell you."

"Where are the kids?" I ask, suddenly fearful.

"Your dad… he's looking after them downstairs. It's okay… it's okay, Adrienne. He brought me, he's helped me. Let me tell you everything."

I nod. "I'm ready. Tell me everything."

FORTY-SIX

They met at the river's edge, near the King's Head in York as agreed. Taking the packet of money from Luca, David smirked. "All here?"

Luca nodded. "All there."

David Lewis didn't look much handsome. No doubt, the drugs. Drink. Etcetera. Luca was counting on that money sending David into an early grave.

"I thought I was a first-class arse wipe, but not compared to you."

"If you say so, David," Luca said, cool moonlight reflected in his eyes. Sturdy, he stood impatient on the cobbles, ready to say his goodbyes.

"Paying me off... now Violet's finally admitted you pushed her to pursue me. This," David said, shaking the packet of money in his hand, "is dirty, stinking money. We both know it."

"I'm paying you off to protect Adrienne. You did the rest all on your own. Stay away from her. She deserves better."

"Yeah, right!" The younger of them laughed manically. "I confided in you about my marriage... thought you were my friend. And this is what you do! Use it against me!"

In fact David shouted so loud, and so hard, he tripped on his shoelace and fell into the river.

Idiot, *thought Luca. He looked over the rope and bubbles*

rose to the surface, but David didn't.

He failed to surface.

Now, it would have been convenient if he had just died, wouldn't it? But then what about the 10K he now had in his inside pocket? Who would explain David carrying all that cash?

"Did that bloke just jump in?" asked some smoker from behind Luca.

Now there were witnesses.

"Shit," Luca cursed under his breath, and threw his jacket off, jumping in after David.

At the hospital, Luca waited to be discharged after having his vitals taken. He was fine and didn't understand the queuing, the waiting – when he was fine. The administration of this country seemed to him madness, enough to drive a man to violence just to escape the plastic chairs and the sterile beds.

Somewhere nearby, he knew David was having his lungs pumped.

Did he feel guilt?

Any at all?

None.

Luca, while stuck there waiting, had too much time to think. He could have just killed David but no, that would be too dangerous. Luca was under pressure – the police getting closer to nailing where his containers came in. They were watching him, had him under a spotlight. He had to be careful. Like with the money... tracing serial numbers. Anyway, he was prepared to ship himself out at any moment. Fly away and start again if he had to, although he'd rather have settled his debt with Adrienne before that.

Violet was collateral damage but luckily for him, she wasn't a grass. She could also be paid off handsomely. She was a former hooker, druggie... someone he knew he could control. Whereas David... he was another story. David was now dangerous, with nothing to lose. David was also the cleverest man he knew. No. He couldn't just kill him, that would be too easy, like killing Adrienne. That'd be too easy as well. Killing David would only make Adrienne more callous than ever and Luca wouldn't stand a chance. With David dead, she'd grieve, be unhappy – and Luca had bigger plans for her. Like raising her up, then stripping her down. Making her husband watch as he romanced Adrienne instead, maybe put another baby in her. Then he would shatter the lives of all that loved them – like he'd been shattered when his only brother – only family – had been stripped from him.

He just had to get her away from David – but now, all that was in disarray. He had a sneaking suspicion Ade would already be flying up in her car to rescue the fucker.

Luca remembered the day he first met Adrienne. It was dinner with the Lewises, an informal business get-together. Prior to that night, David had mentioned she was a peach but Luca hadn't been braced for the fact she was no peach – but a goddess dripping in natural gold. Dominating blonde hair. Lavish, piercing blue eyes. Well spoken. Elegant. Tall. Ample breasted. No photo did her justice.

Pity she was pregnant.

And a murderer.

Luca had to constantly remind himself of that.

A murderer, not the asset to society she appeared to be.

The first woman to make a devastating impact on Luca had to be gorgeous, breathtaking, pregnant with David's child – and his brother's killer.

Luca had called up for David's criminal record the day he employed him – and was impressed he'd stayed out of prison even after three arrests for possession and one arrest for intent to supply which was quashed by a local, well-known barrister.

Luca vowed the day he saw them both so happy together, he would quash all that they had.

He'd wait it out.

He'd waited long enough already to avenge Marco.

What was a few more months or years?

He'd have fun with his concubines while he waited for the chance to rip David and Adrienne's marriage apart.

He would wait for the day David was well and truly out of the picture.

And then pounce.

Dr Benitez entered Luca's treatment room sometime later and told him he was finally free to go. No trauma to worry about. Just go home and have a warm bath or shower.

"The fuck-up I brought in," Luca asked, "is he going to be alright and am I allowed to go in and see him yet?"

The doctor raised his eyebrows, sighing. "He's resting. I take it you know one another?"

"Yes." Luca mirrored the doctor's weary sigh. "I was trying to tell him to get clean–"

"About that," the doctor paused, "he's going to be sectioned."

"No," Luca exclaimed, fearing Ade would sympathise and once again be drawn in by the fuck-up. "Why?"

"Isn't it clear? He threw himself in! He's in restraints... a danger to himself until he's evaluated."

Luca squared up to the doctor. "Five minutes. Please."

"No. No visitors. Sorry."

Luca thought David could be bought, could be tempted to go away and quietly die in a hovel somewhere, drugged up but content. This was a much worse scenario.

***

Meanwhile in David's treatment room, he listened as a detective told him everything. About Adrienne and the connection between Luca and Marcus/Marco. The danger this presented... not only to Adrienne and David, but their

Sarah Michelle Lynch

kids too. David was shown pictures of Violet laid in a hospital bed, a gunshot wound to her abdomen. Apparently she refused to talk. The police officers warned him that could be him next... unless he agreed to their plan.

"We have him under surveillance. He knows we're watching and he won't slip up. The only way to get closer... is through her, Adrienne. For that reason, we need to make you appear dead... so he makes his move quicker," the detective argued. "We'll protect you."

David merely nodded his head; it had become too much of an effort for him to speak or use facial expressions following his dip into the river.

"He is a dangerous man but we will do everything we can to protect her. We don't want this anymore than you but... pretty much, we're out of options... this seems to be the only way. We are desperate to nail this man. Violet can't have children because of what he's done. She's not the only ex-employee of his to wind up injured... or dead."

David nodded, lip trembling. Truly, he was too exhausted to fight all this.

Hewn in two.

Savaged.

Mauled.

By lies.

By love.

Ready to quit.

Give up.

Do whatever they say, a little voice told him. Just anything to end this never-ending agony.

Maybe he didn't want the opportunity to come back. Maybe he was already dead. Maybe this was him, done.

"She'll want to see the body," David told the men conspiring beside his bed.

"You already look dead," the detective said, "and the doctor here's going to give you something to rest deeply."

"How will you pull this off?" David asked the policemen.

374

"*Usually there's a John Doe or two down in the morgue.*"

"*I see. There's just one thing...*" *David began to suggest.*

"*Yes?*" *the senior officer asked.*

"*If I die, she dies too. She won't let him near her.*"

"*Time heals... and time's on our side. He will make a mistake... and we'll be waiting.*"

"*Did I mention I snore when I sleep?*" *David mumbled, sarcastic, even as he realised his fate was out of his own hands.*

When Adrienne came in to see David laid on his deathbed, he tried not to breathe. He lay still, remembering how his swimming teacher taught him to hold his breath: expand the diaphragm and squeeze the nasal passage so no air escapes. He tried to look peaceful even though he knew Luca was a psycho – a man to be reckoned with. But this was the only way – only through death could he one day come back to life. Adrienne had to know the truth for herself – but right then – words didn't seem to be a good enough explanation. She'd have to see for herself what Luca was really like.

He heard her breathing as she stood looking down on him and he bitterly fought the urge to leap from the bed and throw his arms around her.

But then he heard her heartbroken words, "I love you, David," and that was all he needed to know to keep him going.

FORTY-SEVEN

As I absorb the gist of what he just confessed – being forced into hiding by the police – he adds, "We all thought he would be right in there, comforting the widow, but he steered away. Right away. I was in rehab, they forced me into rehab. They found bags of powder in my pocket, they said I needed help. I'd go to prison otherwise. All this stuff, they just kept piling it onto me, stuff I had no control of. I was protected, but I knew you weren't. Eventually, I wanted out... but it was a waiting game."

"Fucking bastards," I growl, "I'll take their names and have my lawyer tear them to pieces."

He shakes his head. "I wanted out. When it was clear Luca wasn't gonna make his move, I wanted out... but they said impossible. It was all off the books, I was properly dead. They were breaking the rules and they knew it... but it all had to look real for Luca to believe it. They had to have evidence of danger for me to come back to life and prove I'd died for a reason. Otherwise, I could go to prison for that too. I had no choice."

"So, why now?"

He nods. "So, after a year of nothing, I threatened to walk... leave my safe house. I was going fucking insane. They said I could go free... if I had a guarantor. Someone who'd vouch for me. Keep me hidden for the time being–"

"My father."

He nods faster, speaking rapidly. "The police found him in London. He came up to the safe house in York and met us and we explained everything. I've been living in his granny flat in Kensington since then, free to come and go. He's rarely there himself. He just works. It's all he does. Apparently he's a business advisor to the Chancellor of the Exchequer now."

"No wonder they let him be your guarantor. I bet he's as bent as the pigs, yeah?"

David laughs. "He saved me, I know that. I couldn't go to Mum's. She doesn't know how to keep her mouth shut."

"You were following me, weren't you? I thought I was going barmy. I kept... having this feeling, that you were with me. I thought once or twice, I saw your face in a crowd..."

He pants. "I couldn't stay away. God Ade, our girls are so beautiful, almost as beautiful as you. I couldn't stay away, baby."

He kisses my mouth and tugs me close, holding me, his little noises making tears bead behind my eyes. I want to put my claws in him and never let go.

Then reality hits and I remember that only a few days ago, I shared a bed with *that* man.

"What the hell do we do now, David? Won't you be in trouble, coming here?"

"Maybe," he agrees, "I just know the police won't leave us alone until they have *him*."

I take to thinking about Lake Como and Milan, wracking my brain for any clues. Anything that might give him away.

"Luca has everyone at the hotel we stayed in terrified. The Palazzo. How come all these people know what sort of man he is, and yet still he gets away with it... doing whatever he wants."

"Why would there be any laws if there were no criminals?"

I nod slowly. "What do you think he wants with me?"

A shadow falls across David's face. "Who made Marcus the way he was?"

I bite my lip, shaking my head. "But Luca seems... the opposite. He seems... a gentleman!"

"I know it's hard to believe, but people like him don't want to admit who and what they are because they weren't always like that. Maybe he can be saved... but look at all the damage he's done."

I shake my head. "You didn't have to sleep with her... and the police forced you to die. All Luca has done so far is..." I pause to think, about what he's actually done that's bad, "...is shoot Violet in the stomach. And actually, I'm not that sorry about that."

David chews his lip. "It's what he *could* do that we have to worry about. He is so careful, his business network so tight-knit, it's only something personal that might undo him and he's always known it. He always has... you're that thing. The cops know you're straight, they know you'd not tolerate corruption... they know because of you, Luca might come undone. The police monitor him... they monitored him when you and he were first together... his movements changed. He..." David doesn't want to say it, so I say it for him: "Stopped shagging whores, you mean? Like he actually loved me."

Shaking my head, I leave the bed, pulling on my dressing gown. The open window beckons me and I try to embrace the fresh, cleansing feeling of air running through my lungs. While I look down onto the green land and the beeches beyond, I muse, "I could go back to him, yes. Pretend to be happy with him. If you give me six months, I'll worm my way into his accounts and find something solid. Something the police can pin on him... something real."

"You can't!" he exclaims.

I turn and nod my head. "I *could*, I *could*. Like you said, this is all about things people could do, and I can take care of myself. Besides, he doesn't want my children… he only wants me. He doesn't have a clue you're alive?"

"No. Not at all."

"I could say I've seen sense, left my kids with my parents, and come to make anew with him. He'll buy it."

"Ade. Listen, okay? He fell for you, I know it. I've looked into his eyes… seen into them. I know what a man in love looks like. Luca fell for you when he didn't mean to. He wanted you for himself. Can't you see? It's why he starves himself of you, like I do with my drugs, but as soon as I go back I'm hooked. That's what addiction is."

"That's not love or addiction, David," I whisper, looking into his eyes, "it's obsession… what he feels for me isn't real. I'm part of the sadness he won't submit to. He hasn't dealt with his feelings over Marco. He needs me to keep the pain contained. He won't hurt me."

"He could still turn at any moment. Any time."

"I know that, but what else are we supposed to do? You'll go to prison if we have no evidence to pin on him and explain why you had to fake your death."

"A catch-22."

Shaking my head, I ask, "So what have you been doing? Just, hiding?"

"Yes… mostly… waiting to see what he'd do next. I did the rehab which was fucking hideous. Me… crying over my father… crying… non-stop… it was awful. I wanted drugs so bad… I wanted sex. I had to abstain… I had to look into myself. It was like a horror show. I'm surprised I put weight on since then. During, I lost about two stone after what happened… with the stress, the fatigue… the depression. It was awful."

My eye twitches and I sit on the edge of the bed, taking his hand. "Rob explained… at your funeral… he… he's had counselling, too."

He looks away, hating the pity in my eyes. I understand that completely. "When I was there, in rehab, I realised that for so many years, I was shunning my true self, just fucking about… because I was scared I was him. I was so terrified I was him, I never gave up my heart to anyone because I decided my limits were the same as his limits. I just screwed women meaninglessly because I was avoiding who I am, and what I am scared of the most… being like him and living a lie, unable to help myself even when I loved you. With Violet, some part of me told myself that all this stability in my life, like with you and the kids and jobs and everything, was bound to come undone, so why not undo everything before it undid me. I can't explain myself any better except to say inside, I felt like filth, and someone like Violet played to that part of me, made me feel better about myself. With you, I felt like I was a stain on your innocence, your purity, and I didn't think I could ever match you for your strength and resolve. Now I've had therapy, I know that it's not my fault I lived the life I did. He left me scarred, on my heart, because he made me lie, he made me betray my mother, he made me watch… he made me think men are like that and it was terrifying to think that that's what I would become too… so I ran from myself, ran from commitment… until you, Adrienne. I couldn't help myself… it was true love. I've always loved you. If you think about it, none of this would've happened if I never worked for FMP… but then, I would never have put my demons to bed, either. My past. My nightmare, my childhood lost, my innocence forever stained and tainted. I grew up in fear, so scared of the notion relationships were based on lies, I avoided them altogether. Always have… always will. Never even kept a best mate."

I swallow. "We're the same, aren't we? I mean, with our mistrust, with our… with everything."

"I agree, and I realise now… we are very similar. Since I've been gone, I've been writing a lot. It's helped. I've also been finishing off my second PhD, not that I'll ever be able to hand it in… not until I can come back to life!"

"Do you think…" I pause, drawing circles in the palm of

David's hand, "…Dad's sorry… do you think he is?"

"As sorry as I am… probably more," he tells me, his face flushing with encroaching tears.

I have to stand up and walk away. I don't want to cry because of the way I feel about my father.

"We don't have to make any decisions right away… let's just be, for a couple of days at least, let's just be together," he asks, "as a family. When you fainted earlier, I snuck you upstairs… the kids haven't seen me yet. I just want to be with my family. We'll make decisions later."

"Okay, let's dress and go down. It's nearly dinner anyway."

Creeping down the corridor in our summer clothes, we run into my mother and Viola.

"Adrienne? Who's this?"

"Oh, David. My husband."

She blinks. "Oh yes, as you were."

She frowns the frown and walks down towards the stairs, shaking her head at herself.

"The little ladies are still napping, their grandfather has lots of energy, yes?" Viola gestures, nodding at the bedroom door opposite mine.

I pick the girls out of bed and like marmosets, they cling to me. They're tired out, no doubt because Granddad had them swimming lengths. He's always been so strong, so impenetrable, and I realise now that I'm older how much like him I am.

David's in tears before he's even touched his daughters. Their eyes still closed as they wake slowly, they don't see he's here.

Next we head downstairs and find my father and Billy hunched over a football annual.

"Mum? What…? Who…? It's not…!"

My son leaps from his seat and into his father's arms. They both cry and shudder.

Slowly, as the girls wake, they realise their father is back and while Marissa remembers little, Lucinda remembers her dad and says, "Oh, you're back. Gone long time."

We all huddle together and I wish this was the same for all kids who'd lost their parent; that one day the lost mother or father just magically comes back, and everything is magically okay again.

I still think magic belies the truth, and I don't trust it. It doesn't last forever.

With that thought, I leave the room telling David, "I had better check in with you know who... to avoid suspicion."

"Don't call him," Dad says, "he might trace it. Send him an email. The fewer words, the better."

I nod slowly. I do feel something for Luca still, but love isn't one of the emotions I associate with him now. Anger, confusion, hurt and misplaced affection, I think. We have unfinished business – like me needing to tell him about what his brother was really like.

In my bedroom I pull out my phone and check the signal. It's weak but viable. Slowly, I tap out an email:

Dear Luca,

I had an unexpected visit from my father and we're spending a few days catching up. My mother's ill and I just want to make sure everything is okay. If you don't hear from me, I'm not being antisocial, I'm just spending some time, that's all.

See you soon,
Adrienne x

As I read the email to myself before I send it, I realise Luca might become suspicious about me going quiet on him. First of all because I mention my father, second of all because there's no love…

When it's done, I walk downstairs into the hive that is my mother's kitchen. Viola's piling fruit in front of the children and a realisation hits. My mother grew up on a market stall in Manchester, where her mother used to sell fruit and vegetables, even with my mother attached to her front.

***

We spend the rest of the evening trying to explain to Billy why David had to go away. Billy doesn't understand and tells us he knows we're lying about things. He tells us nothing makes sense and we partially admit we are lying, but only to protect him. My son is mostly in tears, wondering if he's hallucinating, something I also feel too. David's still David but he's older and stockier and hairier.

At bedtime the kids don't want to be parted from either of us so we all climb into bed together. When they're all fast asleep, we peel ourselves out of their arms quietly and head down to the kitchen. Asking Viola to keep an ear out while we go out for a walk, we leave her sitting in the kitchen, watching over my mother walking circuits of the dining room, wondering where she left her knitting needles. Viola warns us it's best to leave her be and as we pass out of the house, we spot my father sat on the porch drinking hard liquor with a cigar in his hand. He says nothing, only nods in acknowledgement. I read the look in his eyes – he's plotting.

Holding hands, David and I walk downhill towards the nearest bay and peeling our clothes off, we skinny dip in the starlit sea. David's dark eyes fill with twinkles and his strong body cups me against his, treading water for the both of us. We spin and swirl in the inky black waters and with nobody around, we find our very own escape, our very own pool of happiness and contentment.

David carries me out of the water and lays me on some of our clothes. Slowly, he kisses my face, every crevice and every line. He tugs gently on my lips with his teeth and sinks his finger inside me, making me come, crying out his name to the stars and heavens above.

My arms above my head, I lie back in utter exaltation as he worships me thoroughly, kissing almost every inch of me, rolling me and turning me, cupping me and stroking me. Caressing. Burning indentations on my heart, mind, skin and soul.

Licking between my legs, he spits out tiny grains of sand and laughter peels from both of us. Eventually he gives up and uses his fingers to prepare me for him.

On the ground, he pins me beneath him and fucks me with long strokes, hard strokes, short, battering strokes. It's metaphysical, it's extracting, it's beyond real.

I revel in his skin to my skin, every inch of our bodies' largest organ moulded together. He catches my breaths in his mouth, my cries, my gasps as I feel my lower back scraping the shoreline floor.

I feel his heaving body, his weight working hard above me. He's alive, he's real. He's everything.

I always wondered if I'd ever love again, and now I know, even if he has to leave me once more I will never love another man more.

He's ingrained in me, through our kids, through the memories we've made and the steps we've taken together. We pledged like swans to never mate with anyone else and we meant it, we meant it more than any other people on Earth. We'll never love again like we've loved one another.

I open my eyes and see his hair ransacked from me fisting it, spread out over his face and neck. He laughs and his neck twitches and I laugh too, pressing my finger against his pulse to feel him feeling, so that I might feel too.

Sensing I'm growing uncomfortable on the ground, he hikes me up onto his lap and rocks us together, my hair in his arms as and I sweep over his lap. He reaches between us, pressing my clit gently, and I take big gulps of air. Staring into his eyes, I watch as he bites his lip and moans, waiting for me – but desperate to claim me only when I claim him.

I slam my breasts against his chest and hold him tight, my

body cascading around his, rendering me temporarily immobile. He pulls me close as only a man can hold his lady, firmly and yet tenderly too, so I slot perfectly inside his wonderful arms.

Resting my head on his shoulder, I beg, "Tell me you love me, David."

"I love you."

FORTY-EIGHT

When I wake the next day, it's all imprinted on my mind; last night and the hours we spent on the beach, making love in our own private cove. When I roll over into his arms, it feels like heaven, and without even opening my eyes I know I'm home. In our huge queen bed, we're joined by the kids to David's side which means we're both wearing t-shirts and pants.

I open my eyes and look into David's big brown ones. He's been waiting for me to wake, I see, from the smile in his cheeks.

"Are we still legally married?" I whisper.

He purses his lips. "I think we should do it again... properly."

"Me too."

I lean in a little and wrap my arms around his neck. Laid side by side, we kiss gently, eyes wide open.

"Hiya!" Lucinda screeches, breaking us apart as she jumps on David's head.

"Ufff, could you please give me warning next time kiddo?"

She lurches into his arms and smooches his lips as he tussles her curls with his fingertips. Marissa is soon trying to break them apart and get her own time with Dad.

Surprisingly Billy crawls over them and gives me a

cuddle, whispering in my ear, "Thanks for bringing him back."

"Thank Granddad," I whisper back, and he nods slightly. I get the feeling Billy meant something else with his words, but I'm not sure... this must be confusing for a kid, I guess. Maybe he thinks I'm some sort of witch, I don't know.

"Sooo hungry," Luce complains.

"Let's all go down then. I'm sure Viola will have rustled something up; she loves looking after us all."

We all head downstairs in shorts and t-shirts and I get the shock of my life when I find my mother, father and Viola tied to chairs.

"Get the children back... back, David," I say, pleading.

He sees the scene, having been behind me on the stairs, and backtracks. "Quick, up, upstairs!" he yells.

"Stay with them, David."

I reach for a knife from the block and hold it out in front of me, wondering where the captor is hiding. The tall wooden beams around the room obscure my view somewhat and shadows in corners seem deceiving. Dad jolts his head, gesturing he's outside by the pool.

I untie my parents and Viola and tell my father, "Upstairs. Stay there. If he wants me, he'll have to fight for me."

Dad shakes his head. "I won't go through this again with you."

I square up to him as Viola holds my frightened mother tight and directs her towards the stairs. "How did he even get here?"

His chin wrinkles, his bottom lip out. "No idea. None."

"He won't hurt me. He's sick but some part of him loves me. Trust me on that."

My father rolls his shoulder. "I'll kill him, give me the knife. I'll take the rap. I don't care. Just leave... take the kids."

I search my father's eyes and ask, "Why's he out there?"

His neck twitches. "He went upstairs and saw you all cuddled in bed together... I don't think he has the bollocks... but we still don't know for sure, Ade."

"Let me talk to him. I can handle it. I promise you."

"He has a gun."

"He won't shoot me. He only wants to torture me."

"I don't like this," he insists, "let me call some guys to come and dispose of him, let us all be rid of this once and for all."

The truth is, I care for Luca, and part of me thinks he cares for me too. My gut feeling is that he can be reasoned with. I have to try.

"You have to trust me, Dad. Let me try."

"I wish you wouldn't."

"He won't hurt me, I promise."

"Okay," he sighs, and kisses my cheek as he leaves me.

Alone, I take some deep breaths and ready myself to face Luca. Walking out to the pool area, I find him with his head in his hands, sat on a sun lounger. Hunched over, his eyes are fixed on the aqua-blue waves splashing lightly against the poolside, a light breeze sweeping through the courtyard.

"Luca," I whisper.

"Don't come any closer," he demands, the gun on the seat beside him.

"You've had a shock."

I tiptoe toward him and sit on a deck chair a few spaces away from his.

Minutes pass as the breeze revives and awakens my senses. A part of me cares for this man, who spoke kindly to me in private, who gave me a great weekend last week after so many months alone. Another part of me despises him, for all the obvious reasons.

"He used to buy me boxes of chocolates and after I'd eaten them, he'd thrash me with a belt, without consent. He'd tell me I was greedy and needed discipline. He wiped the blood off me with such care, I thought he loved me but needed to break me to feel secure. He wasn't as handsome, nor even half as intelligent as you... but I loved him. He said all the right things. Lavished me in the beginning, treated me like a princess. I was young, impressionable, trying to spread my wings... show my father I was independent... and here was a man who offered me that, and more. Marcus was the first guy to confidently take me on his arm, show me the town, and my young, naïve, underdeveloped heart bought into it all."

Luca turns his face to peer at me through angry eyes. "You don't fool me. You told me what you did. I know what *you* are."

"Yep," I admit, keeping his gaze, "you know what I am. A survivor. Like you. We do what we have to."

Luca turns away, his eyes avoiding mine again. Squeezing his fingers in his eye sockets, I know he's wiping away tears.

"Why was he so bad?" I ask Luca.

Hands clasped together, he shakes his head, waging an internal war with himself. "He watched me... he saw what I had to become, but Marco couldn't distinguish between the job and the man. I could keep the two separate, but not him... I couldn't save him... and do you know why?"

"No."

"Because you took him before I could help him be better. I was working, slaving, aiming to get us both out... and then you ruined any chance of me rectifying all my wrongs."

"No man like him can be redeemed."

"You don't understand, Adrienne..."

"Enlighten me."

He shakes his head, still hunched over. "Your second chance is upstairs, but where's mine? Huh? Laid buried in the ground because of you. We have to settle your debt to me."

"No."

He picks up the gun and taps the barrel against his knee.

"I call the shots, not you."

"I owe you no debt. He threatened to hurt my son and I stopped that. There's not a jury in the land that would convict me."

"Except me," he growls, "except me!"

"Then tell me what you want."

He turns his crimson face to mine and his lip curls when he demands, "An eye for an eye."

I stand, arms outstretched. "Then kill me, take me. I'm yours. I was almost dead anyway, the day Marcus died. Dead from all the hurt... all the pain, in here," I tap my head, gesturing the bullying was the worst affliction I bore.

Luca stands suddenly and points the gun at me, releasing the catch. It looks like a vintage weapon, something special – reserved for a special killing.

"Before you pull the trigger, think about whether this is going to make you feel any better. Think about whether this excuses you for being the man who created a wife beater."

The gun shakes in his hand. "You bitch, you've never known real pain in your life. Not like we did."

"I don't fucking care about your *pain*," I groan, "I don't fucking care. Just kill me, c'mon, get it over with. DO IT!"

He can't shoot, I can see it in his eyes.

Lowering the gun, he admits laughing, "I had to fall in love with you, didn't I?"

I swallow hard. "Part of me loves you, too."

He pinches his temples with his free hand, fingers outstretched.

"Did you know he was alive, did you?"

"No," I immediately reply, "I only found out yesterday. The police had him protected."

A tear peels from his eye. "Come with me. Nobody need get hurt. Just come with me."

Shaking my head, I tell him slowly, "I can't leave my children. I can't abandon them."

His eyes squeeze shut and I watch as he grapples with the

reality: I was never his to take – love or no love. I've always been David's. Always will be.

The police want Luca and I won't give them David. He's the best father my children will ever have.

"What's the point of anything?" he throws his face up to the sun, begging for mercy, for enlightenment – answers.

"Everyone always has a choice. Like me. I decided I'd rather be alone, be poor, be hungry, destitute even, than spend another night with *him*. I was ready to face the music for what I did. I gladly would've done time if it meant freeing my son from the future he faced with Marcus as his father."

Luca lifts the gun again. "Don't, Ade. Fucking don't."

"I consigned myself to a life of loneliness, of nothing, of shoddy existence… because of the way he made me feel. I was still dead, inside, when David found and rescued me. He's the love of my life and I will never leave him. You may as well kill me now. My legs won't carry me away from him."

"You don't know about what people will do for love, Adrienne. What *I* did to give my brother a better life than the one we had."

"I'll tell you about love, shall I? Shall I, Luca?"

He smirks, his mouth curling into an ugly, snarling smile. No words fall out.

"Love is free. It cannot be bought. It creeps up on you when you're least expecting it. Love is holding someone's hand, looking into their eyes, praying on your knees by the side of their bed when they're ill. Staying with them even when it's murder to. Hanging on even when it burns. Turning yourself inside out for another. Crawling on your belly just to give them a day of happiness and save them from the pain you harbour. Love is something you don't know… don't understand. You don't know love. You only know childish arrogance, ignorance and want. You don't know love. Love is smiling even when you hurt, it's caring even when you feel bitter, it's negating everything you are to be better, to be more, and to live up to the person you adore, without question – without conceit."

My words don't sink in; his expression doesn't change, and he won't be reasoned with. "I have a debt to collect. Tell me a name, and I will be gone."

I shake my head. "Me. Do. It. I'm ready. I was dead once before, I'm ready. It's nothing new."

He stares, agape, growling, "A name! Or I'll chose one."

"Me," I repeat, "me. Take me. As if you don't know I mean it. You know as well as I do what it means to feel dead. You and I are the same, it's why you love me. We're not just survivors, we're master and mistress of our worlds. We're rulers. I'm not afraid. Do it. I'd die a hundred times over for them. In fact, killing me will absolve me, so do it!"

We both hear rattling and look up. One of the doors of the bedrooms on the galleried landing above is receiving a beating from someone.

"The first one out up there, gets it," he warns, "maybe Billy, your help… your father, *him*, it's a lottery."

I begin walking forward, ready to ask him to put the gun at my chest and just shoot. "David and I spent last night on the beach. What we enjoy together, most people don't experience in a lifetime. I can die happy. Do it."

He shakes his head at me. "You are fucking crazy."

"You should go, before I call the police. They only took David to lure you… so you'd make your move, the one you're making right now. You're lured. Captured. You should've realised you couldn't outwit me. I did what you couldn't… and clipped the bastard that was your brother."

He whacks me with the gun, splitting my cheek open. The force of his attack sends me to the floor, shrieking in pain. His chest heaving, he mumbles, "I'm sorry, I didn't mean to."

"*He* used to say that, too."

"Adrienne!" my mother screams from up above, on the

galleried balcony, her waist pressed up against the metal railing. Her nightdress and gown waft around her.

It all happens so fast, I have no way of stopping it.

As Viola races out to bring my mother back from the edge, Luca raises his arm and shoots her through the heart.

Blood splurges, seeps, and I see her instantly die.

No.

No.

No.

"Mum."

As David and my father rush the courtyard together, Luca has the last laugh. "Just remember who really killed her, Adrienne."

He puts the pistol in his mouth, and that's that.

FORTY-NINE

6 Months Later

Back where it all began, I huddle in the sheets, on the bed of the house I never sold. Our Harrogate house I put up for rent and now we're back. Like nothing bad ever happened. Like life goes on – and it does – but not in here where I lay day after day.

I can't find the strength to lift myself from my pillow most days.

I live in my mind. My brain is saturated in bandages and I can't bear to peel off even one plaster, in case when I do, everything spills and I no longer exist.

David's a professor. He deals with everything. Without him and Rachel and my father, my children would go hungry, go without clothes, warmth and love. I'm incapable. All the pills in the world couldn't remedy my pain, my responsibility. I carry this mantle of guilt because I deserve it. I own it. It's the only thing that's really mine, because I chose it, and the rest was chance and circumstance.

Voices echo around me, a man sleeps next to me every night, but I shut my eyes and trap myself in my own world. Rerunning conversations with Mum, with Luca, with myself.

David carries me to the bath now and again, shaves me, washes me, whispers to me while I remain unresponsive. Unfeeling.

On the merry-go-round of insanity, I search for something – some morsel of truth – just something I can peel a bandage off and partially stomach. But none of what happened to me is palatable. I refuse to feel *anything*.

I imagine meeting Luca when I was seventeen. Marcus never even existed. A true entrepreneur as opposed to a mule, Luca would have swept me off my feet. I'd have swept him off his, too. I'd discover his dodgy sidelines and encourage him to go legit and it'd be beautiful. We'd have loads of children and he would repent. He'd love me forever. Everything would be beautiful because we saved one another. Endlessly, I dream of him, wishing him alive – wishing he was okay. Wishing we'd never met, wishing we'd met first, wishing David had never committed adultery. I wish for all sorts of realities – anything except the one I'm currently dealing with.

I'm numb. I watch the shadows of the room travel across the walls, and everyday, I document little changes in the way the sun moves over the earth with the changing of the seasons. I revel in the current November daylight, short and low. My mind like a stencil, I know where every little shadow is at whatever time of the day. Therefore I can count down quicker to sleep and I can sleep, longer. Rachel spoons cereals and bowls of fruit in my mouth and I focus on the shadows while she does, while she talks like I give a shit about stuff going on in the world. Everything's a countdown to more sleep, more dreams, where I can construct a world I can control. Absorbed by walls and wood, I feel safe. I feel contained. I'm dangerous. I shouldn't go out. I'll cause chaos, it's all I'm good for. I started it. I finished it. I killed my own mother.

I can't look at my husband. I can't stomach him, most of all. Loving him as I do, beyond reason, I know he doesn't deserve a witch as poisonous as me and I want him to leave and find himself someone better. He could break free, start again, begin anew. He can take the kids and give them a mother they deserve. He can have a new romance and make everything shiny and bright for them, all over again. They can be free. I'll take this pain and wield it for all of us if they can be free, finally. I'd like to give them all that. A new mummy who doesn't disgust them, a new lover for David who isn't tainted by sin, lies and murder.

I'm shattered inside, but as strong as asphalt on the outside. You'll have to roll over me a million times before I reveal the imperfections, the distortions, beneath the surface.

That fated day, I should have got in Luca's car with him and drove away. Then none of this would've happened. We wouldn't have buried my mother and I wouldn't have had to watch the brains of my other lover fly out the back of his head.

Funny how a corpse can leave behind so much pain, so much anguish. Laid inert, his soul gone, his legacy was more potent and powerful than ever. He was right as well, my mother only died because of me.

I see no end to this torment, to this purgatory.

I'm nothing to anybody. I'm just an object buried beneath sheets, buried inside my self.

The merry-go-round twirls again and I see in sharp, kaleidoscope focus another set of circumstances I might have survived:

David died in the river and Luca and me married. I wore a huge dress, sweeping up a large staircase like Cinderella. Not quite glass slippers, but some silver, strappy sandals I got from Milan. A hillside wedding and my children, clean and untainted, too. We all lived happily ever after.

Then my memories remind me – he was no father figure. I try to batter down the reasoning and tell myself he'd have been a great father with my influence. I could have saved him, I could have! He just needed my love. He needed me.

I picture myself with Luca, laid in his arms, his black, bulbous heart pulsing beneath my ear. The black recedes the more I hold him and the whole romance swirls around me in Technicolor. Little children with Luca's eyes and hair. A house by Lake Como. A classic car. Travel. Laughs. Love. I wish he hadn't gone. I wish he wasn't so tormented he had to leave. I could have saved him. He was the other half of myself – someone tossed out into the world with no blanket of love to protect him. No cloak of invisibility. All the world knew what he was, but I saw a tiny corner of the man he used to be before the world got hold of him and mutilated his soul. David's always had Rachel but Luca and me had nobody. He was the only other person who truly understood what it was like to be totally alone in the world, without someone of your equal to pick up the slack – just someone you can entrust everything to.

Sometimes I lie here crying but no sound comes out. The pain's unbearable. It's like Luca's knelt by the side of the bed, whispering he loves me. He wants me to wake, wants me to hold him. Lift myself out of bed and get dressed, put on some make-up. "Millionaires don't wear jeans and t-shirt Adrienne," he chuckles. I giggle and put on £1,000 lingerie sets beneath jeans and t-shirts, and then the vision blurs, because it was David who never cared what I wore, as long as I had something racy beneath. I realise the two men I've loved blur into one and I don't know what's what anymore. Where does separation and cohesion begin? Or end? It's all a muddle.

I'm on this merry-go-round, my bed my vehicle through the annals of my mind, and I don't want to get off this ride. If I do that, I'll have to face up to what I'm left with:

A world without the one person who meant more to me than the very air I breathe.

Mum.

FIFTY

David

I'm at a loss as to what to do. She barely moves. Barely eats. Hasn't talked since the day of her mother's funeral.

In Spain, she rallied everyone, organised everything. Made arrangements for bodies to be flown. Statements to be given to the police. A severance fee for Viola.

On the flight home, she was calling up our lawyers, getting advice. Threatening the police who never forced me to die – but said it was the only way. They were right. Killing Luca was the only way to also kill his nefarious business activities in their tracks.

She watched her mother lowered into the ground and this time – something snapped – when she realised Josephine was really never coming back. Never, ever.

Ever since, Adrienne has been trapped in this dark despair of hers.

"She lays for hours, in the same spot, not moving," I tell my family doctor.

"So…" he stares straight into my eyes, the epitome of duty, "…you've been administering pills. She refuses to talk. Are you sure she's swallowing them?"

"We grind them into her food, well my mother does."

"She doesn't vomit?"

"No," I shake my head, "she eats, drinks, then lies down again."

"There's a treatment. I could come to your house and explain it to her?"

"I don't know if she hears anything we say."

He puts his hand on my arm and in a soft voice, assures me, "Anything is worth a try."

***

The next morning, Dr Bayliss arrives at the house. The kids are all out at school or nursery and my mother is in the kitchen, keeping out of the way, but here nonetheless. I called Max last night but he said he couldn't make it up here. If Ade agrees to treatment, he says he'll come as soon as he can after that.

"Adrienne, I'm Dr Bayliss. I took over from Agatha Henry's position. Remember? Your old GP."

She lies there, not moving. Same way she always lays; raised up on pillows, watching the shadows on the wall opposite the bed.

"Adrienne, can I talk to you?" he asks.

She doesn't respond.

He nods his head in my direction and I leave the room.

From the other side of the door, I listen in but when she still doesn't say anything, he leaves the room and speaks with me outside, shutting the door on her.

"I'm going to put her forward for ECT without consent. Otherwise she could be a vegetable like this for years."

Sorrow raids my body, my heart... and I break down crying.

The bedsores.

Not taking care of herself.

Making as few trips to the bathroom as possible.

The numbness she must feel.

No interest in her kids.

"Please, push it through as quickly as you can."

He nods swiftly. "I will. Seeing as though there are

399

children depending on her, I reckon we could have a team here tonight."

I wipe my tears. "Please. God. Whatever you have to do."

He drops his doctor's bag by his side and hugs me and I pour out on his shoulder.

I apologise profusely but he says it's okay and I mumble, "I've never been so scared in my life."

When they come for her later, they sedate her and put her in a chair that rolls down the stairs in the house. She doesn't fight it whatsoever. It's like she's learned to switch off everything.

I'm only glad that my mother has the kids at her house so they don't have to see their mother being carted off by the men in white coats.

Once Ade's been taken away and I'm left all alone, I have the chance to finally cry the tears I've been holding in all these months.

I'm in complete and utter despair. If I had never let weakness get the better of me, none of this would have ever happened.

In the same breath, I realise I'd never have faced up to my own demons without everything that has happened. I'm stronger now since rehab, so much stronger, but I had to bear months of painful confessions to get where I am now.

Here was me thinking I was the one with the problems. Not in my wildest dreams could I imagine the depth of Adrienne's despair to bring her to this point in time.

She's literally been to hell and back.

***

A few days later, I arrive on the ward with flowers and a shuffling gait. I'm frightened, sad, and angry. I'm scared. I fear she won't be the same. She'll have changed. She won't want me anymore. A different person might look at me from behind her eyes – and it'll all be over. They'll have taken her and lobotomised her with a different woman.

"I'm David Lewis, for Adrienne," I whisper to the ward sister.

"Right this way," she says, leading me down a grey corridor.

"In here," she gestures, and opens the door for me, letting me inside.

When I walk in, Adrienne's sat up in bed, reading. Her hair's washed and she looks clean and fresh. The door clicks shut behind me and it makes her look up.

"David," she whispers.

"Hey baby."

"Come here."

She puts her book beside her and pats the bed. I sit down and she takes my hand for the first time in months. Searching my eyes, she smiles.

"Thank you," she mutters, "thank you."

"Ah god, Ade," I splutter, and toss the flowers down on her food trolley.

Grabbing her tight, she grabs me back and it's me who's falling apart now. When I eventually pull back to give her a kiss, she whispers, "I'm going to get better, I promise you."

Taking a deep breath, I wipe my eyes. "I love you so much."

"I love you," she whispers softly, her dainty features all grey and pallid, her illness treatable but not gone, yet.

The nurse comes back holding a vase and winks at Adrienne. "I did not believe I could meet a man more handsome than my husband, but you boy, you are testing that notion," she says, whistling, and Adrienne chuckles.

When Ade laughs, the lines around her eyes bulge and the grey shadows reveal themselves from behind the frozen façade she's worn for so long. Still, I know she wants to get better, and that gives me hope. Another knock on the door has the nurse walking back to open it and Max arrives, carrying more flowers. I wasn't expecting him and by the looks, neither was Ade.

The nurse turns her head to look at Ade. "Oh good lord, lady, all these beautiful men. And now we need another vase."

Ade snickers and the nurse leaves the room.

"How are you?" asks Max, shuffling in like I just did a minute ago.

I stand to leave but Ade begs, "Don't go."

So I stay.

"I feel clearer, but I still need more treatments. They're trying me on different tablets... I feel sick but I'll be okay now I'm here, thanks to David recognising how bad it had got."

Ade's father nods and clasps his hands together. "There's something I'd like to discuss with the both of you."

"Maybe not now, Max?"

He assures us it's not bad with a slight grin. "It'll only take a minute or two."

"It's okay," Adrienne tells him, "go on."

"Your mother wrote you a letter. When she got her diagnosis, she wrote it, just in case she never saw you again. I forgot all about it until I was going through some papers last month. I came to tell you about it but you weren't receptive... but I'm bringing it now."

He digs into the breast pocket of his jacket and pulls out an envelope.

"Shall I read it?" he asks.

"Have you read it already?"

"She dictated it to me."

Ade and I look at one another and we nod together. It doesn't seem like the words will contain anything nasty.

"Dear Adrienne..." Max begins.

Dear Adrienne,
    This is my in case of emergency goodbye letter.

If you didn't know already, I've been diagnosed with dementia and it's only going to get worse.

I don't know how much longer I can even talk coherently, let alone write again. So here we go...

Whatever circumstances these words find you in, just know... that you were the one. I loved you as hard and as fiercely as I possibly could and I don't regret a minute of the energy, time and soul I invested in you.

Whatever happened in the past, nor how ever much hate I had for your father, let go of the past and move on. Take whatever you have left and carry on... and shine. You're the diamond sun of my universe, shining so bright I'm blinded by your brilliance.

Me and your father were stupid people. Stupid. We fought over you. Squabbled like children for something untainted, something not like us. I have so many regrets and you know what? That's life. Nobody ever gets it really right. You just live and hope for the best.

If there's three things I could ask you, it's these:

Forgive your father for his mistakes. Ever since my diagnosis, we've tried to forgive each other. Because you only get one life and what's the point of hating?

Secondly, forgive yourself.

Thirdly, when you find a man who loves even the blackest parts of you, do not let go.

Give Billy a kiss for me, and also, your other children if you have any.

Do the things I never did. Swear. Wear neon colours. Skydive. Climb fences. Ride horses naked. Say obscene things. Make love. Shout at people when they piss you off. Toot your horn. Scream. Become tainted and be proud of it. It's who you are. You came into this world naked and blank, like a canvass, but I want you to go screaming out of it covered in every colour of the rainbow.

I loved you not only because you were my daughter, but because you were the greatest friend and person anyone

*could ever have or know or love. You're my legacy, now go
child... and be free.*
 Only in you do I live now, and I'm content with that.
 Forever yours, Mum x x

Ade gets out of bed and sits in her father's lap, crying
into his coat.

Over her shoulder, I see tears mixed with acknowledgement in his eyes.

He wrote the letter. I know it.

I nod knowingly, because that's what people do when
they love someone: they paint a better picture for them.

After a long time spent discussing how Ade's treatments will
progress, Max and me leave Ade's room behind together.
Outside the building, as we prepare to go to our separate
cars, we shake hands staunchly.

"Tell me about her mother," I beg.

He purses his lips, standing with his hands folded in front
of him. "I met her at a music festival, in 1980. She was
eighteen, I was twenty-six. A cradle snatcher. She was so
beautiful, so unusually intelligent for a market trader's
daughter. Then we married... had Ade. Everything changed.
She was a manic depressive. Paranoid. Only after she had
Adrienne did it show, did I realise what was wrong. She
didn't get the right treatment at first and before I realised she
was ill, I'd already sullied our love with several affairs. It
was too late, I'd gone too far, and I was trapped in my own
self-hate. I couldn't go back, I tried, but I didn't love her
anymore. We didn't divorce because I knew if we separated,
she'd be worse off. I kept her close so I could take care of
her, so she could look normal to Ade, who seemed to be the
only thing that calmed Josie. For Adrienne's sake, I kept
Josie under control, kept her straight. Fed her pills and drove
her to appointments. I knew Adrienne would grow up to be
ambitious, to want everything out of life she could have.

She's like me in that respect. I know she has misunderstood me for a long time, but I did everything I could to try and protect Adrienne, to give her the standing in life she needs. I tried to… do right."

"So, why send her away? Your own daughter?"

"Everything with Marcus… and Ade being abused… the case… tipped Josie over the edge. The dementia began to really show. I'd known for a while she had that, too, but it was slowly progressive with the drugs she took. I didn't want Adrienne to watch her get worse, which she was starting to. So I sent her packing, with lies… to get rid of her, so she didn't have to watch her own mother die of that fucking dreadful disease. I barely knew Josie towards the end. For the past ten years… she wasn't herself. I gave Adrienne money and told her to go, because I didn't want her to waste her life fretting about her mother, watching her die a slow, painful death of disintegration. You know, in recent years Josie overcame double pneumonia several times… it was only a matter of time before she died. In a way, Luca gave her an exit from her own prison. We have to see it like that, don't we?"

Looking into his clear, blue eyes it's like seeing Adrienne. Now I see where she gets her strength from. "I'm sorry, Max."

"Me too," he says, lip trembling, "I know about my mistakes, and now I know… I can make up for them… if she'll let me. If you'll let me?"

Hand rubbing my mouth, I decide, "Ade's not the same, is she? Not like Josie?"

"No," he shakes his head, "Ade's just been rebooted, that's all. We took everything from her… and now we need to give it all back."

"I agree."

"We do," he says, and instead of a gentleman's handshake, we hug instead.

"I have something to ask you," I state, feeling awkward

as we pull back.

"Name it."

I smile, embarrassed. "I want to ask for your daughter's hand in marriage. Do it properly this time… when she's all better, of course."

He bursts out laughing. "For a second I thought you were going to ask me for money."

Folding my arms, I stare him in the eye. "Why would I?"

"Well… I don't know. I guess that's what most people want from me!"

I grin. "Adrienne has a few quid, Max. All grown up, remember?"

"Oh yes!" he exclaims, throwing a hand over his mouth. I'm sure this is the most shocked he's ever looked and he's even shocked by feeling shocked. His grey hair even stands on end.

"She made a few 'mil at Berken but I've been opening her mail and she recently got a letter saying one of her stocks has shot through the roof. It's worth millions. She invested in Apple in 2004, just £100,000. I assume using her trust fund money? Or a pocket of it?"

"Fucking hell."

"I know. That girl… she's not stupid."

Hands in his pockets, he asks with a wry grin, "So, why do you want to marry my daughter?"

I wipe my hands over my mouth, laughing, my legs spread wide apart in case he thumps me one.

"Well, Max," I chuckle, "there's one simple answer to that question. I want to marry Adrienne because she's the light and soul of my world… and she's fucking gorgeous."

He pats me on the back and directs me to the car park. Hand tight around the scruff of my neck, there's amusement in his warning voice when he walks me away. "Let's get a drink, then we can talk properly. Hmm?"

"Let's."

EPILOGUE

David, 2016

"Yes, you." I point at someone with their hand up.

"Mr Lewis, where would you say your inspiration comes from?"

"Other writers," I reply, folding my arms. I pick another. "And you, yes."

"Mr Lewis, is it true your work is inspired by real life events?"

"Ah, a more precise question," I respond, taking off my reading glasses.

The young twat looks pleased as punch I gave him more than a two-word response and I continue, "Real life is much, much stranger than fiction... so in answer to your question, if there were any part of this book which was real... I'd have to say real life must be pretty fucking frightening in comparison."

Laughter is raised from my avid audience at the Waterstones book store I'm signing and doing a reading at today. My first crime fiction was popular, but this most recent one has been a bestseller.

"Yes, you," I say, picking another.

"Any plans to write something a bit different?"

I tap my knee and choose my words carefully. "My wife wants me to write a romance next. Personally I think myself incapable in that arena."

More laughter.

I neglect to mention that the story of my life with Adrienne is something I've written about... in secret... a story so heartbreaking, she could never write it herself, like I once suggested she might. Only I could write what for her was an unbearably sad time of her life. She was never black inside, whereas I am, and always will be. Which is why I could write our story, on her behalf, because I am the towering strength she clings to. Behind every beacon of hope, is someone like me, someone who can tell it like it is and get away with it for some reason.

"Next, yes... you."

"Is it true you once died and came back to life?"

I take a swig of the water on the small table beside me and swill it around my mouth. "Good question. A Christian question, if you ask me. In a manner, I did resurrect and resurface, reborn. Next... ah yes... you..."

Driving home after the event, I wish I were being chauffeur-driven and had Ade on my lap in the back of some fuck-off vehicle, swigging champagne. Pity it's never been as glamorous as all that for writers. My wife's the rich one and she spends all her money on making more and more investments, bettering this country's financial stability by buying into eco technology and all that jazz.

My Jaguar (yeah, it's not a bad life) winds down the long drive of our palatial home in the West Yorkshire wilds and I spot all the lights on in the house. Pity nobody at the signing today was clever enough to do their research and realise today's my fortieth birthday... the load of slackers.

More is the pity that going by the illuminated house I'm heading for, there's no doubt a party in the offing.

"Crap," I whisper to myself.

I told her no parties.

The bloody woman.

I slot my car in beside her Discovery and peer through

the windows but I can't see any bodies inside. I just want to unwind with a sherry and my wife. I don't want fuss or anything of the sort.

Walking into the large, open-plan hallway of our sprawling country retreat, I hear no voices. No guests waiting to spring out at me. Looking around, I'm suspicious. Where are they hiding?

I throw my over-arm bag and jacket, keys and phone and all the necessary shit of modern life into my office off the hallway and as I'm about to climb the stairs, I notice a note taped to the banister rail.

Fooled you. I'm waiting upstairs.
Naked.
Wearing filthy, horrible things for you to peel off me.
Kids are at Rachel's baking you a cake.
They'll be back at eight.
Quick!

I race, fucking feet slipping on the polished granite stairs. That only gives us two hours to screw the living daylights out of one another.

"Adrienne, you are in so much trouble!" I shout as I near the upper landing leading to our bedroom.

"You have to catch me first, big boy," she giggles, and I hear her chasing through the house, wearing god knows what.

"Where the bloody hell is she?" I ask, when I find our suite empty of her long legs and sleek arms – the only things I need to keep me safe.

"Freezing, absolutely sub zero," she calls.

I pop my head out of the room and think about where she could be. Surely not any of the kid's rooms…

I snicker to myself and realise where she is.

She's playing me, she knows just how to as well.

"Adrienne, I'm warning you…"

"Slightly warmer," she calls, "getting there… warmer… hotter… steamier… filthy hot. Ripe hot, I'd say…"

I find her laid on the carpeted stairs leading up into the loft where we keep the gym and games room. Loosening a few buttons on my shirt, I ask in a warning tone, "You want a staircase fucking?"

"Here's just the start, honey bun."

I bark with laughter and strip the shirt off my back. "Fucking hell, woman."

She's wearing silk and satin. Navy and sky blue patterns. I can't really distinguish what's what. I'm panting and the swell of her breasts, her hips and her belly are what really capture my attention, outlined by her beautiful lingerie.

I crawl up three steps shirtless and nuzzle my nose on her ankle.

"How was it?" she asks.

"Abhorrent."

She tuts. "All your language… and that's all you've got."

I laugh, licking her ankle. "I do what I must. Now, I can do what I want."

"Oh yes."

I smooth my hands up her legs and spreading them, nibble at her sex over her panties. Smelling sweet and ready for me, I recall it's been a few weeks since our last proper session. We fit quickies into our routines but from the smell of her, she's been really looking forward to this.

Trailing kisses across her belly, I realise she's more convex than normal.

"I have a present for you, sweetheart."

"This lingerie isn't it?" I whisper against her breasts as I expose her nipple to the air.

"I love you," she moans.

"Oh, but… I know that!"

By the time I begin kissing her throat, she's wrapped her legs around me and I'm straining against my trousers. She unzips me and pulls me free. Slipping her thong to the side, I slide sweetly into her fiery warmth and bite her bottom lip, gazing into her bright eyes.

"I'm having a son, your son," she says, and I still inside her, hugged by her wet tightness gripping me.

"How do you know? I thought we weren't having anymore."

"Me too," she giggles, "but then I found out last month... and so close to your birthday... I decided to save the surprise for now. I had the five-month scan yesterday. It's a boy."

I burst out laughing. "God I love you."

She grips the sides of my head as I lift and push deeper inside her, eliciting pure cries of joy from her mouth. No wonder she smells and feels so fragrant, she's got the mad hormones I love so much rushing through her.

Adrienne runs her finger over the tattoo on my side which depicts some string tied around my rib. I got it for our second wedding in place of another ring which didn't seem to say it like this does. Whenever she stands by my side, the twin tattoo she got on her ribs corresponds to mine. On her body, a tiny hand holds her side of the string, never letting go.

I take her fingers and kiss them, murmuring, "You're my foundation, my rock, Adrienne."

"You're my love," she whispers, and I lean down and lap her nipple into my mouth, hungrily devouring, enjoying her.

"You're my docking station... the only place I feel truly safe. Fuck, you're wet!"

"Oh, David," she groans and makes love with me, her hands in my hair and on my arse.

"I'm so close. So horny," she whimpers.

Pinning her hands above her head, I ram into her despite carpet burn and she bucks hard beneath me. Swallowed whole by her, she comes around me and drags my climax screaming from my guts.

Panting in her ear, I remind her, "You said this was only the start of the entertainments."

She giggles. "Carry me to the shower, wash me down… and whatever happens, happens."

Lifting my head, I zero in on her starry eyes. "Whatever happens, happens."

We'll always be bound tight and our faith in that has kept us going. Kept us alive. The world threw everything it had to throw at us, and still, one thing always remained apparent at the end of each and every day:

We still loved one another, even when it was murder. I know everything about this woman, everything, and yet I still love her. In fact, I grow to love her more everyday and now we're happy, we have no more story to tell. Only happiness to hold onto, lives to live, hearts to cherish – even mine, black as it is – is free of the same disease which killed my father. Some things simply can't be broken, like us, and this story I've written…

It remains eternal.

A Song To Be Sung By A Lake On A Midsummer's Evening

Let us take this spot and cry out for stronger passions,
May we always have this heat and flavour.
Raise your voice to the soul of good time,
Be not still, but burn out and let all be conquered.

The humming fireflies beg you, be out of tune,
For that is better and ageless and perfect.
Throw the seconds into the freshness of the tides,
The candles shall always burn brightly here.

It did not start, it continues merry merely,
And love shall make minstrels of us all.
Blithe and bonny and in a steady heartbeat,
Broken and together, opposite and one.

That bounce of lapping creature, near us,

Hopping and scouting the water's pallid top.
Inviting us to make all things blush with roses,
We are not devils, but one with the looming, dripping sky.

Soft and steady, with no crescendo ceasing,
This now is our time and our tempo.
Lilting and dancing in the white velvet moon,
Our figures shall be remember'd always.

Peace me, as we chant of undone things,
In the flutter'd reeds of unselfish thinking.
I shall record it all here, in these delights,
For I know it happened, but was a song without
music or words...

THE END

ABOUT THE AUTHOR

Sarah wrote extensively on the Brontës for her degree, writing a dissertation on the entire canon. Without their works, she probably wouldn't have had the notion that one day she could become an author, too. Sarah almost became a teacher, using a presentation on the lives of the three sisters and brother to secure a place on a teaching course. However, journalism is what eventually brought Sarah to where she is right now.

Sarah currently resides in East Yorkshire with her husband and daughter. She works as an editor by day, a dreamer by night.

You can find out more here:

www.sarahmichellelynch.net